Timothy Shay Arthur

The Angel of the Household

And Other Tales

Timothy Shay Arthur

The Angel of the Household
And Other Tales

ISBN/EAN: 9783337026035

Printed in Europe, USA, Canada, Australia, Japan

Cover: Foto ©Andreas Hilbeck / pixelio.de

More available books at **www.hansebooks.com**

THE

ANGEL OF THE HOUSEHOLD,

And Other Tales.

BY T. S. ARTHUR.

PHILADELPHIA:
J. W. BRADLEY, 48 N. FOURTH STREET.
1860.

PHILADELPHIA:
PRINTED BY KING & BAIRD,
ANSOM STREET.

PREFACE.

In the "Golden Age," angels were the companions of men, holding their spirits in immediate relationship with heaven. But, as the gold of celestial innocence became dimmed by the breath of self-love—the parent of all evil—angels receded; and farther and farther they removed themselves, as men darkened their spirits with sin, until even a perception of their existence faded from the mind.

As it was in the "Golden Age" of the world, so is it in the first, or "Golden Age" of each individual life, when the innocence of infancy finds angel-companionship. Whoever holds a babe to her bosom, and holds it there lovingly, comes within the sphere of angelic influences; for, with infants and little children, angels are intimately near. This is seen in the tender love that fills the heart of even a wicked mother, when she clasps her helpless offspring in her arms—a love flowing forth from heaven, and breathed into her spirit by the angels who are with her babe.

Into every household angels may enter. They come in through the gate of infancy, and bring with them celestial influences. Are there angels in your household? If so, cherish the heavenly visitants.

THE

ANGEL OF THE HOUSEHOLD.

CHAPTER I.

"BEDLAM let loose!" exclaimed Mr. Harding, passionately, as he started up from the corner, near the fire, where he had been sitting moodily since supper-time. "Silence! or I'll break some of your bones!"

The children, who had been wrangling, suddenly ceased their noisy strife, and shrunk back from their angry father, who, advancing toward them, seemed half inclined to put his rough threat into execution.

"There, now! don't talk and act like a savage!" sharply ejaculated the wife and mother, throwing from her coal-black eyes a scornful glance upon her husband. "If I couldn't speak to children in a better way than that, I'd not speak at all."

We will not put on record the brutal retort of Jacob Harding, as he almost flung himself from the room; throwing over, in his mad haste, little Lotty, the youngest member of his unpromising flock, who happened to be in his way. The loud slamming of the door, and the wild screaming of the child, mingled for the excited mother's ears their sounds discordant.

7

"He'd better break my bones!" said the oldest boy, Andrew, in looks and attitude the picture of defiance. "I'd just like to see him try it."

"Hush this instant, you little vagabond! How dare you speak so of your father?"

"I don't care! He's not going to break my bones." And the young rebel, not over eight years of age, drew himself up, while his eyes, black as his mother's, flashed with boyish indignation.

"If you say that again, I'll box your ears off!" And Mrs. Harding took two long strides toward the lad, who, knowing something about the weight of her hand, shrunk, muttering, away, and contented himself with thinking all manner of rebellious things, and purposing all kinds of disobedience.

For a few minutes, after Lotty ceased crying, there was silence in the room; not a pleasant, but a gloomy, forced silence. Then Lucy, six years old, and Philip, between four and five, who had been frightened from their play by the scene just described, drew together once more, and commenced rebuilding a block house, which Andrew had wantonly thrown down. Their work, as it again progressed, this bad boy watched with an evil eye, and, just as it was near completion, wantonly swept again the fabric into ruins. Unable to control their indignation at this second unprovoked violation of their rights, the outraged brother and sister, as if moved by a single impulse, threw themselves upon Andrew, and with fists, nails, and teeth, sought to do him all the injury in their power. Fierce was the struggle, and long would it have continued, but for the mother's interference. She did not stop to separate them, but, with her open hand, dealt each such rapid and vigorous blows about the head and ears, that they were soon glad to retreat, crying with pain, into opposite parts of the room.

"Now, off to bed with you this instant!" exclaimed

the angry mother, "and if I hear a word between you, I'll come up with a switch and cut you half to pieces."

Andrew, Lucy, and Philip glided from the room, keeping silent through fear, for they understood their mother's present mood well enough to know that it would be dangerous to provoke her further.

"Come! let me undress you," said Mrs. Harding to Lotty. There was nothing gentle, nothing of motherly love in the tones of her voice. The waters of her spirit were agitated by a storm, and the sky above them was dark.

"I don't want to go to bed," answered the child, fretfully.

"Come here this instant, I say!" cried the mother, with threatening look and tone.

"I don't want to go to bed," repeated Lotty.

"D'ye hear? Come this minute!"

But the child, instead of obeying her mother, shrunk away into the farthest corner of the room.

"If I have to come to you, miss, you'll be sorry; now, mind!"

Most children would have been frightened at the dark, threatening eyes that almost flashed with cruelty; but Lotty was self-willed, and strong to endure, though but a child. She inherited a large portion of her mother's peculiar spirit. Instead of yielding to this threat, she crouched down in the corner, and cast back at her mother a look of defiance. Mrs. Harding was in no mood for a long parley. There were times when the mother in her was strong; and then, for the sake of her wayward, self-willed child, she would patiently strive with her, and use all gentler efforts to bend her to obedience. But now the mother had given place to the passionate woman. It was one of her hours of darkness, when all the evil of her perverse nature had sway. A few moments she fixed her eyes upon those of Lotty, throwing into them, as she did so, a fiercer light; but this failing to intimidate the stubborn child, all patience gave way, and she darted toward her with something like a tiger's spring. Seizing the still resisting little one, Mrs. Harding jerked her from the corner into which she had retreated, and as she lifted her up into the air, struck her three or four hard blows in quick succession.

Did Lotty lie still now in her arms, or stand passively by her side? Not so. The spirit of rebellion was like a young giant in her heart, and blows only quickened this spirit into more vigorous life. The child screamed and struggled, and even struck her mother in the face. Such resistance to her will only made Mrs. Harding blindly resolute. More smarting and longer continued blows were returned, and to these was added such a mad shaking of the child, as she held her out with both hands in the air, that Lotty, losing her breath, became frightened, and ceased her struggles.

"I'll break that stubborn spirit of yours, if I kill you!" said the mother, with cruel triumph in her tones, as she set Lotty down upon the floor heavily. With impatient hands the garments were almost torn from the little one's body, and replaced by her night-gown. Then, without an evening prayer, a kiss, or a kind good-night, she was placed in bed; her only benediction an almost savage threat of consequences, should a single word pass her lips.

All was silent now in the house. The older children had fallen quickly to sleep, and Lotty, subdued by the power of fear, restrained the rebel cries that were almost bursting her heart for utterance. She, too, soon passed into the world of dreams. Was it a beautiful world to her, poor child? or did haunting images, terrible in shape, follow her there from the real world in which she daily struggled and suffered?

Alone, with not a sound on the air but an occasional

sob from Lotty, the tumult of whose feelings even sleep had not entirely subdued, Mrs. Harding's state of mind underwent a gradual transition. There are few in whose spirit subsiding anger does not leave its debris of sad emotions, or painful self-condemnation. It had ever been so in the case of Mrs. Harding, yet had she not seemed to grow wiser by suffering. With every new cause of excitement, her quick temper fired up and burned its little hour fiercely; and, ever as the fire died out, her spirit felt colder than before, and groped sadly in a deeper darkness. And it was so again. How rebukingly upon this state came, now in a single deep sigh, and now in fluttering sobs, the grief of her self-willed child, prolonged even into slumber. So painful was this sound at length, that Mrs. Harding went softly and closed the door that opened into the room where Lotty was sleeping. But, through the shut door, came, ever and anon, the sigh or sob, each time smiting her ear sadly, and adding to the gloomy depression from which she was now suffering. Nor was this the only cause of self-upbraiding. She was alone, and why? Sharp, insulting words, striking on the ears of her impatient husband, had driven him, as the same cause had before, times without number, from home, to spend his evenings at the tavern, among scenes and associates of a degrading character. Ah! how often and often had the unhappy wife, as she sat through the lonely evening hours, wept far the absence of him whom her blind passion had driven forth—even from the hearth her presence might have made warm and attractive.

Alas! that suffering taught not this ill-governed woman its lessons of wisdom. That remembered anguish did not act as a stimulus to self-control. Ever as a leaf in the wind was she, when the gust of passion arose. As it had been with her many, many times, so was it now. She was too unhappy for any thing but tears; and so, letting the work she had taken up fall into her lap, she drew her hands over her face, and sat idle, weeping, and miserable. A knock on the door disturbed her wretched mood. It was night, and their house stood at some distance from the nearest neighbour. Mrs. Harding was no timid woman; yet this summons startled her, not because it was bold and imperative; on the contrary, it was low and hesitating.

"Who's there?"

She had risen up quickly, and now stood in a harkening attitude.

No voice replied, but the same singular knock was repeated.

"Who's there, I say?"

Sharp though her tones were, a slight tremor betrayed a secret fear.

No answer.

"Come in."

A hand was on the door knob. It seemed like the hand of a child, and failed in the apparent effort to gain admittance. Mrs. Harding distinctly heard the rustle of a woman's garments. She tried to repeat the words "Come in;" but a strange fear prevented utterance. Almost as fixed as a statue, she stood gazing at the door, which, after a little while, swung quietly open. Her eyes caught a momentary glimpse of a white garment, and then she looked vainly into the deep darkness There was no form visible.

"Who's there?" she cried, after a brief pause; but silence was the only answer.

As she still gazed through the open door, her eyes, penetrating farther into the gloomy vail of night, saw dimly an object on the ground. Advancing across the room a few steps, she was able to perceive distinctly that this object was a large basket, covered with a cloth.

"Who's there? What's wanted?"

Again she sought an answer; but no response came.
Boldly now she stepped to the door, and bending her
body out, peered farther into the darkness; but there
was no movement nor sound that indicated the presence
of friend or stranger. Close by the door-step stood the
basket. She stretched forth a hand, and made an effort
to raise it from the ground; but to do this required the
exercise of considerable strength.

"This is strange! What can it mean?" said she to
herself, again searching with her eyes into the surround.
ing darkness.

"Jacob! Jacob!"

A thought that her husband might have brought the
basket, flitting across her mind, prompted her to call his
name.

But no answer came back upon the quiet air, that bore
her voice afar off, until it died in the distance. Why
does she start so? A low smothered cry, like that of an
infant, has come suddenly upon her ear; from whence,
she is in no doubt, for already she has lifted the basket,
and is bearing it into the house.

How wildly excited was the countenance of Mrs. Harding, as she stooped down, and with unsteady hand removed the white napkin that covered the basket. The
sight revealed would have touched a harder heart than
hers. A babe, only a few weeks old, lifted to hers a
pair of the softest blue eyes that ever reflected the light;
and as it did so, fluttered its little hands, and showed all
the instinctive eagerness of an infant to be clasped to a
mother's bosom

Now, with all the hardness and passionate self-will of
the woman, up into whose face this helpless, innocent
stranger looked, there was a warm chamber in her heart,
over the door of which was written "mother;" and the
hand of an angel opened this door to admit the babe so
cruelly abandoned. Her first impulse was obeyed—that

2

prompted her to lift the child quickly from the basket, and fold it in her arms. A sweet, confiding smile played softly around its lips; and its large, beautiful eyes rested in hers with an expression so full of loving confidence, that she felt her whole bosom warming with love, and yearning toward it with inexpressible tenderness. The kiss that could not be withheld from the rosy lips that parted to receive the salutation, was the kiss of a mother.

Ere there was time for reflection or observation, the babe had won its way into the heart of Mrs. Harding. The door still remained open as she had left it in the excitement incident to bearing in the basket. Mrs. Harding, now aware of this, arose, still holding the child in her arms, and crossed the room to shut the door. Was it really so; or did her imagination create the picture? Be this as it may, just in the dusky extreme of the circle of light made by the rays pouring out from her lamp, she saw the form of a woman. The face was distinct, and its expression never to be forgotten. It was a young face, very sad, very full, and very beautiful. The hands were clasped tightly together, and the figure seemed bending forward eagerly. For a moment or two the vision was distinct; then it faded slowly, and the eyes of Mrs. Harding saw nothing but darkness

Closing the door, with a strange feeling about her heart, she went back to where the basket stood upon the floor, and, seating herself beside it, the babe on her lap, commenced an examination into its contents, with the hope of gaining some light on the mysterious circum stance. But nothing here gave her the least clue to the parentage of the child, or made clear the reasons for committing it to her tender mercies. In the basket were four or five full changes of clothes, most of them made of good, but not very fine material, except the white flannel skirts, which were soft as down, and of the choicest quality. These were not so new as the other articles. No letter was to be found in the basket; nor did it contain any money.

While Mrs. Harding was thus seeking for all possible light in regard to the babe, it had fallen asleep in her arms, unconscious that any great change had taken place in its fortunes or friends, and as happy in its slumbers as when it nestled on its mother's bosom—if, indeed, it had ever known that blessed privilege. Perceiving this, and affected with a new tenderness as she gazed down upon its face—one of uncommon sweetness, even for a babe—she sat for many minutes with her eyes upon its countenance. Her gaze seemed held there as if by a kind of fascination. What a yearning love grew up in her heart, gaining strength every moment! She wondered at her own feelings.

Rising now, and holding the child with exceeding care, she passed into the next room—her own chamber, where Lotty was sleeping—and gently laid the sweet young stranger in her bed. Here she lingered for some time, leaning over and looking upon the child. Once or twice she left the bed, and went as far as the door, purposing to leave the chamber. But a strange attraction drew her to the babe again and again, and each time it seemed that its face had acquired a newer beauty.

At last, Mrs. Harding compelled herself to leave the apartment; and as she did so, she closed the door softly. Sitting down by the basket, she commenced a new examination of its contents. This was as fruitless of intelligence as the first. Not a mark nor sign was there, to tell from whence the infant came.

Half an hour elapsed, and still Mrs. Harding sat musing over the basket, her mind incapable of finding, for the present, interest in any thing but what appertained to the babe.

Thus she was sitting, when the heavy tread of her husband startled her into painful consciousness of coming trouble. Jacob had never been very fond of children—not even of his own, toward whom he had shown but little tenderness. That he would manifest only ill-nature, perhaps give way to violent passions as soon as he learned that a strange infant had been left at his door, she had too good reason to fear.

He came in roughly, as was his wont—shutting the door heavily behind him.

"Hush!"

Mrs. Harding raised her hand involuntarily, to enjoin silence. But her rude husband strode noisily across the floor, heedless of her warning.

"What's that?" he said, as his eyes rested on the strange-looking basket.

"You would hardly guess," answered Mrs. Harding, speaking with a forced pleasantness of tone, very unusual with her when addressing her husband.

"I shall hardly try," said he, gruffly.

"A strange thing has happened to-night."

The voice of Mrs. Harding was not as steady as she wished it to be.

"How, strange? What has happened? Who's been here?"

"That basket was left at our door to-night."

"By whom?"

"I cannot tell."

"With somebody's cast-off brat in it, I suppose," said Harding, with a flush of anger in his face, for now he saw the baby clothing which his wife had taken from the basket and laid on the table. "Is it so?"

The flush had deepened to a fiery glow, and his eyes burned with indignation.

"The basket contained a young babe," said Mrs. Harding calmly, and with a mother's tenderness in her voice; "the sweetest, loveliest babe your eyes ever rested upon."

"Pshaw!" And Harding averted his face, on which was a look of supreme contempt. "I'd like to know," he added, menacingly, "who has dared do this thing!"

"That we are not likely soon to know," said Mrs. Harding. "The basket contained only infant clothing."

An almost savage imprecation leaped from the tongue of Jacob Harding. For a little while he stormed about the room like a madman. Under almost any other circumstances, his conduct would have kindled up in the mind of his wife as fierce a flame as that which burned in his own. But a woman's true instincts subdued her passionate nature, usually so quick to gather all its forces for combat. Silently she waited for the fire to burn out in her husband's mind for want of fresh fuel, that she well knew how to supply.

"It is such a sweet baby," said Mrs. Harding, in as calm a voice as she could assume, after her husband's fierce indignation had in a measure consumed itself.

"Humph! sweet!" How the selfish, cruel animal growled! What a look of disgust was on his countenance—scarcely human in its expression!

Harding had come home from the tavern, ripe for a quarrel; and he was doing all in his power—impotent of effect so far—to raise a storm. He had not been drinking much: only enough to deaden all of true manhood that he possessed, and to quicken into active force the evil of his nature. He now perceived the change in his wife, and at once divined the cause. The foundling had won its way into her heart, and she was already purposing to adopt it as her own. The thought enraged him anew.

"Where is the brat?" he exclaimed, starting up with a fresh burst of anger. "I'll throw it out of doors!"

"Better replace it in the basket, poor thing!" answered Mrs. Harding. "It has done us no harm."

'Very well. Put the duds back into the basket, and

2*

the child with them. They shan't stay in my house to-night!"

Conscious that, if she gained over her husband at all, it must be through apparent yielding, rather than resistance to his will, Mrs. Harding commenced slowly replacing the baby clothes, as if about to do his bidding. A little wondering at this passive acquiescence on the part of his wife, Harding stood looking on while she laid in garment after garment.

"It is dark out, Jacob, and will be cold before morning. And then the dogs, or some other animal, might hurt the poor helpless thing."

"I don't care. It shan't stay in my house to-night. I'll teach people better than to leave their brats at my door—I will!"

The man's stubborn spirit was roused by the remonstrance of his wife.

A deep sigh heaved the breast of Mrs. Harding, as she bent once more over the basket, and, to gain time, made some new arrangement of the baby clothes.

"Don't be all night about it!" growled the savage.

Mrs. Harding, without a word in reply—a circumstance that excited the especial wonder of her husband—took up the basket, and passed into their chamber, as if to do his bidding. Acquiescence like this he had been far from anticipating. Yet was he, in the blindness of evil passion, bent on thrusting the babe from his house. The very thought of it was an offence to him.

"Jacob!" It was the voice of his wife, calling to him from the adjoining room, where she had been for several minutes.

"What do you want?" he answered, gruffly.

"Come here a moment," Mrs. Harding spoke, in a mild, subdued voice.

"You come here. You're as able to walk as I am," he retorted

"Just a minute. I want to show you something."

Harding arose and went into the room from which his wife had called to him. In the middle of the floor stood the basket, and lying in the basket, with its beautiful face uncovered, was the sleeping infant.

"There it is, Jacob," said Mrs. Harding, in a low, steady voice. "Cast it forth, if you have the heart to do so—I have not."

How suddenly were the man's steps arrested! The moment his eyes fell upon the placid face of the infant, so innocent, so peaceful, so heavenly in expression, he felt himself within the circle of some strange power that stilled the waves of passion in his heart.

"Cast it forth, Jacob, if you can," repeated his wife. "My hands would be powerless were I to make the effort."

A little while Harding struggled with himself and the new influences that so suddenly pervaded the atmosphere around him; then, with an effort, he turned himself away, and went back into the room from whence his wife had called him.

Tenderly, very tenderly, did Mrs. Harding lift the sweet babe, still sleeping, from the basket, and replace it in the bed, the moment her husband retired, vanquished by weapons his fierce manhood despised, yet against which he had no shield of defence. For some time she bent over the baby, gazing upon its face; and it was only with an effort that she could tear herself away.

"You'd better keep it all night," said Harding, as his wife entered the room where he was sitting. His voice, though untouched by gentler feelings, was not so harsh and cruel as before. "Some harm might come to it, and then we'd be blamed. To-morrow I'll have it sent to the poor-house, if no owner can be found."

Mrs. Harding sighed, but said nothing in reply. She

was afraid to express what was in her mind, for, by years of sad experience, she knew that for her to express a wish, or to approve a measure, was to insure her husband's opposition; and, in truth, it must be told, that she had proved no inapt scholar in the same bad school where he had learned his lessons of ill-nature and bootless contention.

"I only wish I could find out who has dared to do this miserable deed," resumed Harding, his anger growing warm again. "A wild beast never deserts her young. The wretch should be gibbeted alive."

As he said this, a cry arose from the chamber.

"There it is! A nice time you'll have with it to-night."

Mrs. Harding went quickly in to the babe, that was now awake. She lifted it gently in her arms, and, as she drew it to her breast, it commenced nestling there, seeking for the fountain of its life—alas! so suddenly and so cruelly cut off. How deeply was the heart of its new friend stirred by this movement! What a yearning pity pervaded her bosom!

"Dear, dear child!" she murmured, as she bent down her face, and placed that of the infant's closely against it. Holding it thus, she went out into the room where her husband still remained.

"Won't you get me a little milk in a cup, and some sugar and warm water, Jacob? The poor child is hungry."

Harding, with considerable reluctance, went off, grumbling, to do as his wife desired. The milk and warm water were brought, and, as he set them on the table, he could not restrain the utterance of an ill-natured remark. To this no answer was returned.

Much to the relief and pleasure of Mrs. Harding, the babe drank freely from the spoon which was placed to its lips. Evidently, it had been prepared for this great change in its life by those who contemplated abandoning it to strangers. Somehow, Harding's eyes remained riveted on the face of the child, as it took the food prepared by his wife; and, strangely enough, the longer he gazed upon it, the gentler became his feelings. The human in him began to rise above the bestial.

"No punishment is bad enough for the wretch who could desert a child like that," said he, his ready indignation taking a new direction. "It was fiend-like."

"You may well say that, Jacob," returned his wife, as she drew the babe's head back upon her bosom, and looked down tenderly upon its face. "Isn't it beautiful?"

"I never saw any thing very beautiful in babies," said the man, a little impatiently. He was worried with himself because of the involuntary interest in the little stranger that was awakening in his mind.

"Oh! how can you say so?"

Something of the sweetness of bygone years was in the voice of Mrs. Harding, and something of the maiden beauty in her face that had won the heart of her husband in the long-ago time; at least so it seemed to Jacob Harding.

"It is true, Mary," he answered, even smiling briefly, as he spoke.

"There is beauty here—beauty that even your eyes can see. Dear little angel! It has come to us like a ray of sunshine, Jacob. You don't know what strange feelings I have had ever since I looked into this sweet countenance. More like a heaven-born than an earthly child the babe seems to me; and now, as it lies so close against my bosom, I feel such a pleasant thrill going deep, deep, even to the centre of my heart, that I wonder as to the cause."

"You are foolish, Mary," said Harding, kindly.

"Maybe I am," she replied, "but I can't help it

Now it is fast asleep again! Did you ever see such perfect lashes for a babe? They lie in a dark line upon its
cheeks like the long lashes of a woman   Let me place it
in bed again."

Mrs. Harding arose and turned to go into the bed-
room.   As she did so, her foot caught in the carpet,
and she would have fallen forward had not her husband,
whose eyes were on her, or, rather, on the babe, sprung
instantly forward and caught her.

"Don't let it fall," he cried, eagerly, stretching his
arms around and beyond her, so as to save the child.
The act was involuntary; but it betrayed, both to his
wife and himself, the strong hold that weak, helpless,
unconscious infant had already gained upon his rugged
heart.   How this betrayal caused the warm blood to
leap joyfully through the veins of Mrs. Harding!
When she returned from the bed-room, and addressed
her husband, he answered in milder tones than he had
spoken to her in many days—weeks and months we
might almost have ventured to affirm.

"There's something uncommon about the child, that's
certain," he said, as they talked together; "and I shall
not feel just right about sending it off to the poor-house.
But it can't stay here, for we've enough of our own, and
it's as much as I can do to fill *their* mouths."

To this Mrs. Harding answered nothing.   So far, the
babe had been its own all-sufficient advocate, and she
felt that words from her might prejudice rather than
advance its cause.

As husband and wife laid their heads upon their pillows that night, each felt a calmness of spirit hitherto
unknown.   Selfish passions were at rest, and higher and
purer emotions—so long held down by evil—stirred with
a new life, and opened the windows of their hearts for
the influx of celestial influences.

CHAPTER II.

As Mrs. Harding lay watchful and musing on her pillow that night, she wondered at her state of feeling. Could the mere presence of a babe effect so great a change? Four times had she been a mother, and four times she had felt, as a helpless babe, just born into the world, was laid against her heart, an indescribable joy. Too soon had this passed away—too soon had her briefly slumbering passions awakened to fresh activity—too soon had the trials and temptations of her position changed the heavenly tenderness that pervaded her spirit into harshness or indifference. She remembered all this, and wondered how she could ever have indulged in anger toward the little ones for whose gift her heart had felt such deep thankfulness.

How distinctly present to the eyes of her mind were Andrew, and Lucy, and Philip, and Lotty! Not with faces marred, as was, alas! too often the case, by selfish and cruel passions, but with each young countenance beautified with loving affections. With what a new impulse did her heart go out toward them! All the mother in her was stirred to its profoundest depths. While she thought and felt thus toward her own children, involuntarily she raised her head, and bending over, lay, partly reclining, with her eyes fixed upon the calm face of the sweet, young stranger.

"Baby—dear baby!" She could not keep back the low utterance; and, as she spoke, she lifted the sleeper in her arms, and, hugging it to her bosom, commenced rocking her body, and murmuring a tender lullaby.

"Don't be foolish, Mary!" Jacob Harding spoke

more roughly than he felt, but in tones less reproving than he had meant to use. "You'll waken the child, and then we shall have a time of it."

"She is so sweet," said Mrs. Harding, as she kissed the babe, and then replaced it in the warm nest from which it had just been withdrawn. She did not know that her husband was awake: he had been lying so very still, that she believed him sleeping. But busy thought excited by a new current of feeling, had driven slumber also from his eyelids.

"One would think you'd never seen a baby before!"

There was no ill-nature in the voice of Jacob Harding, notwithstanding he tried to speak unkindly. The fact was, he had been so long in the habit of speaking harshly to his wife, that, to address her with any thing like tenderness, seemed an unmanly weakness. And so he put on a rough exterior to hide the softness within. He could not entirely hide it, however. Mrs. Harding perceived all the change he, too, was experiencing, and it but increased her wonder and delight. She did not venture a reply, lest something in her words should quicken the perverse temper of her husband.

Never in her life before did Mrs. Harding fall asleep in such a state of mind, or with thoughts so full of all tenderness and loving-kindness; and never before came to her a dream so strange and beautiful. Last in her thoughts, as all waking perceptions died, were the singular incidents of the evening; and, as fancy began to mingle her airy forms with the things of actual life, the strange vision—real or ideal—that fixed the eyes of Mrs. Harding, as she gazed through the open door into the surrounding darkness, was most prominent. Across this warp, fancy threw her shuttle, and strange figures were soon made visible in the dreamy fabric she wove.

Again Mrs. Harding was alone in the family sitting-room No babe was in her lap; but, in the open door

stood a beautiful woman, and she knew her to be the
same whose white, sad, yearning face had been revealed
to her a moment on the background of shadows. Tender and serious, but not sad, was her face now, as she
beckoned with her hand. Mrs. Harding arose and followed the lovely apparition. As she stepped beyond the
threshold, she became aware that the earth lay in sunlight, and that the scenery around was new and more
beautiful than any thing she had seen. Here were soft,
green meadows, dotted with snow-white lambs; there,
leafy avenues, along which the eye ranged to an almost
interminable distance, and yonder towered up, even to
the spotless heavens, mountains as blue as the sky itself.

"The land of innocence and essential love," said the
stranger, as they gained an eminence and looked down
upon the scene spread out in beauty before them. "The
angels of childhood dwell here. Whenever a babe is
born upon the earth, two angels from this world are appointed to its guardianship, and they remain near the
child through all the days of its tender infancy; and
near the mother, also, filling her heart with love for her
helpless offspring. It is their presence that so often
changes the selfish and cruel woman into the tenderest
of mothers. They flow into her mind through love for
her babe, and fill it so full of what is gentle and good,
that evil passion has no room for activity. But, gradually, as the minds of infants are opened, through the
senses, to a knowledge of the world into which they
have been born, and as the will, gaining strength, is
moved by inherent evil, the angels gradually recede from
both the child and the mother; not because they wish to
abandon their charge, but because their gentle influence
is no longer perceived. With some they remain longer
than with others; for some children are born with fewer
perverse inclinings, and some mothers love their babes
with a divine rather than an earthly love."

3

As the fair stranger ceased speaking, Mrs. Harding perceived that they were standing in one of the porticos of a building, the architecture of which, in its grandeur, exceeded any thing ever reached by the boldest imagination. The walls were of translucent gems, and everywhere the ornaments, that seemed living forms, gleamed with gold and sparkled with precious stones of wonderful brilliancy. Into this magnificent palace they entered, and the stranger led the way to a large east room, where a small company of beautiful virgins stood near a window, from which they were gazing earnestly.

"Let us approach them," said the stranger; and they moved over to where the virgins were assembled by the window.

"Pride and human fear have hardened her heart." Thus spoke one of the virgins. "And she is about to desert the babe. See !"

All bent near and gazed from the window. To the eyes of Mrs. Harding every thing looked dark and sad. It was some time before she was able to distinguish objects; but, when her vision was clear, she recognised all the prominent features of the scene. Dimly revealed from out of the murky shadows, was the neighbourhood where she dwelt, and she seemed to be looking down upon it, as from an eminence. It was night, for all was in half obscurity, and the stars were shining from the sky. Here and there stood a house—she knew them all —and there was her humble abode, the only one from the window of which light streamed forth upon the gloomy darkness. As she continued to look, an object moving along one of the roads became visible. Gazing more intently, she saw a woman, and in her hand she carried a basket. A thrill passed along every nerve, as she recognised the face that had looked so wildly upon her from the fading circle of light, and she turned

quickly toward the stranger who had led her thither—
but she was now alone with the virgins.

"Not there," said one of the company.

The woman had paused before a house, the inmates
of which Mrs. Harding knew to be best esteemed in all
the neighbourhood for goodness of heart and kindness of
action. In this home there was ease and comfort; and
the babe, if left there, would find love and tenderness.

"Why not there?" she asked aloud.

"Even a babe has its mission of good to the world,"
answered one. "A household angel will this babe be,
wherever it is received; for to the best of Heaven's
angels has been committed its guardianship. If the
mother, hearkening to evil counsel, casts it from her,
the blessing of its presence must be for those who need
the blessing. No, not there."

And the woman, who had paused before the dwelling
of peace, took up the bundle, and passed on slowly,
wearily, and in tears.

"Not there," said one of the virgins, as she stopped
before another dwelling.

The woman seemed to hear the words, for she raised
the basket again, and kept on her way. As she did so,
her eyes received the light, streaming forth from the
Hardings' window, and she turned her step thitherward.

"The angels of childhood are about to leave that
dwelling," said one of the virgins; "for innocence has
almost died in the hearts of the children. A dark
shadow is resting over them, for the powers of evil have
prevailed over the good. Let the babe go there."

"There? Not there!" answered one of the virgins
"The innocent, helpless lamb must not be left in a den
of wild beasts."

"It will not go alone," was replied. "Angels have
gathered their protecting arms around it; and its own
sphere of innocence will be a wall of defence."

A low cry reached the ears of Mrs. Harding—the cry of a babe. Instantly the vision faded, and she became aware that a small, soft hand was nestling in her bosom. There was a love, more than human, in her heart, as she gathered the half-waking infant in her arms, and felt that she had been, and still was, in the company of angels.

How vivid remained the impression of her dream—not to her a mere phantasm, but a real vision:

"For this great blessing, Father, I am thankful," said she, as she lifted upward her heart to heaven.

Strange fact! Not, perhaps, since the days of innocent childhood until now, had she felt that God was near to her, and near as the Giver of good; and that she should address God in a thankful spirit! She wondered, even while she gave involuntary thanks.

When Mrs. Harding slept again, it was to dream of the babe, and to have a consciousness of deep peace, such as she had never experienced in her waking moments. New purposes and better states of mind had been formed during both the waking and sleeping hours that passed since the little stranger first greeted her with its winning smiles. The morning found her calm, thoughtful, yet sad. What a trial was before her! Ah! how clearly she saw her difficult position! How sunk her heart, as one hard, harsh fact after another, of that position, looked her sternly in the face! She had as much to fear from within as from without—from her ungovernable passions as from the tempers of her husband and children.

Dimly the morning broke, the cold light creeping slowly into the chamber where she lay. Her husband and Lotty still slept; but the babe was awake, and its large blue eyes were looking up into hers. How sweetly it smiled! How trustful and loving the whole expression of its young face!

"Blessed baby!" she said tenderly.

And it responded to her greeting with a curving lip, and the low, cooing sound of a dove, as she talked to it, forgetful of every thing in the pleasure of the moment. Harding awoke suddenly, and starting up in bed, muttered some incoherent words, and threw his eyes hastily around the room. His voice chilled the heart of his wife, for she dreaded his waking mood. Scarcely thinking of what she did, Mrs. Harding drew the bed-clothes over the child, and so placed her body as to shield it from his observation.

"I've been dreaming, I believe," said Harding, as he laid himself back on the pillow.

"Dreaming of what?"

Mrs. Harding spoke very gently. In half wonder, her husband turned his head to look into her face—the tone was so unusual.

"I never saw any thing so real."

"Was it a pleasant dream?"

Harding looked over at his wife again. It was the old voice that, in times gone by, had sounded to him so musically.

"Yes, Mary," he answered, mildly, "it was a pleasant, though a singular dream. I thought some one left a baby at our door"——

He paused abruptly, looked serious for a moment or two, and then said—

"But *that* was no dream, Mary."

He now raised himself up, and, as he did so, Mrs. Harding drew down the bed-clothes, and showed him the smiling infant.

"It was no dream, Jacob," she said, kindly.

For some time, Harding gazed upon the little face, and the longer he gazed, the softer grew his heart. He said no more of the dream; yet, as well to him as to his wife, had come a vision—though not in all things alike.

3*

He had seen the little abandoned one in sleep, and under circumstances that impressed his mind powerfully.

It was now broad daylight, and Lotty, as was usual with her, awoke in a bad humour. She commenced crying even before her eyes were fairly open.

"What do you want, Lotty?" asked Mrs. Harding.

But Lotty cried on, not seeming to have heard her mother's voice.

"Lotty! Lotty!"

The crying did not cease for an instant.

"See what I've got here, Lotty!"

"You ain't got any thing!"

By such words the child had been so often deceived, that no confidence remained even in her mother. And so she kept crying on.

"Will you hush, now?"

The father's patience was gone, and he spoke in a quick, angry voice. How the little stranger babe started! What a frightened look was in its face! Harding saw the effect of his harsh tones; and, for the sake of the babe, regretted the sudden passion to which he had given way.

"But I *have* got something here, Lotty," said Mrs. Harding. "It is the dearest little baby you ever saw in your life."

Instantly the voice was silent, and, springing from the bed in which she lay, Lotty stood beside her mother. Harding watched her face, and saw how suddenly it changed.

"It is wonderful!" he said to himself, as he arose and commenced dressing—"wonderful. It seems even now as if I must be dreaming. 'A heaven-sent child.' These were the very words that sounded in my ears as I awoke; and I verily believe the babe is from heaven."

"Baby! baby! dear, sweet baby! O mother! where did it come from?"

There was such a gush of delight in the voice of Lotty, who was usually cross in the morning, as she stood on a chair, and bent over the infant, that Mr. Harding's wonder increased. A spell about the babe subdued all who came near. To him it was a new life-phenomenon, the mystery of which filled him with surprise, not unmingled with a heart-pervading sense of pleasure.

Mrs. Harding now arose, leaving Lotty and the infant equally delighted with each other, and commenced hurriedly dressing herself. It was her business to prepare the morning meal; for the earnings of her husband were not sufficient to allow her help in the family. With many earnest injunctions to Lotty not to hurt the babe, she left the chamber for the kitchen, in order to make up the fire and get breakfast. Somehow or other, the fire kindled with unwonted quickness; and every touch and movement of her hand seemed to accomplish her purpose more readily than usual. By the time the milkman was at the door, she had the table set, and the kettle was almost ready to boil. The babe's breakfast was her next thought. It was scarcely the work of a moment to dilute some new milk with warm water, to add a little sugar, and a few crumbs of bread, and to bear it into the chamber where she had left the little stranger.

As she came in noiselessly, she saw her husband stooping over the infant, whose two white, chubby hands were fluttering about his rough face, and heard the cooing, dove-like voice that had sounded once before to her so sweetly.

As soon as Harding perceived that his wife was present, he left the bedside, half ashamed of his weakness in thus toying with a mere babe.

"The child must be hungry," he said, with as much indifference as he could affect.

"I've brought her something to eat," answered Mrs. Harding. "And won't you, Jacob, while I feed her, call the children, and bring me in an armful or two of wood? Breakfast will be all ready in a little while."

There was no resisting the manner of Mrs. Harding. If she had always spoken to her husband as now, he would always have been to her a kind husband. Her power over him for good might have been complete, had she been wise, gentle, and forbearing. But she had exercised no self-control, and almost from the beginning of their married life, had excited the evil in him, rather than the good. How much she had lost, and how much she had suffered in consequence, can hardly be imagined. Her life, for the last six or seven years, might almost be called a living martyrdom.

Harding did not answer, but went out from the chamber promptly to do as his wife had requested. Ordinarily, in calling the children, he spoke, to use the strong words of his wife, "as if he would take their heads off." He corrected this bad habit in the present instance; for, instead of ordering them roughly and angrily to get right up, or he would be after them "with a stick," he ascended to the room where they lay, and spoke kindly, yet firmly, to each one, subduing their waking impatience, by the quiet pressure of his own voice and manner.

"Andrew," he said in a tone that, exciting no opposition in the boy's mind, left the consciousness that he must obey—"dress yourself before you come down, and do it quickly."

"Yes, sir," was answered cheerfully, and Andrew sprang from his bed.

"Philip! Lucy!" The two younger children rose up. "Go down to your mother. She wants to dress you."

The voice and manner of their father were so unusual,

that the little ones felt both surprise and pleasure. They obeyed instantly, and Mr. Harding had the strange satisfaction of witnessing an act of ready and cheerful obedience in his children.

A great surprise awaited Lucy and Philip, and they were just in the state of mind for its full enjoyment.

A stranger, who had looked in upon Harding's family at the early meal on the previous day, and who looked in again upon them as they assembled around the breakfast-table on this morning, could hardly have believed that his eyes rested on the same individuals. In her usual place was Mrs. Harding, the stranger babe on her arm, and looking so beautiful and happy, that all eyes and hearts were drawn toward it. Little Lotty, from the moment its bright eyes looked into hers, had not once left its side, and now, as she sat close to her mother, she could not eat for pleasure.

"Has it any name, mother?" asked Andrew, from whom had not proceeded a single ill-natured word or act, since he came down and saw the baby.

Mrs. Harding did not reply, but looked at her husband. A name had been floating in her thoughts, but she hesitated about giving it utterance.

"Dora," said Mr. Harding. "Let us call her Dora."

Now, that was not the name about which Mrs. Harding had been thinking; nor was it a name that pleased her ear. It was on her tongue to say, "Oh, no;" but she kept silent. Her eyes were bent down upon the little one's face, and there she read her duty. For its sake, she refrained from objecting, because she feared that any want of accord with her husband would produce a state of opposition; and so she said nothing.

"Shall it be Dora?" Harding spoke in a pleasant voice.

"Yes, if you like the name." And Mrs. Harding looked up and smiled as she answered

"Have you thought of one, Mary?"

"A name has been in my mind ever since I awoke this morning. But if Dora sounds pleasant to your ears, let her be called Dora."

"What name did you think of? Perhaps I will like it best," said Harding.

"Grace." Mrs. Harding spoke the word softly and tenderly.

"The very name!" said her husband. "It is much better than Dora. Let her be called Grace."

"Grace! Grace!" All the children echoed the name; and the baby, as if conscious of a new importance, tossed its little hands, and smiled.

So touched was Mrs. Harding by this unexpected acquiescence of her husband, that tears came into her eyes. For the first time in months, it might be years, Harding had deferred to her wishes—but not in consequence of resolute persistence on her part. Had she contended for the name that pleased her best, he would never have seen in it a beauty and fitness above the one he preferred himself; and she would, in the end, have been compelled to yield, or have the babe thrust out from the home into which its presence had already brought so many rays of sunshine.

And so the babe was named Grace.

"What will you do, Mary?" said Harding to his wife, as, after sitting longer than usual at the table, he arose to leave the house. As he spoke, he looked toward the child that still lay in her arms. Mrs. Harding understood, and answered quickly—

"Oh, I shall get on very well. Breakfast wasn't late a minute this morning, and I'm sure every thing has gone on pleasantly. No hurry nor confusion. The children never behaved better in their lives."

And the mother glanced at them approvingly.

'But you can't attend to an infant, and do all your work into the bargain?"

"You see if every thing isn't in order, and dinner smoking on the table when you come home," answered Mrs. Harding, cheerfully, and with smiles.

Harding lingered. There was a fascination about little Grace, from the circle of which it seemed as if he could not break.

"What are we to do with this child, Mary?" said he, his manner becoming serious. "We have more children now than we can well take care of."

"Has it brought us trouble or pleasure, so far?" asked Mrs. Harding, looking up earnestly into her husband's face. He did not answer.

"Would you like to see it taken to the poor-house?"

"No, no. It shall not go there!" Harding spoke quickly and strongly

"It is a heaven-sent child, Jacob," said Mrs. Harding, in a low but impressive voice. "I know it from the dream that came to me last night. Let us accept the boon thankfully. He who sent it to us will see that it shall prove not a burden, but a blessing."

Harding answered not a word, but drew nearer to his wife, and, bending down, laid his finger upon the babe's soft cheek. He would have stooped lower and kissed the cheek, but felt ashamed to betray what seemed to him a weakness.

When that hard, harsh, passionate man went forth into the world of strife and labour, he carried in his thoughts the beautiful image of a babe. Men with whom he had been used to come in rough contact, saw a change, but divined not the cause. He was less coarse in speech, and rude in action—less contentious—less overbearing. The consequence was, that men who had always treated him roughly, because he was himself rough, instantly changed their manner, so that fewer things than usual occurred to chafe his spirit. Not during all that morning was the image of the babe once wholly obliterated, though many times obscured.

"What does it all mean?" said Harding to himself, as he reflected on the change. "Am I the same man that I was yesterday? What is there in a little helpless babe to cast a spell like this?"

But he questioned in vain. He could not understand the mystery. With lighter steps and a lighter heart than usual, he took his way home at dinner-time, looking for sunshine there. And he did not look in vain, for it lay broader and brighter over his threshold than it had lain for many years.

CHAPTER III.

THERE was quite a stir in the neighbourhood when the news got abroad that an infant had been found at the door of the Hardings. The gossips had a "world to say" on the subject; and all agreed, that a more unfortunate selection of a home for the little one could not have been made.

"It don't matter much as far as that goes," said Mrs. Margaret Willits, the storekeeper's wife, as she chattered over the tea-table with Mrs. Jarvis and Miss Gimp; "for the truth is—all among ourselves, remember—Harding can't support his own children, let alone other people's. Somebody will have to take the child off their hands, or they'll send it to the poor-house."

"But he does support his own children," replied Miss Gimp.

This was ingeniously remarked, in order to draw Mrs. Willits out.

"I'm not so sure of that," said the storekeeper's wife, mysteriously.

"Who does support them?"

Mrs. Jarvis put the question direct.

"I guess we do our part—this among ourselves."

"Oh, I understand," said Miss Gimp, a light breaking over her countenance. "He doesn't pay up at your store?"

"You've hit it right—but it's all among ourselves, remember."

"Oh, of course," returned Miss Gimp. And——"

"Of course," said Mrs. Jarvis. "We wouldn't speak of it on any consideration."

4

"Don't, if you please; for they're bad kind of people, and I wouldn't get their ill-will on any account. Mrs. Harding has an awful tongue in her head; and what is worse, I verily believe she would seek to do me some harm, if she knew I'd said a word against her."

"Don't be afraid," said both of the ladies at once.

"And so Harding owes your husband?" Miss Gimp spoke insinuatingly.

"Oh, yes. He's been getting things off and on now, for a year. Every little while he comes and pays something on account; but manages to let his bill keep getting larger and larger. Mr. Willits says it must stop soon. He was going to refuse them trust last week; but thought he would wait a while longer. He knows that the moment he stops them off, Harding will be terribly angry, and that he will not only lose the custom of the family, but all the money that is owed to him into the bargain."

"Rather a hard case," remarked Miss Gimp.

"Isn't it? And so, as I was saying, it doesn't matter much for the child, that it was left at their door. They'll never dream of keeping it."

"When was the infant abandoned?" asked Mrs. Jarvis.

"Three nights ago," replied the storekeeper's wife.

"Indeed! I never heard a syllable of it until to-day. And the child is still with them?"

"For all I know to the contrary," said Mrs. Willits.

"They've been very quiet about the matter, that's certain," remarked Miss Gimp, who was dressmaker and assistant gossip for the neighbourhood. "Three nights ago—and not a breath of it to reach my ears until last evening! It looks mysterious. Why should they be so very still about it?—they, of all people in the world! I shouldn't wonder, now that I think of it, if they knew more about the matter than they care to

tell. There's something wrong, depend on't. I'm as
sure of it as that I am sitting here."

"Wrong in what way?" asked Mrs. Jarvis, manifesting a new interest in the subject.

Miss Gimp affected a mysterious manner, as if she
knew more of what was going on in the neighbourhood
than she felt at liberty to tell.

"Have you any suspicion as to where the child came
from?" inquired Mrs. Willits.

"I have my own thoughts," said Miss Gimp, with a
gravity that so well became her. "But thoughts cannot
always be spoken."

"We are all friends, you know, Miss Gimp." Mrs.
Jarvis put on her most insinuating manner. "Old
friends, who can trust one another."

"I'd trust you with any thing I knew certain," replied Miss Gimp. "But it's all guess-work here. Wait
a few days. I'm bound to sift this matter to the bottom.
At present, I'll just give it as my opinion, that the
Hardings know a great deal more about the child than
they care to tell."

"You may be right there, Miss Gimp," said Mrs.
Willits—"else, why have they kept so still about it?"

"Exactly! Why have they kept so still about it?"

"Did you hear," inquired Mrs. Jarvis, "whether
there was a letter in the basket with the child?"

Mrs. Willits shook her head.

"Of course, there must have been," said Miss Gimp.
"There always is, in affairs of this kind. Take my
word for it, the parentage of that child is no secret to
the Hardings. And"—her imagination was taking a
freer range—"I shouldn't at all wonder if the basket
contained something more than a baby."

"What?"

The two ladies bent closer toward Miss Gimp.

"Money!"

"Money?"

"Yes: a handsome sum of money; and a letter besides, promising a regular payment of more every month or quarter, as long as they keep the child. Depend upon it, this is the case; I'm as sure of it as if I had seen into the basket myself."

"You've guessed it as certain as fate," said Mrs. Willits, with animation. "No one would have trusted a little helpless infant in their hands, without some strong hold, like this, upon their selfishness. Well, all I can say is, that, in the first place, they didn't deserve any such good fortune; and in the second place, whoever selected them as guardians of the child, have made a cruel experiment."

In this the other ladies fully agreed, Miss Gimp remarking, "It is an ill wind that blows nobody good. Your husband, Mrs. Willits, may now stand some chance of getting his money."

"Sure enough! I didn't think of that. It takes you, Miss Gimp, to see all the bearings of a subject."

Miss Gimp was flattered by this compliment, and drew her head up in a way peculiar to herself when pleased.

"Has any one seen the child?" inquired Mrs. Jarvis.

"I have not," answered Mrs. Willits; "nor have I met with any one who has called on Mrs. Harding since it was left at her house. There's neither pleasure nor comfort in visiting her; and so people stay away. I haven't been in her house for three months. The fact is, the last time I called on her, she was in an awful humour about something or other, and as snappish as a turtle. I'm sure she boxed the ears of every child she has, three times over, while I was there, and, if the truth must be told, they richly deserved all they got; for a more ill-mannered, quarrelsome brood I never saw. Andrew, their oldest boy, is a perfect little desperado.

The way he knocked the other children about was dreadful. I was in fear every moment of seeing some of their limbs broken or eyes put out."

"Just as it was when I called there last," said Miss Gimp. "I went to fit a dress for Mrs. Harding. The house seemed like a perfect bedlam. The children quarrelled all the while, and their mother stormed at them incessantly. I was too glad to get away."

"Do you expect to go there again very soon?" asked Mrs. Jarvis.

"I ought to have gone there a week ago, to take home the cape of her last new dress. She wants it, I know. There isn't more than half an hour's work on it, and I'll do that this very evening."

"Then you'll see her in the morning," said the storekeeper's wife.

"Yes."

"Just drop in on your way back, Miss Gimp; that's a good soul. It's such a strange affair, I really feel curious about it. Take a good look at the baby, and see if you can trace a likeness to anybody. And then, be sure to find out if any money came with it, or is promised. I want to know about that, of all things."

"Never fear for me," said Miss Gimp, looking unusually bright. "I'll gather up every crumb of information."

"And you'll call in as you go by?"

"Oh, certainly."

"Do, if you please," said Mrs. Jarvis; "for, as I have an errand out in the morning, I'll manage to be here— at what time?"

"Say ten o'clock," replied Miss Gimp.

Little else was talked of by the ladies during the hour they remained together after tea.

On the next morning, at ten o'clock, Mrs. Willits and Mrs. Jarvis sat together, awaiting the arrival of Miss

Gimp, who had looked in upon the storekeeper's wife, as she passed on her way to the Hardings, to say that she would call on her return and make a report. Sooner than they expected the dressmaker, she came in. Her face did not look very animated.

"Good morning, Miss Gimp!—good morning!" said the ladies.

"Good morning."

Miss Gimp tried to look important and well satisfied with herself, but the effort was wholly unsuccessful.

"Well, Miss Gimp, did you see the baby?"

"I did."

There was an ominous gravity in the gossip's tones.

"Is it a nice-looking baby?" inquired Mrs. Willits.

"A very nice-looking baby, indeed. In fact, it's the dcarest, sweetest little thing I ever saw."

"Why, Miss Gimp! You don't say so?"

"It's the truth, every word I tell you."

"Well, really! It's a nice baby, then?"

"You may believe it. And then, it's so good! Mrs. Harding says it hasn't cried an hour since it came into the house."

"You don't tell me!"

"I can well believe her; for, while I was there, it did nothing but smile and coo, and try its best to talk to every one who came near the cradle where it lay."

This information was not half so satisfactory to the two ladies, as the report of its being cross and disagreeable would have been.

"Well, so much for the baby," said Mrs. Jarvis. "And now, Miss Gimp, tell us all you learned about it. Where do you think it came from?"

"Haven't the least idea in the world," replied Miss Gimp.

"Really!"

"Really!"

"Could you trace a likeness?"

Miss Gimp shook hear head.

"Doesn't it look like somebody you have seen?"

"No one that I can remember; and yet the face is strangely familiar. It seems as if I had met it only yesterday; but, for my life, I cannot tell where."

"What does Mrs. Harding say?"

"Nothing."

"Nothing?"

"Or next to nothing. She's very quiet and very reserved. Something has come over her and the whole family."

"Indeed!" Both the ladies spoke at once.

"In what respect?" asked Mrs. Willits.

"I didn't hear a cross word while I was in the house, either from mother or children. The last time I was there, Lotty, the youngest, did nothing but fret, and snarl, and cry. But this morning she sat on the floor, beside the cradle, looking fondly on the baby, or playing with it in the gentlest manner. The fact is, that baby seems to have brought a charm into the house. I could hardly believe I was with the same people."

"You don't tell us so?"

"It's the truth, just what I say."

"Was there any letter or money in the basket?" inquired Mrs. Willits, whose interest in that aspect of the case was particularly strong.

"Not that I could find out," answered Miss Gimp. "I felt my way, and hinted, and did every thing except put the question direct; but Mary Harding either could not or would not understand me. She was always a little close-mouthed, you knew."

"Why didn't you ask her right up and down? I would have done so," said Mrs. Willits.

"It was on my tongue's end more than once; but every time I was about to speak, she seemed to know what was in my mind, and made some remark that threw me off."

"How provoking!"

"It was provoking," said Miss Gimp, looking particularly annoyed.

"What does she intend doing with the little stranger?" asked Mrs. Jarvis.

"Keep it," replied Miss Gimp.

"She's got a house full of her own now—more than her husband·is able to support," said Mrs. Willits. "I don't understand the woman."

"I think I do," returned Miss Gimp, assuming a knowing look. She was good at surmising. "As to there being any disinterested feeling toward the babe, that is not admitted for an instant."

"Of course not."

Miss Gimp resumed—"You may rely upon it, then, as I suggested in the beginning, that she knows all about where the child came from, and is well paid for taking care of it."

"But how do you account for the singular change in her temper, and, above·all, for the change in the temper of her children?"

"I've thought of all that," answered the dressmaker, "and own that I am puzzled. It has occurred to me, that her young savages may have been tamed, as they tame wild beasts, by hunger and stripes. If she has a motive strong enough to make her resolute, Mrs. Harding is not the woman to hesitate about the adoption of any means for the accomplishment of her purposes. It has, no doubt, been made her interest to keep this child, and to keep it right. If this is really so, she will make all bend to her will in the matter."

And so, after all, the dressmaker had failed to learn any thing about the babe, that was satisfactory either to herself or her friends, Mrs. Willits and Mrs. Jarvis. As

might be supposed, the report of Miss Gimp excited still
more the curiosity of the two ladies, who had urged the
visit to Mrs. Harding. They were really troubled, because of their inability to penetrate the mystery that surrounded the affair. Over one bit of information, reserved to the last by Miss Gimp, they became excited;
but it left them still in the dark.

"Harry Wilkins saw the person who left the basket
at Harding's door," said the dressmaker.

"What!"

"I was talking with Harry Wilkins last evening, and
he says, that on the night the child was left at Harding's, he went to Beechwood. On the way, he met a
woman carrying a basket. She was young, and had
something strange-looking about her. It struck him
that she was in trouble, for she seemed very irresolute—
walking on for a time hurriedly; then stopping as if in
doubt; and once or twice turning back toward Beechwood. His curiosity was excited, and he watched her
for some time. On his return, he met her again, but
without the basket. He passed very close to her—
close enough to get a glimpse of her face, which he
says looked like the face of one in deep distress."

"And she came from Beechwood?" said Mrs. Jarvis,
breathing deeply.

"She came from that direction, Harry says."

"The child's mother, no doubt. What a wretch she
must be! From Beechwood? That's something to
know. I've got a cousin living in Beechwood, and I'll
go over and see her this very blessed week. I shouldn't
wonder if she could trace the whole affair."

Saying this, Mrs. Jarvis arose, and made a movement
to go, at which Miss Gimp remarked that she must run
home also, as she had promised a dress on that very
day, and the scissors were not into it yet. Nearly five
minutes elapsed before all their parting words were said;

then they separated, with mutual promises to sift the matter more closely, and to communicate, one to another, any thing new that might happen to be learned.

CHAPTER IV.

A WEEK passed, and, notwithstanding Mrs. Willits, in league with Miss Gimp and Mrs. Jarvis, had been all eye and all ear, so to speak, yet they had not been able to learn any thing satisfactory to themselves about the stranger babe. Each of the ladies had, during the time, made a call upon Mrs. Harding, and each came away, more strongly confirmed in her first conclusion, that she knew a great deal more about the child than she had cared to tell. As for the babe itself, there could be but one opinion. Miss Gimp said it was "lovely;" and when she spoke of an infant so decidedly, you might be sure there was something about it more than common.

Meantime, singular changes were progressing in the home where the little offcast had found an asylum— changes that as much surprised the inmates as those who looked on from a distance. Grace had won all hearts from the beginning; even selfish, rude, ill-natured Andrew, who had been the pest of the family, stood subdued and gentle in her presence. Before she came, his greatest delight was in annoying and oppressing the other children; now his chief pleasure consisted in holding the babe, carrying her about, or playing with her as she lay in the cradle. So attentive was he, that Mrs. Harding scarcely perceived any new demand upon her time, in consequence of so important an addition to her family. Left more to themselves, by the diversion of Andrew's attention, the other children—whose almost incessant strife owed its origin mainly to their older brother's interference—rarely gave way to a wrangling spirit. When it did occur, a word from their mother subdued their angry feelings.

Often and often did the hands of Mrs Harding pause in her work, as she thought intently on this new order of things, and wondered how it was, that a single word could calm the stormy passions of her children, when only a little while before, nothing but a more violent storm on her part could allay the tempest on theirs. How greatly she was herself changed, did not come with clearness into her apprehension—changed, we mean, in her external aspects; for, internally, no real change had yet taken place : there was only the beginning of a change. Nor was she aware how different were her words and manner of speaking, when addressing her children, to what they were a little while before.

One thing the children did not fail to notice. It was this : the marked difference in their mother when Grace was awake and in the sitting-room, and when she was asleep in the adjoining chamber. She was always gentler and more forbearing toward them when the babe was present than when absent. Nor did Mrs. Harding fail to remark, that the children were more gentle and obedient when Grace was in the room with them than when she was sleeping.

Quite as remarkable was the change in Mr. Harding. He never came in, now, with a heavy, horse-like tread, nor banged the door behind him, as had been his custom. Nor did he reprove the children, when in fault, with his former angry violence. Always he went first to look at the babe, as if that were uppermost in his thoughts. And what seemed to please him particularly, was the fact, that little Grace began to flutter her tiny hands the moment he appeared, and never seemed better satisfied than when in his arms. Not once, since she came to them, like a gift from heaven, as she was, had he left home in the evening, to spend his time at the tavern. In his favour it may be said, that his associations at the tavern had never presented a very strong attraction; and he had only gone there, because every thing in the home-sphere, owing to the incongruities of temper between him and his wife, was disagreeable and repulsive.

We have omitted thus far to mention that Jacob Harding was a carpenter by trade. His shop stood at no great distance from the store of Willits the grocer, and not far from the tavern kept by a worthless fellow named Stark, who was doing more harm in the neighbourhood in a single month than he had ever done good in his life. The absence of Harding from the bar-room of Stark, for so many consecutive evenings, did not fail to excite the tavern-keeper's attention, who, not liking to lose so good a customer, made it his business to call in at the shop of Harding, and in a familiar, hale-fellow, well-met sort of a way, inquire if he had been sick. This was about a week after the appearance of little Grace in the carpenter's family. Harding answered in the negative, and with a slight coldness of manner.

"What's the matter, then?" said Stark. "Any thing wrong at home?"

"Nothing."

"We wanted you, particularly, last night. Tom Ellis, from Beechwood, and Jack Fleming, from Avondale, were both here. They had a jolly time of it, I can tell you; and if they asked for you once, they did a dozen times. You don't know what you lost. They're coming over again this evening You must be sure and meet them, for I promised that you would be on hand."

"You were a little too fast in that," said Harding, as he tightened the blade in his jack-plane, and then sighted the edge to see if it was at the true cutting distance.

"Why so?" asked Stark.

"Because I shall not be there."

"And why not, pray?"

"Because I'm better off, and better contented, at home," was replied.

"Tied to your wife's apron-string."

This was said pleasantly, yet with just enough of sarcasm to touch the quick feelings of Harding, without giving offence.

"I never was tied to a woman's apron-string in my life, and never expect to be. Mary Harding knows me far too well to attempt any thing of that kind."

The tavern-keeper shrugged his shoulders, and arched his coarse eyebrows in a way that said, "I can believe as much of that as I please."

The quick temper of Harding took fire, and he was about making a sharp retort; but, singularly enough, the image of little Grace came suddenly before the eyes of his mind, and something in her innocent face subdued and tranquillized him.

"Look here, Harding." Stark spoke in a coarse, rough way. "What's this I hear about somebody's brat being left at your door? Is it so?—or only Gimp-gossip?"

"A young babe was left at my door," Harding answered, coldly, and, at the same time, commenced driving his plane over a rough board that lay on his work-bench.

"You don't tell me so! Well, what have you done with it?"

"Kept it."

"Kept it! You're joking! I thought you had a

house full of your own—more than you could get bread for without making a slave of yourself."

Harding felt annoyed, as well at the tavern-keeper's words as his manner, and an angry retort was on his tongue. But he controlled himself, and merely answered, with assumed indifference—

"We haven't found it in the way, so far."

"Whose is it?" inquired Stark, still in his rude manner.

"Don't know," replied Harding.

"Why don't you send it to the poor-house? I'd do it in less than no time."

"When we are tired of keeping it, perhaps we will do so."

Stark began now to see that his way of speaking to the carpenter was not altogether relished; and, as it was by no means his interest to offend one of his customers, he changed, somewhat, his manner of addressing him. But he failed altogether in his effort to restore the old state of feeling that had existed between them.

From the shop of Harding, Stark went to the store of Mr. Willits, where he bought a barrel of sugar and a bag of coffee. He was about the only man in the neighbourhood whose pocket-book was sufficiently well filled to warrant the purchase of groceries in such liberal quantities.

"Make out the bill and receipt it," said he, in a self-satisfied voice.

"I like that," was the pleasant response of the store-keeper. "I wish all my customers were as ready to put the cash down.'

"Pay as you go—that is my motto," returned Stark. "You'll not find my name on anybody's books."

"It's the safest kind of a motto, and one that I shall have to suggest to two or three people about here even should I offend them," said Willits. "Harding, for instance, between you and me."

"Jacob Harding! Why, is he running behindhand?"

The storekeeper, before answering, threw open his ledger, and, after glancing rapidly along a column of figures on one of the pages, said—

"Yes; to the tune of a hundred dollars in six months."

"Whew! And he's the man that takes in stray babies? He can afford to be generous—at your expense."

"Not any longer. Thank you for that hint. I'll act upon it at once."

And so he did; for, at that moment, Andrew Harding entered the store, with a wooden pail in his hand, and said that his mother had sent him for six pounds of flour and two pounds of sugar.

"Have you brought the money?" asked Willits.

"No, sir. Mother says, charge it."

"Tell your mother that I can't charge any thing more."

The boy looked bewildered. He did not clearly understand the storekeeper.

"Tell your mother that she must send the money. I can't trust any more."

Andrew retired slowly, his mind in considerable perplexity, and bore the message to his mother.

"That's right," said Stark, approvingly. "It's the only safe way to do business. I rather think Harding will be as mad as a March hare. You may look out for a squall before night."

"Let it come; I'm not at all concerned," replied Willits.

"I hope," said Stark, growing serious, "that nothing I have said has caused you to take this stand with

Harding. "We've always been on good terms; and I wouldn't say any thing to injure him for the world."

"Oh, no. My mind was pretty well made up before you came in. That baby business decided me. Mrs. Willits and I were talking it over last night, and we both came to the conclusion that, if he couldn't make both ends meet before, there was no hope for him now. We did think, at first, that a money inducement caused him to keep the child; but Mrs. Harding assured my wife, yesterday, that not a farthing came with it, nor was promised at any future time. If they are fools enough to take up a burden like this, they mustn't expect me to bear it for them."

"This refusal on your part may do them good," said Stark. "It will, at least, open their eyes to their true position. I rather think the child will find its way into the poor-house before it is a week older."

"I don't care where it goes, or what becomes of it," answered the storekeeper, "so I get my money."

Soon after Stark left the shop of Jacob Harding, the latter put on his coat and hat, and went over to the house of a farmer, named Lee, about a quarter of a mile distant. This Lee, a rather thriftless sort of a man, who spent far too large a portion of his time and money at Stark's tavern, owed the carpenter a hundred and fifty dollars for new roofing his house, and doing sundry repairs to his dilapidated old barn. The account had been standing for some months. On the payment of this money, Harding had intended settling his bill at the grocer's. The manner of Willits, on the day before, when he had called to get half a pound of tea and some corn meal, annoyed him considerably. He saw that the storekeeper was getting uneasy at the size of his account, which, but for the failure to procure a settlement with Lee, would have been long since paid off. He had brooded over this until a sort of desperate feeling took possession of him; and, in this state of mind, he went over to see the farmer.

"Can't do any thing for you," said Lee, in the coolest way imaginable, on Harding's asking for a settlement. "Haven't ten dollars in cash to bless myself with, let alone a hundred and fifty."

Harding felt exceedingly fretted at this way of treating him, and said, quite sharply—

"Pray, Mr. Lee, when do you intend settling my account?"

"Some of these days," replied the farmer, indifferently.

"That way of doing business don't suit me. I want something definite. I paid the cash down for the shingles that cover your roof; and now I want my money."

"Don't get excited, Harding: it won't do any good," said Lee. "The man doesn't live about here that can drive this horse; so *you* needn't try."

This was more than the carpenter could bear. Bitterly did he retort upon the farmer, and left him, finally, with threats of an immediate resort to law for the recovery of his bill.

When Harding and his wife met at dinner-time, each perceived in the other's countenance a troubled aspect. Harding's heavy brows were drawn down; and about his wife's mouth was the old look of fretfulness that had so often repelled him. For the first time, he passed the cradle without even looking at Grace, whose round, white arms had commenced flying the moment she heard the sound of his footsteps across the threshold; and, going into the yard, he took up the axe, and commenced splitting up a stick of cord wood. This done, he came back into the house, again passing the cradle, and sitting down, in moody silence, at the dinner-table, on which their meal had already been served. While cutting up the meat, and helping it around, the low, sweet, coaxing murmur of the baby's voice sounded in his ears. The cradle was only a little way from him, and so turned that Grace could see him. And there she lay, fluttering her arms, and cooing, and trying all means in her power to arrest his attention. Yet, resolutely, he kept his eyes turned away from the imploring little one. But weaker, each moment, became his resolution; for her voice came to his ears like the music of David's harp to Saul, driving out the evil spirit. At last he could resist the babe's pleadings no longer. Almost stealthily, he turned his eyes upon her. One look was enough. The tenderness of a mother filled his heart. So sudden was the revulsion of his feelings, that, for a few moments, he was bewildered. But of one thing he was soon clearly conscious, and that was of having Grace in his arms, and hugging her almost passionately to his heart.

CHAPTER V.

THE suddenness with which Harding arose from the table and caught up the child, which he had not seemed to notice since he came in, and the eager way in which he held it to his heart, naturally excited the surprise of his wife, who looked at him wonderingly. His indifference toward Grace had not been unobserved by Mrs. Harding. She saw that he was in one of his unhappy moods—that a dark cloud was on his spirit—and that only a word was needed to awaken a fierce storm. And, more than all this, the message brought from the storekeeper by Andrew had so deeply angered her, that her mind was still panting under the excitement, and still fretting itself with indignant thoughts; so that she, too, was ready for strife. It had been as much as she could do to keep back from her lips words of sharp reproof, for the cruel indifference manifested by her husband toward the pleading babe : most probably, a few minutes longer of forced neglect on his part, would have brought down upon him a storm of words that would have marred every thing for little Grace, and made her presence, in the household, ever after, a cause of angry contention. Happily, the quick-tempered wife controlled her struggling impulses long enough for better influences to prevail. As she looked at the singular exhibition of feeling in her husband, she was touched by softer emotions. The incident gave her a deeper insight into his character, while it quickened her own thoughts into self-reproaches for the misjudgment which had wellnigh fanned a few embers into fiercely burning flames of discord

As for Harding, now that the repressed tenderness of his heart had free course, he found himself carried away as by a flood. The babe in his arms felt more precious to him than life itself; and it seemed as if he could never be done hugging it to his heart. When, at length, he reseated himself at the dinner-table, with Grace on his knee, and looked over to his wife, the cloud had passed from her countenance.

"What possessed you," she said, smiling, and in a pleasant voice, "to neglect the sweet child so? She was almost dying to have you notice her."

Harding did not answer, but merely drew Grace close against him, and, bending over, talked to her in fond, childish language.

A calm followed this little exciting episode, in which both Mr. and Mrs. Harding looked and felt sober, but not ill-natured. After dinner, as Harding was preparing to leave the house, he took some silver change from his pocket, and handing it to his wife, said—

"Our bill at the store is getting rather large. Don't send for any thing without the money. Here are two dollars and a half for any little thing you may want."

The change in his wife's countenance as he said this arrested Harding's attention.

"What's the matter?" he asked, abruptly.

"Nothing much," she replied, her face flushing as she spoke. "Only I'm glad you've left me some money, for we're out of flour, and—and"——

"And what?" She paused, stammering, and Harding saw that something was wrong.

"Nothing, only Willits sent word this morning, that he wouldn't let us have any thing more, unless we paid the money down!"

"He did!" A fierce light burned instantly in the eye of Jacob Harding, and his lips were drawn back against his teeth.

"Yes,' said his wife, forcing herself to speak in a mild and soothing way; "but no matter, Jacob. Let us try to get on without asking for credit anywhere. I'll do my best to economize in every thing. It chafes me to be under obligations to anybody, and especially to the Willits. I don't like any of the family."

"That's talking outright, Mary!" said Harding, the threatening scowl on his heavy brow suddenly breaking away; and, as he spoke, he thrust his hand a second time into his trousers pocket, and drew out a handful of small change, which he counted over.

"Here are three dollars more," he added. "It's all the money I have just now, and may be all I shall receive this week. Make it go as far as you can."

"You may be sure I will do that, Jacob," replied his wife, kindly and earnestly.

"Wouldn't trust us any more!" Harding's mind returned to this hard, unpleasant, mortifying fact. "Very well—so let it be. He's had a good deal of my money in his time—I hardly think he will get as much in the future. Don't you buy any thing there that you can do without. The next time I go over to Beechwood, I will lay in a good stock of things, if I happen to have the money. I saw Lee to-day, and tried to get him to settle that bill of his; but he put me off again, and is more indifferent about it than ever. I got out of all patience, and threatened to put the sheriff on him. It will have to come to this sooner or later; and the quicker it is done, the quicker I shall get my money."

"Couldn't you trade off the account to Willits, and thus save a world of trouble?" suggested the wife.

Mr. Harding caught at this suggestion, and, after turning it over in his mind for a few moments, said—

"I don't know, Mary, but that might be done. Now that I come to think of it, I remember hearing some-body say that Willi's was about buying that house and

acre lot where Jones lives. You know it belongs to Mr.
Lee. There's no doubt in the world but that he could
settle my account in the transaction. I'll see him about
it this very afternoon."

"Do, Jacob," answered his wife, encouragingly. "It
will be such a relief to have this all off our minds."

In spite of his indignation against Willits, Harding
went direct to his store. The latter, on seeing him
enter, made up his mind for a sharp passage of words
with the fiery tempered carpenter. Still, he managed to
receive him with a forced smile.

"How much have you against me on your books?"
inquired Harding, speaking firmly, and with a sober
countenance, yet repressing, as far as possible, all appearance of anger.

The storekeeper, affecting a pleasant manner, turned
over his ledger, and, glancing at the account, which was
already footed up, replied—

"One hundred and fourteen dollars."

"So much as that?" Harding showed surprise.

"I will make you out a bill of items, day and date,
and you can examine the account. I presume you will
find every charge correct."

"I expected to have paid this long ago," said the
carpenter, "but have been disappointed in getting a
large bill. To-day I tried my best to collect, but I'm
afraid there's no chance for me, unless I go to law, and I
don't want to do that."

"Whose account is it?" inquired Willits.

'The one I have against Lee for roofing his house,
and repairing his barn."

"Is it possible he hasn't paid that yet?"

"Not a cent of it."

The storekeeper looked serious for a few moments,
then, shaking his head, he remarked—

"That's not right in Lee."

"No, it is not right," said Harding, warmly. "If he had paid me, I would not now be in debt a single dollar."

"Have you any objection to transferring your account to me?" Willits hesitated a little, as if fearful the proposition would not be received with favour. "I have some business transactions with Lee, in which, most probably, I could manage to include your bill."

"The very thing I thought of proposing to you," said Harding. "I understand you are about buying the property now occupied by Jones; and it has occurred to me that you might save my account in the purchase, thus obliging me and getting a settlement of your own bill at the same time."

"It can all be done, no doubt," replied the store-keeper. "Lee has offered the house and grounds at a fair price, and is anxious for me to buy—so anxious, that a proposition to take your claim against him in part payment will be no impediment to the bargain. The best way for you to proceed will be to get his note in settlement. He'll give that readily enough, in order to gain time, and get rid of the annoyance of being dunned. This note you can endorse to me, and I will pay it over to him."

Perfectly satisfactory to both parties was the proposed arrangement, and the two men separated in much better humour with themselves and each other than when they met. During the afternoon, Harding called again on Mr. Lee, who readily acceded to his request, and gave him his note, at six months, in settlement of the account.

"Pleasant news, Mary," said the carpenter, as he came home at sundown. "My name is off of Willits' books."

"Off of his books! How, Jacob?" Mrs. Harding did not see his meaning clearly

"I've settled his account."

"Have you? Oh! I'm so glad."

"And better still, Mary: he owes me thirty-six dollars, which I have agreed to take out of his store, as we want things in his line."

"It *is* pleasant news, indeed, Jacob. But how did all this come to pass?"

"Just in the way you suggested. Willits has taken my bill against Lee, and credited me with the difference between that and the account on his books."

"Oh! I am so glad: it has taken such a load off of me," said Mrs. Harding. "I don't believe Mr. Lee would ever have paid the bill without your suing him; and I dread lawsuits above every thing: they always bring trouble to both sides."

Already, Grace was in the great, strong arms of the carpenter; and Lotty, between whom and her father a new and gentler relation had existed ever since the stranger-babe came to them, was leaning on his knee and playing with the happy little one.

At this moment, a form darkened the door. It was the form of a woman, just past life's middle age. Her countenance was strongly marked—the lines as indicative of patient endurance as great suffering. She was tall in person, with the carriage of one who had moved in polished circles.

"Can you tell me," said she, as she advanced one foot inside of the door, "how far it is to Beechwood?"

"Nearly two miles, ma'am," replied Mrs. Harding, who had turned, on perceiving the presence of a stranger.

"So far away?" said the woman, in apparent concern "I can't possibly reach there before dark."

"You certainly cannot," replied Mrs. Harding. She then added "Won't you come in and rest yourself?"

"Thank you," returned the stranger, stepping across the threshold, and advancing a few paces into the room.

"What a dear, sweet babe!" she said, as, on taking a chair, she fixed her eyes, with a tender, admiring gaze, upon the babe that still remained in Harding's arms. She could not have offered a remark better calculated to make a favourable impression on the minds of the carpenter and his wife.

"What is her name?" she asked, after a moment's pause.

"We call her Grace," replied Mrs. Harding, all her countenance lit up with pleasure.

"Grace—Grace," said the woman, half speaking to herself, in an abstracted way. "A beautiful name," she added; "none more beautiful." And then she bent forward, and gazed at the child with such an earnest, tender expression, that Mrs. Harding, who was observing her intently, felt a troubled consciousness that she knew something of the child, and did not now look upon it for the first time in her life.

There was about the stranger a bearing that inspired involuntary respect. Her calm, intelligent eyes looked into those of the carpenter and his wife in a way that caused them to feel a singular deference; and when she referred again to the long distance she had still to go, and spoke, in a troubled voice, of the gathering darkness, Harding said, looking at his wife—

"If the lady will accept what poor accommodations our house will afford, she need not go to Beechwood to-night. What say you, Mary?"

"She is welcome to the best we have to give," was the answer of Mrs. Harding.

"I did not expect this," said the woman, evidently touched by the proffered hospitality; "nor do I know whether it will be altogether right for me to trespass on

6

your kindness. If there is a respectable tavern in the neighbourhood"——

Harding shook his head, as he answered—

"There is no tavern about here but Stark's, and I couldn't advise you to go there. If you will remain in our poor home, believe yourself entirely welcome."

"Let me take your bonnet and shawl," said Mrs. Harding, encouragingly; and she reached out her hands to receive them.

The woman hesitated only a moment, and then removing her bonnet and shawl, gave them to her hostess, who took them into the adjoining chamber. As Mrs. Harding returned to the apartment she had just left, she was struck with the singular beauty of the woman's countenance—bearing though it did the marks of time—as well as by the depth and brilliancy of her eyes, that were fixed, almost as if by fascination, on the infant which still lay against the bosom of her husband.

All parties were now, for a time, in a state of embarrassment. Harding felt a little uncomfortable in the presence of the woman, whose eyes, whenever they rested upon him, seemed as if trying to read his very thoughts; and the stranger, conscious of the effect her entrance had produced, did not feel altogether at ease.

"Let me have that dear babe," said the woman, reaching out her hands toward Grace.

The little one shrunk closer against the breast of Harding, while a shade, almost of fear, darkened her face.

"Won't you come?"

The woman spoke in soft and winning tones, and still extended her hands; but the babe could not be lured from its place.

At this moment, Andrew came in, rudely, dashing his hat upon the floor, and pushing his sister Lucy aside so roughly as almost to throw her down. Lucy gave an

angry scream at this violence, and called her brother
some vile name. The woman turned, half startled, at
this sudden outbreak, and fixed her dark, penetrating
eyes on Andrew, who, now first conscious of the presence of a stranger, became quiet, and shrunk away into
the farther part of the room, the eyes of the woman still
following him.

"Is that the place for your hat, sir?"

Anger, as well as mortification, caused Harding to
speak roughly to the boy. The woman seemed quite as
much startled by the voice of the father as she had been
by the rudeness of the son. The look she threw upon
him was timid—almost fearful; and her eyes passed
rapidly from his dark, threatening face, to the calm,
sweet, confiding countenance of the infant, who seemed
not in the least disturbed by the sudden gust of passion
which had come sweeping over the little household.

Andrew looked sulky and stubborn for a few moments
only; then he returned to the place where his hat lay
upon the floor, and taking it up, hung it upon a nail.
In the next minute he stood beside the baby, who, the
instant she saw him, arose from her reclining position, reached out her little hands to him, and almost
springing into his arms, gave voice to her pleasure and
affection in sounds as well understood as if the utterance
had been in words. Andrew bore her in a sort of
triumph about the room; while the stern features of his
father gradually relaxed, as his eyes followed the happy
babe, until no trace remained therein of the anger which
disfigured it a little while before. Lucy, too, forgot her
indignation against Andrew, and, moving close beside
her brother, clapped her hand at Grace, and talked to
her with a voice so full of tenderness, that the stranger
looked at her in wonder, hardly crediting the fact that
she was the same little girl who, scarcely a moment before, had startled her with a shrill cry of anger.

Silent, yet attentively observant of all that passed, did the visiter now remain, until supper was ready, and she was invited to join the family in their evening meal.

"Do you reside in Beechwood?" inquired Harding, addressing the stranger, soon after they had gathered around the table.

"No, sir," was her simple answer, somewhat coolly made, as though she wished to repel inquiry.

"You have friends there?" said Harding, who, as he observed the stranger more narrowly, felt his curiosity in regard to her increasing. Particularly did her manner of looking at the child excite his attention: to him it seemed as if she made an effort to conceal the interest really felt by her in the little one.

"Yes, I have friends there," she replied; and then said, almost in the same breath, "How old is your little Grace?"

Harding looked at his wife, and she looked at him. Both seemed taken by surprise at the question; and both were slightly confused.

"How old is it, Mary?" asked Harding.

"About nine weeks," replied Mrs. Harding, her face receiving a shade of colour as she spoke.

The stranger looked at her intently. Mrs. Harding's eyes fell under the steady gaze.

"A bright child for nine weeks old," remarked the woman.

Then she seemed to lose herself in thought, and once or twice sighed deeply. After the supper-table was cleared away, and the children were all in bed, her manner underwent a change. She was now entirely at her ease, and conversed in so attractive a way with the carpenter and his wife, that both found themselves strangely drawn toward her, and ready to answer freely in regard to their personal affairs, about which she inquired with an interest they felt to be genuine. About people in the neighbourhood she also asked questions; and when reference was made to Stark the tavern-keeper, she spoke strongly of the danger of visiting such houses as he kept.

"It gratified me more than I can express," she said, looking at Harding, "to find you at home, during the evening, with your family. There is every thing to hope, for a sober, industrious man. . Your struggle with the world may be hard for a time, but keep a brave heart. With temperance, industry, and frugality at home, you are sure to rise above your present position. It is our first meeting, and it may be our last; but if we ever do meet again, I shall expect to find that Andrew Harding has taken a long stride in the way of prosperity."

There was more in her manner than in her words that impressed the mind of the carpenter. But no matter in which lay the influence, Harding felt new purposes growing up in his heart; and he even said to himself, "If ever we do meet again, it shall be as you predict."

At an early hour, Mr. and Mrs. Harding retired, after having shown their guest to the little spare room kept for visitors.

"I must have one look at that dear babe of yours," she said, as she was about leaving them for the night.

Mrs. Harding led her into her own chamber, where Grace was sleeping, and drew down the bed-clothes from the face of the infant. The woman bent low over it, and, for a time that seemed long to Mrs. Harding, stood gazing upon the calm face before her, so full of heavenly innocence. There were tears on her lashes, when, with a deep, quivering sigh, she lifted herself from the babe. Placing a hand on the shoulder of Mrs. Harding, and

6*

raising a finger slowly upward, she said, in a tone so solemn, that it thrilled to the heart of her auditor—

"God has committed to your care one of the precious ones whose angels are ever before his face. Oh! never forget your high responsibility. Love, cherish, keep the dear one."

The woman's voice faltered. She made an attempt to say more; but, as if conscious that she was betraying too much feeling, turned away quickly, and retired to the little chamber that had been assigned to her.

On the next morning, breakfast was all ready, ere the stranger joined the family.

"Had you not better call her?" said Harding to his wife.

Mrs. Harding stepped to the door of the guest-chamber, and tapped lightly. She tapped a second time, for there was neither movement nor reply; yet all remained silent. A louder summons was answered only by its own echo.

Wondering at this, Mrs. Harding lifted the latch, and pushed open the door.

"There is no one here, Andrew," she said, in a startled voice.

"No one, Mary!"

"Even the bed is not tumbled! What can it mean?"

The carpenter now stood beside his wife, and both entered the room together. There was no evidence whatever that any one had passed the night there. On the little dressing-table was a narrow slip of white paper, which Mrs. Harding caught up. On it was written simply these words—

"Grace Harding. Ten weeks old to-day. June 4th, 18—."

"It is very strange!" said the carpenter, with a look of doubt and wonder on his countenance.

"Very strange!" echoed his wife, in a troubled voice.

"Who can she be?"

"One," answered Mrs. Harding, "who knows all about our little Grace. I felt that it was so last night."

And weak, pale, and trembling, she sunk into a chair.

CHAPTER VI.

THE sudden appearance of the woman, her singular conduct, and mysterious departure, were new facts in the strange series of events, that were almost bewildering the minds of Mr. and Mrs. Harding. Something in this woman's manner had strongly impressed them both, and now, when they thought of her, it was with a certain sense of constraint, as if she were present, and closely observing their actions. That she bore some kind of relationship to the babe was no longer a question in their thoughts; and it was equally clear, that her visit was by no means accidental or purposeless.

A pressure upon the feelings was a natural consequence; not so much a troubled pressure, as a certain thoughtful sobriety, favourable to self-control, and productive of wiser counsels in the minds of both the carpenter and his quick-tempered wife. Each had need of a preparation like this, for the day was to prove one of more than ordinary trial.

From some cause, Andrew, their oldest boy, naturally of an exceedingly perverse temper, was ill-natured and quarrelsome beyond his wont, on this particular morning. Since rising, he had not ceased to interfere with Lucy and Philip, and this created a strife among the three, which the mother vainly sought to subdue. Not until the father, with a stern threat and a smart blow, commanded the overbearing lad to cease from his annoyance of his brother and sister, was the discord abated. And then the evil in the boy's heart remained strong as ever. Only the fear of instant punishment kept down the spirit of rebellion.

Soon after his father left for the shop, his mother said to him—

"Andrew, go over to the store, and get me two pounds of sugar and two pounds of rice; and go quickly, for it's nearly school-time now."

"Where's the money?" Andrew spoke very rudely.

"Never mind the money," said Mrs. Harding. "Go and do as I tell you."

"'Taint no use. Mr. Willits said yesterday that you needn't send for trust any more."

"Go, this minute, you little"——

The angry mother caught the profane epithet just leaping from her tongue, and kept it back from utterance.

"'Taint no use, I tell you," persisted Andrew. "He said"——

"Off with you, this instant!"

And Mrs. Harding, unable to restrain her indignation, made two or three rapid strides toward the boy, who, seeing from her face that he was in danger, darted from the house, and went away toward the store. After being gone long enough to have done the errand twice, he came loitering back, without the articles for which he had been sent.

"Where's the sugar and rice?" asked his mother, looking at him sternly as he came in.

"I told you so," was his irritating reply.

"Told me what?" said Mrs. Harding.

"Why, that you needn't send there for trust any more."

"Have you been to Mr. Willits'?" asked his mother, growing suddenly calm, and speaking very firmly.

"Yes, ma'am, I have," was the unhesitating answer.

"And you saw Mr. Willits?"

"Yes, ma'am."

"And asked him for the sugar and rice?"

"Yes, ma'am."

"What did he say?"

"He wanted to know where my money was; and when I said I had none, he told me to go home and tell you that he didn't charge things any more."

All this was spoken by Andrew with a steady voice and eye, and in a manner that but ill concealed a spirit of triumph.

For a little while, a tempest of indignant anger raged in the breast of Mrs. Harding.

"He'll be sorry for that, or I am not a living woman!" she muttered to herself, as soon as a little self-possession was obtained, and thought ran partially clear once more. "Here's the money," she added, aloud, speaking to Andrew, as she drew from her pocket some change; "go back, as swift as your legs will carry you, and get two pounds of rice and two pounds of sugar."

The boy took the money, and went loitering indifferently away; but, ere he had gone ten paces, a switch was laid smartly over his shoulders by his mother, who could no longer control her anger against him. The effect was all she wished to produce. He sprung from her like a frightened young deer, and ran the whole distance to the store. In returning, he resumed the old pace, and managed to get back at least half an hour after school-time.

"It's so late, mother, can't I stay at home to-day?" This was his response to a hurried order to start off immediately for school. "Mr. Long will keep me in."

"I don't care if he does. It will serve you right. No; you can't stay home."

The lad threw himself down on the door-step, and began to cry.

Poor Mrs. Harding! Notwithstanding the influence of recent events, the causes of irritation were too many and too strong for her. Almost since daylight had this perverse boy been making assaults upon her patience. Several times she had lost the self-control she was struggling to maintain, and given way to bursts of passion, and as often had she striven to force back into quietude the disturbed impulses that darkened her spirit. Now, her pent-up anger blazed forth like a fierce flame. Seizing a stout switch, she sprung toward Andrew, and commenced lashing him with all her strength. Her countenance was that of a fury. For a short time, Andrew, who had great powers of endurance, bore the smarting strokes, thinking to tire his mother out; but in this he was mistaken. She was possessed of cruel spirits; and, in the blind passion with which they inspired her, would have struck on, even to the endangering of his life. At last, with a yell of pain, that sounded more like the cry of some animal than a human being, Andrew started up from the door-step, and ran off beyond the reach of his mother's arm.

"Now, away to school with you, or I'll give you as much more!" cried Mrs. Harding, as she advanced resolutely toward the place where Andrew paused on getting out of her way.

Finding that contention with his mother, under present circumstances, was rather too serious a business,

Andrew yielded to forces he was not able to resist, and started off to school, conquered, but not subdued in spirit. The fire of his mother's anger had hardened instead of softening him. Rebellion grew rank in his young breast, as he moved on his way; and no sooner was he out of sight, than he sat down on the roadside to deliberate on the question of going to school or playing the truant.

It was some time after Mrs. Harding returned into the house, before she was sufficiently calm to reflect at all. The storm, though brief, had raged fiercely, and sad were the wrecks it left behind—wrecks of peace and good resolutions. Never in her life had she suffered such intense mental pain as now—never experienced a state of mind so sad and self-condemnatory. New and better states had been forming, and they had brought her within the sphere of higher and holier influences. It was violence to these that occasioned such anguish of spirit. Good, having gained a place in her heart, might be overshadowed, but not cast out. When the storm raged, it could retire and hide itself far down in the calmer depths of her spirit, to come into perception again when the tempest abated. And thus it was now. The good was hidden, not extinguished, and its low voice was heard as soon as the wild shrieking of the storm was silent. It was not strong enough to contend with evil when evil had full sway; but, like the sunshine and the gentle dews, it possessed a restoring and creating power; and, like them, in the peaceful days and quiet nights, it went on with its heavenly work of restoration and recreation.

What a deep calm reigned in the household, as Mrs. Harding came back among her younger children, who received her with frightened looks, and went shrinking away into distant corners—a calmness which, by its contrast, only made more apparent the wild, half-insane ex-

citement from which every nerve of her spirit was still
palpitating. The revulsion in Mrs. Harding's mind was
great. The first rebuking image that arose in her
thoughts was that of the stranger, whose coming and departure were almost like the changes in a dream. So
vivid was this impression, that she almost expected to
see the woman enter, and fix upon her those deep, sad
eyes, whose expression she could never forget.

An unwonted sound came now upon her ears. It
arose from the cradle. The eyes of Mrs. Harding
sought instantly the child. Sweet one! There was a
look of fear on her baby face—grievingly her lip was
curled—a low murmur of pain was audible.

Tenderly, very tenderly, was the infant lifted from its
cradle-bed; and lovingly was it pressed to the bosom of
Mrs. Harding. Soothing words in soothing tones were
poured into its ears from lips that touched them softly.

As Mrs. Harding sat with the babe held close against
her heart, all the exciting incidents of the previous half
hour passed before her mind in rapid review. The conduct of Andrew had been very bad, and he needed correction; but she could not justify her own action in the
case, nor quiet the voice of self-reproach. She saw that
the evil in her only excited the evil in him—that angry
words hardened him into stubborn resistance. She felt
sad, too, as she thought of the cruel stripes she had
given him—stripes laid on with the full strength of her
strong arm. In angry resentment, not sorrowing love,
had she grasped the rod, and its strokes excited only a
spirit of rebellion. Oh! how unhappy she felt—unhappy even to weeping. Her indignation against the
storekeeper was but a feeble flame now. She felt too
deeply humiliated in consequence of her own misdeeds
to cherish anger against others.

In this state of mind the morning passed. At twelve
o'clock, Andrew came in from school, gliding through

the door silently, and with an evident desire to avoid notice. Mrs. Harding said nothing. She was glad to see him subdued in spirit, and felt more of pity toward the boy than anger. Her husband soon followed, as it was dinner-time. His brow was clouded. Something had gone wrong with him during the forenoon. Silently and moodily he sat at the table, eating hurriedly, and taking no notice of any one. In a shorter time than usual, he finished the meal, and, rising, was about leaving the house, when Mrs. Harding said—

"Didn't you tell me to send to the store for any thing I might want?"

"Certainly I did. Why?"

"Because Willits refused to let me have some sugar and rice, this morning, without the money."

"Oh no! He couldn't have done that. There are thirty-six dollars to my account on his books, as I told you."

"Well, he did, then; and I had to send the money before I could get what I wanted."

Harding waited to hear no more. "I'll soon settle that!" he exclaimed, as he went hurriedly from the house. A rapid walk of a few minutes brought him to the store of Willits, into which he strode with a heavy, resolute tread.

"What do you mean," was his angry interrogation, "by sending such messages to my wife?" And, as he spoke, he confronted the storekeeper with a threatening scowl.

The latter was startled, as well he might be, for Harding was in a fierce mood of mind, and stood before him with his hand clenched, and meditated violence in his look and manner.

"Say! What do you mean?" repeated Harding.

"I sent no insulting message to your wife," said the storekeeper

"It's false! You did!" exclaimed Harding.

"And I say that I did not," retorted Willits, whose reddening face showed his rising anger.

"Why didn't you send her the sugar and rice this morning?" said Harding.

"I did send it," replied the storekeeper.

"Not until she furnished the money."

"I beg your pardon, neighbour Harding. Andrew came for two pounds of sugar and two pounds of rice, which I have charged in your account."

"Didn't you refuse to let him have them without the money?"

"No, sir, I did not. Haven't you a balance on my books in your favour? Here are the articles charged."

And Willits opened his day-book and pointed to the recent entry.

"I don't understand this," said Harding, looking bewildered.

"There's some mistake. Who told you that I refused to send these articles without the money?'

"I must see further into this. Can't comprehend it."

And as the carpenter said this, he turned away abruptly, and went back home.

"Mary," said he, "didn't you tell me that Willits refused to let you have the rice and sugar to-day without the money?"

"Yes, I did; and I had to send the money before I could get them."

"He denies it, and has the sugar and rice both charged to me."

"What!"

"He says that he didn't refuse to let you have the articles without the money."

"Andrew!"

Mrs. Harding called to her oldest boy, in a quick,

peremptory voice, turning around as she spoke; but there was no answer.

"Andrew!" she called again.

"He's gone to school, mother," said Lucy.

"It isn't school-time yet."

"But he's gone. I saw him put on his hat, and go out through the back gate a little while after father went away."

Mr. and Mrs. Harding looked at each other for a few moments in a kind of blank amazement. To both came a dim foreshadowing of the truth.

"Did Andrew bring you that message?" said Harding, in a stern voice.

"He did; and then I gave him the money to get the things I wanted."

"And he went back with it to the store?"

"Yes."

"That will do."

How the heavy brow of the carpenter contracted! There was something savage in his face.

"He'll remember this while he has breath in his body," he said fiercely, as he left the house.

On his way to his shop, he called in again at the store of Willits, and, by a few questions, satisfied all lingering doubts as to the guilt of Andrew.

As soon as two o'clock came, he went to the school-house and asked for his son.

"He hasn't been here to-day," was the teacher's reply to his question.

"Are you certain of that, Mr. Long?"

Harding was not prepared for this.

"Altogether certain," answered the schoolmaster. "Was Andrew here this morning?" He now addressed the scholars.

"No, sir"—"no, sir"—"no, sir"—ran all around the room.

"Have any of the boys seen him?" inquired Mr. Long.

"I saw him," spoke up one of the scholars, "as I came to school just now."

"Where?"

"Sitting on the fence over by Miller's woods."

"Did you speak to him?" inquired the schoolmaster.

"Yes, sir. I asked him what he was doing; and he said, 'Nothing.' Then I asked him if he wasn't going to school; and he said, 'Maybe so—after a while.' As I walked along, I saw him going over into Miller's woods."

"That will do," said the schoolmaster. And then he directed two of the older boys to go over to Miller's woods, and if they saw Andrew, to bring him to school.

Harding went back to his shop in a state of profound agitation. A new cause of anger against the boy was added—namely, the disgrace to himself of standing before the assembled village children as the father of a boy who had meanly played the truant.

During the afternoon, every thing seemed to go wrong with the carpenter. A man for whom he had done some work disappointed him in regard to the payment; while another, for whom work had been promised at a certain time, rated him soundly for not being up to the letter of his contract. Moreover, Stark the tavern-keeper called in and abused him for having said, as reported to him, that he was doing more harm to the neighbourhood than a gang of thieves. Maddened by this assault, coming, as it did, upon his unbalanced state of mind, Harding threw a mallet at his head, which, happily, glancing by, went smashing through a window. The frightened tavern-keeper beat a hasty retreat.

Toward evening, the teacher called in to say, that the boys sent for Andrew had found him, and that he refused to return with them to school. This was the last crushing pound laid on the carpenter's panting self-control. The savage imprecation that fell from his lips, startled the teacher, who turned off from him instantly, and went on his way, oppressed by a feeling of troubled concern.

CHAPTER VII.

WHEN Jacob Harding came home from his shop a little after sundown, he was blind with passion. The more he had thought of Andrew's conduct, the stronger had grown his indignation against him; and he was now prepared to mete out to him a degree of punishment cruel in the extreme. Grief for the evil he had done was not so prominent a feeling with Harding, as anger at the boy for having dared to venture upon the commission of such flagrant outrages. "Liar! thief! truant!" Such were the bitter words that came, every few moments, through the excited father's shut teeth, as he strode homeward. "That a boy of mine should be guilty of such things!" he repeated over and over again. "A boy of mine to disgrace me in this way!"

And he would stretch forth his arms, with his large hands gripped so tightly, that the nails almost penetrated the callous skin, clutching, in imagination, the guilty child.

"Where's Andrew?" he asked, almost fiercely, as he entered the house.

Mrs. Harding lifted to his her troubled face, and answered, in a sad voice—there was no trace of anger about her—

7*

"I haven't seen him since dinner-time."

"Not home yet?"

"No."

Harding passed through the house into the yard, where he cut from a tree a stout, tough rod—far too stout and strong for his vigorous arm to wield in the chastisement of a tender child—and returning with it, laid it in full sight of the younger children, on a table.

"A liar, a thief, and a truant!" he exclaimed, in a voice of angry excitement. "It will be the sorriest day of his life! I just want to get my hands on him!"

Mrs. Harding answered nothing. She too had felt strong anger toward the boy; but as the day wore on, and imagination pictured him writhing in the cruel hands of his passionate father, anger changed to yearning pity. Not that she felt like excusing him, or even palliating his crime and disobedience; but in her heart revived the mother's tenderness, and this made her perceive, clearly, that in a blind indignation against the boy, his father would destroy the salutary effects of punishment, through an excessive administration.

Slowly crept on the dusky twilight, and thicker and thicker fell the evening shadows, closing in nearer and nearer to the carpenter's dwelling, so that the disturbed inmates, constantly on the watch for Andrew, found their circle of vision growing momently narrower.

And now, sharp flashes of lightning began to stream forth from a heavy bank of cloud that lay piled up in the west, and the freshening winds rustled the leaves in the old elms that stood around the humble cottage.

"There's a gust rising!" said Mrs. Harding, in a troubled voice, going to the door and gazing anxiously around. "Where is that unhappy boy?"

"Skulking in some of the neighbours' houses," gruffly replied the husband. "But he might as well come home first as last He can't escape me."

Mrs. Harding sighed, and was about retiring from the door, when a heavy peal of distant thunder jarred on the air.

"Oh! I wish he was home!" she said; "we're going to have a terrible storm."

The thick bank of clouds had now covered so large a space in the west, that all the sun's retiring beams were hidden, and darkness was closing around her heavy curtains.

"The storm will bring him home," was all the reply made by the father.

"I wish, Jacob," said Mrs. Harding, after waiting for nearly half an hour longer, during which time the heavy concussive thunder sounded nearer and nearer, "that you would step over to Mrs. Aaron's, and see if Andrew is not there. He goes with John Aaron a good deal, and it may be that he is loitering with him now, afraid to come home."

Harding made no answer, but took up his hat and went out. The dwelling of Mrs. Aaron was distant nearly an eighth of a mile, and thither the carpenter directed his steps, walking rapidly. It had become very dark before he reached there—the darkness invaded, every few moments, by brilliant streams of light from the cloudy west.

"Have you seen any thing of my Andrew?" inquired Harding, on reaching the neighbour's house.

"I have not," replied Mrs. Aaron, as she stood with the door held partly open.

"Is your John at home?" was next asked.

"My John? Oh yes, indeed! He's never away after dark.'

John came to the side of his mother.

"Have you seen my Andrew to-day?" Harding spoke to the boy.

"No, sir; I have not. He wasn't at school either in the morning or afternoon."

"Are you certain about not having seen him to-day?"

"Oh yes, sir. He hasn't been anywhere around here."

"Where can he be?" said Mrs. Aaron, now manifesting a woman's concern.

"Dear knows!" answered the carpenter, with some impatience of manner. "I only wish I had my hands on him."

"How long has he been away?" asked Mrs. Aaron.

"Ever since dinner-time," was replied.

"Maybe he is over at Mr. Lawson's," spoke up John. "Neither Henry nor Peter Lawson were at school this afternoon. I shouldn't wonder if they'd all gone a fishing in Baxter's mill-dam."

"I'm obliged to you!" was almost roughly said by Harding, as he turned off abruptly, and strode away in the direction of Lawson's farm-house, which was at least a quarter of a mile from his own dwelling.

The darkness was now so deep, that he could see only a few steps before him, save when the broad-sheeted lightning threw its mantle of flame over the earth for an instant, and then left the night blacker than before. The flashes came in quick succession, and by their aid he walked on as steadily as if day had been abroad. At Lawson's he gained some intelligence of his truant boy. Andrew had been with Henry and Peter fishing, as was suggested by young Aaron, and had stayed there to supper. But it was more than half an hour since he started for home.

"You'll find him safe and sound when you get back," said Mr. Lawson; "so you needn't give yourself any more uneasiness about him. I didn't notice that he was staying so late, or I would have sent him away earlier. I told the boys to go with him a part of the way, but he said he wasn't at all afraid, and went off by himself."

It did not take Harding long to retrace his steps homeward. Not in the least was his anger against the child abated, nor had he changed, in the smallest degree, his cruel purposes regarding him. He had often punished him severely; but the severity now meditated was something far beyond any prior infliction.

He was only a short distance from his dwelling, when a lightning gleam, that made the air light as noonday, showed him the form of Andrew crouching down against a large tree that stood a little off from the road. He saw it but for an instant: for, in the next moment, the blackness of darkness was around him.

"Andrew!" he called, sternly.

Ere his voice died on the air, another flash quivered along the ground; but when the lad's form had just been seen, no object was visible. Mr. Harding stood still, and awaited, in silence, the next recurring flash It came, but Andrew was not in view.

"Andrew!" he cried again. "Andrew! why don't you answer me?"

The echo of his own voice was all the reply that came He now advanced to the tree, felt about it in the darkness, and searched all around with his eyes, as flash after flash lit up the scene. But the form of Andrew was not again descried. He called, threatened, and called, again and again. He searched around for a considerable distance, but to no purpose. Concluding that the boy had gone home, he kept on his way, and soon arrived at his dwelling.

"Is he here yet?" was his sharp interrogation, as he stepped over the threshold.

"Haven't you found him?" asked Mrs. Harding, with a blanching face.

'He was over at Lawson's until dark, and then

started for home. I'm very sure I saw him up at the turn in the road, sitting by the foot of an old beech-tree. A flash of lightning made it as clear as day; but, when the next flash came, he was not there. I called, and called, but he wouldn't answer me. He'll come creeping in here before long. The rain will soon be pouring in torrents, and he'll never stand that."

"O Jacob!" said the mother, in a tone of distress, "I'm afraid something has happened to him."

"Never fear. He's too bad for any thing to happen to him," was the harsh response.

"Don't talk so, Jacob. It's a fearful night. There! Oh, what a sharp flash! Go out and call to him. Maybe he is close by, and afraid to come in. Tell him not to be afraid—that you won't punish him. Do, Jacob!"

"I *will* punish him, though! and I'll *not* lie about it," firmly answered Harding. "The moment I get my hands on him, I'll flog him within an inch of his life, the desperate little vagabond! A pretty race he has run me, after all his ill-doing—as if that wasn't enough."

"What a crash!" exclaimed poor Mrs. Harding, her face blanching still whiter. "Hark! is that wind or rain?"

"Both," replied her husband, coolly. "He'll not be away long now."

But the unyielding father erred in his prediction. The storm came down with fearful violence, howling among the tall elms, crashing its thunder through the air, and pouring out a deluge of rain; yet the boy ventured not to the door of his father's house, where a more dreaded evil awaited him. He could bear the elemental wrath, wild and fierce though it was, as something less to be feared than the cruel anger of his justly incensed father.

Nine, ten, eleven o'clock came; still the fearful tempest roared without—still the harsh thunder boomed along the sky, or came sharply rattling down, and still nothing was seen or heard of Andrew. Almost sick with anxiety and alarm, Mrs. Harding, who had moved about the rooms incessantly—now listening at the door or window, now gazing into the darkness, and now calling the name of the boy—at length sunk down into a kind of hopeless state. That something terrible had happened to Andrew, she felt certain; for she was sure he would not remain out in storm and darkness, if he could make his way home. If softened at all toward his erring son, Harding did not manifest the change. He had walked the floor restlessly for a greater part of the evening, every now and then opening the door to look out, and calling sternly the name of Andrew, who was, he persisted in affirming, skulking somewhere near at hand. It was all in vain that the lad's mother strove to turn aside the harsh anger of his father.

"Ill not let him go to swift destruction, Mary," he would answer, with knitted brows. "I'll not be a foolish father, and spare the rod. Come when he will, he has got to feel the weight of this arm. It is all well enough for you to pity him; but I have a stern duty to perform, and mean to execute it fully."

"Try and not feel so angry against him, Jacob," pleaded the mother, laying her hand on his arm. "We know not where he is, nor how dreadfully he may be suffering. What if he should be dead! The lightning has struck very near, several times."

"I would rather see him dead now, than swinging on the gallows 'twenty years hence," said Harding, as he drew himself away from his tearful wife. "If he is dead, he will be safe from the evil to come; but if alive, it shall be my business to check the course of evil."

It was between eleven and twelve o'clock, when Mrs. Harding went from the family sitting-room into the adjoining chamber, leaving her husband pacing the floor, and nursing his anger against the absent boy. The height of the storm had passed. At more distant intervals, the feebler flashes came, and the far-off thunder had a muffled roll. The winds were fast dying away, and no longer swept through the air, in howling gust, or bore the fast descending rain in fitful torrents against the windows. Every moment the rushing sound without grew less; and by the time Mrs. Harding returned from the chamber—scarce three minutes had elapsed since she left her husband—a deep stillness had succeeded the tempest's wail. She came in with so changed a countenance, that her husband could not help exclaiming—

"Why, Mary! what is it?"

"Jacob!" There was a depth of emotion in the voice of Mrs. Harding, as she grasped with both hands her husband's arm, and lifted to his face her moistened eyes, that surprised and subdued him. "Jacob," she repeated, gently drawing him toward the chamber-door, "I want to show you something."

Harding followed, passively.

"Look there, Jacob!" And she pointed to the low bed on which Grace was laid every night beside Lotty, and where she usually slept soundly until Mrs. Harding retired.

Harding started at what he saw, with a quick ejaculation; but his wife clung to his arm, saying, in a half whisper—

"Hush, Jacob!—don't wake them now—don't!"

The pause was fatal to his stern purpose. The face of Andrew was before him, pale and shrunken with suffering; and close beside, almost touching it, on the same pillow, was the calm, sweet, heavenly face of the babe. The boy had crept in through the window, in the height of the storm, and, after putting off his wet clothes, laid himself down beside little Grace, evidently

with the hope that her dove-like innocence would soften
the fierce indignation of his father against him, and
there had fallen asleep. His hair was wet, and tear-
stains marked his cheeks.

"Poor boy!" almost sobbed Mrs. Harding. She was
overcome with tenderness. As she breathed the words,
a deep sigh parted the lips of the sleeping child, and, at
the same moment, Grace, moving in her sleep, drew her
little arm across his neck, and laid her warm, bright
cheek to his.

It would have required a harder, sterner heart than
Jacob Harding's—hard and stern as that was—to with-
stand the softening influence of a scene like this, coming
as it did after long hours of intense excitement, and in
the solemn hush succeeding a fearful tempest. A little
while he stood as if spell-bound, and then turning suddenly away, left the chamber. When his wife followed
him into the next room, she found him sitting in a
chair, with his head bowed upon his bosom. She came
up to where he sat, and leaning against him, laid her
hand upon his shoulder.

"Jacob," she said, softly. It was the old, old voice
that now entered his ears—the voice that had sounded
sweetest of all in the days when young love filled his
mind with dreams of an Elysian future. He neither
moved nor spoke; but his heart was melting.

"Jacob—husband—dear husband!" How many
years had passed—desolate, dreary years to both their
suffering spirits—since Mrs. Harding had spoken to her
husband so tenderly, and in words like these!

"Say on, Mary!" And as the words passed his lips,
he leaned toward her. How naturally glided her arm
from his shoulder to his neck, as her heart leaped with a
delicious impulse! The old, old voice, once so full of
music, was ringing n her ears again It was the voice

8

of her young lover—that in which he had wooed and won her in the days of innocent, confiding girlhood.

"Say on, Mary," he repeated. How gently, almost humbly, he spoke! There was not a trace of bitterness or passion in his tones.

"Think of what the poor boy has suffered to-night, Jacob. A tender child, only eight years old, exposed to such a fearful storm! Think of him as suffering and repentant, Jacob—not as stubbornly bent on continuing in wrong. He looks so pale and frightened, even in his sleep, that the sight of him makes my heart ache."

"And think, too, Mary," answered Harding, "of his great offence. Will it be right to let him go unpunished?"

"Why should he be punished?" asked Mrs. Harding.

"For his own good. He must be taught that evil deeds bring inevitable pain."

"And have they not brought pain to-night?" said Mrs. Harding. "Think, Jacob, whether, for any wrong, you would have doomed him to the anguish and fear he must have suffered to-night? I am sure you would not."

"O Mary! I dare not let him escape my severe displeasure," replied Harding, his voice taking a troubled tone. "For him to go on in this way, is certain ruin."

"It is for us to save him from evil, if in our power, Jacob. But how shall we save him. Severity, I fear, will not do it. He has been scolded, and driven, and whipped, until I sometimes think he is hardened. A number of times I have noticed of late, that when I speak mildly to him, he obeys more readily than when I am out of patience. If I order him to do any thing in an angry or imperative voice, he moves off sulkily, and, unless I follow him up, is certain to disobey me. But if I say, 'Andrew, go and do so and so, that's a good boy,' he springs away and does the errand in the shortest time, and with evident pleasure."

"I wish to do right, Mary," said Harding, in an irresolute voice.

"No one knows that better than I do, Jacob," answered Mrs. Harding. "But what is right? Ah! that is the question. How ignorant and erring we are! We have tried hard and harsh means with our children from the beginning, and they do not seem to grow better. Let us try some gentler methods."

"But what are we to do with Andrew? Let the past go unpunished?"

"Unpunished, at least by the rod, Jacob. He expects that, and is, in some degree, prepared for it. If we deal more gently by him, and let him understand that we are grieved rather than angry at his conduct—that our punishment, whatever it may be, is given in love, not indignation—he may repent far more deeply of his evil deeds, than if stubborn anger be aroused through painful chastisement. Hush!"

Mrs. Harding raised herself up and listened, as a voice came from the room they had left a little while before. It was Andrew's voice. "O father!" they heard him say distinctly, and in a tone of fear.

Both arose quickly, and went into the chamber where he was lying.

"Don't cut me so hard, father!—don't; oh, don't" His tones were full of agony.

"I'm so wet and frightened!" he murmured, a little while afterward. "Won't the lightning strike me? Oh dear! oh dear! If father wouldn't cut me so hard!"

The heart-full mother could not keep the tears from raining over her face; and even Jacob Harding felt a woman's weakness stealing through his breast. He was about moving away from the bed where his children slept, when Andrew started up, wide awake almost as soon as his eyes were opened.

"O father!" he exclaimed, the moment his bewildered mind was able to comprehend his 'rue position—"don't whip me—please don't! I've been very bad; but if you don't whip me, I'll try and not be bad any more."

And he stretched forth his hands imploringly, while his colourless face had such a look of fear and sorrow, that the heart untouched by its expression must have been of adamant.

"You have been very wicked, Andrew," said his mother, in a low, serious, grieving voice; "and I do not see how your father can help punishing you."

"O mother! mother!" cried the child, bursting into tears, and bending over toward her—she had stooped down by the bedside—"I know I have been wicked, and I'm so sorry. I don't know why I did it. It seemed as if I couldn't help it. O mother! how dreadful it was out in the woods, with the thunder and lightning all around me! I was so frightened! But I was afraid to come in. I saw the candle in the window, and heard you and father call me; but I didn't dare to answer. Once, when the lightning made all as bright as day, I thought I saw Grace just a little way before me on the ground. I ran right up to the spot, but she wasn't there! Then I thought I'd get into the window, and lie down on the bed, just here, alongside of her. Maybe, I said to myself, father, who loves little Grace so much, won't whip me for her sake, if I promise not to be bad any more."

"And do you promise, Andrew?" Mrs. Harding spoke very seriously.

"I'd promise, if I thought father would believe me," sobbed the poor child.

"Promise in earnest?"

"Oh yes, mother!"

"Then ask him to forgive you, my son!"

There was a deep silence for some moments.

"Father!" Timid, hesitating, almost fearful was the voice that broke on the hushed air of the chamber.

Harding neither moved from the spot where he stood, with averted face, nor answered.

"Father! O father!"

The stern man was too much softened to resist the pleading anguish of that broken voice.

"Well, my son?" He did not mean to speak so gently; but his heart flowed into his tones.

"I've been very wicked, father." His utterance was choked, and he could say no more.

"Speak to him, Jacob," said Mrs. Harding, bending toward her husband.

"Lie down, my son, and go to sleep. You *have* been very wicked, and I intended to punish you severely; but if you *will* be a good boy, as you promise, I may forgive you."

Harding tried to speak calmly, and even a little sternly; but his voice was scarcely steady, and betrayed the powerful struggle that was going on within. As Andrew fell back, sobbing, on the pillow, from which, a little while before, he had started up in fear, his father left the chamber, deeply agitated. He wished to be alone, in order to recover his manly self-possession. His face was calm and elevated when he rejoined his wife. In both their hearts, what a wild tempest had raged, symboling the fierce storm that darkened the face of nature! But the azure depths of their spirits were clear again—clear as the starry heavens that arched above their lowly dwelling

8*

CHAPTER VIII.

MR. LONG, the village schoolmaster, after leaving the carpenter, took his way homeward, oppressed by a troubled feeling. He was a man of humane impulses, and these were excited by the cruel threats and savage looks of Harding. Andrew's offence was heinous, deserving more than ordinary marks of displeasure; and he had, himself, been thinking over various modes of punishment, in order, if possible, to select that which would be most efficacious, when the young truant presented himself in the morning. Miss Gimp, the dressmaker, was at his house when he returned home. She was doing some work for Mrs. Long, and dropped in with it a little before supper-time. Very naturally, she was invited to remain until after tea. Indeed, Miss Gimp was generally a welcome guest, for she was chatty, and knew the weak side of every woman in the neighbourhood. She was, moreover, in possession of all the current gossip—good-natured and ill-natured—floating about, far and near, and had a way peculiar to herself, and racy withal, of telling every thing she knew, and a little more sometimes.

"You look sober, Edward," said the schoolmaster's wife, as her eyes rested on her husband's face, soon after he came in. "Don't you feel well?"

"Something has happened that troubles me," replied Mr. Long. And then he looked more serious.

How quickly was the head of Miss Gimp elevated! What a sparkling interest was in her two bright eyes!

"Trouble you, Edward? What is it?"

A shade of anxiety flitted across the pleasant face of Mrs. Long.

"Nothing that particularly concerns myself," replied the schoolmaster.

"Any thing wrong in the school?"

"There's something wrong about one of the scholars. Andrew Harding has been playing truant."

"The ne'er do well!" exclaimed Miss Gimp; not so much in sorrow or anger, as from a species of unconscious satisfaction at hearing a piece of bad news.

"I'm afraid that boy will come to an evil end," remarked Mrs. Long.

"He'll come to the gallows, without doubt," said Miss Gimp. "I never saw his match. Not for a mountain of gold would I live in the house with him. I pity his poor mother; but, then, she has herself to blame. I never saw a woman have so little management with children. She lets them do as they please, and make as much noise and disorder as they like, until she gets so worried she can't stand it any longer; and then she screams at them, and boxes their ears right and left, in a way to make one's blood cold. That's no way to bring up children."

"Indeed, it is not," was the quiet response of the schoolmaster's wife.

"Why, d'ye know," ran on Miss Gimp, "that on one occasion of my being there to fit a dress for Mrs. Harding, Andrew—a little imp of Satan he is—forgive me for saying so—Andrew threw a large case-knife at his sister Lucy. It came as nigh cutting her ear off as could be—just touching it with the edge as it glanced by. If you had seen the passion of his mother! It was awful! She grew almost black in the face; and I thought she would never get done beating the boy. It made me sick at heart. Oh! she is a woman of an awful temper!

I wouldn't have her tongue on me for the world. And
so Andrew has been playing the truant, ha!"

How the voice of Miss Gimp changed, as she recol-
lected herself!

"I am grieved to say that he has," answered the
schoolmaster, gravely.

"Does his father know it?" asked Mrs. Long

"Yes; and I am sorry to say, is in a most dreadful
passion about it. I called at his shop as I came home
just now, and the way he looked and spoke made me
really shudder."

"He's a cruel-tempered man," said Miss Gimp. "I
know all about him. His father was little better than a
savage, and used to beat his children about as if they
were dogs."

"I pity Andrew, from my heart," said Mr. Long.
"He has acted very badly; but he is only a tender
child, needing correction for his fault, but not able to
bear the cruelty in store for him. I feel unhappy
about it."

"How would it do," suggested Mrs. Long, "for you
to go over, after tea, and try to soothe his father, and
thus break the heavy weight of his displeasure?"

"Just what I was thinking about," said Mr. Long.

"I wouldn't do any such thing," spoke up Miss Gimp,
quickly. "Take my advice, and don't go near him.
He's a very strange man. As sure as you do, he'll
insult you; and, what is worse, beat Andrew twice as
badly, from a fresh excitement of angry feelings."

"There may be something in that," remarked the
schoolmaster's wife.

"There is something in it," said Miss Gimp.
"People like them can't bear interference from others;
and always repel intrusion by broad insult. Let them
alone, Mr. Long, to do with their own as they please.
More harm than good will arise from any attempt you

may make to screen the young rebel. It's all very
kind, very humane in you, Mr. Long, and does great
credit to your heart; but you can't help them any."

"There may be truth in your suggestion," answered
the schoolmaster, in some doubt and irresolution—he
was flattered, in spite of himself, by Miss Gimp's compliment—"and yet it does not seem right to leave a
helpless child in the hands of a man insane from anger,
and not make an effort to save him from excessive
cruelty."

Tea was soon after on the table. Mr. Long, still undecided in his mind, sat thoughtful and nearly silent
during the meal, while Miss Gimp rattled on, much to
the edification of Mrs. Long, who, in her agreeable tittle-
tattle, quite forgot poor Andrew Harding. A sudden
roll of distant thunder interrupted the voluble play of
the gossip's tongue.

"What's that!" she exclaimed—"not a gust coming
up?"

Mr. Long went to the door, and threw a glance around
the horizon.

"There are some heavy clouds in the west," said he.

"And it threatens rain," added Miss Gimp, who now
stood by his side. "Get me my bonnet, if you please.
Mrs. Long," said she, turning to the schoolmaster's wife.
"It's growing dark fast, and I must run home."

"Don't be in a hurry. It isn't late. I'm sure it
won't storm to-night," said Mrs. Long, affecting a great
deal of reluctance at parting with Miss Gimp, who, in
her turn, had just enough self-esteem to believe that the
schoolmaster's wife felt really bad about her "going
away so early."

Often, during the fearful storm that raged that night,
did Mr. Long think of Andrew Harding, and wonder
how it was with him. He could not forget the cruel

face and words of the boy's father: they haunted his imagination and his thoughts.

On the next morning, he went early, as was his custom, to the school-house. He was sitting at his desk, engaged in study, when the sound of footsteps caused aim to look up. It was too soon to expect any of the scholars, and he was, therefore, prepared to see a stranger. He almost started, as he saw the carpenter leading his son, and within a few steps of the door.

"Mr. Long, I have brought Andrew to school this morning."

Harding had paused with one foot across the threshold. He spoke in a steady voice, rather below his ordinary tone. "I preferred coming early, before the other scholars arrived, as I wished to say a word about the lad."

"Won't you step in?" said the schoolmaster, quite taken by surprise at the manner of his visitor, in which was nothing of the fierce indignation apparent at their last interview.

"No, I thank you. You can go in, Andrew."

The boy entered quietly, and went with a stealthy step to his usual seat.

"I called to say, Mr. Long," resumed the carpenter, "that Andrew promises, if you will forgive him, never again to be guilty of such bad conduct. I think his punishment has already been severe enough, and of a character not likely soon to be forgotten. He has been very wicked, but, I think, repents sincerely."

"I am not angry with him," said the schoolmaster, "but grieved that any scholar of mine should commit that most disgraceful of all offences—playing the truant. If you think he has been sufficiently punished, and sincerely repents, the matter can rest where it is; but I will not promise, for the future, should he offend again, The example would be too pernicious."

"I think you can trust him," answered the carpenter, as he moved back a few steps from the door. "Good morning," he added, after standing silent for a moment or two, and went away.

Mr. Long felt rather strangely on finding himself alone with the boy, after this brief interview with Harding. In both the father and son, a striking change was apparent. As to the basis of the change, he was altogether ignorant. The natural conclusion to which his mind came, almost without reflection, was, that the carpenter had punished his child with a measure of severity from which his own better consciousness now revolted, and that, as some reparation for his cruelty, he now sought to screen him from further consequences. That both were greatly subdued, was apparent at a glance.

"Andrew," said the schoolmaster. He spoke kindly but seriously.

The child looked up timidly.

"Come here, Andrew."

The boy left his seat, and came toward the schoolmaster, with a slow movement, his eyes fixed earnestly and inquiringly upon his face.

There were unmistakable marks of suffering and fear in that young countenance; and, as Mr. Long noted them, pity for the lad and a new interest in regard to him were awakened in his mind.

"Poor boy!" It was his involuntary mental ejaculation. Scarcely thinking of what he was doing, he took Andrew, by the hand, and said, kindly—

"I am sorry you were so naughty yesterday. How came you to do so?"

The child's lips quivered a moment, and his eyes fell to the ground. A little while he stood silent.

"How came you to do so, Andrew?" The voice that said this was kind and encouraging.

"I don't know, Mr. Long," was answered; and now

the boy's clear eyes—the schoolmaster was struck with
the softness of their expression—were raised to his.
"It seemed as if I couldn't help it. I didn't think
much, at first, what I was doing; but when I got a
going, it was like running down hill. I could not stop
myself."

"You are sorry about it, are you not, Andrew?"

"Oh yes, Mr. Long. I can't tell you how sorry I am
I wish I hadn't done it."

"You will never do so again?"

"Not if I can help it, Mr. Long."

"You can help it, Andrew," said the schoolmaster, in
a serious voice. "Every one can help doing wrong."

"I don't know." The child spoke half to himself,
and in a tone so sad, that the schoolmaster was touched
by it. "It seems as if I couldn't help it, sometimes."

"Do you ever say your prayers, on going to bed at
night?" asked the schoolmaster, after a few moments of
thoughtful silence.

"I used to say them a good while ago; but I never
do now," was answered.

"You must begin again, Andrew, if you desire to be
a good boy. Begin this very night. Do not get into
bed until you have knelt down and said, 'Our Father
who art in heaven.' Do Lotty and Philip say their
prayers at night?"

"No, sir. Mother doesn't teach any of us to say our
prayers."

"Do you ever read in the Bible?"

"Mother won't let me have the Bible."

"Why not?"

"She says I dirty the leaves and pictures."

"Have you no Testament?"

"No, sir."

"If I give you one, will you read in it?"

"Yes, sir."

"Very well, Andrew, I will bring you a Testament this afternoon, and it shall be yours if you will learn a verse in it every day."

The lad's face brightened with real pleasure.

"Not all evil—no, not all evil!" were the schoolmaster's earnestly, inward spoken words. "The innocence of childhood has been trampled on and overlaid; but there is good ground still, ready for the hand of culture."

"Andrew," said he, after a slight pause, "you must be on your guard when the other boys come to school. It is known that you have played truant, and some of them will be sure to say unkind things to you about it. Try and not get angry—try hard, and I'm sure you can help it. Don't seem to mind what they say, and they'll soon let you alone."

The form of a boy darkened the door at this moment, and the conference of Andrew and the schoolmaster was at an end.

CHAPTER IX.

It was evening. Lotty and Grace were sleeping, side by side, and Philip, a restless, rather fretful child of four years, had some time since been taken off to bed. Mrs. Harding, having cleared away the supper things, now busily plied her needle. Her husband was near her, by the table, his head resting on his hand, and his mind busy with a new train of thoughts that occupied it almost per force. Side by side, on two low chairs, sat Andrew and his sister Lucy, younger by two years. Andrew held open in his hands the Testament given him, according to promise, by Mr. Long, and he was reading from it in a low voice, while Lucy leaned toward him, listening intently. The mother's ears were open, as well as Lucy's, and took in every word; and it was not long before Harding began to listen also. Andrew was reading of the birth of Christ in the city of Bethlehem, and of the wise men who came from the East, guided by the star that heralded his wonderful advent. It was many, many years since the words of this strange history had been in his thoughts; and now they came to him with a newly awakening interest. Andrew read on—of the angel who appeared to Joseph in a dream, warning him of the evil designs of Herod—of the cruel slaughter of the Innocents—of John the Baptist preaching repentance in the wilderness of Judea—and of the baptism of the Saviour in Jordan.

All unconscious that his father and mother were listening, the boy continued to read. What a power was in the divine word, coming to their ears, as it did, borne on the voice of a child! There was a wonderful fascination about every fact and every holy sentiment. They saw, in imagination, Jesus led up, of the Spirit, into the wilderness, to be tempted of the devil; and when the rebuked tempter left him, they felt a sense of pleasure at the triumph of good over evil, that passed with a low thrill to the profoundest depths of their being. In the call of Simon and Andrew, and James and John, the sons of Zebedee, they almost seemed to hear the Lord speaking to them, and calling them to a new life. They saw him going about through Galilee, teaching in the synagogues, and preaching the gospel of the kingdom, and healing all manner of sickness and all manner of disease among the people. And when he went up into a mountain, and taught from thence the multitude, the divine words he uttered came to them with a spirit and power that lifted their souls into higher regions, and gave them perceptions of truths such as had never come to them before.

"Blessed are the merciful, for they shall obtain mercy. Blessed are the pure in heart, for they shall see God. Blessed are the peacemakers, for they shall be called the children of God."

Many times, in earlier days—days in which some rosy gleams from the morning of childhood mingled with the colder light of selfish maturity—had they heard these beautiful sentences; but never had the words so penetrated their souls; never had they felt such a sad, almost hopeless yearning to rise into the holy states of the merciful, the pure in heart, and the peacemaker.

Still Andrew read on, unconscious that other ears than Lucy's were hearkening to his utterance intently.

"Let your light so shine before men, that they may see your good works, and glorify your Father which is in heaven."

A low sigh from the mother's heart trembled, scarce audibly, on the air.

"Again, ye have heard that it hath been said by them of old time, Thou shalt not forswear thyself, but shalt perform unto the Lord thine oaths. But I say unto you, Swear not at all: neither by heaven, for it is God's throne; nor by the earth, for it is his footstool; neither by Jerusalem, for it is the city of the great king. Neither shalt thou swear by thy head, because thou canst not make one hair white or black; but let your communication be yea, yea; nay, nay: for whatsoever is more than these, cometh of evil."

"Cometh of evil—cometh of evil." How the words sounded in the ears of Jacob Harding, over and over again, as if spoken directly to him!

"But I say unto you, Love your enemies, bless them that curse you, do good to them that hate you, and pray for them which despitefully use you and persecute you: that ye may be the children of your Father which is in heaven; for he maketh his sun to rise on the evil and on the good, and sendeth rain on the just and on the unjust. For if ye love them which love you, what reward have ye? do not even the publicans the same? And if ye salute your brethren only, what do ye more than others? do not even the publicans so? Be ye therefore perfect, even as your Father which is in heaven is perfect."

Tired with reading aloud, Andrew now closed his Testament, and said, in a kind way, to his sister—

"Come, Lucy—let's go to bed."

Lucy made no objection, and the two children, who had learned to wait on themselves, took a candle, and went off to their chamber, up stairs, without a cross or angry word—something so unusual, that both father and mother noted it with surprise.

Plying her needle, sat Mrs. Harding, and near her, his hand shading his face from the light, was her husband, almost motionless. In the minds of both lingered

passages just read from the Word of Life, while a deep
calmness pervaded their spirits. Not so much rebuked
were they by the truths, condemnatory of the past,
which seemed spoken anew, as inspired by a dawning
hope of something better in the future. A dim foreshadowing of better and happier states came to both, and
with it an awakening tenderness each for the other, and
a deeper, purer, more unselfish love for their children.

A little while they had heard Andrew and Lucy
moving about in the chamber above; then all was still.
Presently there stole down a low murmur. The mother's
hand rested in her lap, and she raised her head to listen.

"What is that?" she said, rising and going to the
foot of the stairway.

"Give us this day our daily bread, and forgive us our
debts"——

This much she heard distinctly, in the voice of
Andrew.

The murmuring sound was continued for a little while,
and then all was silent.

"What was it?" asked Harding, as his wife came
back to her seat by the table.

A moment or two Mrs. Harding gazed into her husband's face, as if to read his state of mind, and then
answered—

"It was Andrew, saying his prayers."

The hand that had been withdrawn from between the
light and his face, was quickly restored to its position by
Harding, who turned himself a little farther away from
observation, and did not speak for nearly half an hour.
That time was spent in an almost involuntary review of
the past, and in partially formed purposes to live a better
life in the future; if not for his own sake, at least for
the sake of his children.

Very gently did sleep draw her dusky curtains around
the weary heads of Mr. and Mrs. Harding that night.

Morning found their spirits calm, hopeful, and yearning for the better life, of whose beatitudes came to them some partial glimpses as they listened to the words of the Saviour, teaching the multitudes that gathered to hear, as he sat upon the mountain of Galilee.

CHAPTER X.

ONE day, a few weeks later in the course of events we are recording, Miss Gimp was a little fluttered by seeing a handsome carriage draw up before her humble dwelling. She looked, of course, for a richly dressed lady to emerge from so elegant a vehicle; but, instead, a plainly attired girl, evidently a domestic in some family, stepped upon the ground. The dressmaker was already in the door.

"Does Miss Gimp live here?" asked the girl.

"That is my name: will you walk in?" said the dressmaker.

The girl entered, and took the chair that was proffered.

"Are you very busy at this time?" she inquired.

"Not very," answered Miss Gimp.

"Have you a week to spare?"

"I don't know about that," replied the dressmaker. "Who wants me for a week?"

"Mrs. Barclay."

"Mrs. Barclay, over at Beechwood?"

"Yes. You made a dress for her last fall, I believe."

"Yes. When does she want me?"

"Right away, if you can come."

Miss Gimp considered a little while.

"I have two dresses to finish," said she; "after that, I can go to Mrs. Barclay."

"How long will it take you to finish these dresses?" asked the girl.

"To-day and to-morrow."

"Then you can come the day after to-morrow?"

"Yes."

"Very well. I'll say so to Mrs. Barclay. At what time in the morning will you be ready?"

"As early as you please."

"Say nine o'clock?"

"Yes."

"Very well," said the girl; "I will be over for you, in the carriage, by that time."

Miss Gimp was very good at promising, and at performing also, when it suited her to keep her engagements. In the present case, she meant to be as good as her word, even though in keeping her word to Mrs. Barclay, she broke it to her very particular friends, Mrs. Jarvis and the storekeeper's wife, for both of whom she had promised to make dresses, as soon as the work on hand was finished. The Barclays were wealthy people, and she could afford to disappoint her less pretending neighbours, for the sake of making favour with them.

According to appointment, the handsome carriage drew up before the dressmaker's door exactly at nine o'clock on the day agreed upon, and Miss Gimp, conscious of having acquired a new importance, was soon reposing among its luxurious cushions. Past the dwelling of Mrs. Willits drove the elegant vehicle, and Miss Gimp did not fail to lean from the window, to throw a smile at the storekeeper's wife, who exclaimed to herself—

"Why, bless us! What does all this mean?"

A brisk drive of half an hour brought them to the stately residence of the Barclays—the finest within a circle of twenty miles. Mrs. Barclay, a handsome but dignified woman—her age was not over thirty-five—received the dressmaker kindly, but with a manner that at once repelled all gossipping familiarity. She had sent for her as a workwoman, to perform a needed service, and wished for nothing beyond; and it was but a little while before Miss Gimp understood this clearly. Two or three times during the first day, she tried to draw Mrs. Barclay out; but it was of no use—the lady wanted her skill as a dressmaker; but, beyond this, neither asked nor received any thing.

"Proud—haughty—stuck up!" Many times did Miss Gimp repeat these words to herself, by way of consolation in her disappointment at not being questioned by Mrs. Barclay about people for whom she had worked. There were the Wilsons and the Mayfields—she had made dresses for them, and quietly intimated the fact—of whom, considering their position, Mrs. Barclay must want to hear the dressmaker's opinion. But not the slightest sign of interest was manifested by the lady. Once or twice Miss Gimp alluded to them, in a way that she believed would draw Mrs. Barclay out; but the allusion was met by a frigid silence.

Mrs. Barclay had a daughter in her fifteenth year, who, though but a child, was as reserved to the dressmaker as her mother. Miss Gimp tried hard to win her confidence by a chatty familiarity; but Florence repelled all these advances—politely, yet effectually.

On the second day of Miss Gimp's rather uncomfortable sojourn in this family, where she was appreciated only for her skill in mantua-making, she heard Mrs. Barclay remark to her daughter in a low voice—

"Your aunt Edith Beaufort will be here to-morrow."

"She will!" There was a tone of surprise in the voice of Florence that instantly quickened the ears of Miss Gimp, who bent closer to her work in order to seem entirely absorbed therein.

"Yes. I got a note from her a little while ago. Jacob brought it over," answered the mother.

"I thought she was going back to Clinton, after finishing her visit to Mrs. Larch"

"She intended doing so when she left here; but she wants to see your father about some business matters that she says needs his attention."

"How long is she going to stay?" inquired Florence.

"A week, she says."

"I don't like aunt Edith, and I can't help it," remarked Florence. "I never feel pleasant when she is here; and am always relieved from a kind of pressure on my feelings when she goes."

"You should try to overcome this," said Mrs. Barclay. "Your aunt is always kind, and, I think, much attached to you. She has her peculiarities, as we all have; and toleration of individual peculiarities, as I have often said to you, is a common duty we owe to each other."

"I often wish, mother," replied the girl, in a gentler tone, "that I were more like you—that I could forget and deny myself for the sake of others, as much as you do."

"It is not in our power," answered Mrs. Barclay, "to love others and seek their good by a mere effort of the mind. Desire is fruitless, unless it flows into action What we have to do, is to be externally kind and forbearing—to do that good for others which reason and religion enjoin upon us. This may require some effort and self-denial in the beginning; but acts, from right principles, form vessels in the mind, into which affections can flow and find a permanent abiding place.

What is mere duty at first, becomes ultimately a delight."

Florence bent her head, listening attentively, and seeking to find, in her mother's earnestly spoken words, the power to overcome. And she did receive strength.

Miss Gimp, whose ears had taken in every word of this conversation, was puzzled to comprehend its entire meaning. The words she understood; but to hear such words from the lips of Mrs. Barclay, whom she had regarded only as a proud woman of the world, bewildered her. Could they be spoken sincerely? Yet there was no room for doubt. They were the utterance of a mother—made only for the ears of a beloved and confiding child. In spite of her wounded self-love, Miss Gimp could not but feel respect for Mrs. Barclay. From that time, she was subdued and reserved in her presence.

On the next day, aunt Edith Beaufort came. She was a woman past the middle age; tall and dignified in person; somewhat proud and stately in her carriage; and with an eye that, when it looked at any one steadily, seemed to reach inward to the very thoughts. A close observer would not fail to observe a certain cloaking of her own purposes. While she sought to penetrate every one, she as sedulously kept herself impenetrable.

Mrs. Beaufort had none of the high-minded scruples that prevented her sister-in-law, Mrs. Barclay, from listening to the idle or malicious gossip of the dressmaker. On the other hand, she rather encouraged Miss Gimp to talk. On the morning after her arrival, Mrs. Barclay and her daughter rode out. They were gone a couple of hours, and a portion of this time was spent by Mrs. Beaufort in the department where the dressmaker was at work.

"What kind of a man," said she, during a pause in

Miss Gimp's tittle-tattle, "is your carpenter? Harding, I believe, is his name."

"Oh, a very bad sort of a man," promptly answered Miss Gimp. "The worst man I ever knew."

A slight shadow flitted over the countenance of Mrs. Beaufort, and there was a perceptible huskiness in her voice as she said—

"Bad in what way?"

"Why in every way."

"Bad-tempered?" inquired Mrs. Beaufort.

"You'd think so, if you'd ever seen him among his children. He came near killing his oldest boy two or three weeks ago."

"How?"

"He stole money, and lied, and played truant into the bargain. His father beat him almost to death."

"He did!"

"Yes, indeed! The poor little fellow is only eight years old, and if he did do wrong, wasn't to be treated like a dog or a vicious horse."

Mrs. Beaufort sighed, and fell into a state of mental abstraction, from which the dressmaker soon aroused her, by saying—

"The strangest and saddest thing of all is, somebody left a little helpless infant at their door not long since."

Mrs. Beaufort started.

"Well, what of it?" she said, partially averting her face.

"What of it? They might as well have placed a lamb among wolves."

"You speak strongly, Miss Gimp." Mrs. Beaufort now fixed her eyes upon her with a searching look. "Have you heard of their ill-treating the child?"

"Not particularly," answered Miss Gimp. "The fact is, nobody hardly ever goes there But what are you to expect of people who treat their own children as if they were wild animals, instead of human beings?"

"Have you seen the stranger baby of whom you speak?" inquired the lady.

"Oh yes."

"What kind of a baby is it?"

"One born for a better lot than that which has been so cruelly assigned to it. The mother who could desert that child had a heart of stone. It is the sweetest, loveliest little darling that ever I saw; and everybody says the same."

"Does no one suspect from whence it came?"

Miss Gimp looked knowing, as she answered—

"Every one has the liberty of guessing, you know, madam."

"True. But what ground for guessing is there in the present case?"

"We know one thing for certain," replied Miss Gimp "It came not a hundred miles from Beechwood."

"Ah!"

Mrs. Beaufort manifested some surprise.

"What reason have you for saying this?"

"The woman who left it at Harding's was seen."

"Who saw her?"

There was, on the part of Mrs. Beaufort, an evident desire to conceal the interest she felt in the subject, which did not escape the quick penetration of Miss Gimp.

"Harry Wilkins, a neighbour of mine, saw her. He met her carrying a basket, as he was going over to Beechwood. She acted strangely, and this caused him to notice her. As he was returning home, he met her again, without the basket. It was on the very evening the babe was found."

"And that is all you know about it?" said Mrs.

Beaufort, the earnestness of manner, shown a little while before, all gone.

"All I know now, certainly, but not all I expect to know," replied Miss Gimp. "Harry Wilkins says that he got a good look at the young woman's face, and that he would know it again among thousands. He thought he saw her about two weeks ago, and, if it hadn't been just where it was, he would have been sure of it."

The interest of Mrs. Beaufort reawakened.

"Where did he think he saw her?" she inquired.

"Over at Clifton."

Mrs. Beaufort started. The eyes of Miss Gimp were fixed intently upon the lady, in whose face she read much more than Mrs. Beaufort wished to reveal. The two looked earnestly at each other for some moments, and then their eyes fell to the floor. Nearly a minute of silence followed. Mrs. Beaufort then said, with apparent indifference—

"Over at Clifton?"

"Yes, ma'am. He was riding over there to see a man on some business, when, just as he came in sight of the village, a carriage drove by, having in it two ladies. One of them, he is almost sure, was the woman he saw on the night the child was found. If her vail hadn't been partly over her face, he would have been in no doubt. He says he turned his horse, and rode after the carriage until he saw where it stopped."

"He did?"

"Yes, ma'am."

"Did he describe the house?"

"Yes. It was a large, old-fashioned stone house, with beautiful grounds about it."

"Didn't he ask who lived there?"

"Yes; but he forgot the name. He's going over there in a few weeks, and then he will learn all he can

about the people who live in the house. So you so—,
ma'am, we're likely to find out something."

Mrs. Beaufort made no answer, but sat lost in the
tangled maze of her own thoughts for a long time. Ever
and anon the dressmaker would cast stealthy glances
toward her, but the lady seemed all unconscious of observation. Her face, now in repose, and taking its hue
from the tenor of her thoughts, was one to puzzle a
wiser physiognomist than Miss Gimp. Its expression,
even, she could see, was bad—bad, as indicating the
long predominance of selfish purposes and an overmaster-
ing self-will. And yet it contained traces of an old
beauty. The lines were sharpened by pride and passion,
not rounded by a debasing sensuality. Yet was not all
bad. A softness about the delicately formed mouth and
gently receding chin, showed that all the true woman in
her had not suffered obliteration. Without speaking,
she at length arose, and went from the apartment with a
slow, stately step.

"I'll read that riddle before I'm done with it," said
the dressmaker, letting her hands fall into her lap, the
moment she was alone, and raising her body into an
erect position. "My lady knows all about this matter,
or I'm mistaken. Let me see. Clifton? Didn't Florence Barclay say something. about her aunt's going
back to Clifton? Be sure, she did! I remember it now
distinctly."

What a light came into the shrivelled face of Miss
Gimp!

"And then," she continued, "what interest, I wonder, could a woman like her feel in a man like Harding,
if there were not something behind the curtain? How
did *she* know there *was* such a man? It's all clear as
daylight. I see it as plain as I do that butterfly on the
window. I'll call at Harry Wilkins', as soon as I go
home, and tell him to be sure and find out the name of

them people the next time he goes over to Clinton. I wouldn't be much afraid to bet"——

The door opened, and Mrs. Beaufort re-entered. She had a silk dress in her hand, one of the breadths of which had received an ugly fracture.

"Can you mend that neatly for me?" said she, as she held the dress toward Miss Gimp.

The latter examined the rent.

"The edges are very much frayed out; but I will do the best I can."

"I would like you to do it now. I wish to wear the dress this afternoon."

Miss Gimp laid aside the work on which she was engaged, and commenced repairing the damaged silk, while Mrs. Beaufort sat by, looking on.

"You think," said the latter, speaking as if she were continuing a conversation, "that your neighbours will ill-treat the babe?"

"If they ill-treat their own children, what can you hope for other people's that fall into their hands? It's my opinion that the neighbours ought to take it away from them, and send it to the poor-house; and I've said so from the beginning. But what is everybody's business is nobody's business."

"Is Harding getting along pretty well?" Mrs. Beaufort inquired, after a pause.

"Men like him never get along well," answered the uncompromising dressmaker.

"Isn't he a good workman?"

"The best in twenty miles round, I've heard it said. But what does that signify?"

"Does he drink?"

"He's seen too often at Stark's tavern, if that indicates any thing. I can't say that he gets drunk; but you know to what tavern-going leads."

"He's in debt at the store. Mrs. Willits told me this herself, and that her husband was going to stop trusting him. That doesn't look very much to me as if he was beforehanded."

Mrs. Beaufort sighed gently, as if some unpleasant thought had flitted across her mind. Then she changed the subject, and did not once again allude to it, even remotely. After the torn dress was mended, she thanked Miss Gimp, with a reserved and dignified air, and withdrew from the room. The dressmaker did not see her again, and only learned, incidentally, that she left for her home on the next morning.

CHAPTER XI.

THE feeble aspirations for a better life, which had been awakened in the breast of Jacob Harding, struggled not toward activity without frequent assaults from the tempter. Too deeply interwoven, in the very texture of his moral nature, were evil inclinations, made strong by long indulgence, for good to gain an easy victory. His life, for years, had been one of disorder, internal as well as external; and now, when there came to him faint and far-off glimpses of the beauty and desirableness of order, virtue, and religion, the new creation—it could be nothing less—seemed so near to an impossibility, that his heart bowed, at times, hopeless—almost despairing.

External causes of disturbance were added to the

awakening conflict within. ...n some days, every thing
would go wrong with him, and he would return to his
home, when evening closed, in so fretted a state of mind,
that his coming fell upon his household like a shadow.
But the shadow darkened only for a little while. The
presence of Grace was a perpetual sunshine; and even
the dense clouds that gathered, at times, around the carpenter's stormy spirit, could not shut out the light and
warmth diffused so genially around her. With the babe
in his arms, or lying against his breast, the enemies of
his spirit assaulted him in vain. Deeply disturbed
though he might have been by the conflicts of the day,
peace now folded her wings in his heart. However
much doubt and despondency, arising from worldly dis-
appointments, had overshadowed him with gloom, the
soft cheek of the little one was never laid against his
own without his feeling a tranquil confidence that, even
as God was providing for the helpless innocent, so would
he provide for him. In the clear depths of her beautiful
eyes, he always saw a light that seemed to make plainer
the way before him.

But, had not the babe's influence been felt by others
of his household, as well as by himself, Harding would
have struggled for self-conquest in vain. Happily, over
all, the silent power of her beauty and innocence continued to prevail; and, in a marked degree, over Mrs.
Harding. Thus, in the better life, up to which all were
voluntarily or involuntarily aspiring, a kind of equipoise
was established. The disturbed forces had received a
new and better adjustment. One great gain on the part
of both Harding and his wife was this: each had learned
to repress the utterance of captious or ill-natured words.
In former times, unkindness of thought found ever a
quick outbirth in harsh, exciting language, that never
failed to produce a storm of passion. These storms, and
their often fearful ravages, each remembered too well;

10*

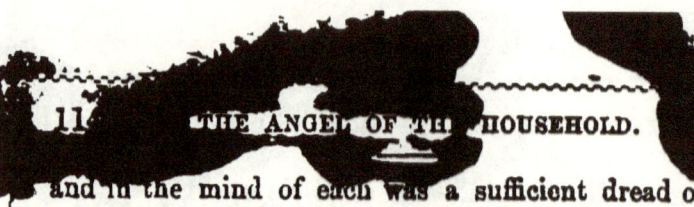

and in the mind of each was a sufficient dread of their recurrence to induce a watchful self-control.

Since the fearful night in which Andrew suffered so many terrors, there had been a marked change in this wayward boy. Mr. Long, the schoolmaster, seeing the impression that remained, and feeling for him a kind interest, made it a point to notice him, and, as carefully and judiciously as was in his power, awaken and foster his self-respect. At least once a week, he would drop in at the carpenter's, and never failed, on these occasions, to speak a word in praise of Andrew's good conduct and studiousness. The lad's gratified look, whenever this was done, gave him broad ground of hope for the future.

The change in Andrew was another readjusted weight in the balancing of moral forces to which we have referred. Without this particular readjustment, the new equipoise seen in the carpenter's family could hardly have been maintained. Little trouble was required in the management of the younger children, now that Andrew's baleful influence over them was, in a great measure, withdrawn; and this left a diminished evil pressure on the temper of Mrs. Harding.

A man like Jacob Harding is never a popular man. He is sure to offend in his business intercourse with others, and to make enemies. Of the carpenter, there were few to speak a good word, beyond the fact that no better workman than he was to be found. This reputation had insured him work that otherwise would have found its way to the shop of a better-natured, but in no way so reliable a mechanic, who lived in Beechwood. But there are men who will sacrifice their interests quicker than their feelings. Two of this class, who had employed the carpenter for some years, and given him a good deal of work in that time, becoming offended in consequence of some hasty words on the part of Harding, withdrew their patronage and influence, and gave both to a young beginner in a neighbouring village. One of these men was about erecting a handsome dwelling, for which Harding had furnished a part of the plans, and in the building of which he had expected to make a better profit than usually fell to his share. On learning the decision that had been made in favour of a rival workman, the carpenter was oppressed with a sense of discouragement so great, that it seemed to him as if a high mountain were suddenly thrown across his path. Not as had been usual with him, when things went wrong, did he give way to a burst of passion, when the fact was announced that his old customers had withdrawn their work.

"All right," he answered, in a voice of forced calmness; and the messenger who brought the intelligence left his shop, little dreaming that the seemingly unmoved carpenter had wellnigh staggered under his words as if they had been heavy blows. Upon these two customers, Harding had depended for the best of his season's work. All his other engagements were of minor importance, and the profit to accrue therefrom scarcely sufficed to provide food for his table. Of the causes leading to this result he was by no means ignorant. In his last interview with both of the parties, he had suffered himself to get very much annoyed at certain propositions which he thought involved a question of his honesty. Rough and plain spoken, he flung back upon them the fancied imputation in so offensive a manner as to make them angry, and they left him under a good deal of excitement. This, he doubted not, would pass off, and leave them ready to complete arrangements with him as before. But the sequel showed his error.

Never before had the carpenter's way seemed so closely hedged—never had he felt such an oppressive sense of doubt and fear as he looked into the future.

Work he had usually had in plenty. It came crowding in upon him from all sides, and he was oftener worried on account of its superabundance than concerned for its continuance. He had not always executed with promptness; and to this fact might be traced one of the causes of his want of thrift.

It was nearly half an hour after this unpleasant intelligence had been received, and Harding stood leaning on his work-bench, the chisel with which he had been cutting a mortice resting idly in his hand, when a form darkened his shop-door, and a familiar voice said—

"Good afternoon, friend Harding!"

The carpenter lifted his eyes, and met the pleasant, always cheerful face of Mr. Long, the schoolmaster, who was on his way home after the close of his afternoon session.

"You seem troubled," said the latter. Harding had looked at him, without replying. "There's nothing wrong with you, I hope? I thought I'd just drop in to say that Andrew is getting on finely."

"I'm glad to hear it." There was a huskiness in the carpenter's voice, that betrayed his unhappy state.

"None of your family sick, I hope?" said Mr. Long, with a kind interest that won upon the carpenter's feelings.

"All reasonably well, I thank you."

"Any thing wrong in your business?"

"I'm sorry to say that there is," replied Harding. "I have just lost my whole season's work."

"How comes that?" said Mr. Long.

"Two buildings that I had engaged have gone into the hands of another carpenter, and I am left without a single contract of any importance."

"This is bad," remarked the schoolmaster.

"It is bad for a man in my situation, with a large family on his hands. What I am to do, Heaven only knows!"

Mr. Long was struck with the tone of despondency in which these words were uttered. Obeying the prompting impulse of the moment, he answered—

"You may trust in Heaven, Mr. Harding. He that feedeth the ravens will not suffer you to want."

The words of the schoolmaster produced a momentary disturbance in the mind of Harding, who replied, with some bitterness of manner—

"Oh! as for me, I don't pretend to have any claims on Heaven."

"All men," replied Mr. Long, "have claims on their Maker for things needful to sustain life, and give them the ability to perform useful service in the world. For these you may look with confidence. Providence never hedges up a man's way in one direction, without seeing that it is opened in another. All will come out right, neighbour Harding—never fear."

"But I do fear," was the desponding answer. "To my knowledge, no one else is going to build this summer. Unless there comes a hurricane, unroofing half a dozen barns and houses, I see no chance of a sufficiency of work during the season."

Harding said this with affected humour; yet his tones failed to conceal the bitterness and distrust within.

"Not a good direction for any one's thoughts to flow," said Mr. Long, seriously. "Providence will open the way before you, I trust, without the aid of hurricanes, or any other ministers of destruction."

"I hope so; but I see little to encourage me."

Even while the carpenter said this, a neighbouring farmer entered his shop, and asked the question—

"Are you very busy just now, Mr. Harding?"

"Not particularly so," was answered.

"Will you call over, and see me in the morning? I wish to talk with you about putting a new roof on my barn. I did think of trusting it until next spring but

I've been examining it rather closely to-day, and don't think it will be safe to run the risk, especially as there is every prospect of large crops this summer. In fact, I've decided to have a new roof. So, if you'll call over to-morrow morning, we will arrange to have it done."

Harding promised to see the farmer bright and early on the next morning. Receiving this assurance, the latter departed. The schoolmaster had remained during this brief interview, and when the farmer left, remarked, with a smile—

"It is true as I said, neighbour Harding. Providence never hedges up a man's way in one direction, without opening it in another."

"But what's the use of it all?" replied the carpenter. "I would call this kind of business mere child's play. Smith's money is just as good as Jones's, and will buy as much pork and corn meal. And as for the work, one job is about as easy as another."

"Did it never occur to you," said Mr. Long, "that in the dealings of Providence with men, something beyond the provision of mere food and raiment was involved. Have your thoughts never reached beyond the question of pork and corn meal?"

"I don't understand you." The carpenter looked slightly bewildered.

"Man has two lives," said Mr. Long: "a life of the body and a life of the mind. To one of these lives has been appointed a comparatively short duration; the other is unending."

The carpenter leaned his head in an attitude of attention; seeing which, Mr. Long continued—

"God is an eternal being; and it is plain, from the fact that he has given to the spirit of man an eternal existence, that he must regard the wants and destiny of the spirit as in every way of primary account, when compared with the wants and destiny of the body. Let this thought find a distinct resting-place in your mind, neighbour Harding, and then you will begin to have some glimpses of higher truths."

The schoolmaster paused for some moments, in order to let his words make their due impression.

"From which have you suffered most in life?" resumed Mr. Long. "From sickness of the body, or sickness of the mind?"

"Sickness of the mind?" Harding did not clearly apprehend the question; and the schoolmaster modified it thus—

"I should have said, from pain of body, or pain of mind?"

"I've never had much sickness," said Harding, beginning to have a dim perception of the schoolmaster's meaning.

"And yet you have suffered deeply. Mentally—or in your spirit—you were in great pain only a little while ago."

"True, very true." The carpenter spoke partly to himself, as if new thoughts were coming into distinct perception. "Yes, indeed, I have suffered pain of mind. I always suffer pain of mind. As for bodily suffering, I can bear that; but mental suffering drives me, at times, almost beside myself."

"Did you never think of this before?" asked the schoolmaster; "that is, did you never separate so distinctly, in thought, your mind from your body, and see in each a distinct capacity for pleasure and pain?"

"Never. And yet it seems strange how I could have failed to do so."

"If pain of mind is more acute than pain of body," said Mr. Long, "is it not fair to conclude that the mind, or spirit, is capable of far higher pleasures than the body?"

"Yes, I suppose that it is."

"Let us take it for granted—and this is no difficult matter—that God, our Creator, Preserver, and Redeemer, is a Being of infinite benevolence—that love is his essential nature: it will follow as a consequence, that he not only desires, but seeks the good of his creatures. You are one of this number; and one toward whom his heart must be moved with pity, for your spirit has suffered much. Thus far in life, you have known little of the true enjoyment that God desires for all the children of men. Vainly have you sought for pleasure in sensual delights: they have proved only serpents to sting you. What a dark, weary way it has been to you!"

"Yes, dark as Egypt at times," muttered the carpenter.

"Let us go back a little," said the schoolmaster. "It is plain, that in the way you have been going, matters have not improved much. You are no happier now than you were six months ago."

"I don't know about that," answered Harding. "I don't know about that. Maybe you may think me foolish, but I can't help it. Since that strange baby came into our family, I have felt like another man. I don't know how it is, but the dear little thing has crept right into my heart, and brought with it something of its pure and gentle nature. The truth is, Mr. Long, I'm not the same man I was before Heaven sent that child to my door."

"Heaven sent it. You have used the right words, neighbour Harding. All good gifts are from Heaven In love to you, God bestowed this blessing; not to give ease, or comfort, or pleasure to your body, but for the health and joy of your spirit. Ah! I am glad to hear this confession from your lips. And now let me suggest a thought. May not the disappointment you have suffered to-day, and which was for a time so bitter, be productive of higher benefits than any you could have received, had all things gone according to your wishes?"

"I do not see your meaning clearly," said the carpenter.

"Our present conversation would otherwise hardly have occurred," suggested Mr. Long.

"No; I think not."

"Is it not clear, then? Think."

"Perhaps you are right," said Harding, in a thoughtful manner. "You have certainly filled my mind with new ideas. Come over and see me in the evening sometimes, won't you? I'd like to talk with you again of these things. They sound strangely—and yet my mind assents to them as true."

"Nothing is truer," replied the schoolmaster, "than that the eyes of God are over all his works, and that he leadeth his erring creatures by ways that they know not, ever seeking to bring them from the darkness of natural evil into the pure light of his truth. And thus he is seeking to lead you, neighbour Harding. Ah! resist not, but gently yield yourself to the divine guidance. But I have said enough for the present. Yes, I will call over and see you, and if you still find interest in these subjects, we will talk of them again."

What a change had taken place with the carpenter in the brief space of half an hour!—a change from deep agitation of mind, and a paralyzing distrust, to a calm and hopeful spirit. Not to the fact of work having come from an unexpected quarter, was this chiefly to be ascribed. That was but the foundation, so to speak, on which a higher and juster conception of Providence had been erected. His step was firmer, his head more elevated, and his countenance marred by fewer lines of care, as he took his way homeward. No shadow fell across the threshold as he entered; and no heart shrunk with fear at the sound of his voice, that seemed to have found new tunes and gentle modulations.

11

CHAPTER XII.

THE schoolmaster's words, only dimly apprehended at first, lingered in the mind of Harding; and, as he pondered them, new suggestions came, and new light seemed to break in upon him. There was a higher and better life than the life of the body—wants that no natural sources could supply—sufferings that no earthly physician could alleviate. How clear all this became the longer his mind rested on what his neighbour had said! and he half wondered that, until now, no perception of such important truths had come to him.

Happily, all things at home harmonized with the carpenter's state of mind on that evening. Andrew he found, on his return, busy over his lesson; Lucy had dear little Grace in her arms; and Lotty and Philip, who rarely disagreed if no one interfered with them, were playing together, and singing to themselves as happily as if nothing had ever ruffled the quiet surface of their feelings. The influence of Mr. Long over Andrew, since his particular interest in him had been awakened, and since he had discovered the right avenue by which to reach his feelings, was remarkable. Having secured the good opinion of Mr. Long—to have the good opinion of any one was a new experience for the lad—Andrew was particularly desirous to retain it. A kind look—an approving word—what ample rewards were they for all effort and self-denial! In these he found a pleasure far above any thing that evil indulgence or wrong-doing gave; and, best of all, they left no sad, painful after-consequences.

"That's right Andrew," said Mr. Harding, approvingly, as he came in and saw how the boy was occupied. "It gives me real pleasure to see you studying your lessons."

What a glow of delight did these words send to the heart of the boy! What a beaming smile irradiated his countenance, as he looked up, gratefully, into his father's face!

Mr. Harding laid his hand gently upon Andrew's head. The act was involuntary, and sprung from a passing mood of gentler feeling. How the touch thrilled along every nerve in the child's being! Memory was at fault in her efforts to recall the time when that hand rested upon him in affectionate approval before. Lower bent his head, and closer to his face was the book lifted. None saw that his eyes were suddenly dimmed, and none but he knew that the page before him was wetted by a tear.

A cry of pleasure from the babe now greeted the ears of Harding; and, in the next moment, Grace was in his arms, and hugged tightly to his heart. At this instant, a shadow fell across the threshold—the twilight was already gathering—and the strange woman, who had visited them a few weeks previously, stood in the door. Her dark, keen eyes took in the whole scene presented to her at a glance.

"Good evening, friends," she said, half familiarly, half respectfully; and, without invitation, she entered.

"Good evening, madam," returned Harding, approaching her by a step or two. Grace had laid her head close against his breast, and was nestling there with a happy, confiding look on her sweet young face.

"Will you take a chair, madam?"

The chair was proffered and accepted. At the same time, the woman laid off her bonnet.

"You were so kind at my last visit, that I hardly feel like a stranger," said she, as she adjusted her cap, and pushed back under it a portion of her black hair, in which gray lines were visible.

"That dear babe, again," she added, as she fixed her eyes intently on Grace. "I never saw a lovelier creature."

Mrs. Harding entered, at this moment, from the kitchen, where she had been preparing supper. At sight of the woman, she started, and looked disturbed.

"Good evening, ma'am."

The stranger fixed her eyes penetratingly upon her.

"Good evening," was coldly replied.

"In passing this way again, I could not resist the inclination to call, if for no other reason than to thank you for your former kindness, and to apologize for my abrupt departure. It was necessary for me to be at Beechwood at a very early hour, and I did not wish to disturb you, or tax your hospitality for an early breakfast."

The blandness and easy self-possession with which this was said, in a measure overcame the instinctive repugnance of Mrs. Harding. Still, she did not like the woman, and felt ill at ease in her presence. With as good a grace as possible, she bade her welcome. From the woman's manner, it was evidently her intention to remain to supper, and, in all probability, through the night. Indeed, she soon intimated this to the carpenter and his wife, who could do no less than invite her to remain with as much show of cordiality as possible. The object of her visit was matter of little question to them. Too distinct was their remembrance of her conduct on a previous occasion—and of the intimations then given by her—to leave any room to doubt that she had a personal interest in Grace, and now came solely on this account.

All eye and all ear was the stranger to every thing that passed in the family of Jacob Harding. The carpenter's face she scanned with so close a scrutiny, that he often found his eyes drooping beneath the singular gaze that was fixed upon him. The movements of Mrs. Harding were also closely observed, and not a word passed between the children that she did not weigh its meaning.

Whether it were from the presence of this dignified stranger, or from the subduing effects of better states of mind, the children were unusually well-behaved and orderly during supper-time. Lucy proposed to wait and be the nurse of Grace during the meal; although her mother said that she could hold the babe and attend the table well enough.

After supper, the woman succeeded, after many ineffectual attempts, in alluring Grace from Mr. Harding. The little one looked half frightened as she passed to the arms of the stranger, and then immediately reached out her hands to go back. But, being retained, her lips began to curve, and a low murmur of fear was audible.

"Come back, then, darling!" said the carpenter, lovingly; and he took her from the woman almost by force. What a happy change was seen instantly in the sweet young face, and with what a manifest joy did the little one shrink to the manly breast, and cling there as if it had found a home of safety!

"You love that child?" said the woman. Her tones were grave, and her proud lips firm.

"Yes; better than any thing in this world."

"It is not your own child?" added the woman.

"It is mine by the gift of God," said the carpenter, with a depth of feeling in his voice that surprised his auditor. "Some one—I do not think she is worthy the name of woman—deserted it at our door."

The woman moved uneasily, and partly averted her face.

"Abandoned," continued the carpenter, "by her to whom God had given a precious gift, the guardianship was transferred to us. We have accepted it gladly—thankfully. And who will now *dare* say the child is not ours? Such words must not be spoken here!"

The natural warmth of Harding's temperament betrayed him into an indignant vehemence, which caused the woman to shrink back from him a little way, and to look surprised, almost fearful.

"We cannot hear such words spoken," repeated the carpenter, in a gentler voice. "God sent an angel to our household when he sent this babe; and we have made room for her—room for her in our home, and room for her in our hearts."

The woman sat for some time with her eyes upon the floor. She was evidently in deep thought.

"Rather say"—thus she spoke in a low voice—"that God *lent* her to you—lent her, it may be, only for a little while. It is not well to fix the heart too idolizingly upon a child. What if her real mother were to come and claim her at your hands?"

"There is her *true* mother," said the carpenter, firmly, and he pointed toward his wife. "A woman gave her life, but *she* gave her *love*—a mother's love. Her *real* mother! Madam! I would spurn from the door the wretch who dared say that she brought into existence this sweet young cherub, and then abandoned her to perish, or, mayhap, find an unwelcome home among strangers."

"Can an evil tree produce good fruit?" asked the woman, looking at the excited carpenter almost sternly.

"It is said not," he replied.

"Could an evil-hearted mother give birth to so angelic a babe? Think, Mr. Harding."

"Could a good-hearted woman abandon her nursing infant? Think, madam."

The woman's glance cowered beneath the steady eyes of the carpenter

"Can a sweet fountain send forth bitter waters?"
The man spoke half to himself. "No—no—no."

"State the case as you will," said the woman, "and
the difficulty is the same. Here is a babe in which
all goodness seems concentrated—I cannot believe,
nor can you, that the mother who gave it birth was all
evil."

"Why did she abandon it?" replied the carpenter.

"Ah! there lies the question. Do you know?"

"You need not ask."

"She may not have acted freely. There may have
been an array of circumstances that crushed out, for a
time, her true life. I can more easily believe this, than
that her heart was all evil. The baby in your arms
contradicts that assumption."

"Mercy!"

This was the startled exclamation of Mrs. Harding, as
she arose quickly to her feet. Her eyes were fixed on
the door, which had swung slowly open. Every glance
followed her own. A beautiful young woman, with face
as white as marble, stood there, motionless—statue-like.
That face the carpenter's wife remembered but too well.
She had seen it once before, as it stood out on the background of darkness, and every feature was daguerreo-
typed on her memory.

"Edith! You here! What madness! Go! go!"

The woman started up, and raising both hands,
motioned her energetically to be gone.

"Baby! baby! Oh, my sweet baby!"

And the young creature bounded forward. Ere the
bewildered carpenter had time to recover his self-possession, she had lifted Grace from his arms, and was
hugging her wildly to her heart.

"Oh baby! Grace! Darling!" What a passionate
tenderness was in her voice! "I was wicked, wicked,
wicked to give you up! But you are once more against

my heart, and we will live or die together! Baby! Sweet one! Oh! darling! darling!"

She had moved about the room like one half crazed; but now, as a shower of tears fell over her face, she dropped into a chair, and leaning over the child, which she held close to her bosom, she mingled kisses, sobs, and tears, for some minutes, in a very tempest of emotion.

Meantime, the elder of the two women showed strong agitation, that was repressed only by a vigorous effort. Now her face was dark with struggling passion; and now so pale and ghastly, that it seemed as if her very life's love were suffering its final assault. As soon as the first bewildering excitement was over, she went up to the young woman, and laying her hand upon her with a firm grasp, said, in a tone of remonstrance—

"What madness has come over you, Edith? Give back the child, and come away. It is as well cared for as you or I could desire."

The other waved her hand with an imperative gesture as she replied—

"It is useless, mother! My resolve is taken. I will not part with my child. Mine it is—mine, born in lawful wedlock, and there is no earthly power strong enough to drag it from my arms. You may turn from me, if you will. You may shut up your heart against me; but mine shall be open to my child—my darling, darling child! Sweet, sweet baby!"

And she again hugged it to her heart.

"The fountain is not dry yet, love," she murmured, in a low, tender voice, as she bared her bosom, and drew the babe's soft face against it. "Drink again—drink! I have kept it open for this hour—this hour that my heart told me would come—must come. There—there. Drink, baby—drink. Drink, and God bless you!"

And as the babe commenced drawing sweet life from

this fountain of life, the mother's eyes were lifted heavenward. Her cheeks glowed, and a thrill of exquisite joy trembled along every fibre of her soul.

"Father," she sobbed, "let my tears and thankfulness for this hour of restoration, obliterate the record that darkens one page of my life's sad history."

This scene was more than the woman she called her mother could witness unsubdued. Hitherto her imperious will had ruled her complying child. But nature—free nature—had now asserted her right, and swept aside all opposing forces. In Edith's heart, the mother's love was stronger than the daughter's fear.

"Edith, what am I to understand by all this?" said the woman, speaking with a resolute calmness.

"That I am ready to give up all for my child."

"Give up me?"

The woman held her breath for an answer. Edith did not reply, but bent lower over her babe, and drew it closer to her heart.

"Give up me?" repeated the woman.

"Mother! As God liveth, I will keep this child. If you turn from me—if you cast me off—well; but, as God liveth, I will keep my child!"

For a little while the frame of the other quivered, as if attacked by a sudden ague fit. Then stepping back a pace or two, she stood a few moments irresolute. The door of the adjoining room was partly open. Into this she now passed with a quick movement. A struggle had commenced that she wished to sustain all apart from observation. Nearly ten minutes elapsed before her reappearance. Scarcely a change of position or relation had occurred during her brief absence. Her face was very calm, her step deliberate, and her manner self-possessed, like one who has passed from doubtful questionings to a certainty.

Going up to her daughter, she laid her hand again upon her, saying, as she did so—

"Edith, my child!"

The voice was low, calm, and even tender.

"Mother!"

It was the bowed creature's simple response. She did not look up.

"Edith, I may have erred—I know not. If so, it has been for your sake. Love and pride have both been strong. But we will contend no longer. In the future, your own heart must lead you: I will oppose nothing."

An electric thrill seemed suddenly to awaken the half-dormant sensibilities of the young mother. She looked up with a blending of joy and surprise in her countenance.

"What do I hear? Speak the words again."

"We will contend no longer, Edith. In the future, your own heart must lead you: I will oppose nothing."

The eyes of Edith closed as she leaned her head back against her mother, whose arm now clasped her. How placid was her pale young face!—how soft, and tender, and loving the sweet lips just parting with a smile!

"You have made me happy. Can a mother ask more for her child?"

It was all she said; but the words went trembling down into the agitated heart of that strong, self-willed woman of the world, and accomplished their mission.

A kiss—long and fervent—sealed the reconciliation and new compact.

CHAPTER XIII.

WHILE this scene was passing, little Lotty had crept into her mother's lap, and was lying with her head close against her bosom. Since Grace came among them, Lotty had found a new pleasure. She never tired of being with the babe, and the babe never seemed happier than when Lotty was bending over her, and talking to her in a language that only they understood.

"Is she going to take Grace away from us?" she whispered two or three times to her mother, as she looked on wonderingly, yet with an instinct of the truth.

Mrs. Harding did not reply, for she could not; but, at each renewal of the question, her arm drew, with an involuntary pressure, the little one closer to her breast.

"I'll be your little Grace, mother."

These words, so unexpected, thrilled a new chord in her heart.

"Grace is so sweet and so good," she answered, more from impulse than thought. The words were scarcely uttered, ere she felt that they were spoken unwisely.

"I will try to be good."

There was a pleading softness in Lotty's tones that touched the mother's sensibilities. She was asking for a love, deeper, purer, truer than she had ever known—such a love as she had seen given to another.

"I will try to be good, mother. I will try to be like Grace. But they won't take her away, will they mother?"

"I hope not, dear."

"If they do, mother, shan't I be your little Grace?"

"Yes, if you will be good, like Grace."

"I can't be good just like her. But I'll try, mother. And you won't scold me so, will you, mother? Talk to me sweet and good, just as you talk to Grace—won't you, mother?"

And now the child's arms were stealing around the neck of Mrs. Harding, and her eyes were looking up into her face, pleading and filled with tears.

What language could have been more rebuking, more softening, more subduing? It penetrated to the very inmost of her consciousness. Her only answer was a strong embrace. How her heart enlarged toward Lotty!

"You will love me, mother, if I'm good?"

The child was not satisfied with mere dumb show.

"Oh yes, my dear one!" answered Mrs. Harding, in a voice whose tenderness satisfied the heart of Lotty. "I will love you. Be a good little girl, and I will love you just as well as I love Grace."

"I will be so good, mother," murmured the happy little one, as she hid her face, and wept for very joy.

Thus she was lying, when the elder of the two strangers, turning from her daughter, between whom and herself so singular a reconciliation had taken place, said, addressing Mr. Harding in a calm voice—

"My friend, there was a meaning in the words I spoke a little while ago, that went beyond my own thoughts. This young woman—the mother of Grace—is my child. I did not expect her here this evening—nothing could have been farther from my anticipations. I knew that she was almost dying to see her child—to have it again in her arms, and I feared that its restoration might become necessary. Why she abandoned it at your door, cannot now be explained; neither can we reveal who we are, or where we came from. That secret, for the present, must remain with ourselves. Enough, that the child is ours, and now returns to its true home and its true mother You and your excellent wife will never be forgotten. My daughter has a heart that can feel gratitude—bad as you have pronounced her—and this you will, ere long, know. Let me ask of you one thing, and that is, silence as to the occurrences of this evening."

The carpenter sat with his eyes upon the floor, during all the time that the woman was speaking.

As she ceased, he arose, and crossing the room, stood before the young woman, who still held Grace in her arms.

Reaching out his hands, and smiling, he said, in a voice of tender persuasion—

"Come, Grace—come, love—come."

The little one lifted her head from the woman's breast, bent toward the carpenter, and smiled, in return, one of her sweetest, most loving smiles. The woman instantly drew the child back, while a shade of fear went over her countenance.

"Don't be alarmed, madam," said the carpenter, in a respectful voice. "If she will come, let her come. You may take her again. Grace, darling! Sweet one! Come!"

Again the babe raised herself up, and leaned toward the carpenter. Again she smiled sweetly, fluttered her tiny hands, and seemed anxious to get into his arms. He reached out for her; but just as she seemed ready to spring to him, her eyes wandered up to the loving face, so full of unutterable tenderness, that bent over her; and then she fell back upon the bosom she knew to be her mother's.

A shadow darkened on the carpenter's face.

"Come, darling!" he repeated, extending his hands.

She lifted her head again, stretched out her arms, and in the next instant was tightly clasped to the carpenter's bosom.

"Heaven bless you, sweet one! Bless you! bless you! An angel of love you have been to us all! How can we give you up? Oh! no, no! It must not be! God gave you to us; and shall we let any but the death-angel take you away?"

The mother had started to her feet, and was now moving by the side of Harding, as he paced about the room, her face full of alarm and anxiety.

"Oh, sir! give me back my babe!" she cried, in a voice of deep supplication. "Grace! Darling! Come to your mother!"

Harding paused, and, by an effort, repressed the strong upheaving of emotion. As he relaxed the tight clasp of his arms, the little one raised her head, and now reached out her hands toward her mother.

"Go back, then," he said, kissing her tenderly. "Go back. I cannot say nay, if it is in both your hearts."

As Grace returned, with a baby murmur of joy, to her mother's arms, the carpenter's strength seemed to leave him, and he sunk into a chair, where for some time he remained, with his head drooped upon his breast. From this state he was aroused by hearing the elder of the two women say, addressing her daughter—

"You came in the carriage?"

"Yes."

"How far is it away?"

"About a quarter of a mile, on the road to Beech wood."

"It is growing late. We must leave here."

"You will not leave to-night?" said Harding, as he arose and came forward.

"Oh yes; we must go," was answered.

"To that I cannot consent"—the carpenter spoke firmly—"unless you go alone."

"Alone!"

The mother of Grace looked frightened.

"Yes—a one. Did you think, for an instant, that I would stand passive and see her taken away by strangers, no matter what their claim? If so, you have mistaken Jacob Harding. Who are you? Where do you live? These are questions that must be fully answered."

There was a manly dignity about the carpenter that compelled respect, and a firmness of manner that showed him to be entirely in earnest.

The two women looked at each other with troubled glances.

"You shall know all in good time," said the elder.

"Now is the good time," was answered. "Believe me, when I say, that I love that babe too well, to trust her even with her mother, when all the past is considered, unless I know where to find that mother. I must hold you both to a higher responsibility than your own consciences."

"What is to be done?" almost sobbed the distressed young woman. "Oh that I were once more at home with my babe! Kind sir"—and she turned to the carpenter with a pleading look—"do let us go. I have the means of being generous to you, and I will be generous. Gratitude for your kindness to my child has already suggested ample benefits. Oh, sir! withdraw your opposition. There are reasons why we desire to remain for the present unknown. Say that we may leave, and I will never cease to ask for you Heaven's choicest blessings."

"It cannot be," said the carpenter, with unwavering firmness. "That child never leaves here unless I know all about those who take her away. Rely upon it, nothing will turn me from this purpose."

The two women now communed with each other, apart, for some minutes. The elder then approached Harding, and said—

"My name is Hartley; and I live in Overton."

There was an unsteadiness of voice and eye as she spoke, that did not escape the carpenter's notice.

"It will not do," replied Harding, shaking his head.

"What *will* do, then?" exclaimed the woman, in a quick, demanding voice.

Her whole manner changed. The fretted will, so used to reaching its purposes in spite of all hinderances, could tamely brook this opposition no longer.

Five times did Jacob Harding pace the room backward and forward before answering. Then pausing before the woman, who had remained standing, he said—

"One thing I have fully decided."

"What?"

The woman spoke eagerly.

"That Grace does not leave here to-night."

"Oh sir, don't say that!" cried the younger of the two strangers. Her pale face blanched whiter.

"I have said it, and will not change," answered the carpenter. "You can both remain if you will. We will give you the best accommodations our poor abode can offer. As for me, I want time to consider this matter. It is far too weighty to receive a hurried decision. I must have a night's sleep upon it."

"Oh, for patience!" exclaimed the elder of the women. "You may repent this, sir! You know not whose will you are thwarting."

"I confess my ignorance," said Harding, with a shade of irony in his voice; "and therefore it is that I hesitate, and choose to act with circumspection."

"We cannot remain here to-night. Impossible!"

"Very well. You will find us all here to-morrow, or the day after."

Seeing that Harding was not to be moved, the two women drew together in a distant part of the room, and remained in whispered conversation for a long time.

"My daughter cannot be induced to leave her child,"

said the mother, as she left Edith, and came forward to
where Harding was now seated by his wife. "She will,
therefore, remain, at least, until to-morrow. Then, I
trust, you will permit her to depart with her babe.
Further hinderance on your part will be cruelty. Think
of what she has already suffered, and spare her further
anguish. As for me, I will go to-night."

"You are welcome to stay, if it so please you," returned the carpenter.

"My daughter's health has been feeble for some
time," said the woman, "and she is now quite overcome
by fatigue and excitement. If you will let her retire
early, she will take it as a kindness."

Mrs. Harding arose at this time, and laying the now
sleeping Lotty in her father's arms, passed from the
room. In a few minutes she returned, and said the
chamber was ready, if the lady wished to retire. The
mother and her daughter went in together, and shut the
door behind them. Mrs. Harding intended to enter
the room also, but the door closed so quickly, that she
was left without. For a moment or two she stood confused and undecided. Then turning to her husband,
she said—

"Jacob, what is to be done? How can we give her
up?"

"We will not, unless we know more of these persons
than we now do," replied Harding.

"It is her mother," said Mrs. Harding.

"Yes; that is plain. But who and what is she?"

"If we only knew."

"We must know." Harding spoke firmly. "Not
until I have the fullest intelligence in regard to them,
will I consent to let them have the child. Hark! what
is that?"

The carpenter listened.

"What do you hear?"

Mrs. Harding was startled by her husband's manner.
"I thought I heard a noise."
"What was it like?"
"I don't know."
Both listened for some moments.
"Where was it?"
"I can't tell whether it was in the house or out doors.
It was nothing, probably. I'm excited."
Still they listened in a kind of breathless suspense.
"I wonder if they have fastened that door: they are
very still," said the carpenter.
Mrs. Harding stepped lightly to the door, and tried
the lock.
"It is fastened," she whispered back.
"They must have turned the bolt very silently," re-
marked Harding. "Suppose you knock, and ask if
they want any thing."
Mrs. Harding tapped gently. There was no answer
She tapped again, but louder. Still all remained silent
within. She now rattled the lock, and called to the inmates. The answer was fruitless: no answer to her
summons was returned.
"I don't like this," said Harding, starting up, and
advancing to the door, against which he threw his body
with a force that broke the fastenings within. As the
door swung open, his eyes rested upon the open window.
In an instant, all was comprehended. Flinging the
sleeping child he held in his arms upon the untumbled
bed, he sprung through the open window, and disappeared in the darkness.
"A quarter of a mile from here, on the road to Beechwood." He remembered these words, and ran swiftly in
that direction, hoping to overtake the fugitives. The
sky was overclouded, and the night intensely dark. In
vain the eye sought to penetrate the thick vail of shadows For more than half a mile, Harding pursued his

way toward Beechwood, and then stopped, with a heart-sickening consciousness that longer search in that direction was hopeless. Returning with rapid steps, he swept around in a wide circle, vainly seeking for the two women who had disappeared so noiselessly, taking with them the dear angel of the household. But all was of no avail. Under cover of the darkness, they had effected their escape. After an hour spent in fruitless search, he came back, looking pale and distressed. To the eager questionings of his tearful wife, he only answered—

"Gone! gone! and not a trace of them left behind!" dropping into a chair as he spoke, and trembling from exhaustion of body and mind.

"Oh, Jacob! Jacob!" It was all the heart-stricken wife could say, as she leaned over him, and wept bitterly.

"Mary," said the carpenter, after he had grown calmer, "I have never had any thing to hurt me like this. It seems almost as if a hand were grasping my heart, and striving to tear it from my breast. Dear baby! And to lose her thus! I cannot bear it, Mary!"

"If we only knew where she was; if we could go to her sometimes," sobbed Mrs. Harding.

"If she had died and passed up into heaven," said the carpenter. "But to be stolen from us, and taken, we know not where, perhaps to be abandoned again, and to suffer, who can tell, what cruel treatment! Oh! the thought drives me half distracted."

"I do not think, Jacob, that her mother will part with her again. She loves her child too deeply. My heart ached, as I looked at her, to think of what she must have borne since she tore it from her bosom, and left it at our door. I wonder that she was not bereft of reason. For her sake, I will try to bear the pain I feel. Oh! if I only *knew* that all would be well with the babe."

"That I must know, Mary," replied the carpenter,

with regained firmness. "The woman said her name was Hartley, and that they lived at Overton. This may be true or false; but to Overton I will go early in the morning. If the statement prove false, so much is settled, and I can turn with more confidence my eyes in another direction. Of one thing I am certain—they do not live very far from Beechwood."

As best they could, the carpenter and his wife sought to console each other, and, in the act, drew closer together in heart, and felt a mutual sympathy. How deserted the house seemed to them! and their chamber, when they retired for the night, felt lonely and cheerless. If the baby had died, and, a little while before, been carried forth from that room to its mortal resting-place, the feeling of sadness and desolation that oppressed them could not have been stronger. Sleep did not visit their pillows early. They were kept awake by thoughts of the sweet babe that had so grown into their hearts, that it seemed a part of their life. But, at last, their heavy eyelids closed, and then this dream came to Mrs. Harding :—

She was sitting in her own chamber, with an infant lying close against her bosom. It had soft, brown, silken hair, curling in glossy circles about its forehead and temples, and eyes down into whose blue depths she gazed until it seemed that heaven was opening to her vision. It was not Grace—not the angel babe whose coming and going were shrouded in mystery—but a new gift to her mother's heart. Full of love and joy she bent over the lovely innocent, while her spirit uplifted itself in thankfulness for a boon so precious. As she sat thus, a pale, sweet-faced woman entered, also clasping an infant in her arms. She knew them both at a glance—the mother of Grace, with her newly-regained treasure in her arms. Coming up slowly to Mrs. Harding, she stood, for some moments, gazing upon her with a tender smile. Then her lips parted with the words—

"Our household angels!"

A thrill of such exquisite pleasure went through the sleeper's mind, that she awoke. Lotty was in her arms, and she drew her to her heart with a feeling of maternal tenderness deeper than she had ever known for her child.

"I'll be your little Grace, mother."

The words seemed spoken in her ears again, and she raised herself up to see if Lotty were not really waking. But no: Lotty was in the world of dreams.

"Bless you, my baby!" murmured Mrs. Harding, as she laid her lips against the warm cheek of the sleeper. "You shall be my little Grace."

"Dear mother! I will be good if you will love me"

She was dreaming.

Gathering her little one closer in her arms, Mrs. Harding lifted her voice to heaven, and prayed that she might be to her children a true mother. And her prayer, rising from an earnest, yearning heart, did not return to her fruitless.

CHAPTER XIV.

"Quick!" ejaculated the elder of the two wolen, as she closed the door of the little chamber into which the carpenter's wife had shown them, and slipped the bolt silently. Gliding past her half-bewildered daughter, she raised the window, which opened only a few feet from the ground, and springing out with the agility of a girl, was ready to help Edith through the narrow way of egress they had chosen.

"Quick! quick! Step lightly."

And the mother drew her arm around the slender form of Edith, and bore her onward as if she had been only a child. Sweeping around the house, the two women gained the road that passed only at a short distance from the door, and then pressed forward, as fast as the darkness would permit, in the direction of Beechwood. They were only a short distance away from the carpenter's dwelling, when the young woman said, in a voice of alarm—

"Hark! What is that?"

Both paused to listen, and instantly became aware, by the sound of swiftly approaching footsteps, that they were pursued.

"O mother! what shall we do?" said Edith, in a frightened voice.

Her companion answered not, but passing an arm around her waist, drew her off from the road to a clump of bushes that opportunely offered a place of concealment. Behind this they crouched just in time to hide their figures, which, from portions of white in their garments, would, in all probability, have attracted the eyes of

Harding, whom they doubted not to be the individual approaching with such hasty speed. He passed within only a few feet of them—so near, that his muttered words reached their ears.

"Come," said the elder of the women, as soon as Harding's heavy footsteps sounded faint in the distance.

"Not that way," objected her daughter.

"Why not?" was sharply inquired.

"He has just passed."

"Is not the carriage in this direction?"

"Yes."

"Concealed in the woods?"

"Yes."

"He will not find it, but we must. Come! In this deep darkness lies our safety. Here—give me the child."

"No—no."

And Edith resisted the attempts of her mother to get possession of Grace.

"Why don't you give her to me? Foolish girl! I am stronger than you," said the woman.

"She is as light as a feather in my arms," replied Edith, who still kept hold of the babe. "You lead the way, and I will follow as fast as you desire."

The woman, with a slight murmur of impatience, gave up the brief contest, and moved on again in the direction taken by the carpenter, her daughter following close in her footsteps. Stopping every little while to listen, and then pressing on, the two fugitives continued their way for about ten minutes, when Edith said—

"This is the place, mother. I told Mark to wait for me in the woods, off to the left."

Leaving the road, the two women sought for the carriage, but, to their dismay, it was nowhere to be found.

"Are you certain about the place, Edith?"

Edith was very certain in the beginning, but the

darkness was so bewildering, that her mind began to waver.

"I think it was here, mother."

"O Edith! and so much at stake!" exclaimed her companion, rebukingly. "When will you learn to rightly guard the future?"

"The darkness is so deep," said Edith.

"You should have thought of that, and taken a closer observation. What are we to do?"

"Mark!" called Edith.

"Hush! Mad girl! Your voice may reach other ears than his."

"Listen!" Edith spoke in a quick, eager tone. "What is that?"

"It is the carriage, thank God!"

And the excited young creature leaned her head against her mother, and sobbed violently. Her voice had reached the coachman, who was only a short distance from where they were standing, and his horses were in motion. But a few moments elapsed before the two women were in the carriage.

"Home, Mark—home!" whispered the mother, "and as swift as our horses' feet will take us."

"It is very dark, ma'am," answered the coachman.

"You know the road, Mark," was the brief and significant answer.

For a few minutes the carriage crept along almost noiselessly, until the road was fairly gained; then, at a word from Mark, the horses sprung away at a speed that satisfied even the impatient riders.

For nearly two hours this speed was maintained, and then the foaming horses were turned into a wooded lane that wound up to a fine old mansion, around which clustered many evidences of wealth, taste, and aristocratic pride. Into this the two women passed, and here, for the present, we will leave them.

The morning that broke after that eventful night, found Mr. and Mrs. Harding in trouble, grief, and great perplexity of mind. A tearful vail was over their whole household. Not one of the inmates but grieved after dear little Grace, with a sorrow that knew no words of comfort—no ray of consolation. All questioned, but there was none who could answer.

"What shall we do?"

That was the doubtful inquiry of the carpenter and his wife, asked often of each other, and answered only by troubled looks.

"Shall we at once make it known to the neighbourhood?" asked Harding. "This it is necessary for us speedily to determine. The child will be missed, sooner or later, when we shall have to account satisfactorily for its absence."

"Suppose you see Mr. Long, and ask his advice," said Mrs. Harding. "He is a good man, and discreet."

"Well suggested, Mary," said the carpenter. "I will see him without a moment's delay."

But even the schoolmaster failed to see the matter clearly on its first presentation. To bruit the whole thing abroad, might prove a serious error; but, in what way, a total ignorance of the parties concerned left altogether in doubt. It was plain that they had acted with a desperation which only the gravest considerations could justify. The crime of having abandoned an infant involved the deepest disgrace, and it was no cause of wonder that they sought to escape the penalty. On the other hand, the absence of the babe from the family of Harding would not fail to attract attention, and the neighbours would have a clear right to demand an explanation of the fact.

"What had we best do, Mr. Long?"

This was the earnest question of Harding, at the conclusion of his conference with the schoolmaster.

"Say nothing to any one else, at least for to-day," was the answer. "I will testify, if necessary, to the fact that you came to me, and related the whole of the strange circumstance, and that I advised you to keep silent for a day or two, while you made earnest search for the parties who carried off the child. My word, I am sure, will be all that is needed to screen you from suspicion of wrong."

"I am very sure of that, Mr. Long, and will do as you suggest," replied the carpenter. "And now, my first search must be made in the neighbourhood of Overton, although I have little hope of finding them there. I saw deception in the woman's unsteady eyes, when she mentioned this as her place of residence. One step brings us to the point from which the next can be taken. I will regard this as the first step in a search that must not be fruitless."

"And it will not be fruitless, I trust," said the schoolmaster, as Harding turned from him, and went back home to advise his wife of the conclusion to which he had arrived, after consulting with Mr. Long.

Mounted on a good horse, the carpenter was soon on his way to Overton, a small town some two miles beyond Beechwood. A widow lady, with whom he had some acquaintance, resided there, and at her house he alighted on reaching the village. After the customary greetings, and brief questions about family matters, Harding said—

"Do you know a lady, in Overton, by the name of Hartley?"

"Oh yes! very well," was the answer.

With what a strong throb did the heart of the carpenter bound at this reply, so little expected!

"Is she an elderly lady?" he next inquired.

"She is past the middle age; yet no one would call her old."

"Where does she live?"

The woman took him to the door, and pointed to a fine old mansion, almost hidden by majestic elms, that stood not far from her dwelling.

"Has she a daughter?"

"Yes; an only daughter."

"Grown up?"

"Yes."

"The person I wish to see," said the carpenter; "and as my business is somewhat urgent, I must bid you good morning."

Turning almost abruptly from the woman, he sprung into his saddle, and galloped away in the direction of Mrs. Hartley's, his mind already strongly excited in anticipation of an interview, the termination of which involved so much, and was yet so full of uncertainty. Passing from the public road into a gravelled lane, lined on each side by tastefully cut cedars, he advanced toward a beautiful dwelling, around which was every thing to indicate the possession of a cultivated taste by the owner, and wealth for its gratification. But at these external beauties he scarcely glanced. Too deeply was he absorbed by thoughts of the approaching interview.

Dismounting and fastening his horse, Harding advanced to the hall-door, and lifting the heavy knocker, brought it down with a strong hand. The sound reverberated loudly within. In a few moments, a servant answered his summons.

"Is Mrs. Hartley at home?" asked the carpenter. The suspense from which he was now suffering made his voice falter.

"She is," was the quiet answer.

"Can I see her?"

"Will you walk in?" said the servant, politely.

The carpenter entered, and was shown into one of the elegantly furnished parlours.

"What name shall I say?"

Harding was about to give a wrong name, but his quickened moral sense instantly objected, and he said—

"No matter. Say that I wish particularly to see her."

The servant hesitated for a few moments, and then left the apartment. Soon the rustle of a lady's garments was heard on the stairs. Harding arose to his feet, involuntarily, and stood almost holding his breath. A tall, dignified, middle-aged woman, with a mild countenance, presented herself. It was not her of whom the excited man was in search. The lady bowed, as she entered, and said—

"My name is Mrs. Hartley."

'Not the Mrs. Hartley I wish to see," replied the carpenter, in a tone that betrayed the depth of his disappointment.

"I know no other by my name," the lady answered. "You seem to be under some mistake, sir. Perhaps, if you explain yourself, I may be able to set you right Will you not be seated ?"

As Harding resumed his chair, he said—

"A woman was at my house last night—it is the second time she has called there—who told me that she lived in Overton, and that her name was Mrs. Hartley."

"Ah !" The lady was surprised. "What kind of a looking woman was she ?"

"In person, near your size, and, to all appearance, near your age."

The lady's face flushed.

"Near my size and age ?"

"Yes, ma'am; but, in countenance, you bear no resemblance," said the carpenter.

"And she said her name was Hartley, and that she resided at Overton ?"

"She did; but I questioned, in my own mind, her truthfulness at the time. Ah ! how cruelly have I been deceived !"

' Deceived! In what way, sir?" asked the lady.

"Pardon me," said the carpenter, "if I decline an explanation: the reasons are imperative."

"You are the best judge of that. And yet, as my name has been used in so strange a manner, it seems only right that I should be made acquainted, at least in some degree, with the occasion of such an unwarrantable liberty. Can you describe the woman to me?"

Harding gave as accurate a description as possible of the person of whom he was in search.

"Did you observe a mole on her right cheek?" asked the lady.

"Oh yes, madam! I remember that distinctly," said the carpenter, starting to his feet. "Tell me! Do you know her?"

"And she said her name was Hartley?"

"Yes."

"And that she lived at Overton?"

"Her words, as my visit here attests."

"A very singular statement," said the lady.

"Oh, madam! tell me if you know her: do not keep me in suspense," urged the carpenter, growing more excited.

"I cannot imagine the reason of such singular conduct." The lady spoke to herself. "Gave her name as Mrs. Hartley! What does it mean? There is some mystery here," she added, addressing the carpenter; "and as my name has become connected with it, I have a right to ask for explanation. For what purpose did this woman come to your house?"

"From the description I have given, do you identify her?" asked Harding.

"I do, clearly."

The carpenter struck his hands together, exclaiming—

"So much gained! so much gained! Oh, madam! tell me where I can find her!"

13*

"Not unless I know why you are in search of her. If you will not trust me, neither will I trust you," replied the lady, firmly.

Deeply perplexed was the carpenter again. He saw that the woman was right; and yet he was as much in doubt respecting her, as she was respecting him. It was plain that she knew the persons who had carried off the child; but what good or evil might flow from a revelation of the strange facts connected with them, she was unable to divine.

"Does she live in Overton?" he asked, hoping to gain some admission.

"I shall communicate nothing," said Mrs. Hartley, "unless I know the ground of your inquiries. If, as I said before, you will not trust me, I will not trust you."

"We never know how far it is safe to trust an entire stranger," remarked Harding.

"Very true; and that is my reason for not giving information to a stranger, of whose object I am entirely ignorant."

"Will you answer me these questions?" The carpenter spoke in an anxious tone. "Is the lady in good social standing? And is she known as virtuous and honourable?"

"I can answer you freely. She is in good standing, and I have never heard any thing against her of so grave a nature as this that you now allege—the assumption of my name. This, sir, is a most serious allegation. The wherefore must involve something more serious still."

"That it certainly does," said the carpenter. "And this being so, it is but just toward her that I should keep my own counsel until I see her face to face. That she desires secrecy, is apparent in the fact, that she has misled me by assuming a name that belongs to another. Ah, madam! if you would only give me the information I seek"

The lady mused for some time; then, shaking her head, she answered—

"I cannot meet your wishes."

Harding sighed deeply. Rising, he moved toward the door of the apartment, his face strongly marked by disappointment.

"May I ask your address?" said Mrs. Hartley.

It was given without hesitation.

"Your errand here this morning is a very singular one, Mr. Harding," remarked the lady, evidently unwilling to have him depart, without some disclosure of facts about which her curiosity was in no small degree excited. "Is it not possible for us so far to trust each other, as to impart the information each desires?"

"Not at present, I fear," answered the carpenter. "Too many grave considerations force themselves upon my mind, and enjoin circumspection. But of one thing I can assure you: I shall not long remain in this suspense. Should the search of to-day not prove successful, you will see me in the morning—perhaps this evening, when, to gain the information I desire, I will disclose what now discretion warns me to conceal."

Bowing to the lady, who made no further effort to detain him, Harding withdrew, and, mounting his horse, rode off at a quick pace. It was not his purpose, now, to make further search in this direction. First, he wished to consult with Mr. Long, and get his advice as to the propriety of disclosing to Mrs. Hartley the facts of the previous evening, in order to get the information so much desired. And so, turning his horse's head homeward, he pressed the animal to his utmost speed.

CHAPTER XV.

IMMEDIATELY on his return from Overton, the carpenter went to see Mr. Long.

"One step taken in the right direction," said the schoolmaster, after Harding had finished his narration of what passed between him and Mrs. Hartley.

"But what of the next?" asked Harding. "That is the question I am unable to answer. A wrong step may involve most serious consequences. The parties in this strange and disgraceful business evidently occupy a high social position, and are exceedingly anxious to remain unknown. If I reveal all to Mrs. Hartley, in order to gain the information I seek, it may be the cause of an irreparable injury. The mother of Grace has, it is plain, acted under an influence from her imperious mother that she was unable to resist; and the latter, moved by family pride, or some other strong consideration, has taken an extreme step, the knowledge of which, if it get on the wings of common report, must ruin her in the good opinion of every one."

"It is but just," remarked the schoolmaster, "to weigh every thing with the nicest care, where so much is involved. I think you were altogether right in withholding from Mrs. Hartley the information she asked, and I cannot blame her for being equally discreet."

"But what step can next be taken? I have not a single clue by which to trace out the fugitives. They escaped in the darkness, and left no sign of their departure."

"Did not the young woman say something about her carriage being near at hand, on the road to Beechwood?"

"Yes. She said it was a quarter of a mile away."

"It might be worth your while," said the school-master, "to examine the ground, a little off from the road, and see if you can find the mark of wheels. The carriage, most probably, was withdrawn from the public way, in order to escape observation."

"Of what use will it be?" said the carpenter.

"Possibly, the direction taken may be ascertained."

Harding shook his head doubtfully.

"Very small indications are sufficient often to lead to important results," remarked the schoolmaster. "When we are altogether in the dark, we accept the feeblest ray, and hail it gladly, as the harbinger of approaching light. But some other course may have suggested itself to your mind."

Harding shook his head, saying—

"I am, to use your own words, altogether in the dark. Not a single beam of light is on the way before me."

"Then do as I suggest, my friend."

"I very seriously doubt," said the carpenter, "the the truth of what they said about the carriage being in the direction of Beechwood. I followed them quickly, but saw nothing of either them or the carriage, although I kept on for at least half a mile."

"The carriage was, of course, withdrawn from the road, and concealed from view. I do not wonder at your not seeing it. The women, most probably, heard you coming after them, and hid behind some sheltering object, until you passed. The distance you went gave them an opportunity to gain the vehicle, and make their escape. As you did not meet the carriage on returning, the inference is plain, that the direction taken was not toward Beechwood. Now, if you can only find where it turned off from the road, and can thence follow the wheel-marks to the place of concealment, you may be able to trace them still farther, and thus determine, with

more or less certainty, the course taken. It will be
something gained, to know that they did or did not go
toward Beechwood."

"I will act at once upon your suggestion," said the
carpenter. "No time is to be lost."

Just about the place which had been indicated, Harding found the deep impression of wheels in the soft turf,
turning off abruptly from the beaten road. Following
these, he discovered the spot where a carriage had been
standing for some time, as was clear from the hoof-marks
on the ground. It was behind a clump of trees. Beyond this, he could follow the tracks, until they were
again lost in the road. One thing he was able to determine clearly: the carriage neither came from nor returned toward Beechwood. Between the place at which
it had been stationed and the little settlement where the
carpenter lived, a road leading to the town of Clifton
branched off. He tried to follow the wheel-marks in the
road, in order to be sure that the vehicle actually went
toward Clifton; but the hard, beaten surface, and the
mingling of other wheel-tracks, made this impossible.

It was now midday, and Harding returned home, intending, immediately after dinner, to start for Clifton,
and devote the remainder of the day to searches in that
direction. He found his wife waiting him in troubled
suspense. A few words sufficed to give her the meager
result of his efforts to discover their visitors of the previous evening. Her sad face and red eyes told but too
plainly how she had spent the hours since his departure.
The children were subdued in manner, and their sober
faces showed how sincerely they were grieving for the
loss of their sweet little playmate. Lotty had kept close
beside her mother during all the morning; and whenever
the latter sat down, overcome by her feelings, to weep,
the child would come and lean against her, or draw her
tiny arms about her neck and say—

"If they don't bring her back, I will be your little Grace, mother."

How the words went thrilling to the mother's heart, going deeper and deeper every time they were repeated, until at last she could not help clasping the little one passionately to her bosom.

Harding, after eating a few mouthfuls of the dinner which he found awaiting his return, had left the table, and was preparing to leave the house, when Miss Gimp, the dressmaker, who had only half an hour before got home from Beechwood, came in with a look of importance on her thin face.   In that particular crisis, she was far from being a welcome visitor; the more especially, as it was inferred by them from her manner, that she had by some means gained intelligence of what had occurred. She felt the reserve with which they treated her, and was somewhat piqued thereat; nevertheless, she could not keep back from them all that was in her mind, and said, soon after she came in, in order to introduce the subject—

"How is that dear little babe?" glancing around the room.   "Asleep, I suppose?"

Was this a ruse to bring them out?   Both Mr. and Mrs. Harding thought so; and therefore made no reply.

"I met a lady over at Beechwood," said Miss Gimp, "who asked about you and that babe with a good deal of interest."

"Indeed!"

Both Mr. and Mrs. Harding's indifference was gone.

"Who was she?"

Miss Gimp looked mysterious

"I don't feel at liberty to mention her name," she answered, with affected gravity.

"Was she an elderly lady?" inquired the carpenter.

"She was ne'ther very old nor very young," said Miss Gimp.

"Though somewhat past middle age," remarked the carpenter, who saw that it was necessary to excite a little the dressmaker's curiosity, by appearing to have some knowledge of the person to whom she referred.

"Yes," said Miss Gimp, looking at the carpenter rather warily.

"With dark, penetrating eyes, and a peculiarly dignified, almost commanding manner."

"I found her pleasant and affable enough," said Miss Gimp.

"She can be so when it suits her purpose."

"Ah! you know her, then?" remarked the dressmaker, thrown off her guard.

"I have met her, I presume."

"She did not intimate this."

Miss Gimp looked a little puzzled.

"It was not necessary, I presume. Did you meet her in her own house?"

"Me? No, indeed. I haven't been to Clifton."

"Ah! True enough. You were at Beechwood?"

"Yes. At Mrs. Barclay's. Mrs. Beaufort"——

The dressmaker stopped suddenly; for she saw by the eager manner with which the carpenter bent toward her, that he was merely leading her on to tell what she knew about the lady to whom she had referred.

"Mrs. Beaufort of Clifton, the widow of General Beaufort?" said Harding, pressing on to the dressmaker so closely, that she could only answer in the affirmative.

"Yes; it was Mrs. Beaufort," she replied. "She is a sister of Mrs. Barclay, and was making a short visit at Beechwood while I was there."

"Did she leave yesterday?"

The carpenter asked the question in so indifferent a tone, that Miss Gimp was altogether deceived as to the amount of interest he felt.

"Yes She went away some time in the afternoon,

I believe. Her going was thought rather sudden by the family. In fact, I heard Mrs. Barclay say to her daughter—the words were not meant for my ears—tnat she couldn't conceive what motive Mrs. Beaufort had for leaving so abruptly, and at so late an hour in th: day."

"You will excuse me, Miss Gimp," said the carpenter, partly turning away, and taking up his hat from a chair.

"Men are always excusable," returned Miss Gimp "Business has the first claim. So make no apologies."

"Mary!"

Harding looked at his wife, and she arose and followed him to the door.

"I am going over to Clifton," said he, "and will come back as early as possible. In the mean time, be on your guard with Miss Gimp, and do not, on any account, let her know what happened last night."

"Never fear, Jacob; she will learn nothing from me," returned Mrs. Harding. "But do you think that that woman was Mrs. Beaufort of Clifton?"

"I am sure of it."

"Don't be too certain, Jacob. The disappointment, should the supposition prove untrue, will only be the greater."

"There is not a shadow of doubt on my mind, Mary —not a shadow. Good-by! I will be back as early as possible."

And the carpenter hurried away.

"You know, then, all about this Mrs. Beaufort?" said Miss Gimp, in the most insinuating way, as Mrs. Harding came back into the room.

"The lady about whom you were speaking to my husband just now?"

The utter indifference with which Mrs. Harding said this, surprised in no small degree the dressmaker.

"Yes. Mrs. Beaufort, who resides at Clifton."

Mrs. Harding shook her head. "On the contrary, I know nothing about her."

"Nothing? Well, that's strange! I'm sure your husband does, if you don't."

Miss Gimp was puzzled, disappointed, and a little fretted.

"That may all be," answered Mrs. Harding. "He sees a great many people who never come in my way."

"But, really, now, Mrs. Harding, just in confidence" —Miss Gimp leaned toward the carpenter's wife, and put on her most insinuating look—"don't you know something about Mrs. Beaufort? I'm sure you do She had a great deal to say about you."

"Had she?"

"Yes, indeed; and about the baby in particular. Where is it?" and Miss Gimp's eyes looked around, searchingly.

"What about the baby?" said Mrs. Harding.

"And you don't know her at all?"

Mrs. Harding shook her head.

"It's my opinion, then, that she knows a great deal more about that baby than you do."

Almost impossible did Mrs. Harding find it to repress the strong desire she felt to question Miss Gimp closely and to gain all she knew at the price of entire confidence; but her better judgment gave her self-control.

"That may be," she answered; "for we know nothing of its history. All I can say is, that I hope she may have as clear a conscience about the child as we have."

"Clear a conscience! How?"

And Miss Gimp's eyes went searching about the room again, and even tried to penetrate the adjoining chamber, through a small opening in the door.

"We have done our duty by the babe."

Miss Gimp was puzzled.

"How is the sweet little cherub?" she asked.

"Well," was the brief answer.

"Asleep, I suppose?"

"When did you leave Beechwood?" asked Mrs Harding, not appearing to notice the dressmaker's question.

"This morning."

"How long were you there?"

"Several days."

"At Mrs. Barclay's, you said, I believe?'

"Yes. She sent her carriage for me, and took me over."

"And returned you in the same way?"

"Of course. She's very much of a lady, only so cold and reserved. Mrs. Beaufort, her husband's sister, is a very different kind of woman."

"In what respect?"

"Oh! she's so pleasant and talkative."

"What kind of a looking person is she?" asked Mrs Harding.

"Tall, and very dignified. I never saw such a penetrating pair of black eyes in my life. They seem to look right through you sometimes. She takes a great deal of interest in you, let me tell you."

"Does she, indeed? I wonder why!"

How hard was it for the carpenter's wife to maintain her exterior indifference!

"No, you don't wonder," said Miss Gimp, whose close observation detected the hidden excitement the other was so anxious to conceal. "You know that you are dying, this minute, to hear all I can tell about Mrs. Beaufort."

"If you really think so," remarked Mrs. Harding, forcing a smile, "pray have compassion on me, and relieve my great suspense."

The dressmaker was at fault again.

"Oh!" she replied, with ill-concealed vexation, "if

you are so indifferent about the matter, I shall not trouble myself to enlighten you. I thought you would naturally feel an interest in learning something about a person who evidently knows a good deal more than you do about little Grace, and who, it is plain, has her eyes pretty closely fixed on you."

Saying this, Miss Gimp arose, and made a movement toward the door. She was very confident that this act would break down, at once, the assumed indifference of Mrs. Harding. But she erred. The latter was too clearly aware of how much was at stake to suffer herself to be thrown from her guard. All the information of any value possessed by Miss Gimp had been communicated. She saw this, as her mind grew calm and clear, and she was pleased that the prying gossip was about to depart. It was in vain that the dressmaker lingered, and tried to strike some new chord of interest. Nothing vibrated to her touch; and she withdrew, utterly disappointed in the object of her visit, and in a very bad humour with both the carpenter and his wife, whom she failed not to abuse, in round terms, during three neighbourly visits paid by her ere reaching her own dwelling.

CHAPTER XVI.

IN a large chamber, the costly furniture of which was in the fashion of an earlier day, sat a pale but beautiful young woman, gazing fondly upon the lovely face of a sleeping child. She had no eye, no ear, no thought for any thing but the babe; for, as she sat thus, an elderly woman entered, and moved across the room, without attracting observation, until she stood close beside her.

" Edith !"

The young woman started, and her face slightly flushed.

" I did not hear you come in, mother," she said.

" You can neither hear nor see any thing, now, but that child."

The mother spoke with some harshness of manner.

Edith raised her eyes—they were not tearful, but calm and resolute—and fixing them on the face of her mother, she said, speaking slowly, yet firmly—

" Have I not said, mother, that this babe is dearer to me than life? Believe me, they were no idle words, uttered under excitement. For her sweet sake, I am prepared to give up every thing—to endure every thing. Let us, then, contend no longer."

" Think of the consequences, Edith ! Cannot you think of these? Remember that Colonel D'Arcy will be here next week."

" Well ?"

" And that he comes to claim your hand."

" Claim my hand ?"

" It is promised," said Mrs. Beaufort.

" By whom ?"

"By yourself. He has your written acceptance of his marriage offer."

"My written acceptance?"

"Yes. But why need you be reminded of this?"

Edith raised one hand, and clasping it tightly against her forehead, sat for some moments with a bewildered look.

"My written acceptance of Colonel D'Arcy's hand! Why do you say that, mother?"

"Because it is the truth. You wrote the letter of acceptance yourself."

"I did! When?"

Edith looked more surprised than ever.

"Scarcely two months have passed," was the firm answer.

"Ah!" A gleam of light shot across the young woman's face. "That, too," she added, with a sigh, "is becoming clear. By what dark spirit was I possessed? Mother! I have been on the very brink of insanity. The extorted pledges then made I now repudiate, as I have already repudiated the cruel act of abandoning my precious babe. Had I been in my right mind, I dare not now pray for forgiveness. The act of accepting Colonel D'Arcy is yours, mother, not mine. Your thought—your purpose—guided my hand when I wrote the letter, as it guided and controlled my actions on that day, of all days the darkest in the calendar of my unhappy life. But I have returned into my own proper self. I am clothed and in my right mind again; and, Heaven helping me, from this day forth I yield to no influence but that of my own sense of right and duty! I can work and suffer, mother. I can bend to any hard necessity that may come; but false to my woman's heart I will not be! The widow's tears are not yet dry on my cheeks, and shall I turn my heart from all its pure love? You need not scowl at me, mother—I did love him with a full heart, tenderly. He was my husband, my excellent, true, noble-minded husband, poor and in humble station though he was; and the duty of public acknowledgment that I owe to his memory, to myself, and to his child, I am resolved to make, and that right speedily. My first great error was the concealment of our marriage from the world; the second was suffering him to go away alone. Oh that I could have been with him in his last extremity! My hand should have been the one that smoothed his pillow—my voice the last that sounded in his ears. Ah, mother!—hard, proud, exacting mother! With what memories have you cursed your child!"

Gradually had voice and manner deepened, until both displayed an almost fierce energy, before which Mrs. Beaufort—for she it was—felt herself cowering. Hitherto her imperious will had ruled her daughter; but now her power over her was at an end, and she felt that it was so. The darling scheme, to compass which she had trampled the most sacred obligations under foot—making her suffering child a participator, even at the risk of dethroning her reason—had come to naught; and in its hopeless failure, other ruin was involved. Gone for ever—she saw, in this second strong encounter with Edith, that it was so—gone for ever was all power to bend that young spirit to her will. But, what next? Could she turn from her child in proud anger, and go forward on her life-path alone? She asked herself the question; and the very thought caused a quick gasping for breath, as if she were about to suffocate. A little while she remained standing near Edith; then, without replying, she went slowly from the room.

An hour afterward she returned, entering the chamber of her daughter as noiselessly as before. A low, sweet, cooing voice stole into her ears as she passed through the door, and thrilled her whole being with a strange emo-

tion—a mingling of exquisite pleasure and pain. It was
the baby's voice. Little Grace was lying on the bed,
and over her bent Edith.

"Darling! Sweet one! Darling!"

Thus her mother spoke to her, and at each tenderly
uttered word, she answered with a loving response.

"My sweet baby!"

And a shower of kisses followed the words.

The babe still answered, with its sweet, low murmur,
every word and every act of endearment. She lay,
partly elevated on a pillow, and in such a position that
Mrs. Beaufort could see her face, while she remained unobserved by her daughter. The hour passed alone had
been one of strong self-conflict—ending with self-con-
viction of wrong. The proud, unscrupulous woman of
the world chafed for a time against the iron bars of necessity with which she found herself enclosed, and then
gave up the vain struggle.

"Hard, proud, exacting mother! With what memories
have you cursed your child!" How the words continued
to ring in her ears, until chords were thrilled which had
given forth no sound for years. Calmness succeeded to
powerful emotion; and with this subsiding of the storm,
came touches of gentler feeling.

"My poor child!" she sighed to herself, as some vivid
realizations of what Edith had suffered startled her into
a new consciousness.

This was Mrs. Beaufort's state of mind when she entered Edith's chamber. It was not the first time that
the voice of Grace had awakened echoes in her heart.
None but she knew the struggle that it cost to part with
the babe, when cruel pride and worldly interests demanded its abandonment. Angry as she had been at her
daughter's secret marriage with a young man in humble
life, when the fact was made known to her, and almost
driven to madness when the babe came to mar all the

well-schemed future—still, in its lovely innocence, that babe had glided into her heart, and made for itself a place there in spite of all her efforts to keep it out and to cast it out. Witness her two visits at the carpenter's, in venturing which so much was endangered.

In full view was the babe's face, as she entered the room of Edith. What a heavenly beauty radiated therefrom! What a winning sweetness was in her murmured replies, as she answered to the voice of her mother!

"Edith!" said Mrs. Beaufort.

Edith started, as before, and a shadow fell on her countenance, as she turned toward her parent.

"Edith, my daughter!" There was a tremulousness in the tones of Mrs. Beaufort, that betrayed her softened feelings. A few moments Edith looked into her face, doubtingly; then she saw that her eyes were dimmed by gathering tears.

"Oh, my mother! my mother!" she exclaimed, in a voice of passionate entreaty; "will you not take this precious darling to your heart, as once you took me?" And she lifted Grace quickly from the bed, and held her toward her mother. "Her hands are outstretched, mother! She asks for a place in your heart. Will you not let her in? A Heaven-sent blessing to us both she will prove—an angel in our home to smile away the darkness that has overshadowed it so long Dear mother! gather us both in your arms! Mother! mother!"

The last brief struggle was over. Around them both the arms of Mrs. Beaufort were flung, and, with a strong compression, she drew them to her heart.

"My child! my child!" she sobbed, as her tears fell over the face of Edith and the babe. "Even so let it be. There is room enough for both. I will take her in. Nay—she is there already."

CHAPTER XVII.

MRS. BEAUFORT, the widow of General Beaufort, a man of wealth, who had attained considerable political distinction during his lifetime, was left with an only daughter, Edith, for whom she had large ambition. A very selfish and self-willed woman, she yet loved this child with an absorbing intensity rarely witnessed. Edith was a part of herself, and she loved herself in its reproduction in her child, with a largely increased vitality.

But very unlike her mother was Edith. In her, the milder, better traits of her father predominated, and this gave room for the acquirement, by such a woman as Mrs. Beaufort, of almost unbounded control over her From the beginning, the most implicit obedience had been exacted; and as it was ever an easy sacrifice for Edith to give up her own will, the requirement of her mother came to be the law of her actions.

While Edith remained a child, the current of these two lives—that of the mother and daughter—flowed on together at the same velocity, and in channels bending ever in the same direction. But there came a time when the surface of that gently gliding child-life began breaking into ripples—when the heart claimed its freedom to love what its own pure instincts regarded as lovely.

From the earliest time, had the thoughts of Mrs. Beaufort reached forward to the period when Edith's hand would be claimed in marriage; but not once had qualities of mind and heart elevated themselves, in the prospective husband, above family, wealth, and high position in the world

As Edith grew up, and the pure young girl expanded into lovely womanhood, her personal attractions, as well as her station in life, drew suitors around her; but all failed to win their way into her affections. Among these was a Colonel D'Arcy, a man of wealth and station, who in every thing satisfied the ambition of Mrs. Beaufort. Well-educated, accomplished, possessing a fine person and a large share of self-esteem, Colonel D'Arcy, on approaching the lovely heiress, might have exclaimed with Cæsar, at the battle of Ziecla, "Veni, vidi, vici!"

But he came, he saw, and did *not* conquer. The heart of Edith was too true in its perceptions to make an error here. Utterly repulsive to her was this confident suitor. The sphere of his quality surrounded him like the subtle odour of a noxious plant, and her delicate moral sense perceived this quality the instant he approached. That he repelled instead of attracting her, D'Arcy saw at their earliest interview. This piqued his pride, and, in the first excitement occasioned by Edith's cool reception, he vowed that he would "win her and wear her." It did not take long to satisfy the gallant colonel that the storming of a fort was an easier task than the storming of a heart. That of Miss Beaufort he found impregnable under all his known modes of warfare.

That the mother favoured his suit, Colonel D'Arcy saw from the beginning; but a proud confidence in his own powers would not let him stoop to solicit her as an ally. Yet he had to do so in the end. Against their joint assault, aware, as he had become, of Mrs. Beaufort's influence over her daughter, he was certain there would only be a short resistance. Here, again, he erred. Edith unhesitatingly declared to her mother that no power on earth would induce her to accept the hand of Colonel D'Arcy, for whom she had the most intense repugnance. Never before had her daughter so boldly set at naught her will. The fiery indignation of Mrs. Beau-

fort burned fiercely for a time, and in her blind passion
she did not hesitate to utter the maddest threats of consequences, if there was not an instant compliance with
her wishes.

"I can imagine nothing so dreadful as to become the
wife of that man," Edith would answer—shuddering as
she answered—every intemperate appeal. And little beyond this did she say; for all her words, she knew, must
fall idly on her mother's ears.

Meantime, at the house of a friend in the neighbourhood, she met with a young man, named Percival, who
was paying a short visit there. He resided in the city
of B——, distant a hundred miles, where he was pursuing the study of law. He was poor, with few interested
friends, and had the world all before him. At their first
meeting, Henry Percival did not know even the name,
much less the social position of Miss Beaufort; and she
was as ignorant of all that appertained to him. But
from the eyes of each looked forth upon the other a congenial spirit, that was seen and recognised.

The progressive steps of their intimacy we will not
pause to relate. On the part of Percival, there was no
design, in the beginning, to win the heart of Edith; and
when he saw that it was his, and reflected on the wide
disparity of their possessions, the discovery saddened his
spirit, for he saw, darkening over both their futures, a
stormy cloud.

On returning home to pursue his studies, he arranged
with Edith for a regular correspondence, which was conducted for nearly a year, without becoming known to
Mrs. Beaufort. At the end of that time, he came back
to Clifton, when he and Edith were secretly married.
The precipitation of this act was caused by Mrs. Beaufort's acceptance of Colonel D'Arcy in the name of her
daughter, and the actual appointment of a day, some two

or three months distant, when the nuptial ceremonies were to take place.

In order to free Edith from the martyrdom in which her life was passed, and to get for ever rid of Colonel D'Arcy, the young couple resolved upon this step. It was taken, and notice thereof at once communicated to Mrs. Beaufort, coupled with the intelligence that the bridegroom and bride would present themselves before her after the lapse of a week, and claim forgiveness and a blessing.

We will not attempt to describe the state of mind into which Mrs. Beaufort was thrown by this undreamed-of intelligence. Her very life's love was assailed and threatened with extinction. No eye but that of Heaven saw her, as, in the secrecy of her own chamber, she endured the wild conflict of passion that succeeded; but marks of the fearful storm were too plainly visible on her altered face, when she came forth in her stately composure.

The week passed, and then Edith and her young husband presented themselves. The first she received with icy coldness; the latter she overwhelmed with bitter denunciation and the most withering scorn.

"Come, Henry," said the young wife, laying her hand upon his arm, and drawing him away—"I will not hear you addressed in such language, even by my mother. You are my husband, and the wide world is ours."

There was a simple dignity, blended with unmistakable purpose in this, that confounded as well as surprised Mrs. Beaufort. Edith had already turned away, and was moving with her husband toward the door through which they had just entered.

"Edith ! Girl !"

The voice of the mother arose almost into a cry of anguish.

Edith paused, and turning, looked back. Her face

15

was colourless, and all its lines rigid from excessive emotion; but it was resolute.

"I have cast my lot in life, and with deliberation, mother," she said. "You left me no other course. Death I could have met calmly, but not the destiny you assigned me. This man is my husband, chosen from all other men, and with him I shall go through the world. If you receive not him, you cannot receive me."

"Mad girl! mad girl!" exclaimed Mrs. Beaufort, as she staggered back a few steps, and sunk upon a chair. "How have you flung to the stormy winds every dearest hope of my life!"

Edith left her husband's side, and going quickly to her mother, laid her hand gently upon her hot forehead, on which the veins were swollen into chords. The touch of that soft hand thrilled magnetically along every nerve. For some minutes Mrs. Beaufort sat entirely passive.

Ah! she could not live without her child; and never did she feel that truth more deeply or more painfully. Indignant pride would have flung her off and disowned her for ever; but intense love clung to her even as the drowning cling to a straw.

"O Edith! my child! what have you done?"

As these words came almost sobbing from her lips, Mrs. Beaufort arose and went from the room with unsteady steps.

When, after the lapse of two hours, she rejoined Edith and her husband, it was to meet them with a kindness of manner that took both by surprise. Below this assumed exterior, Percival, who had a quick, penetrating mind, saw concealed a sinister purpose; but Edith, too happy at so broad a concession, believed that her mother had resolved to make the best of circumstances, which no act of hers could change. The first inquiries made by Mrs. Beaufort were in reference to the publicity which had been given to the marriage. On learning that every

thing had been conducted with the strictest secrecy, and
that the fact was only known to one or two pledged
friends, who were to be relied upon, she expressed much
satisfaction, and at once proposed further measures of
concealment for the present.

To these proposals, Percival and Edith, after some
persuasion, were induced to accede; and at an early day
the young man returned to B—— alone, to enter upon
the practice of his profession, he having been just admitted to the bar.

Six or seven months elapsed, during which time Percival had twice visited Clifton, arriving, by arrangement,
late in the evening, and not showing himself to any
visitor during the brief period he remained. To both
himself and Edith, this secrecy was growing daily more
and more oppressive and repugnant, and it was only
maintained through the powerful influence of Mrs.
Beaufort.

About this time, a gentleman from New Orleans
called upon Percival, and made him liberal offers if he
would go to the South. This person's name was Maris.
He had been in correspondence for some two years with
Percival's legal preceptor, and at his instance made the
proposition to which we have referred. The opening
promised to be so largely advantageous, that the young
man felt bound to accept of it. Previously to doing so,
he repaired to Clifton to consult with his wife and
mother-in-law. Edith made some feeble objections;
but Mrs. Beaufort was so decided in her approval, that
she acquiesced, and immediate preparations for departure
were made.

For three months letters came regularly from Percival, whose residence was New Orleans. He spoke with
animation of his opening prospects, and shadowed forth,
in ardent fancy, a future of brilliant success in his profession   Then came a longer silence than usual; then a

letter from Mr. Maris, announcing Percival's dangerous illness with a Southern fever. Two weeks more—weeks of agony to the young wife—and the terrible news of his death came, with mournful details of the last extremity. In the midst of Edith's wild anguish, a babe was born—the sweet little Grace, in whom the reader feels so tender an interest. Around this event, Mrs. Beaufort threw every possible vail of concealment, even going so far as to bribe to secrecy, by most liberal inducements, every member of her household that became necessarily aware of the circumstances.

Weak in body and mind—prostrate, in fact, under the heavy blow that fell so suddenly upon her—Edith became passive in the hands of her mother, and obeyed her, for a time, with the unquestioning docility of a little child. Even her mind, in its feeble state, became impressed with the idea of secrecy, so steadily enjoined by Mrs. Beaufort; and, in presence of the few visitors whom she could not refuse to see, she assumed a false exterior, and most sedulously concealed every thing that could awake even a remote suspicion that she had been a wife, and was now a mother.

Meantime, under all the disadvantages of its position, the babe was steadily winning its way into a heart that, from the beginning, shut the door against it, with a resolute and cruel purpose. Mrs. Beaufort could never come where it was, without feeling a desire to take it in her arms, and hug it to her bosom; and the more she resisted this desire, the stronger it became, until the conflict occasioned kept her in a constant state of excitement.

A few weeks after the news of Percival's death was received, Colonel D'Arcy visited Clifton. On being announced, Edith positively refused to see him; and her feeble state warranted, even in her mother's view, the decision   He remained only a short time: but, on leaving, placed in the hands of Mrs. Beaufort an epistle for her daughter, couched in the tenderest language, and renewing previous offers of his hand.

Percival out of the way, Mrs. Beaufort was now more than ever resolved to compass this darling scheme of her heart—the marriage of her daughter with Colonel D'Arcy. The first step in its sure accomplishment was to get the child out of the way. But how was this to be done? It was a fine, healthy child, more than usually forward for its age, and in no way likely to die speedily, unless—unless? Did thoughts of murder stir in the mind of that proud, selfish, cruel woman? Such thoughts were suggested, and even pondered! But other thoughts —of disgrace and punishment—came quickly to drive them out. The abandonment of Grace was next determined upon. To effect this, she first induced Edith— who, from grief, sickness, and incessant persecution, had entirely lost her mental equipoise—to write a letter of acceptance to Colonel D'Arcy. Passive hopelessness left her a mere instrument in her mother's hands. For her acts she was scarcely responsible. The letter of acceptance passed speedily from her, and went on its mission, beyond recall. This fact of acceptance was a great power gained over Edith—a power that Mrs. Beaufort, seeing her- vantage ground, used with a heartless rigour, that finally led to the cruel act of desertion already known to the reader.

For two weeks subsequent to Edith's return home, after placing the basket containing her babe at the door of Mr. Harding—she had resisted all persuasion, entreaty, and command of her mother to leave that task for another—she retained but little consciousness of surrounding circumstances. The trial proved too great; and her over-tried spirit sought protection and repose in partial oblivion. Slowly recovering, her first sane thoughts were of her babe; and though she said nothing of her

15*

purpose to her mother, she was fully resolved, the mo
ment strength came for the effort, to regain possession
thereof, publicly acknowledging it and her marriage,
and, if that sad necessity were imposed, go forth from
her mother's house into the world alone.

The meeting at Harding's was quite as great a surprise
to Edith as to her mother; but it was all the better, as
giving occasion for the unqualified declaration of her
future purpose—a declaration that, as has been seen, she
was prepared to sustain.

CHAPTER XVIII.

"If the heart is not satisfied, mother, life at best is a
heavy burden."

Mrs. Beaufort and her daughter were sitting together,
on the day after their recovery of Grace, and talking
calmly of the future. Hopeless of attaining her ambitious ends, the former had given up the struggle, so long
continued. Even though but a few hours had passed
since the unequal strife with Edith, she was becoming
clearly conscious that her course of action toward her
child had been far from just or humane, and that her
position gave her no right to exercise so tyrannical an
influence. No longer compelled, by her own selfish purposes, to cherish a feeling of antipathy toward Grace,
she found her heart beginning to flow forth toward the
lovely infant. Such was the nameless attraction possessed by the babe, that even with all her powerful
reasons for wishing to annihilate her, if that were pos-

sible, Mrs. Beaufort had not been able to resist the sphere of her love-inspiring innocence. Now, when no barrier to affection reared itself, her heart turned toward the infant, and opened itself with eagerness to take her in. Quick to perceive the real change in her mother's feelings toward Grace, Edith placed the little one in her arms, and with a thrill of exquisite delight saw it drawn impulsively to her bosom. In that moment, the work of reconciliation was accomplished. Against the winning attractions of Grace, Mrs. Beaufort had striven from the beginning, but never with perfect success. It was all in vain, that, to satisfy pride and ambition, she had cast her off; even in the separation, her heart had mirrored the babe's sweet image; turned ever and anon toward her; and yearned for her restoration. And now, when she came back to brighten, with her seraphic presence, the darkness of their unhappy home, and no strong motive for thrusting her out remained, her heart leaped toward her, panting with its long-endured thirst to love, and receiving her therein with joy and gladness.

"O mother!" added Edith, as they sat together, each striving for, and feeling the way toward a truer reconciliation, "how vainly do we seek for happiness, if we seek it beyond the range of our own true wants! We must look inward—not outward. We must ask of our hearts—not of the world—how, and where, and with what companionship we are to spend our life's probation. As for me, I desire nothing beyond my own home, and an entire devotion of all I have and all I am to my child. If that will satisfy me, why should any one seek my unhappiness by dragging me into uncongenial spheres, or cursing me with associations against which my whole nature revolts with loathing? As for Colonel D'Arcy— I speak of him now, because you are better prepared to understand me than ever before—his friendship even oppresses me But, when he seeks a nearer association—

presumes to ask of me the love given but once, and never to be given again—I am almost suffocated with disgust. Yield him my hand, mother! Never while I have strength to bind it to my side. I would brave a thousand deaths in preference. He is a bad man—I know it by the quick repugnance that fills my heart whenever he comes near me. Did he possess a single germ of true manliness, he would not pursue me after all that has passed."

A servant interrupted them by announcing that a strange man had called, and asked to see Mrs. Beaufort.

"What is his name?" inquired the lady.

"He wishes to see you a moment; but would not give his name."

"What kind of a looking man?"

The servant described him.

"Say that I will be down in a few moments." As the servant withdrew, the whole manner of Mrs. Beaufort changed. "It is Harding," said she.

Edith started, and turned pale, at the same time lifting Grace from her mother's arms.

"What is to be done? How did he find his way here?"

"We must see him," said Mrs. Beaufort, after a few moments of hurried reflection.

"Both of us?"

"Yes, Edith, both of us. And he must see Grace. Nothing is left now, but to conciliate, and bring him, a certain degree, into our confidence. He and his wife proved faithful to the trust reposed in them. They loved our little Grace truly, and cared for her tenderly; and they must have their reward. There was a fine manliness about his conduct last night, that raised him high in my estimation. I think he can be trusted."

"But he frightened me so, mother: he spoke so harshly, and seemed so cruel."

"Was he not right, Edith, in seeking to prevent our taking away the babe, strangers as we were, and refusing, as we did, to give any satisfaction as to our personality? He was right, and I approved his manly firmness at the time."

"I wish you would meet him alone, mother."

"I do not think that will be best," replied Mrs. Beaufort. "We must not let him see that we are afraid of him. Our relations are very different from what they were last evening; and if we show a consciousness of our real position, he will not be slow to perceive his own."

The room into which the carpenter had been shown was a large parlour, richly furnished, its six windows draped with heavy curtains of red satin damask. Around the walls were hung many pictures, among which his eyes soon recognised his two visitors of the previous night, Mrs. Beaufort and her daughter. The portrait of Edith had been taken some five years previous, and, while it still bore to her a striking resemblance, had all the innocent sweetness of gentle girlhood. As he gazed, with a kind of fascination, upon this pictured countenance, it seemed to change and grow life-like, and he almost started to his feet as he saw the eyes of dear little Grace looking down, with a loving expression, from the canvas. He was scarcely freed from the illusion, when he became aware that footsteps drew near the door. Turning, he met the calm, dignified face of Mrs. Beaufort, and the pale, timid, half-frightened countenance of her daughter, who held the babe he had lost closely drawn to her bosom.

"Mr. Harding!" said Mrs. Beaufort, speaking with entire self-possession, and giving her hand to the carpenter as she advanced to meet him. "So you have found us, my good friend," she added; "and it is, perhaps, as well. We had powerful reasons for desiring to remain unknown. Under the circumstances, this was hardly possible. You, at least, were not to be baffled in your search, as this early visit testifies. Sit down, Mr. Harding. We had better understand each other fully."

Harding was somewhat bewildered by the calmness of his reception. From the dignified countenance of Mrs. Beaufort, his eyes turned to the sweet babe that lay so closely drawn against the breast of its mother: as they did so, a softened expression passed over his rough face

"Grace! Grace!" he said, tenderly, and advancing reached out his hands.

Edith moved off a pace or two; but the little one, the moment she heard the well-known voice, started up, and, with a glad murmur, fluttered her rosy fingers, and leaned eagerly forward, while her whole face was lit up with a joyful recognition. Edith drew her back, while an expression of anxiety and alarm dimmed her countenance.

"Let her come to me, ma'am," said the carpenter, in a respectful voice—it trembled with feeling.

Edith glanced toward the door, fearfully. Harding understood the meaning of this.

"You need not mistrust me, ma'am." He stepped to the door, and closed it. As he returned to where she stood, he continued—"Jacob Harding has gone thus far in life without a treacherous action, and he will not violate his honour now. Let her come to me; oh! let her come! Let me feel the dear one again in my arms, where she has lain so many, many times."

Mrs. Beaufort, seeing that her daughter still hesitated, took Grace from her arms, and placed her in those of the carpenter. As Harding received the precious burden, he clasped her passionately, and spoke to her in the most endearing tones. The little one answered him with her sweet love-language, and even drew her tiny arms about his neck. How wildly he kissed her! Dim were his eyes as he restored her to her mother; and he spoke not, for emotion was too strong.

"I am foolish," he said, as he recovered himself. "It is not manly, I know; but that child has, from the beginning, softened my heart, until it has become weak as a woman's. How you could ever have parted with her"—this thought restored his self-possession, and he spoke with something of a rebuking sternness—"passes my comprehension."

"And it passes mine! it passes mine!" murmured Edith, speaking to herself, as she bent lower over the babe, which the carpenter had restored to her arms.

"As for the past," said Mrs. Beaufort—she spoke with a calmness and self-possession that had its effect on Harding—"that must sleep, my friend, with its errors and sufferings, as far as memory will let it sleep. All I will say of it to you is, that I had ambitious views in regard to my daughter, which she frustrated by a secret marriage. The death of her young husband, a few months afterward, and while I was yet able to prevent the fact from becoming known, revived all my ambitious hopes. The birth of this child I was able to conceal; and, moreover, succeeded in so overshadowing the mind of its mother, as to induce her, in a moment of partial derangement, to abandon it at your door—not yours by choice, but by accident. The rest you know. The mother's heart was too strong in my child. Her babe is again on her bosom, and there it must remain. Her grateful thanks are yours for the tenderness with which you have cared for the babe; and she will not let her gratitude, believe me, rest in her mind a fruitless sentiment. For the present, all we ask of you is discretion. Let the knowledge of our personality in connection with this matter remain wholly with you and your wife. Of course the babe must now be acknowledged, and we shall proceed, without delay, to give public, indisputable evidence of my daughter's marriage. As to the abandonment of the child, with the circumstances attending it, if all becomes known in each minute particular, we shall suffer strong opprobrium. Very naturally, I wish to escape this myself, and especially to save my daughter from the charge of having abandoned to strangers, of whom she knew nothing, her own tender infant. Can we trust in your prudence? Will you not bind your-selves to us—you and your wife—by a new debt of gratitude?"

It was some time before Harding made any answer. His mind was bewildered by what Mrs. Beaufort said. Plain enough was it, that the angel of their household was to return to them no more; and the shadow already on his heart fell colder and darker.

"All does not lie with us," he remarked, scarcely re-flecting on what he said.

"Why not on you?"

Mrs. Beaufort spoke anxiously.

"The dressmaker you saw at Mrs. Barclay's yesterday directed my suspicions toward you."

"What!"

Mrs. Beaufort grew excited.

"Miss Gimp told me that you manifested a singular interest in us and the babe. I asked her to describe you, and knew you by the description in a moment; therefore I am here."

"Bad—bad. That is bad. I was imprudent."

Mrs. Beaufort spoke to herself.

"I have also seen Mrs. Hartley of Overton."

The face of Mrs. Beaufort flushed.

"She knew you by my description."

"Well?"

"But refused to say who you was or where I could find you, unless I gave her my entire confidence."

"Which you——"

"Did not," replied Harding. "Every thing was so much involved in mystery, that I chose to be discreet."

"That was well. But Miss Gimp—does she know of what took place last night?"

"No one knows it out of my family, except Mr. Long, the schoolmaster, whose prudence is altogether to be relied on."

It was now Mrs. Beaufort's turn to be silent. For many minutes she sat revolving in her mind all the difficult aspects of the affair in which she had become involved. At length she said—

"Mr. Harding, all we ask of you now is, entire silence to every one for the present, in regard to what has transpired. We will offer you no personal inducement to secure this, for that would be an insult to your manliness of character. But you have laid us, and can still lay us, under a heavy burden of gratitude. May we trust you?"

"As entirely as you can trust yourselves," was the unhesitating answer. "I see no good that can arise from bruiting the matter abroad. Why, then, shall it be done? But there is one thing I must ask."

"Name it."

"The privilege for my wife of seeing the babe. Ah, ma'am! you know not how she loves it. For many weeks it slept in her bosom, until it has grown to be a part of herself. You know not her distress at its loss. Her eyes have been full of tears ever since. To us all, the child has been as an angel. Strife has ceased in its blessed presence, and the lowest murmur of its sweet voice has been a 'Peace, be still,' to the wildest storm of passion."

"Bring her here to-morrow," said Mrs. Beaufort, with a good-will in her voice, that betokened her earnestness. "We would send our carriage, but for reasons that need not be suggested to you."

"Yes; bring her over," added Edith. "I wish to

see her and know her. She has laid my heart under a debt of gratitude."

Harding arose. "Once more let me feel her in my arms," said he, as he fixed his eyes lovingly on the infant.

The timid mother did not hesitate, but resigned to him the babe, that looked up fondly in his face, and smiled its sweetest smile.

"God bless you and keep you." Harding spoke with deep feeling. He could say no more. Kissing the pure lips and brow many times fervently, he handed the babe back to her mother. As soon as he had recovered his self-possession, he withdrew formally, saying that he would see them, in company with his wife, some time during the next day. A few minutes afterward, he was galloping homeward as fast as his horse's feet would carry him.

CHAPTER XIX.

THOUGH removed from them, as to bodily presence, the angel of their household still remained with the carpenter and his family. Not a member thereof, from the rugged father down to little Lotty, but saw ever before the eyes of their spirits, the dear young face that brought sunlight into their darkened dwelling; but they saw her with tear-moistened vision. She was no longer theirs in physical actuality; but present as in a dream that is never forgotten. Subdued even to sadness, the intercourse between the members of the family was marked by a tender regard, the one for the other. Each felt the other's grief at the loss of Grace, and desired to lighten instead of increasing its pressure. As for Lotty, since Grace left them, she had sought to win for herself that regard in her mother's heart which the stranger had occupied. She was too young for reflection, and only obeyed a heaven-inspired instinct. And as she knocked at the too long closed door of her mother's heart, that door gradually yielded, until at last the rusty hinges opposed no resistance, and it swung wide open to take her in

The intelligence brought back from Clifton, while it set the tears of Mrs. Harding to flowing afresh, because it extinguished all hope of the babe's restoration to her arms, relieved her mind greatly. There was a certainty about this intelligence, that settled the doubtful question of its fate. It was, and would be well with the child. Her love for it could ask no more, though her heart was bleeding from the separation.

To the eager questions of the children—"Where is

Grace?" "Have you seen Grace, father?" "Isn't she coming back any more?"—Mr. Harding answered with as much information in regard to her as he deemed prudent, assuring them, at the same time, that if Grace did not come to them again, they should go to see her.

During the evening, Mr. Long, the schoolmaster, called to learn the result of Harding's visit to Clifton. To him, as a friend fully to be confided in, the carpenter related the occurrences of the day.

"She has been such a blessing, such a comfort to us," said Mrs. Harding, as they sat talking of Grace.

"God has given you many comforts, many blessings," answered the schoolmaster, as he glanced meaningly toward her children, who were all present, quiet, half-wondering auditors. Andrew, over whom Mr. Long had already acquired great influence, was standing beside his teacher, proud of the notice and gratified with the kindness ever extended to him by his judicious friend; while Lotty, who had climbed into her mother's lap was lying close against her breast, looking contented—even happy.

It was on the lips of Mrs. Harding to reply, "If they were only like Grace." But her conscience rebuked her for the thought ere it found utterance, and she remained silent. But she took the lesson to her heart, and as she did so, drew her arm involuntarily tighter around Lotty, who, feeling the pressure, looked up at her mother with a smile of love. In return, the soft cheek of the mother was bent down until it rested on the sunny hair of her child.

The schoolmaster saw that he was clearly understood, and did not mar the good impression of his words by seeking to enforce their meaning.

On the next morning, quite early, Mr. and Mrs. Harding, accompanied by Lotty, started for Clifton. They had to pass the door of Miss Gimp, the dressmaker, on their way, and she failed not to discover the fact that the carpenter and his wife were riding out together—an event too noteworthy to be regarded with indifference.

"What does this mean? Where are they going?"

Such were her rather excited questions, as she laid aside her work, and took her place at the window, to note the direction they would take.

"Over to Clifton? Hardly. Yes—I declare!—if they haven't taken the road to Clifton! Ah, ha! There's something in the wind. I wonder if they can be going over to Mrs. Beaufort's. I thought I could see deeper into the mind of Mrs. Harding than she cared for. I was sure she knew more about Mrs. Beaufort than was pretended. But whose child is it? I'd give my little finger to know."

Unable to work with this mystery on her mind, Miss Gimp drew on her bonnet, and ran over to see Mrs. Willits, the storekeeper's wife, for just a minute.

"Our carpenter is getting up in the world," said she, as soon as she could thrust in the words, after meeting her friend.

"So I should think," answered Mrs. Willits, who had seen Harding go by; "riding out with his wife at a time when other people are at work. My husband can't afford such indulgence."

"They were always a shiftless set."

Miss Gimp spoke with some indignation. She could not forgive Mrs. Harding for the impenetrable reserve she had thrown around herself at their interview on the previous afternoon—a reserve felt to be both a wrong and an insult.

"And will come to beggary in the end," said Mrs. Willits. "It was only last evening that I heard Mr. Grant going on about Harding at a great rate. It appears that he had promised to call over early in the morning to consult with him in regard to a job that Grant, the farmer, wanted done. Mr. Grant waited at

16*

home until dinner-time, but no carpenter came. It made him terribly angry. He stopped at our store in the evening, and the way he talked about Harding would have done you good to hear. He gave it to him right and left, I can assure you."

"Didn't keep his promise with him?"

"Not he—Mr. Indifference or Mr. Independence, whichever you choose to call him."

"Mr. Shiftless, you'd better say."

"Well, Mr. Shiftless, then. And now he's playing the gentleman—riding out with his wife as coolly as if he hadn't lost a good job!"

"Mr. Grant won't have any thing more to do with him?"

Miss Gimp spoke with a kind of pleased inquiry

"Not he."

"Serves him right."

"Of course it does. He said that early this morning he would go to Beechwood and engage a carpenter there; and he swore—for he was in a great passion—that if Harding starved, he'd never handle a dollar of his money so long as he lived."

"I don't blame him," said Miss Gimp.

"Nobody can blame him," responded Mrs. Willits.

"D'ye know," remarked the dressmaker, lowering her voice, and speaking mysteriously, "that in my opinion something more than a mere pleasure ride takes them out this morning."

"What are they after? where are they going?" inquired Mrs. Willits, brightening up at this intimation on the part of Miss Gimp.

"They took the road to Clifton, I'm certain."

"To Clifton! Well, what great and mighty business takes them over to Clifton, I'd like to know?"

"Something about that child they've got, I'll venture my existence." said Miss Gimp

"What of it?"

Mrs. Willits brightened up still more.

"I think I can guess where it came from."

"Indeed!"

"Of course, it is only guess-work; but, in putting this and that together, you know, we often get very near the truth. I've been sewing at Mrs. Barclay's in Beech-wood."

"Yes."

"You've heard of Mrs. General Beaufort, who lives in Clifton?"

"Yes."

"Well, I never knew it before; but she's the sister of Mr. Barclay."

"Is she?"

"Yes. And she came over to see her brother about something while I was there."

"Well?"

"One day, when all the family were out, she came into the room where I was alone, sewing, and made herself quite sociable. After talking around a while, she asked if I knew Harding and his family. I said that I did. Then she wanted to know what kind of people they were. Of course, I couldn't give them a very exalted character, and didn't. It was plain enough to be seen that she had some secret interest in them. Who first spoke of that little foundling baby, I can't now remember; but the moment it was named, I saw that she knew a great deal more about it than she cared me to guess. In order to bring her out, I spoke of Harding and his wife in the strongest manner—taking good care to say, that in placing that child in their hands, it was like putting a lamb among wolves. She grew uneasy and excited at this; so much so, that she clearly felt that she was betraying herself, and left me abruptly. That afternoon she went away, very unexpectedly to the fa mily Depend upon it, Mrs. Willits, she knows all about that baby."

"Why don't you go to see Mrs. Harding, and feel around her?" inquired the storekeeper's wife, who had become much interested in the dressmaker's gossip.

"I've been already," answered Miss Gimp. "I came away from Mrs. Barclay's a day sooner than I intended, and on purpose."

"Ah? Well, what did you make out of her?"

"Nothing certain. I saw Harding and his wife, but they were as close-mouthed as terrapins."

"Did you speak to them of Mrs. Beaufort?"

"Yes; and its just my opinion that they got out of me all I know, and didn't let me see below the surface of their thoughts. I was *so* provoked!"

"And so you learned nothing?" said Mrs. Willits.

"Nothing certain. But it takes sharper people than they are to hide things from my eyes. That both were greatly interested in Mrs. Beaufort, and knew far more about her than they chose to tell, was plain enough; and that their ride over to Clifton, this morning, is to see her, I do not in the last doubt."

"I shouldn't wonder at all," remarked Mrs. Willits. "Mrs. General Beaufort! That is news. Has she a daughter?"

"I don't know," replied Miss Gimp.

"Why didn't you ask Mrs. Barclay?"

"Just what I've said to myself twenty times over. I'm provoked to death at my own stupidity."

"How soon are you going over there again?"

"I can't tell. I don't think Mrs. Barclay will want me very soon."

"We must find out in some way."

"Yes, indeed. I'll not rest until I know all about it. You remember that Harry Wilkins saw a woman carrying a basket on the night the child was left at Harding's?"

"Yes."

"Very well. He told me that he's certain he saw the same woman, riding in a carriage, in the neighbourhood of Clifton. Put this and that together, Mrs. Willits, and it isn't very hard to make out a case."

"I should think not. Depend upon it, you're fairly on the track. Harding isn't riding out, this morning, for nothing. Had they the baby with them?"

"That I couldn't see. I tried my best to look over into Mrs. Harding's arms, but her husband was on the side next to me, and though I got up into a chair, it was of no use. But I shouldn't at all wonder."

"I'll tell you how you can find out."

"How?"

"Just by running over to their house for a minute. Of course, nobody's at home but the children."

"That's it," replied Miss Gimp, starting up. "I'll go this instant." And she stepped toward the door.

"Don't forget to stop as you come back," said the storekeeper's wife.

"Oh! no. I'll be sure to call."

And Miss Gimp left with the sprightly step of a young girl of sixteen. In some twenty minutes, she returned.

"Well?" said Mrs. Willits, as she came in.

"No child there," answered the dressmaker.

"No? Indeed?"

"True as preaching."

"Where is it?"

Miss Gimp shook her head.

"Who was there?"

"Only Philip and Lucy."

"Couldn't they tell?"

"They couldn't, or wouldn't—which, I am at a loss to say. I never saw such mum, stupid little wretches in my life."

"Did you ask them where their father and mother had gone?"

"Yes."

"What answer did they make?"

"Said they didn't know."

"They lied, I suppose—instructed by their parents."

"As like as not," answered Miss Gimp. "But isn't it dreadful to think of? Who can wonder if they go to destruction?"

"Nobody. And so the child is gone?"

"Yes. No doubt they took it with them, this morning. But I'll find out all about it, by hook or by crook, see if I don't."

And with this assurance, the dressmaker, who had a good deal of work on hand, to be ready by a certain time, took her departure to renew her vain efforts at meeting her engagements. To promise was a part of her profession—and not to keep these promises to the letter, the other part. Having the interests of the whole neighbourhood to attend to, it was impossible to be entirely punctual in such unimportant matters.

CHAPTER XX.

IT was past midday when the carpenter and his wife returned from Clifton, each with sober but not troubled countenances. Their anxieties about the babe's welfare were fully satisfied; but they came back with the sad assurance that its sweet smile had faded from their home for ever—that an angel had departed from among them, and with it, they feared, the sweet, angelic influences that, in so brief a time, had made their desert to blossom as the rose.

A hurried dinner was prepared, and then Harding went to his shop, that had now been closed for nearly two whole days. It was his intention to go from there, immediately, to farmer Grant's to make ararngements about the new roof, which he had promised to attend to immediately. He was just on the eve of doing so when a neighbour stopped at the door, and said—

"Why, what's been the matter, Harding? I was about going over to your house, to see if you were sick or dead."

"I've had a little business to attend to, which has taken all my time for nearly two days," replied the carpenter; "but I'm through with it now, and at my post again."

"You've lost a job by it, I'm thinking," said the neighbour.

"How so?"

"I heard Grant abusing you right and left for not keeping an engagement, yesterday morning. He said you promised to come over and see him about a new roof to his barn; and that he waited in for you a greater part of the day. He was dreadfully put out; and in the afternoon, rode over to Beechwood, and engaged a carpenter there."

"Are you sure of that?" asked Harding, as his countenance fell.

"Very sure. I saw him riding over, myself."

"I'm sorry. If he'd known *why* I was unable to keep my engagement, he would not have acted so hastily. I was, this moment, about going to see him."

"It won't be of any use, I can tell you. Why didn't you send him word that it was out of your power to see him?"

"I should have done so, but didn't think of it."

"And, what is more," said the neighbour, "Mr. Edgar was going to engage you to build an addition to his house; but Grant talked so strong about you—saying, among other things, that you were not to be depended upon—that he concluded to employ another carpenter. So you see, this 'little business' of yours has proved rather a bad business. But, good morning! I mustn't stop here."

The neighbour departed. As he turned his back, Harding folded his arms, and leaning hard against his workbench, gave way to feelings of despondency, not unmingled with reproaches toward Heaven for the hardness, even injustice, of these cruel reactions.

"I've done nothing to merit this," said he, in partial utterance of his true feelings. "Nothing! nothing! Then why am I left without work, though my hands are strong and my heart willing? God never hedges up a man's way in one direction without opening it in another —so says the schoolmaster—and so I began to think when Grant came with the offer of one job after I had lost another. But now the way that opened so encouragingly before me is closed, even before I had set my foot therein. I wonder in which direction it will now open?"

The bitterness of distrust was in both Harding's voice and countenance.

"There's no use in folding your arms and standing idle," said a voice, speaking within him.

"Of course, not. But what am I to do? There's not a single stroke of work on hand." The carpenter answered his own thought thus, speaking aloud.

"Do something—make something. There are lumber and tools in your shop."

As the inward voice said this, the eyes of Harding rested on a half-finished pine table, which he had commenced in an idle hour, and thrown aside for other work. It was suggested to him to complete the table rather than not do any thing. This suggestion he resisted for a time, because he had no heart to work, particularly as the work promised no return.

"Finish the table. Somebody will want it."

The voice spoke again. With something like blind obedience to this inward monitor, the carpenter commenced working on the table. The effort naturally relieved his mind from the heavy pressure under which it was bowed down. He felt better, but did not know why. He had yet to learn that in all useful work the mind rests with a degree of calmness; that there is a power in true mental or bodily labour, to sustain the spirit in doubt, pain, or sorrow. Once engaged in his task, he pursued it with a natural ardour, and, at the end of two hours, a well-made table stood finished in his shop. He was looking at it with a certain degree of pleasure, when Stark, who had been very shy of him for some weeks, presented himself at the shop-door.

"The very article I want," said the tavern-keeper, as his eyes fell on the table. "Is it to order, or on sale?"

"Three dollars of anybody's money will buy it," answered the carpenter.

"Enough said," returned Stark, drawing out his purse "Here's the coin. I'll send my Tom over for it in half an hour. And, see here, Harding, if you've got time, I wish you'd make me two good, strong benches, about eight feet long. Some chaps got to skylarking over in my house last night, and smashed one all to pieces for me. How much will you charge for them?"

The carpenter took a piece of chalk, and figured up the cost of the wood.

"Two dollars apiece," said he.

"Very well. Make them. How soon will they be done?"

"As I've nothing particular on hand to-day, I'll get out the stuff this afternoon, and finish them some time early in the morning."

"That will do." And the tavern-keeper went his way, leaving three dollars in the carpenter's pocket, and his mind something easier. The stuff for the two benches was got out, and the work on both nearly completed by sundown, when Harding closed his shop and returned home. On his way, the gloomy, desponding state of mind returned. As he looked into the future, only a wall of darkness loomed up before him. His best customers had left him—the season was advanced—and no ground to build a hope upon was under his feet. Mrs Harding saw the heavy contraction of his brows as he entered, and it caused a shadow to fall upon her heart. Had the evil spirit, which the presence of Grace drove out, come back to him again? Alas! alas! if it were so! Yes, the evil spirit had come back, but, as yet, its power over him was small. It lay in his breast as a live coal, and only waited for the fuel of excitement to kindle a blaze of destructive passion. Happily, that fuel was not supplied. There was nothing in his home to fret or disturb him. His wife spoke to him so kindly, that he could not but answer kindly, and the children were so quiet among themselves, that no cause of annoyance or anger existed in that direction. Still, he remained gloomy, almost entirely silent.

"I don't know what is going to become of us, Mary," said he, as they sat together, after the children had gone to bed. The gentleness and kindness of his wife's manner had gradually subdued the state of irritability that threatened so much of evil; and now he felt like drawing nearer to her—letting her share his anxieties, and offer him his her sympathy.

"Why do you say this, Jacob?" Mrs. Harding raised her eyes to the sober face of her husband.

"I haven't a stroke of work."

"How comes that?" The interrogation was so gently made, that it encouraged, instead of repressing confidence.

"Dear knows! I don't just understand it. To me, it seems very strange, that just now work should all stop, when there's not been a day before, in ten years, that I hadn't as much as I could do. I promised Mr. Grant to call yesterday morning about putting a new roof on his barn. But you know why I couldn't see him. He got angry because I didn't keep my appointment, and gave the job to a carpenter over in Beechwood."

"That's only a single job," said Mrs. Harding, without seeming to be in the least troubled by the gloomy prospect before them. "You're a good workman, that every one knows. And I've often heard you say, that a man who does good work, never need fear but what he'll have enough to do."

"Yes, Mary; but look how far the season is advanced. Every good job that I expected has gone into other hands, and I don't know a soul that now talks of building even a pig-pen this year. I feel completely disheartened. If we were only a little beforehand, I wouldn't feel so bad. But we are not. Every thing is run down, and I haven't ten dollars ahead."

Just then some one knocked at the door. Harding opened it, and found a strange man, with a large bundle in his hand. His own name was inquired for.

"I am the person," he answered.

"Mrs. Beaufort sent this letter to you"—handing a letter—"and this bundle to Mrs. Harding"—reaching out the package.

"Won't you come in?" said the carpenter, as he received the letter and package.

"No, sir. It is late, and I must ride over to Clifton to-night."

The man departed, and Harding turned back into the house. Breaking the seal of the letter with unsteady hands, he opened it, and read—

"I wish to see you to-morrow. Come over early. If I am not mistaken, I can serve your worldly interests materially. I learn that you are a good workman, and faithful in the performance of whatever you may undertake. I am about putting up several outbuildings, and making some important alterations in my house. It is partly in reference to these matters that I wish to see you.   "EDITH BEAUFORT."

Within this letter, another, directed to Mrs. Harding, was enclosed.

"O Jacob! Just see here!" By the time her husband had gathered the meaning of his letter, Mrs. Harding was in full possession of the contents of hers. As she thus exclaimed, she held up two bank bills, each claiming the valuation of fifty dollars, while her face had a bright, joyful, wondering expression.

"Why, Mary!" ejaculated the bewildered carpenter, as he reached out for the letter of his wife. It read—

"Accept, dear madam, from one who can never forget, and never repay the debt she owes you, the enclosed as a first act of justice. Use it for yourself and children. Accept, also, a few small presents for yourself and them I have talked much with my mother about you and your good husband since you left us this morning; and I think, if there is nothing to bind you to your present place of abode, that we shall soon have you near us. We are about making some extensive repairs, improvements, and alterations in and around our home, and my mother thinks that your husband is just the man to whom she can safely intrust their execution. She desires him to see her in the morning. Urge him to come without fail.

"Yours, with gratitude,
                    "EDITH PERCIVAL."

"It is broad daylight now." Such were the carpenter's words, after sitting silent for some moments.

"The darkest hour is just before daybreak, you know," said Mrs. Harding, her eyes filling with glad tears.

"Providence never hedges up a man's way in one direction, without opening it in another. So Mr. Long said to me; and so I tried to believe. But how can one believe with a mountain rising up in his path, and thick darkness on either side of him? I cannot." .

"But let us not forget, Jacob"—Mrs. Harding's voice was subdued, almost humble—"what more the schoolmaster said in his kind and earnest talks with us."

"What did he say, Mary?"

"That the hedging up of our way in life, and the opening of new paths, are not for the alone sake of worldly good."

"Yes, I remember." The carpenter bowed his head thoughtfully.

"But for the sake of heavenly and eternal good," continued Mrs Harding. "How much he talked of our

17*

mental wants, and of our mental sufferings! and as he talked, did we not both see and feel, that mere bodily wants and sufferings were nothing in comparison to these?   The natural event of finding a babe at our door, which we received with reluctance, how much delight of mind it produced!   Now, it was in providence, as Mr. Long said, that the babe was so left at our door; and does it not seem, that it was so provided for, in order that, through this natural event, our spirits might become better and happier?   Surely, we are all better and happier for the presence of dear little Grace among us?"

"Have I not said so a hundred times, Mary?"   There was light in the carpenter's face as he said this.

"And will we not all be better and happier, if we can be where our eyes, every little while, may look upon her angel face?   Oh yes, I know we will, for the sight of that face will lift our hearts upward, and make us desire that spiritual innocence of which, as Mr. Long so beautifully said, she was the perfect bodily correspondent. And the desire will prompt us to resist the evils of our nature; and if we resist evil, you know, it is said that it will depart from us.   Dear husband!"—and as Mrs. Harding, animated with her subject, leaned toward him, and laid her hand upon his arm, the carpenter saw, as of late he had seen so many times, the sweet beauty in her face that had charmed and won his love in the time gone by—"dear husband! let us believe that the hedging up of your way in the old direction, and the opening of it in this, is not so much for the sake of worldly prosperity as for the higher good of our spirits.   Oh! is not peace of mind more to be desired than all earthly benefits? It is, Jacob; my heart—your heart—replies that it is. Let us, then, in accepting the earthly good, look still higher, and claim the better portion that may be ours."

"You are learning these wise lessons faster than I am, Mary," said the carpenter, with a tenderness of manner that went to the heart of his wife. "In the school of good I shall be, I fear, a slow learner. But the apter scholar must have patience with my poor progress. I am hasty, moody, and passionate by nature, Mary, as you know too well. As you overcome, give me aid. If you can keep your heart in the sunlight, mine will not long remain under the cloud. If your sky continues serene, the storm will soon pass from mine. Try and remember this, Mary, and in my darker moods, bear with me. You will surely have your reward."

"And in my darker moods, Jacob," answered his wife—"and they will come—for I, too, am hasty and passionate: you must bear with me. Oh, let us help one another!"

The pledges and promises of that hour were never forgotten, as the brighter, happier future attested. On examining the package sent by the mother of Grace, it was found to contain various articles of clothing for Mrs. Harding and her children, besides a handsome vest pattern, and a dozen fine silk handkerchiefs for the carpenter. They were gratefully received, coming, as they did so timely, and under circumstances that did not make the gift a burdening obligation. Tranquil was their sleep that night, and the morning of a new day found them looking hopefully into the brightening future.

CHAPTER XXI.

A MONTH later in the progress of events, and we find the carpenter and his family residing in a small, neat house, on the estate of Mrs. Beaufort, happily relieved from all anxiety about the "bread that perishes," and surrounded with more of taste and comfort than they had ever known. Harding had already entered, actively, upon the execution of such work as Mrs. Beaufort first desired, and, thus far, was giving every satisfaction. Why should this not be? for he was quick and skilful in all the branches of his trade, and perfectly honest in the execution of whatever might be intrusted to him. All that could be done to make Mrs. Harding's new home a pleasant one was done by Mrs. Percival, who came over, almost daily, to see her, accompanied by her babe, whose visits to the carpenter's family ever seemed like the shining in of sunbeams. Grace was still the angel of their household, beating back through her sweet presence to their bodily eyes, or, when absent, to the eyes of their spirits, the natural passions, which, like evil beasts, were striving to devour the innocent affections just born in their hearts, and which were daily gaining strength and beauty. Bright moments to Harding, in the day's circle of hours, were those in which the babe, borne in the arms of her nurse, came out to see him at his work. If he laid down his axe, his saw, or his plane at such times, that he might take the happy little one, and hold her against his heart, who could blame the act, or deem him an idler from his tasks? Not a stroke the less was given for these moments of self-indulgence—if we may call them by so cold a name—for they sent new

life through the carpenter's nerves, and fresh vigour to
his willing hands.

Only a few weeks were permitted to pass ere the
public announcement of Edith's marriage was made, accompanied by such evidence to all interested friends, as
removed even the shadow of doubt or suspicion.   The
fact of the babe's abandonment by its mother at the door
of a stranger, was never clearly understood.   That it had
been in the carpenter's family was known; but under
what peculiar circumstances it came there, was a matter
of question even to the neighbours of Harding.   Beyond
this narrow circle, it was taken for granted, that in order
to conceal the marriage and birth of the child, Mrs.
Harding had been selected as the nurse, and pledged to
secrecy in regard to its parentage.   Even among the carpenter's old neighbours, this theory finally prevailed, in
consequence of its adoption by Miss Gimp.

"I always said"—so the dressmaker gossiped, after
having settled to her own satisfaction all the difficulties
presented by the case—"that Mrs. Harding knew a
great deal more about the child than she cared to tell.
I said this in the beginning, and I've never altered my
mind.   You can't make me believe that people like the
Hardings would take a strange babe into their house, and
treat it even better than one of their own, unless well
paid for it.   It isn't in nature, much less in the nature
of such people."

And this solution of the matter was pretty generally
adopted, thus saving the young mother that crushing
odium which must have followed the clear annunciation
of her act, even done as it was in a state of partial
derangement.

Two months only had passed, since Edith was presented to her friends in her true character, when Colonel
D'Arcy, not to be baffled in the pursuit of her hand,
wrote her a long, earnest letter of sympathy and con-

fidence, begging forgiveness at the same time for the ardour of his attentions at a period when she must have been bowed to the earth with sorrow—a sorrow of which he was "necessarily ignorant"—and asking the privilege of occasionally visiting at her mother's house as a friend. Not to leave the matter solely to her unbiassed decision, the gallant colonel wrote also to Mrs. Beaufort, mentioning his letter to her daughter; and frankly saying to her that, notwithstanding the secret marriage of Edith, and birth of a child, now that her husband was dead, he was ready again to offer his hand. Instantly, the smouldering ambition of this proud woman was fanned into a blaze; and, once more, she resolved to compass, if possible, the long-desired marriage of her daughter. The acknowledgment of Edith's true relation—that of the widowed wife of an obscure, young adventurer—would, she had not doubted, at once settle all so far as D'Arcy was concerned; and this was why she strove so desperately to prevent its taking place. In consenting to publicity, she had abandoned her ambitious hopes. Now, they all started again into vigorous life. The hand of her daughter was yet deemed worthy of possession, even by Colonel D'Arcy; the marriage, so dear to her heart, might yet be accomplished; and she instantly resolved that its failure should not be in consequence of any want of effort on her part.

The two letters came by the same post. Edith had just finished reading hers, when Mrs. Beaufort, the ardour of whose reawakened purpose impelled to an immediate interview with her daughter, entered the room where she sat, with the flush of outraged womanhood yet warm upon her cheeks.

"Is your letter from Colonel D'Arcy?" inquired the mother, slightly hesitating, in the conscious conviction that the subject would be disagreeable.

"It is," was Edith's simple yet firm response.

"He knows of your marriage?"

"Yes."

"May I see your letter?"

Edith handed the letter to her mother, who, after reading it, said—

"What answer will you make?"

"None," was replied.

"None! That will be uncourteous."

"He is entitled to no courtesy from me," was the decisive answer, "and will get none."

"But, Edith"—Mrs. Beaufort's face was flushing, and her eyes beginning to glitter.

"Mother!"—Edith interrupted her—"what I have said to you, hitherto, about this man, was said from the heart; and I give it a repeated utterance, hardly repressing a cry of abhorrence. His very name is an offence; and his presence here, if you permit him to come, will be to me an outrage. I understand the hidden import of his glossing letter clearly; but he writes to me in vain. No—not even as a friend will I receive him. Mother!——"

A hurried step was heard this instant in the hall, and Edith, checking the utterance of what was on her tongue, started, with eager eyes and changing cheeks, to the floor. With hands raised and partly extended, and her gaze riveted on the entrance to the room, she stood, her ear bent to the sounding tread of a man's approaching feet. An instant more, and uttering wildly the cry—

"Henry! Oh, my husband! my husband!" she threw herself upon the breast of a tall, handsome, embrowned young man, who sprung forward to receive her, and catching her eagerly in his arms, covered her face with kisses.

"O Henry! am I dreaming?" sobbed the bewildered young creature, as, disengaging herself partly from his arms, she gazed into his face, pressing the hair back with both hands from his ample forehead.

"Not dreaming, Edith, dear," he answered. "The dream is past—this is the glad awakening."

"My husband! My dear, dear husband!" And, fondly, Edith laid her head upon his bosom. A moment only it rested there; then, starting up, she caught him by the arm, and, drawing him toward a door that opened into an adjoining room, said—

"Come."

He followed, as she led.

"Look!"

They had entered, and were beside a cradle in which their babe was sleeping.

"It is ours, Henry!—our sweet, precious one!—our darling Grace!" And lifting it tenderly, she laid it in his arms.

As if a blasting spectre had met her vision, Mrs. Beaufort fled to her chamber at the sight of Percival, and was now hidden from all eyes but those of her Maker. She had fully believed him dead, and had rejoiced in his death; his sudden appearance, therefore, was as of one risen from the dead. His coming, too, just as old schemes, so long cherished, were about being reconstructed, to scatter all her mad ambition to the wind, seemed so like Heaven's mockery, that, with a crushed, helpless feeling, she shrunk into herself, and bowed her spirit in the bitterness of forced submission.

Two hours afterward—Edith, who knew her too well to intrude during the time, had not even tapped at her chamber-door—she came forth, and received the nusband of her daughter with a degree of cordiality altogether unexpected.

"We believed you dead, Mr. Percival," said she. "Can you explain why we were deceived by false intelligence? Mr Maris wrote to us, first, that you were very ill, and soon after, that you had died of a malignant southern fever"

"I was ill, very ill, for a time," the young man answered, "but not of a malignant southern fever. The physician at the hospital to which I was sent to die, and where, in providence, I was permitted to recover, strongly suspected that I had been unfairly dealt by—some of my symptoms resembling in a marked degree the effects of poison."

"Poison!" Mrs. Beaufort looked startled as she gave almost involuntary utterance to the word.

"Yes; and I have now but little doubt that such was the case; for I learn, with no small surprise, that after my reported death, Colonel D'Arcy renewed his offers for the hand of Edith."

"Colonel D'Arcy! What of him? What had he to do with your sickness?" Mrs. Beaufort's countenance became suddenly clouded.

"I know not that he had any thing to do with it," replied Percival; "but this I know, he was a friend of Mr. Maris, and visited him on the night I was taken sick. They drank wine together, and both urged me with such gracious kindness to take a glass of sherry with them, that I could not refuse. Colonel D'Arcy touched his glass to mine, and said, in a singularly altered voice, so it struck me at the moment—

"'Your good health, Mr. Percival.'

"I did not like the man, for out of his eyes an evil spirit had ever looked at me. On this particular occasion, that spirit seemed to glare upon me with a kind of malignant triumph. Soon after drinking the wine, I felt an unusual heat in my stomach, which gradually pervaded my system. My head grew heavy and painful, and my body hot and sluggish. On complaining of indisposition, Mr. Maris advised me to go home, saying that a few hours' rest would restore me. But so far from that, I was in a raging fever all night, and early on the next morning, at his suggestion, as I afterward learned of Mr. Maris, I was sent to the hospital to die. An ordinary fever would have run to its crisis, terminating in favour of or against the patient, in a certain number of days; but the fever which had seized upon me was altogether different, and seemed as if it would never tire drinking at my vitals. When, at last, its fire abated, I was left so much exhausted, that small hope of recovery was felt by either physician or attendants. It was more than two months before strength sufficient to bear the weight of my body was gained. Then the life-current began to flow more freely; and a few weeks of rapid convalescence placed me so near to health, that I ventured to make this homeward journey. Soon after I was taken to the hospital, a man named Henry Percival died in one of the sick wards. Mr. Maris, I suppose, took it for granted that my death was the one reported, and immediately communicated the fact to you."

For a considerable time after the young man ceased speaking, Mrs. Beaufort sat with her eyes upon the floor, evidently in deep and troubled thought.

"There's a dark mystery here," she said, at length, speaking partly to herself. "Mr. Maris, then, is a particular friend of Colonel D'Arcy?" she added, raising her eyes.

"They appeared to be very intimate. I often saw them together."

"It's a strange story." She again seemed speaking to herself. "And I can't make it all out. Colonel D'Arcy?—Mr. Maris?—poison?"

As Percival looked at her fixedly, he saw a low shudder pass through her frame. A dark suspicion entered his mind on the instant, but he resolutely thrust it out; and, in doing so, he was but just to Mrs. Beaufort. If he had been dealt by foully, of which there was small reason to doubt, she was no party to the wicked deed.

A few days afterward, Colonel D'Arcy, following up his letters with a degree of confident assurance, made a visit to Clifton, in order to throw the weight of his personal influence in the scale, and thus secure a preponderance in his favour.

Mrs. Beaufort, now that all blinding antagonism toward Percival was laid aside, and closer contact gave her a better view of his character and a clearer appreciation of his worth, began to find herself drawn toward him with a power of attraction, at first resisted, but hourly gaining strength. His intelligence was of a different order from that by whose glitter she had been attracted through life. It was not the obtrusive intelligence which is assumed for effect—illustrating only the pride of its possessor— but had in it a soul of moral wisdom—a beautiful humanity, warm with a higher life. Often, as he talked, she listened with something akin to wonder; and, as her eyes rested upon his animated countenance, she saw in it a manly beauty, caught from the inspiring soul, that compelled a half-reluctant admiration. Not unfrequently, at these times, would the face of Colonel D'Arcy present itself before the eyes of her mind with singular vividness, yet ever marred by an expression, well remembered as peculiarly its own, but now, as seen in contrast with the fine countenance of Percival, *felt* to be cruel, selfish, and debasingly sensual. Almost with a shudder, at such times, would she close her bodily eyes, seeking to destroy the unpleasant vision. It was on an occasion like this that the servant announced Colonel D'Arcy.

"Impossible!" exclaimed Mrs. Beaufort, thrown entirely from her guard.

The name was repeated.

"Tell him that I will be down in a few minutes," she said, recovering herself.

For some moments the three looked at each other in doubt and irresolution. All of them knew well the object of his visit. Percival was the first to speak.

"Let us," said he, "go down together and receive him. He thinks I am dead, if he thinks of me at all. Should my suspicions be true, at sight of me he will be thrown from his guard and betray himself. Come! Let us go at once."

And he arose, moving on a pace or two in the direction of the door. Mrs. Beaufort and Edith followed, as if impelled by his will—the latter carrying Grace in her arms.

Side by side they entered the parlour where D'Arcy sat awaiting some member of the family.

"Colonel D'Arcy!"

Mrs. Beaufort inclined her body gracefully, and smiled upon her visitor with a bland smile. But he saw not the motion nor the smile, for his eyes were riveted instantly on the calm face of Percival, who, with his young wife shrinking to his side and holding her babe against her bosom, looked at him steadily and sternly. Only for a moment did he stand in the attitude of astonishment assumed as the unexpected apparition confronted him—then, with a look of dismay and an exclamation of terror, he swept past the little group and fled from the house.

"I did not err in my suspicions," said Percival, speaking with entire self-possession. "He is guilty of having sought my life. Dear Edith!" he added, as he drew an arm around her, and pressed his lips to her pure forehead—"how thankful am I for your dear sake that his wicked purpose failed."

"My children!"

The arms of Mrs. Beaufort were flung suddenly around them both.

"My children!"

Her voice choked, and what she would have said further,

remained unspoken.   Pride could not suffer her to betray the strong agitation she felt.

There were a few moments of silence.   Then she disengaged her arms, and turning from them, retired with slow and stately steps to her own apartments.

One scene more, briefly sketched, and the curtain must fall upon our characters.

A few months have glided pleasantly by.   The nearer view that Mrs. Beaufort now had of the son-in-law accepted with such an intense reluctance, enabled her to see the higher qualities of mind with which he was endowed ; as well as the sterling virtues already developed in one so young.   Her estates were large, and needed the intelligent care of a man who had some acquaintance with legal and landed affairs.   This knowledge, the education of Percival had in a measure supplied; and his calm judgment and integrity of purpose were a guarantee for the rest that Mrs. Beaufort was very ready to accept : and the result involved no measure of disappointment.

So well pleased was she with our friend the carpenter, that she soon made a contract with him to remain as overseer on her estate, at a liberal salary.

It was a warm afternoon near the close of the ensuing May, that Mrs. Percival stepped across the broad green lawn that sloped gently from her mother's fine old mansion, and took her way to the pleasant cottage-home of the carpenter and his family, that stood only at a short distance.   On entering, she found no one in the sitting-room; but, with the familiarity of a friend who knows the awaiting welcome at all times, she pushed open the door of the adjoining apartment, when a sight met her

eyes that made the blood leap warmer from her heart.
A week before, had been born in that chamber, another
babe; and it was to see the mother and inquire after her
wants, if any were unsupplied, that Mrs. Percival had
now come. She supposed that Harding was absent at
work; but this was not so. The fact was, scarcely an
hour passed during each day, since the little stranger
came, that he did not run in to look at its fair young
face, or take it in his great, strong arms, and bear it about
the room. He was sitting now near the bed, where lay
his happy wife, with her face turned toward him and the
babe; and he was holding the tender little one on his
arm, and gazing with a look that could not be mistaken
for love, down upon the sweet image of innocence.
Around were grouped the children, and little Lotty,
standing between her father's knees, was laying her white
finger softly on the baby's cheek, and talking to it
fondly.

As Mrs. Percival swung open the door, and at a glance
comprehended the scene, she said, with a pleasant familiarity that her previous intercourse with them warranted—

"Ah! nursing that baby again, Mr. Harding? Why,
one would think you'd never had a baby in your house
before!"

"We never knew the value of a baby," replied the
carpenter, "until yours came to us and won our hearts.
Ah! She was the Angel of our Household, and it was a
hard trial to see her go forth never to return again. But
God has given us another angel."

"And may she be dearer to you than the one you have
lost," said Mrs. Percival, as she reached over and took
the precious burden from the arms of Mr. Harding.
"Have you chosen a name for it yet?"

Mrs. Harding glanced toward her husband.

"It was chosen the hour of her birth," answered the carpenter.

"Is it Grace?"

Mrs. Percival smiled as she made the inquiry.

"No other name would express our love for her. Yes, it is Grace!"

"May she indeed prove, as I am sure she will, the Angel of your Household," said Mrs. Percival, with touching solemnity.

An audible "Amen" broke the stillness that followed; and, as we repeat the word, the curtain falls.

THE END.

THE

HOME MISSION.

By T. S. ARTHUR.

PREFACE.

IF it were possible to trace back to their begin-
nings, in each individual, those good or evil impulses
that have become ruling affections, in most cases
the origin would not be found until we had reached
the home of childhood. Here it is that impressions
are made, which become lasting as existence itself.
But the influence of home is not alone salutary or
baneful in early years. Wherever a home exists,
there will be found the nursery of all that is excellent in social or civil life, or of all that is deformed.
Every man and woman we meet in society, exhibit,
in unmistakable characters, the quality of their
homes. The wife, the husband, the children, the
guest, bear with them daily a portion of the spirit
pervading the little circle from which they have
come forth. If the sun shines there, a light will
be on their countenances; but shadows, if clouds
are in the sky of home. If there be disorder, defect of principle, discord among the members,
neglect of duty, and absence of kind offices, the
sphere of those who constitute that home can hardly

be salutary. They will add little to the common stock of good in the social life around them. We need not say how different will be the influence of those whose home-circle is pervaded by higher, purer, and truer principles.

A word to the wise is, we are told, sufficient. He, therefore, who speaks a true word in the ear of the wise, has planted a seed that will surely spring up and yield good fruit. May we hope that all into whose hands this little book is destined to come are wise, and that the few suggestive words spoken therein, as "hints to make home happy," will fall into good ground. If this be so, "The Home Mission" will not be fruitless. Though no annual reports of what it has accomplished are made, its silent and unobtrusive work, we trust, will be none the less effectual.

HOME MISSION.

A VISION OF CONSOLATION.

THE tempest of grief which, for a time, had raged so wildly in the heart of Mrs. Freeland, exhausted by its own violence, sobbed itself away, and the stricken mother passed into the land of dreams.

To the afflicted, sleep comes with a double blessing —rest is given to the wearied body and to the grieving spirit. Often, very often, the Angel of Consolation bends to the dreaming ear, and whispers words of hope and comfort that from no living lips had yet found utterance.

And it was so now with the sleeping mother. A few hours only had passed since she stood looking down, for the last time, on the fair face of her youngest born. Over his bright, blue eyes, into whose heavenly depths she had so loved to gaze, the pale lids had closed for ever. Still lingered around his lips the smile left there by the angels, as, with a kiss of love, they received his parting spirit. In the curling masses of his rich, golden hair, the shadows nestled away, as of old, while his tiny fingers held a few white blossoms, as with a living grasp. Was it death or sleep? So like a sleeping child the sweet boy lay, that it seemed every mo-

7

ment as if his lips would unclose, his eyes open to
the light, and his voice come to the listening ear
with its tones of music.

If to the mother had come this illusion, it remained
not long. Wild with grief, she turned away as the
sweet face she had so loved to gaze upon was hidden
from her straining eyes for ever.

Hidden from her eyes, did we say? Only hidden
from her natural eyes. Still he was before the eyes
of her spirit in all his living beauty. But, to her
natural affections, he was lost—even as he had faded
from before her natural eyes; and, in the agony of
bereavement, it seemed that her heart would break.
Back to her darkened chamber she went. Her
nearest and dearest friends gathered around, seeking
lovingly to sustain her in her great affliction; but
she refused to be comforted.

At length, as at first said, the tempest of grief,
which, for a time, raged so violently in the heart of
Mrs. Freeland, sobbed itself away, and the stricken
mother passed into the land of dreams.

For the most part, dreams are fantastic. Yet
they are not always so. In states of deep sorrow or
strong trial, when the heart turns from the natural
world, hopeless of aid or consolation, truth often
comes in dreams and similitudes.

The mother found herself in the company of two
beautiful maidens, in the very flower of youth; and
as she gazed earnestly into their faces, which seemed
transparent from an inward celestial light, she saw
expectation therein—loving expectation. They
stood beneath the eastern portico of a pleasant
dwelling, around which stately trees—the branches

vocal with the song of feathered minstrels—lifted their green tops far up into the crystal air. Flowers of a thousand hues and sweet odours were woven into forms and figures of exquisite beauty upon the carpet of living green spread over the teeming earth, while groups of little children sported one with another, and mingled their happy voices with the melody of birds.

Yet, amid all this external joy and beauty, the hand of grief still lay upon the mother's heart; and when she looked upon the sportive infants around her, she sighed for her own babe. Even as she sighed, one of the maidens turned to her and said, while her whole countenance was lit up with a glow of delight—

"It has come. A new babe is born unto heaven."

And, as she spoke, she gathered her arms quickly to her bosom, and the wondering mother saw lying thereon her own child. The other maiden was already bending over the infant—already had she greeted its coming with a kiss of love. Quickly both retired within the dwelling, and the bereaved mother went with them, eager to receive the babe she had lost.

"Oh, my child! my child!" she said. "Give me my child."

And ere the words had died upon her lips, the maiden who had received the babe gave it into her arms, when she clasped it with a wild delight, and rained tears of gladness upon its face.

For a time, the two maidens looked upon the mother in silence, and in their bright countenances love and pity were blended. At length, one of them said to her, (and she smiled sweetly, and spoke with an exquisite, penetrating tenderness,)—

"Your heart is full of love for your babe?"

"He is dearer to me than life—dearer than a thousand lives," replied the mother quickly, drawing the babe closer to her bosom.

"Love seeks to bless the object of its regard."

There was a meaning in the words and tone of the maiden, as she said this, that caused the mother to look into her face earnestly.

"This is not the land of sickness, of sorrow, of death," resumed the maiden, "but the land of eternal life and blessedness. Into this land your babe has been born. You are here only as a visitant, and must soon return to bear a few more trials and pains, a few more conflicts with evil; but the end is your preparation for these heavenly regions."

A shadow fell instantly upon the mother's heart. Tears rushed to her eyes, and she drew her arms more tightly about her babe.

"Shall we keep this babe in our heavenly home, or will you bear it with you back to the dark, cold, sad regions of mortality?"

"Do not take from me my more than life!" sobbed the mother wildly. "Oh! I cannot give you my child;" and more eagerly she hugged it to her breast.

For a time there was silence. Then one of the maidens laid gently her hand upon the mother, and she lifted her bowed head.

"Come," said the maiden.

The mother arose, and the two walked into the open air, and passing through the group of children sporting on the lawn and in the gardens, went for what seemed the space of a mile, until they came to a forest, into the depths of which they penetrated; and, for a time, the farther they went the darker and more gloomy it became, until scarcely a ray of light from the arching sky came down through the dense and tangled foliage. At last they were beyond the forest.

"Look," said the companion.

The mother lifted her eyes—the babe had strangely passed from her arms. A dwelling, familiar in aspect, stood near, and through an open window she saw a sick child lying upon a bed, and knew it as her own. Its little face was distorted by pain and flushed with fever; and as it tossed restlessly to and fro, its moans filled her ears. She stretched forth her hands, yearning to give some relief; even as she did so, the scene faded from her view, and next she saw an older child, bearing still the linaments of her own. There was the same broad, white forehead and clustering curls; the same large, bright eyes and full, ruddy lips; but, alas! not the soft vail of innocence which had given the features of the babe such a heavenly charm. The fine brow was contracted with passion; the eyes flashed with an evil light; and the lips were tightly drawn, and with something of defiance, against the teeth. The boy was resisting, with a stern determination, the will of the parents—was setting at naught those early salutary restraints which are the safeguard of youth.

"Oh! my unhappy boy!" cried the mother.

The scene changed as she spoke. The boy, now

grown up to manhood, once more stood before her. Alas! how had the light of innocence faded from his countenance, giving place to a shadow of evil, the very darkness of which caused a cold shudder to pass through the mother's frame.

"Look again," said the maiden, as this scene was fading.

But the mother hid her face in her hands, and turned weeping away.

"Look again." And this time there was something so heart-cheering in the maiden's voice, that the mother lifted her tearful eyes. She was back again in the beautiful place from which she had gone forth a little while before, and her babe, beautiful as innocence itself, lay sweetly sleeping in the arms of the lovely maiden who had received it on its first entrance into heaven. With a heart full of joy, the mother now bent over the slumbering babe, kissing it again and again.

"Grieving mother," said the angel-maiden, in tones of flute-like softness, "God saw that it would not be good for your child to remain on earth, and he therefore removed it to this celestial region, where no evil can ever penetrate. To me, as an angel-mother, it has been given; and I will love it and care for it with a love as pure and tender as the love that yearns in your bosom. As its infantile mind opens, I will pour in heavenly instruction, that it may grow in wisdom and become an angel. Will you not let me have it freely?"

"But why may I not remain here and be its heavenly mother? Oh! I will love and care for it

witn a tenderness and devotion equal to, if not exceeding yours."

Even while the mother spoke there was a change.
She saw before her other objects of affection. There
was her husband, sitting in deep dejection, sorrowing
for the loss of one who was dear as his own life;
while three children, the sight of whom stirred her
maternal heart to its profoundest depths, lay sleeping in each other's arms, the undried tears yet
glistening on their lashes.

The wife and mother stretched forth her hands
toward these beloved ones, eager to be with them
again and turn their grief into gladness. But, in a
moment, there passed another change. The pleasant
home in which her children had been sheltered for
years, no longer held them; the fold had been
broken up and the tender lambs scattered. One of
these little ones the mother saw, sitting apart from
a group of sportive children, weeping over some task
work. The bloom on her cheek had faded—its
roundness was gone—the light of her beautiful eyes
was quenched in tears. And, as she looked, a woman came to the child and spoke to her harshly.
She was about springing forward, when another
scene was presented. Her first-born, a noble-spirited
boy, to whose future she had ever looked with pride
and pleasure, stood before her. Alas! how changed.
Every thing about him showed the want of a mother's
care and considerate affection; and from his dear,
young face had already vanished the look of joyous
innocence she had so loved to contemplate.

Again the mother was in the presence of the
angel-maiden, to whose loving arms a good God had

confided the babe, which, in his wisdom, he had removed from the earth. And the angel-maiden, as she looked first at the babe in her arms and then at the mother, smiled sweetly and said—

"He is safe here; will you not let him remain?"

And, with a gushing heart, the mother answered, "Not for worlds would I take him with me into the outer life of nature. Oh, no! He is safe—let him remain."

"And you will return to those who still need your love and care?"

"Yes, yes," said the mother, earnestly. "Let me go to them again. Let me be their angel on earth."

And she bent hastily to the heaven-born babe, kissing it with tearful fondness.

There came now another change. The mother was back again in her chamber of sorrow; and undried tears were yet upon her cheeks. But she was comforted and reconciled to the great affliction which had been sent for good from heaven.

Those who saw Mrs. Freeland in the first wild grief that followed the loss of her babe, wondered at her serene composure when she came again among them. And they wondered long, for she spoke not of this Vision of Consolation. It was too sacred a thing to be revealed, to any save the companion of her life.

THE STEP-MOTHER

THERE are few positions in social life of greater trial and responsibility than that of a step-mother; and it too rarely happens that the woman who assumes this position, is fitted for the right discharge of its duties. In far too many cases, the widower is accepted as a husband because he has a home, or a position to offer, while the children are considered as a drawback in the bargain. But it sometimes happens, that a true woman, from genuine affection, unites herself with a widower, and does it with a loving regard for his children, and with the purpose in her mind of being to them, as far as in her power lies, a wise and tender mother.

Such a woman was Agnes Green. She was in her thirty-second year when Mr. Edward Arnold, a widower with four children, asked her to become his wife. At twenty-two, Agnes had loved as only a true woman can love. But the object of that love proved himself unworthy, and she turned away from him. None knew how deep the heart-trial through which she passed—none knew how intensely she suffered. In part, her pale face and sobered brow witnessed, but only in part; for many said she was cold, and some even used the word heartless, when they spoke of her. From early womanhood a beautiful ideal of manly excellence had filled her mind; and with this ideal she had invested one who proved false to the high character. At once the green things of her heart withered, and for a long time its surface was a barren waste. But the woman was yet strong in her. She must love something. So she came forth from her heart-seclusion, and let her affections, like a refreshing and invigorating stream, flow along many channels. She was the faithful friend, the comforter in affliction, the wise counsellor. More than once had she been approached with offers of marriage, by men who saw the excellence of her character, and felt that upon any dwelling, in which she was the presiding spirit, would rest a blessing. But none of them were able to give to the even pulses of her heart a quicker motion.

At last she met Mr. Arnold. More than three years had passed since the mother of his children was removed by death, and, since that time, he had sought, with all a father's tenderness and devotion, to fill her place to them. How imperfectly, none knew so well as himself. As time went on, the want of a true woman's affectionate care for his children was more and more felt. All were girls except the youngest, their ages ranging from twelve downward, and this made their mother's loss so much the more a calamity. Moreover, his feeling of loneliness and want of companionship, so keenly felt in the beginning, instead of diminishing, increased.

Such was his state of mind when he met Agnes Green. The attraction was mutual, though, at first, no thought of marriage came into the mind of either. A second meeting stirred the placid waters in the bosom of Agnes Green. Conscious of this, and fearful lest the emotion she strove to repress might become apparent to other eyes, she assumed a certain reserve, not seen in the beginning, which only betrayed her secret, and at once interested Mr. Arnold, who now commenced a close observation of her character. With every new aspect in which this was presented, he saw something that awakened admiration; something that drew his spirit nearer to her as one congenial. And not the less close was her observation.

When, at length, Mr. Arnold solicited the hand of Agnes Green, she was ready to respond. Not, however, in a selfish and self-seeking spirit; not in the narrow hope of obtaining some great good for herself, was her response made, but in full view of her woman's power to bless, and with an earnest, holy purpose in her heart, to make her presence in his household indeed a blessing.

"I must know your children better than I know them now, and they must know me better than they do, before I take the place you wish me to assume," was her reply to Mr. Arnold, when he spoke of an early marriage.

And so means were taken to bring her in frequent contact with the children. The first time she met them intimately, was at the house of a friend. Mary, the oldest girl, she found passionate and self-willed; Florence, the second, good-natured, but careless and slovenly; while Margaret, the third, was in ill health, and exceedingly peevish. The little brother, Willy, was a beautiful, affectionate child, but in consequence of injudicious management, very

2*

badly spoiled. Take them altogether, they presented rather an unpromising aspect; and it is no
wonder that Agnes Green had many misgivings at
heart, when the new relation contemplated, and its
trials and responsibilities, were pictured to her
mind.

The earnestly-asked question by Mr. Arnold, after
this first interview,—"What do you think of my
children?"—was not an easy one to answer. A
selfish, unscrupulous woman, who looked to the connection as something to be particularly desired on
her own account, and who cared little about duties
and responsibilities, might have replied, "Oh, they
are lovely children!" or, "I am delighted with
them!" Not so Agnes Green. She did not reply
immediately, but mused for some moments, considerably embarrassed, and in doubt what to say.
Mr. Arnold was gazing intently in her face.

"They do not seem to have made a favourable
impression," said he, speaking with some disappointment in his tone and manner.

A feeble flush was visible in the face of Agnes
Green, and also a slight quiver of the lips as she
answered:

"There is too much at stake, as well in your case
as my own, to warrant even a shadow of concealment. You ask what I think of your children, and
you expect me to answer truly?"

"I do," was the almost solemnly-spoken reply.

"My first hurried, yet tolerably close, observation, has shown me, in each, a groundwork of natural
good."

"As their father," replied Mr. Arnold, in some

earnestness of manner, "I know there is good in them,—much good. But they have needed a mother's care."

"When you have said that, how much has been expressed! If the garden is not cultivated, and every weed carefully removed, how quickly is it overrun with things noxious, and how feeble becomes the growth of all things good and beautiful! It is just so with the mind. Neglect it, and bad habits and evil propensities will assuredly be quickened into being, and attain vigorous life."

"My children are not perfect, I know, but—"

Mr. Arnold seemed slightly hurt. Agnes Green interrupted him, by saying, in a mild voice, as she laid her hand gently upon his arm:

"Do not give my words a meaning beyond what they are designed to convey. If I assume the place of a mother to your children, I take upon myself all the responsibilities that the word 'mother' involves. Is not this so?"

"Thus I understand it.'

"My duty will be, not only to train these children for a happy and useful life here, but for a happy and useful life hereafter."

"It will."

"It is no light thing, Mr. Arnold, to assume the place of a mother to children who, for three years, have not known a mother's affectionate care. I confess that my heart shrinks from the responsibility, and I ask myself over and over again, 'Have I the requisite wisdom, patience, and self-denial?'"

"I believe you have," said Mr. Arnold, who was beginning to see more deeply into the heart of

Agnes. "And now," he added, "tell me what you think of my children."

"Mary has a quick temper, and is rather self-willed, if my observation is correct, but she has a warm heart. Florence is thoughtless, and untidy in her person, but possesses a happy temper. Poor Maggy's ill health has, very naturally, soured her disposition. Ah, what can you expect of a suffering child, who has no mother? Your little Willy is a lovely boy, somewhat spoiled—who can wonder at this?—but possessing just the qualities to win for him kindness from every one."

"I am sure you will love him," said Mr. Arnold, warmly.

"I have no doubt on that subject," replied Agnes Green. "And now," she added, "after what I have said, after showing you that I am quick to see faults, once more give this matter earnest consideration. If I become your wife, and take the place of a mother to these children, I shall, at once,—wisely and lovingly, I trust,—begin the work of removing from their minds every noxious weed that neglect may have suffered to grow there. The task will be no light one, and, in the beginning, there may be rebellion against my authority. To be harsh or hard is not in my nature. But a sense of duty will make me firm. Once more, I say, give this matter serious consideration. It is not yet too late to pause."

Mr. Arnold bent his head in deep reflection. For many minutes he sat in silent self-communion, and sat thus so long, that the heart of Agnes Green began to beat with a restricted motion, as if there was a heavy pressure on her bosom. At last Mr. Arnold looked up, his eyes suddenly brightening, and his face flushing with animation. Grasping her hands with both of his, he said:

"I have reflected, Agnes, and I do not hesitate. Yes, I will trust these dear ones to your loving guardianship. I will place in your hands their present and eternal welfare, confident that you will be to them a true mother."

And she was. As often as it could be done before the time appointed for the marriage, she was brought in contact with the children. Almost from the beginning, she was sorry to find in Mary, the oldest child, a reserve of manner, and an evident dislike toward her, which she in vain sought to overcome. The groundwork of this she did not know. It had its origin in a remark made by the housekeeper, who, having learned from some gossipping relative of Mr. Arnold that a new wife was soon to be brought home, and, also, who this new wife was to be, made an imprudent allusion to the fact, in a moment of forgetfulness.

"Your new mother will soon put you straight, my little lady," said she, one day, to Mary, who had tried her beyond all patience.

"My new mother! Who's she, pray?" was sharply demanded.

"Miss Green," replied the unreflecting housekeeper. "Your father's going to bring her home one of these days, and make her your mother, and she'll put you all right—she'll take down your fine airs, my lady!"

"Will she?" And Mary, compressing her lips

tightly, and drawing up her slender form to its full height, looked the image of defiance.

From that moment a strong dislike toward Miss Green ruled in the mind of Mary; and she resolved, should the housekeeper's assertion prove true, not only to set the new authority at defiance, but to inspire, if possible, the other children with her own feelings.

The marriage was celebrated at the house of Mr. Arnold, in the presence of his own family and a few particular friends, Agnes arriving at the hour appointed.

After the ceremony, the children were brought forward, and presented to their new mother. The youngest, as if strongly drawn by invisible chords of affection, sprung into her lap, and clasped his little arms lovingly about her neck. He seemed very happy. The others were cold and distant, while Mary fixed her eyes upon the wife of her father, with a look so full of dislike and rebellion, that no one present was in any doubt as to how she regarded the new order of things.

Mr. Arnold was a good deal fretted by this unexpected conduct on the part of Mary; and, forgetful of the occasion and its claims, spoke to her with some sternness. He was recalled to self-possession by the smile of his wife, and her gently-uttered remark, that reached only his own ear:

"Don't seem to notice it. Let it be my task to overcome prejudices."

During the evening Mary did not soften in the least toward her step-mother. On the next morning, when all met, for the first time, at the breakfast table, the children gazed askance at the calm, dignified woman who presided at the table, and seemed ill at ease. On Mary's lip, and in her eye, was an expression so like contempt, that it was with diffi culty her father could refrain from ordering her to her own room.

The meal passed in some embarrassment. At its conclusion, Mr. Arnold went into the parlour, and his wife, entering at once upon her duties, accompanied the children to the nursery, to see for herself that the two oldest were properly dressed for school. Mary, who had preceded the rest, was already in contention with the housekeeper. Just as Mrs. Arnold—so we must now call her—entered the room, Mary exclaimed, sharply:

"I don't care what you say, I'm going to wear this bonnet!"

"What's the trouble?" inquired Mrs. Arnold, calmly.

"Why, you see, ma'am," replied the housekeeper, "Mary is bent on wearing her new, pink bonnet to school, and I tell her she mustn't do it. Her old one is good enough."

"Let me see the old one," said Mrs. Arnold. She spoke in a very pleasant tone of voice.

A neat, straw bonnet, with plain, unsoiled trimming, was brought forth by the housekeeper, who remarked:

"It's good enough to wear Sundays, for that matter."

"I don't care if it is, I'm not going to wear it today. So don't bother yourself any more about it."

"Oh, yes, Mary, you will," said Mrs. Arnold, very indly, yet firmly.

"No, I won't!" was the quick, resolute answer. And she gazed, unflinchingly, into the face of her step-mother.

"I'll call your father, my young lady! This is beyond all endurance!" said the housekeeper, starting for the door.

"Hannah!" The mild, even voice of Mrs. Arnold checked the excited housekeeper. "Don't speak of it to her father,—I'm sure she doesn't mean what she says. She'll think better of it in a moment."

Mary was hardly prepared for this. Even while she stood with unchanged exterior, she felt grateful to her step-mother for intercepting the complaint about to be made to her father. She expected some remark or remonstrance from Mrs. Arnold. But in this she was mistaken. The latter, as if nothing unpleasant had occurred, turned to Florence, and after a light examination of her dress, said to the housekeeper:

"This collar is too much soiled; won't you bring me another?"

"Oh, it's clean enough," replied Florence, knitting her brows, and affecting impatience. But, even as she spoke, the quick, yet gentle hands of her stepmother had removed the collar from her neck.

"Do you think it clean enough now?" said she, as she placed the soiled collar beside a fresh one, which the housekeeper had brought.

"It *is* rather dirty," replied Florence, smiling.

And now Mrs. Arnold examined other articles of her dress, and had them changed, re-arranged her hair, and saw that her teeth were properly brushed. While this was progressing, Mary stood a little apart, a close observer of all that passed. One thing she did not fail to remark, and that was the gentle firmness of her step-mother, which was in strong contrast with the usual scolding, jerking, and impatience of the housekeeper, as manifested on these occasions.

By the time Florence was ready for school, Mary's state of mind had undergone considerable change, and she half regretted the exhibition of ill temper and insulting disobedience she had shown. Yet was she in no way prepared to yield. To her surprise, after Florence was all ready, her step-mother turned to her and said, in a mild, cheerful voice, as if nothing unpleasant had occurred,

"Have you a particular reason for wishing to wear your new bonnet, this morning, Mary?"

"Yes, ma'am, I have." The voice of Mary was changed considerably, and her eyes fell beneath the mild, but penetrating, gaze of her step-mother.

"May I ask you the reason?"

There was a pause of some moments; then Mary replied:

"I promised one of the girls that I'd wear it. She asked me to. She wanted to see it."

"Did you tell Hannah this?"

"No, ma'am. It wouldn't have been any use. She never hears to reason."

"But you'll find me very different, Mary," said Mrs. Arnold, tenderly. "I shall ever be ready to hear reason."

All this was so far from what Mary had anticipated, that her mind was half bewildered. Her step-mother's clear sight penetrated to her very thoughts.

3

Taking her hand, she drew her gently to her side. An arm was then placed lovingly around her.

"My dear child,"—it would have been a hard heart, indeed, that could have resisted the influence of that voice,—"let us understand each other in the beginning. You seem to look upon me as an enemy, and yet I wish to be the very best friend you have in the world. I have come here, not as an exacting and overbearing tyrant, but to seek your good and promote your happiness in every possible way. I will love you; and may I not expect love in return? Surely you will not withhold that."

As Mrs. Arnold spoke thus, she felt a slight quiver in the hand she had taken in her own. She continued:

"I cannot hope to fill the place of your dear mother, now in heaven. Yet even as she loved you, would I love you, my child." The voice of Mrs. Arnold had become unsteady, through excess of feeling. "As she bore with your faults, I will bear with them; as she rejoiced over every good affection born in your heart, so will I rejoice."

Outraged by the conduct of Mary, the housekeeper had gone to Mr. Arnold, whom she found in the parlour, and repeated to him, with a colouring of her own, the insolent language his child had used. The father hurried up stairs in a state of angry excitement. No little surprised was he, on entering the nursery, to see Mary sobbing on the breast of her step-mother, whose gentle hands were softly pressed upon the child's temples, and whose low, soothing voice was speaking to her words of comfort for the present, and cheerful hope for the future.

Unobserved by either, Mr. Arnold stood for a moment, and then softly retired, with a gush of thankfulness in his heart, that he had found for his children so true and good a mother.

With Mary there was no more trouble. From that hour, she came wholly under the influence of her step-mother, learning day by day, as she knew her better, to love her with a more confiding tenderness. Wonderful was the change produced on the children of Mr. Arnold, in a single year. They had, indeed, found a mother.

It is painful to think how different would have been the result, had the step-mother not been a true woman. Wise and good she was in her sphere loving and unselfish; and the fruit of her hand was sweet to the taste, and beautiful to look upon.

How few are like her! How few who assume the position of step-mother,—a position requiring patience, long-suffering, and unflinching self-denial,—are fitted for the duties they so lightly take upon themselves! Is it any wonder their own lives are made, at times, miserable, or that they mar, by passion or exacting tyranny, the fair face of humanity, in the children committed to their care? Such lose their reward.

POWER OF KINDNESS.

"Tom! Here!" said a father to his boy, speaking in tones of authority.

The lad was at play. He looked toward his father, but did not leave his companions.

"Do you hear me, sir?" spoke the father, more sternly than at first.

With an unhappy face and reluctant step, the boy left his play and approached his parent.

"Why do you creep along at a snail's pace?" said the latter, angrily. "Come quickly, I want you. When I speak, I look to be obeyed instantly. Here, take this note to Mr. Smith, and see that you don't go to sleep by the way. Now run as fast as you can go."

The boy took the note. There was a cloud upon his brow. He moved away, but at a slow pace.

"You, Tom! Is that doing as I ordered? Is that going quickly?" called the father, when he saw the boy creeping away. "If you are not back in half an hour, I will punish you."

But the words had but little effect. The boy's feelings were hurt by the unkindness of the parent. He experienced a sense of injustice; a consciousness that wrong had been done him. By nature he was

28

like his father, proud and stubborn; and these qualities of his mind were aroused, and he indulged in them, fearless of consequences.

"I never saw such a boy," said the father, speaking to a friend who had observed the occurrence. "My words scarcely make an impression on him."

"Kind words often prove most powerful," said the friend. The father looked surprised.

"Kind words," continued the friend, "are like the gentle rain and the refreshing dews; but harsh words bend and break like the angry tempest. The first develop and strengthen good affections, while the others sweep over the heart in devastation, and mar and deform all they touch. Try him with kind words; they will prove a hundred fold more powerful."

The latter seemed hurt by the reproof; but it left him thoughtful. An hour passed away ere his boy returned. At times during his absence he was angry at the delay, and meditated the infliction of punishment. But the words of remonstrance were in his ears, and he resolved to obey them. At last the lad came slowly in with a cloudy countenance, and reported the result of his errand. Having stayed far beyond his time, he looked for punishment, and was prepared to receive it with an angry defiance. To his surprise, after delivering the message he had brought, his father, instead of angry reproof and punishment, said kindly, "Very well, my son; you can go out to play again."

The boy went out, but was not happy. He had disobeyed and disobliged his father, and the thought of this troubled him. Harsh words had not clouded

his mind nor aroused a spirit of reckless anger. Instead of joining his companions, he went and sat
down by himself, grieving over his act of disobedience.
As he thus sat, he heard his name called. He listened.

"Thomas, my son," said his father, kindly. The
boy sprang to his feet, and was almost instantly beside his parent.

"Did you call, father?"

"I did, my son. Will you take this package to
Mr. Long for me?"

There was no hesitation in the boy's manner. He
looked pleased at the thought of doing his father a
service, and reached out his hand for the package.
On receiving it, he bounded away with a light step.

"There is a power in kindness," said the father,
as he sat musing, after the lad's departure. And
even while he sat musing over the incident, the boy
came back with a cheerful, happy face, and said—

"Can I do any thing else for you, father?"

Yes, there is the power of kindness. The tempest
of passion can only subdue, constrain, and break;
but in love and gentleness there is the power of the
summer rain, the dew, and the sunshine.

BEAR AND FORBEAR.

"Don't talk to me in such a serious strain, Aunt Hannah. One would really think, from what you say, that James and I would quarrel before we were married a month."

"Not so soon as that, Maggy dear. Heaven grant that it may not come so soon as that! But, depend upon it, child, if you do not make 'bear and forbear' your motto, many months will not have passed, after your wedding-day, without the occurrence of some serious misunderstanding between you and your husband."

"If anybody else were to say that to me, Aunt Hannah, I would be very angry."

"For, which you would be a very foolish girl. But it is generally the way that good advice is taken, it being an article of which none think they stand in need."

"But what in the world can there be for James and I to have differences about? I am sure that I love him most truly; and I am sure he loves me as fondly as I love him. In mutual love there can be no strife—no emulation, except in the performance of good offices. Indeed, aunt, I think you are far too serious."

"Over the bright sky bending above you. my dear niece, I would not, for the world, bring a cloud

31

even as light as the filmy, almost viewless gossa-
mer.　But I know that clouds must hide its clear,
calm,. passionless blue, either earlier or later in life.
And what I say now, is with the hope of giving you
the prescience required to avoid some of the storms
that may threaten to break upon your head."

"Neither cloud nor storm will ever come from
that quarter of the sky from which you seem to
apprehend danger."

"Not if both you and James learn to bear and
forbear in your conduct toward each other."

"We cannot act otherwise."

"Then there will be no danger."·

Margaret Percival expressed herself sincerely.
She could not believe that there was the slightest
danger of a misunderstanding ever occurring between her and James Canning. to whom she was
shortly to be married.　The well-meant warning of
her aunt, who had seen and felt more in life than
she yet had, went therefore for nothing.

A month elapsed, and the young and lovely
Maggy pledged her faith at the altar.　As the bride
of Canning, she felt that she was the happiest creature in the world.　Before her was a path winding
amid green and flowery places, and lingering by
the side of still waters; while a sunny sky bent
over all.

James Canning was a young lawyer of some
talent, and the possessor of a good income inde-
pendent of his profession.　Like others, he had his
excellencies and his defects of character.　Naturally, he was of a proud, impatient spirit, and, from a
child, had been restless under dictation.　As an

offset to this, he was a man of strict integrity, generous in his feelings, and possessed of a warm heart.
Aunt Hannah had known him since he was a boy,
and understood his character thoroughly; and it
was this knowledge that caused her to feel some
concern for the future happiness of her niece, as
well as to speak to her timely words of caution.
But these words were not understood.

"We've not quarrelled yet, Aunt Hannah, for all
your fears," said the young wife, three or four
months after her marriage.

"For which I am truly thankful," replied Aunt
Hannah. "Still, I would say now, as I did before,
'Bear and forbear.'"

"That is, I must BEAR every thing and FORBEAR
in every thing. I hardly think that just, aunt. I
should say that James ought to do a little of this as
well as me."

"Yes, it is his duty as well as yours. But you
should not think of his duty to you, Maggy, only of
your duty to him. That is the most dangerous error
into which you can fall, and one that will be almost
certain to produce unhappiness."

"Would you have a wife never think of herself?"

"The less she thinks of herself, perhaps, the better; for the more she thinks of herself, the more
she will love herself. But the more she thinks of
her husband, the more she will love him and seek to
make him happy. The natural result of this will
be, that her husband will feel the warmth and perceive the unselfishness of her love; this will cause
him to lean toward her with still greater tenderness,

and prompt him to yield to her what otherwise he might have claimed for himself."

"Then it is the wife who must act the generous, self-sacrificing part?"

"If I could speak as freely to James as I can speak to you, Maggy, I should not fail to point out his duty of bearing and forbearing, as plainly as I point out yours. All should be mutual, of course. But this can never be, if one waits for the other. If you see your duty, it is for you to do it, even if he should fail in his part.

"I don't know about that, aunt. I think, as you said just now, that all this is mutual."

"I am sorry you cannot or will not understand me, Maggy," replied Aunt Hannah.

"I am sorry too, aunt; but I certainly do not. However, don't, pray, give yourself any serious concern about James and me. I assure you that we are getting along exceedingly well; and why this should not continue is more than I can make out."

"Well, dear, I trust that it may. There is no good reason why it should not. You both have virtues enough to counterbalance all defects of character."

On the evening of that very day, as the young couple sat at the tea-table, James Canning said, as his wife felt, rather unkindly, at the same time that there was a slight contraction of his brow—

"You seem to be very much afraid of your sugar, Maggy. I never get a cup of tea or coffee sweet enough for my taste."

"You must have a sweet palate. I am sure it is like syrup, for I put in several large lumps of sugar," replied Margaret, speaking in a slightly offended tone.

"Taste it, will you?" said Canning, pushing his cup across the table with an impatient air.

Margaret sipped a little from the spoon, and then, with an expression of disgust in her face, said—

"Pah! I'd as lief drink so much molasses. But here's the sugar bowl. Sweeten it to your taste."

Canning helped himself to more sugar. As he did so his wife noticed that his hand slightly trembled, and also that his brow was drawn down, and his lips more arched than usual.

"It's a little matter to get angry about," she thought to herself. "Things are coming to a pretty pass, if I'm not to be allowed to speak."

The meal was finished in silence. Margaret felt in no humour to break the oppressive reserve, although she would have been glad, indeed, to have heard a pleasant word from the lips of her husband. As for Canning, he permitted himself to brood over the words and manner of his wife, until he became exceedingly fretted. They were so unkind and so uncalled for. The evening passed unsocially. But morning found them both in a better state of mind. Sleep has a wonderful power in restoring to the mind its lost balance, and in calming down our blinding passions. During the day, our thoughts and feelings, according with our natural state, are more or less marked by the disturbances that selfish purposes ever bring; but in sleep, while the mind rests and our governing ends lie dormant, we come into purer spiritual associations, and the soul, as well as the body, receives a healthier tone.

The morning, therefore, found Canning and his wife in better states of mind. They were as kind and as affectionate as usual in their words and conduct, although, when they sat down to the breakfast table, they each experienced a slight feeling of coldness on being reminded, too sensibly, of the unpleasant occurrence of the previous evening. Margaret thought she would be sure to please her husband in his coffee, and therefore put into his cup an extra quantity of sugar, making it so very sweet that he could with difficulty swallow it. But a too vivid recollection of what had taken place on the night before, caused him to be silent about it. The second cup was still sweeter. Canning managed to sip about one-third of this, but his stomach refused to take any more. Noticing that her husband's coffee, an article of which he was very fond, stood, nearly cup-full, beside his plate, after he had finished his breakfast, Margaret said—

"Didn't your coffee suit you?"

"It was very good; only a little too sweet."

"Then why didn't you say so?" she returned, in a tone that showed her to be hurt at this reaction upon what she had said on the previous evening. "Give me your cup, and let me pour you out some more."

"No, I thank you, Margaret, I don't care about any more."

"Yes, you do. Come, give me your cup. I shall be hurt if you don't. I'm sure there is no necessity for drinking the coffee, if not to your taste. I don't know what's come over you, James."

"And I'm sure I don't know what's come over

you," Canning thought, but did not say. He handed up his cup, as his wife desired. After filling it with coffee, she handed it back; and then reached him the sugar and cream.

"Sweeten it to your own taste," she said, a little fretfully; "I'm sure I tried to make it right."

Canning did as he was desired, and then drank the coffee, but it was with the utmost difficulty that he could do so.

This was the first little cloud that darkened the sky of their wedded life; and it did not fairly pass away for nearly a week. Nor then did the days seem as bright as before. The cause was slight—very slight—but how small a thing will sometimes make the heart unhappy. How trifling are the occurrences upon which we often lay, as upon a foundation, a superstructure of misery! Had the earnestly urged precept of Aunt Hannah been regarded, —had the lesson—"Bear and Forbear," been well learned and understood by Margaret, this cloud had never dimmed the sun of their early love. A pleasant word, in answer to her husband's momentary impatience, would have made him sensible that he had not spoken with propriety, and caused him to be more careful in future. As it was, both were more circumspect, but it was from pride instead of love, —and more to protect self than from a tender regard for each other.

Only a month or two passed before there was another slight collision. It made them both more unhappy than they were before. But the breach was quickly healed. Still scars remained, and there were times when the blood flowed into these cicatrices so feverishly as to cause pain. Alas! wounds of the spirit do not close any more perfectly than do wounds of the body—the scars remain forever.

And thus the weeks and months went by. Neither of the married partners had learned the true secret of happiness in their holy relation,—neither of them felt the absolute necessity of bearing and forbearing. Little inequalities of character, instead of being smoothed off by gentle contact, were suffered to strike against each other, and produce, sometimes, deep and painful wounds—healing, too often, imperfectly; and too often remaining as festering sores.

And yet Canning and his wife loved each other tenderly, and felt, most of their time, that they were very happy. There were little things in each that each wished the other would correct, but neither felt the necessity of self-correction.

The birth of a child drew them together at a time when there was some danger of a serious rupture. Dear little Lilian, or "Lilly," as she was called, was a chord of love to bind them in a closer union.

"I love you more than ever, Maggy," Canning could not help saying to his wife, as he kissed first her lips and then the soft cheek of his child, a month after the babe was born.

"And I am sure I love you better than I did, if that were possible," returned Margaret, looking into her husband's face with a glance of deep affection.

As the babe grew older the parent's love for it continued to increase, and, with this increase, their happiness. The chord which had several times

jarred harshly between them, slept in profound
peace.

But, after this sweet calm, the surface of their
feelings became again ruffled. One little incongru-
ity of character after another showed itself in both,
and there was no genuine spirit of forbearance in
either of them to meet and neutralize any sudden
effervescence of the mind. Lilly was not a year old,
before they had a serious misunderstanding that made
them both unhappy for weeks. It had its origin in
a mere trifle, as such things usually have. They
had been taking tea and spending an evening with a
friend, a widow lady, for whom Mrs. Canning had a
particular friendship. As there was no gentleman
present during the evening, the time passed rather
heavily to Canning, who could not get interested in
the conversation of the two ladies. Toward nine
o'clock he began to feel restless and impatient, and
to wonder if his wife would not soon be thinking
about going home. But the time passed wearily
until ten o'clock, and still the conversation between
the two ladies was continued with undiminished interest, and, to all appearance, was likely to continue
until midnight.

Canning at length became so restless and wearied
that he said, thinking that his wife did not probably
know how late it was,—

"Come, Margaret, isn't it 'most time to go home?'"

Mrs. Canning merely looked into her husband's
face, but made no answer.

More earnestly than ever the ladies now appeared
to enter upon the various themes for conversation
that presented themselves, all of which were very

frivolous to the mind of Canning, who was exceedingly chafed by his wife's indifference to his suggestion about going home. He determined, however, to say no more if she sat all night. Toward eleven o'clock she made a movement to depart, and after lingering in the parlor before she went up stairs to put on her things, and in the chamber after her things were on, and on the stairs, in the passage, and at the door, she finally took the arm of her husband and started for home. Not a word was uttered by either until they had walked the distance of two squares, when Margaret, unable to keep back what she wanted to say any longer, spoke thus,—

"James, I will thank you, another time, when we are spending an evening out, not to suggest as publicly as you did to-night that it is time to go home. It's very bad manners, let me tell you, in the first place; and in the second place, I don't like it at all. I do not wish people to think that I have to come and go just at your beck or nod. I was about starting when you spoke to me, but sat an hour longer just on purpose."

The mind of Canning, already fretted, was set on fire by this.

"You did?" he said.

"Yes, I did. And I can tell you, once for all, that I wish this to be the last time you speak to me as you did to-night."

It was as much as the impatient spirit of Canning could do to keep from replying—

"It's the last time I will ever speak to you at all," and then leaving her in the street, with the intention of never seeing her again. But suddenly he thought of Lilly, and the presence of the child in his mind kept back the mad words from his lips. Not one syllable did he utter during their walk home, although his wife said much to irritate rather than soothe him. Nor did a sentence pass his lips that night.

At the breakfast table on the next morning, the husband and wife were coldly polite to each other. When the meal was completed, Canning retired to his office, and his wife sought her chamber to weep. The latter half repented of what she had done, but her contrition was not hearty enough to prompt to a confession of her fault. The fact that she considered her husband to blame, stood in the way of this.

Reserve and coldness marked the intercourse of the unhappy couple for several weeks ; and then the clouds began to break, and there were occasional glimpses of sunshine.

But, before there was a clear sky, some trifling occurrence put them again at variance. From this time, unhappily, one circumstance after another transpired to fret them with each other, and to separate, rather than unite them. Daily, Canning grew more cold and reserved, and his wife met him in a like uncompromising spirit. Even their lovely child—their darling blue-eyed Lilly—with her sweet little voice and smiling face, could not soften their hearts toward each other.

To add fuel to this rapidly enkindling fire of discord, was the fact that Mrs. Canning was on particularly intimate terms with the wife of a man toward whom her husband entertained a settled and well-grounded dislike, and visited her more frequently

4*

than she did any one of her friends. He did not
interfere with her in the matter, but it annoyed him
to hear her speak, occasionally, of meeting Mr.
Richards at his house, and repeating the polite language he used to her, when he detested the character
of Richards, and had not spoken to him for more
than a year.

One day Mrs. Canning expressed a wish to go in
the evening to a party.

"It will be impossible for me to go to-night, or,
indeed, this week," Canning said. "I am engaged
in a very important case, which will come up for
trial on Friday, and it will take all my time properly
to prepare for it. I shall be engaged every evening,
and perhaps late every night."

Mrs. Canning looked disappointed, and said she
thought he might spare her one evening.

"You know I would do so, Margaret, with pleasure," he replied, "but the case is one involving too
much to be endangered by any consideration. Next
week we will go to a party."

When Canning came home to tea, he found his
wife dressed to go out.

"I'm going to the party, for all you can't go with
me," said she

"Indeed! With whom are you going?"

"Mrs. Richards came in to see me after dinner,
when I told her how much disappointed I was about
not being able to go to the party to-night. She said
that she and her husband were going, and that it
would give them great pleasure to call for me. Am
I not fortunate?"

"But you are not going with Mr. and Mrs. Richards?"

"Indeed I am! Why not?"

"Margaret! You must not go."

"Must not, indeed! You speak in quite a tone of authority, Mr. Canning;" and the wife drew herself up haughtily.

"Authority, or no authority, Margaret"—Canning now spoke calmly, but his lips were pale—"I will never consent that my wife shall be seen in a public assembly with Richards. You know my opinion of the man."

"I know you are prejudiced against him, though I believe unjustly."

"Madness!" exclaimed Canning, thrown off his guard. "And this from you?"

"I don't see that you have any cause for getting into a passion, Mr. Canning," said his wife, with provoking coolness. "And, I must say, that you interfere with my freedom rather more than a husband has any right to do. But, to cut this matter short, let me tell you, once for all, that I am going to the assembly to-night with Mr. and Mrs. Richards. Having promised to do so, I mean to keep my promise."

"Margaret, I positively forbid your going!" said Canning, in much excitement.

"I deny your right to command me! In consenting to become your wife, I did not make myself your slave; although it is clear from this, and other things that have occurred since our marriage, that you consider me as occupying that position."

"Then it is your intention to go with this man?"

said Canning, again speaking in a calm but deep voice.

"Certainly it is."

"Very well. I will not make any threat of what I will do, Margaret. But this I can assure you, that lightly as you may think of this matter, if persevered in, it will cause you more sorrow than you have ever known. Go! Go against my wish—against my command, if you will have it so—and when you feel the consequence, lay the blame upon no one but yourself. And now let me say to you, Margaret, that your conduct as a wife has tended rather to estrange your husband's heart from you than to win his love. I say this now, because I may not have——"

"James! It is folly for you to talk to me after that fashion," exclaimed Margaret, breaking in upon him. "I——"

But before she could finish the sentence, Canning had left the room, closing the door hard after him.

Just an hour from this time, Mr. and Mrs. Richards called in their carriage for Mrs. Canning, who went with them to the assembly. An hour was a long period for reflection, and ought to have afforded sufficient time for the wife of Canning to come to a wiser determination than that from which she acted.

Not half a dozen revolutions of the carriage wheels had been made, however, before Margaret repented of what she had done. But it was now too late. The pleasure of the entertainment passed before her, but it found no response in her breast. She saw little but the pale, compressed lip and knit brow of her husband, and heard little but his word of disap proval. Oh! how she did long for the confused pageant that was moving before her, and the discordant mingling of voices and instruments, to pass away, that she might return and tell him that she repented of all that she had done.

At last the assembly broke up, and she was free to go back again to the home that had not, alas! proved as pleasant a spot to her as her imagination had once pictured it.

"And that it has not been so," she murmured to herself, "he has not been all to blame."

On being left at the door, Mrs. Canning rang the bell impatiently. As soon as admitted, she flew up stairs to meet her husband, intending to confess her error, and beg him earnestly to forgive her for having acted so directly in opposition to his wishes. But she did not find him in the chamber. Throwing off her bonnet and shawl, she went down into the parlours, but found all dark there.

"Where is Mr. Canning?" she asked of a servant.

"He went away about ten o'clock, and has not returned yet," was replied.

This intelligence caused Mrs. Canning to lean hard on the stair-railing for support. She felt in an instant weak almost as an infant.

Without further question, she went back to her chamber, and looked about fearfully on bureaus and tables for a letter addressed to her in her husband's handwriting. But nothing of this met her eye. Then she sat down to await her husband's return. But she waited long. Daylight found her an anxious watcher; he was still away.

The anguish of mind experienced during that unhappy night, it would be vain for us to attempt to picture. In the morning, on descending to the parlour, she found on one of the pier-tables a letter bearing her name. She broke the seal tremblingly. It did not contain many words, but they fell upon her heart with an icy coldness.

"MARGARET: Your conduct to-night has decided me to separate myself from a woman who I feel neither truly loves nor respects me. The issue which I have for some time dreaded has come. It is better for us to part than to live in open discord. I shall arrange every thing for your comfortable support, and then leave the city, perhaps for ever. You need not tell our child that her father lives. I would rather she would think him dead than at variance with her mother.

"JAMES CANNING.'

These were the words. Their effect was paralyzing. Mrs. Canning had presence of mind enough to crush the fatal letter into her bosom, and strength enough to take her back to her chamber. When there, she sunk powerless upon her bed, and remained throughout the day too weak in both body and mind to rise or think. She could do little else but feel.

Five years from the day of that unhappy separation, we find Mrs. Canning in the unobtrusive home of Aunt Hannah, who took the almost heart-broken wife into the bosom of her own family, after the passage of nearly a year had made her almost hopeless of ever seeing him again. No one knew where he was. Only once did Margaret hear from him,

and that was on the third day after he had parted
from her, when he appeared in the court-room, and
made a most powerful argument in favour of the client
whose important case had prevented his going with
his wife to the assembly. After that he disappeared,
and no one could tell aught of him. A liberal an-
nuity had been settled upon his wife, and the necessary papers to enable her to claim it transmitted to
her under a blank envelope.

Five years had changed Margaret sadly. The
high-spirited, blooming, happy woman, was now a
meek, quiet, pale-faced sufferer. Lilly had grown
finely, all unconscious of her mother's suffering, and
was a very beautiful child. She attracted the notice
of every one.

"Aunt Hannah," said Margaret, one day after
this long, long period of suffering, "I have what you
will call a strange idea in my mind. It has been
visiting me for weeks, and now I feel much inclined
to act from its dictates. You know that Mr. and
Mrs. Edwards are going to Paris next month. Ever
since Mrs. Edwards mentioned it to me, I have felt
a desire to go with them. I don't know why, but
so it is. I think it would do me good to go to Paris
and spend a few months there. When a young girl,
I always had a great desire to see London and Paris;
and this desire is again in my mind."

"I would go, then," said Aunt Hannah, who
thought favourably of any thing likely to divert the
mird of her niece from the brooding melancholy in
which it was shrouded.

To Paris Mrs. Canning went, accompanied by her
little daughter, who was the favourite of every one

on board the steamer in which they sailed. In this gay city, however, she did not attain as much relief of mind as she had anticipated. She found it almost impossible to take interest in any thing, and soon began to long for the time to come when she could go back to the home and heart of her good Aunt Hannah. The greatest pleasure she took was in going with Lilly to the Gardens of the Tuileries, and amid the crowd there to feel alone with nature in some of her most beautiful aspects. Lilly was always delighted to get there, and never failed to bring something in her pocket for the pure white swans that floated so gracefully in the marble basin into which the water dashed cool and sparkling from beautiful fountains.

One day, while the child was playing at a short distance from her mother, a man seated beside a bronze statue, over which drooped a large orange tree, fixed his eyes upon her admiringly, as hundreds of others had done. Presently she came up and stood close to him, looking up into the face of the statue. The man said something to her in French, but Lilly only smiled and shook her head.

"What is your name, dear?" he then said in English.

"Lilly," replied the child.

A quick change passed over the man's face. With much more interest in his voice, he said—

"Where do you live? In London?"

"Oh no, sir; I live in America."

"What is your name besides Lilly?"

"Lilly Canning, sir."

The man now became strongly agitated. But he contended vigorously with his feelings.

"Where is your mother, dear?" he asked, taking her hand as he spoke, and gently pressing it between his own.

"She is here, sir," returned Lilly, looking inquiringly into the man's face.

"Here!"

"Yes, sir. We come here every day."

"Where is your mother now?"

"Just on the other side of the fountain. You can't see her for the lime-tree."

"Is your father here, also?" continued the man.

"No, I don't know where my father is."

"Is he dead?"

"No, sir; mother says he is not dead, and that she hopes he will come home soon. Oh! I wish he would come home. We would all love him so!"

The man rose up quickly, and turning from the child, walked hurriedly away. Lilly looked after him for a moment or two, and then ran back to her mother.

On the next day Lilly saw the same man sitting under the bronze statue. He beckoned to her, and she went to him.

"How long have you been in Paris, dear?" he asked.

"A good many weeks," she replied.

"Are you going to stay much longer?"

"I don't know. But mother wants to go home."

"Do you like to live in Paris?"

"No, sir. I would rather live at home with mother and Aunt Hannah."

"You live with Aunt Hannah, then?'

"Yes, sir. Do you know Aunt Hannah?" and the child looked up wonderingly into the man's face.

"I used to know her," he replied.

Just then Lilly heard her mother calling her, and she started and ran away in the direction from which the voice came. The man's face grew slightly pale, and he was evidently much agitated. As he had done on the evening previous, he rose up hastily and walked away. But in a short time he returned, and appeared to be carefully looking about for some one. At length he caught sight of Lilly's mother. She was sitting with her eyes upon the ground, the child leaning upon her, and looking into her face, which he saw was thin and pale, and overspread with a hue of sadness. Only for a few moments did he thus gaze upon her, and then he turned and walked hurriedly from the garden.

Mrs. Canning sat alone with her child that evening, in the handsomely-furnished apartments she had hired on arriving in Paris.

"He told you that he knew Aunt Hannah?" she said, rousing up from a state of deep thought.

"Yes, ma. He said he used to know her."

"I wonder"——

A servant opened the door, and said that a gentleman wished to see Mrs. Canning.

"Tell him to walk in," the mother of Lilly had just power to say. In breathless suspense she waited for the space of a few seconds, when the man who had spoken to Lilly in the Gardens of the Tuileries entered and closed the door after him.

Mrs. Canning raised her eyes to his face. It was her husband! She did not cry out nor spring forward. She had not the power to do either.

"That's him now, mother!" exclaimed Lilly.

"It's your father!" said Mrs. Canning, in a deeply breathed whisper.

The child sprung toward him with a quick bound, and was instantly clasped in his arms.

"Lilly, dear Lilly!" he sobbed, pressing his lips upon her brow and cheeks. "Yes! I am your father!"

The wife and mother sat motionless and tearless, with her eyes fixed upon the face of her husband. After a few passionate embraces, Canning drew the child's arms from about his neck, and setting her down upon the floor, advanced slowly toward his wife. Her eyes were still tearless, but large drops were rolling over his face.

"Margaret!" he said, uttering her name with great tenderness.

He was by her side in time to receive her upon his bosom, as she sunk forward in a wild passion of tears.

All was reconciled. The desolate hearts were again peopled with living affections. The arid waste smiled in greenness and beauty.

In their old home, bound by threefold cords of love, they now think only of the past as a severe lesson by which they have been taught the heavenly virtue of forbearance. Five years of intense suffering changed them both, and left marks that after years can never efface. But selfish impatience and pride were all subdued, and their hearts melted into

each other, until they became almost like one heart.
Those who meet them now, and observe the deep,
but unobtrusive affection with which they regard
each other, would never imagine, did they not know
their previous history, that love, during one period
of that married life, had been so long and so totally
eclipsed.

THE SOCIAL SERPENT.

A LADY, whom we will call Mrs. Harding, touched
with the destitute condition of a poor, sick widow,
who had three small children, determined, from an
impulse of true humanity, to awaken, if possible, in
the minds of some friends and neighbours, an interest in her favour.   She made a few calls, one morning, with this end in view, and was gratified to find
that her appeal made a favourable impression.   The
first lady whom she saw, a Mrs. Miller, promised to
select from her own and children's wardrobe a number of cast-off garments for the widow, and to aid her
in other respects, at the same time asking Mrs. Harding to call in on the next day, when she would be
able to let her know what she could do.
    Pleased with her reception, and encouraged to
seek further aid for the widow, Mrs. Harding withdrew and took her way to the house of another acquaintance.   Scarcely had she left, when a lady,

named Little, dropped in to see Mrs. Miller. To her the latter said, soon after her entrance:

"I've been very much interested in the case of a poor widow this morning. She is sick, with three little children dependent on her, and destitute of almost every thing. Mrs. Harding was telling me about it."

"Mrs. Harding!" The visitor's countenance changed, and she looked unutterable things. "I wonder!" she added, in well assumed surprise, and then was silent.

"What's the matter with Mrs. Harding?" asked Mrs. Miller.

"I should think," said Mrs. Little, "that she was in nice business, running around, gossiping about indigent widows, when some of her own relatives are so poor they can hardly keep soul and body together."

"Is this really so?" asked Mrs. Miller.

"Certainly it is. I had it from my chambermaid, whose sister is cook next door to where a cousin of Mrs. Harding's lives, and she says they are, one half of their time, she really believes, in a starving condition."

"But does Mrs. Harding know this?"

"She ought to know it, for she goes there sometimes, I hear."

"She didn't come merely to gossip about the poor widow," said Mrs. Miller. "Her errand was to obtain something to relieve her necessities."

"Did you give her any thing?" asked Mrs. Little.

"No; but I told her to call and see me to-morrow, when I would have something for her."

"Do you want to know my opinion of this matter?" said Mrs. Little, drawing herself up, and assuming a very important air.

"What is your opinion?"

"Why, that there is no poor widow in the case at all."

"Mrs. Little!"

"You needn't look surprised. I'm in earnest. I never had much faith in Mrs. Harding, at the best."

"I *am* surprised. If there was no poor widow in the case, what did she want with charity?"

"She has poor relations of her own, for whom, I suppose, she's ashamed to beg. So you see my meaning now."

"You surely wrong her."

"Don't believe a word of it. At any rate, take my advice, and be the almoner of your own bounty. When Mrs. Harding comes again, ask her the name of this poor widow, and where she resides. If she gives you a name and residence, go and see for yourself."

"I will act on your suggestion," said Mrs. Miller. "Though I can hardly make up my mind to think so meanly of Mrs. Harding; still, from the impression your words produce, I deem it only prudent to be, as you term it, the almoner of my own bounty."

The next lady upon whom Mrs. Harding called, was a Mrs. Johns, and in her mind she succeeded in also awakening an interest for the poor widow.

"Call and see me to-morrow," said Mrs. Johns, "and I'll have something for you."

Not long after Mrs. Harding's departure, Mrs. Little called, in her round of gossiping visits, and to her Mrs. Johns mentioned the case of the poor widow, that matter being, for the time, uppermost in her thoughts.

"Mrs. Harding's poor widow, I suppose," said Mrs. Little, in a half-sneering, half-malicious tone of voice.

Mrs. Johns looked surprised, as a matter of course.

"What do you mean?" she asked.

"Oh, nothing, much. Only I've heard of this destitute widow before."

"You have?"

"Yes, and between ourselves,"—the voice of Mrs. Little became low and confidential—"it's the opinion of Mrs. Miller and myself, that there is no poor widow in the case."

"Mrs. Little! You astonish me! No poor widow in the case! I can't understand this. Mrs. Harding was very clear in her statement. She described the widow's condition, and very much excited my sympathies. What object can she have in view?"

"Mrs. Miller and I think," said the visitor, "and with good reason, that this poor widow is only put forward as a cover."

"As a cover to what?"

"To some charities that she has reasons of her own for not wishing to make public."

"Still in the dark. Speak out more plainly."

"Plainly, then, Mrs. Johns, we have good reasons for believing, Mrs. Miller and I, that she is begging for some of her own poor relations. Mrs. Miller is going to see if she can find the widow."

"Indeed! That's another matter altogether. I promised to do something in the case, but shall now

decline. I couldn't have believed such a thing of
Mrs. Harding! But so it is; you never know people until you find them out."

"No, indeed, Mrs. Johns. You never spoke a
truer word in your life," replied Mrs. Little, empha-
tically.

On the day following, after seeing the poor widow,
ministering to some of her immediate wants, and encouraging her to expect more substantial relief, Mrs.
Harding called, as she had promised to do, on Mrs.
Miller. A little to her surprise, that lady received
her with unusual coldness; and yet, plainly, with an
effort to seem friendly.

"You have called about the poor widow you spoke
of yesterday?" said Mrs. Miller.

"Such is the object of my present visit."

"What is her name?"

"Mrs. Aitken."

"Where did you say she lived?"

The residence was promptly given.

"I've been thinking," said Mrs. Miller, slightly
colouring, and with some embarrassment, "that I
would call in and see this poor woman myself."

"I wish you would," was the earnest reply of Mrs.
Harding. "I am sure, if you do so, all your sympathies will be excited in her favour."

As Mrs. Harding said this, she arose, and with a
manner that showed her feelings to be hurt, as well as
mortified, bade Mrs. Miller a formal good-morning,
and retired. Her next call was upon Mrs. Johns.
Much to her surprise, her reception here was quite
as cold; in fact, so cold, that she did not even refer
to the object of her visit, and Mrs. Johns let her go

away without calling attention to it herself. So affected was she by the singular, and to her unaccountable change in the manner of these ladies, that Mrs. Harding had no heart to call upon two others, who had promised to do something for the widow, but went home disappointed, and suffering from a troubled and depressed state of feeling.

So far as worldly goods were concerned, Mrs. Harding could not boast very large possessions. She was herself a widow; and her income, while it sufficed, with economy, to supply the moderate wants of her family, left her but little for luxuries, the gratification of taste, or the pleasures of benevolence. Quick to feel the wants of the needy, no instance of destitution came under her observation that she did not make some effort toward procuring relief.

What now was to be done? She had excited the sick woman's hopes—had promised that her immediate wants, and those of her children, should be supplied. From her own means, without great self-denial, this could not be effected. True, Mrs. Miller and Mrs. Johns had both promised to call upon the poor widow, and, in person, administer relief. But Mrs. Harding did not place much reliance on this; for something in the manner of both ladies impressed her with the idea that their promise merely covered a wish to recede from their first benevolent intentions.

"Something must be done," said she, musingly. And then she set herself earnestly to the work of devising ways and means. Where there is a will there is a way. No saying was ever truer than this.

It was, perhaps, a week later, that Mrs. Little called again upon Mrs. Miller.

"What of Mrs. Harding's poor widow?" said the former, after some ill-natured gossip about a mutual friend.

"Oh, I declare! I've never thought of the woman since," replied Mrs. Miller, in a tone of self-condemnation. "And I promised Mrs. Harding that I would see her. I really blame myself."

"No great harm done, I presume," said Mrs. Little.

"I don't know about that. I'm hardly prepared to think so meanly of Mrs. Harding as you do. At any rate, I'm going this day to redeem my promise."

"What promise?"

"The promise I made Mrs. Harding, that I would see the woman she spoke of, and relieve her, if in need."

"You'll have all your trouble for nothing."

"No matter, I'll clear my conscience, and that is something. Come, wont you go with me?"

Mrs. Little declined the invitation at first; but, strongly urged by Mrs. Miller, she finally consented. So the two ladies forthwith took their way toward the neighbourhood in which Mrs. Harding had said the needy woman lived. They were within a few doors of the house, which had been very minutely described by Mrs. Harding, when they met Mrs. Johns.

"Ah!" said the latter, with animation, "just the person, of all others, I most wished to see. How could you, Mrs. Miller, so greatly wrong Mrs. Harding?"

"Me wrong her, Mrs. Johns? I don't understand

you." And Mrs. Miller looked considerably astonished.

"Mrs. Little informed me that you had good reasons for believing all this story about a poor widow to be a mere subterfuge, got up to cover some doings of her own that Mrs. Harding was ashamed to bring to the light."

"Mrs. Little!" There was profound astonishment in the tones of Mrs. Miller, and her eyes had in them such an indignant light, as she fixed them upon her companion, that the latter quailed under her gaze.

"Acting from this impression," resumed Mrs. Johns, "I declined placing at her disposal the means of relief promised; but, instead, told her that I would myself see the needy person for whom she asked aid. This I have, until now, neglected to do; and this neglect, or indifference I might rather call it, has arisen from a belief that there was no poor widow in the case. Wrong has been done, Mrs. Miller, great wrong! How could you have imagined such baseness of Mrs. Harding?"

"And there *is* a poor, sick widow, in great need?" said Mrs. Miller, now speaking calmly, and with regained self-possession.

"There is a sick widow,' replied Mrs. Johns, "but not at present in great need. Mrs. Harding has supplied immediate wants."

"Well, Mrs. Little!" Mrs. Miller again turned her eyes, searchingly, upon her companion.

"I—I—thought so. It was my impression—I had good reason for—I—I" stammered Mrs. Little.

"It should have been enough for you to check a

benevolent impulse in my case by your unfounded
suggestions. Not content with this, however, you
must use my name in still further spreading your
unjust suspicions, and actually make me the author
of charges against a noble-minded woman, which had
heir origin in your own evil thoughts."

"I will not bear such language!" said the offended
Mrs. Little, indignantly; and turning with an angry
toss of the head, she left the ladies to their own reflections.

"I am taught one good lesson from this circumstance," said Mrs. Miller, as they walked away; "and
that is, never to even seem to have my good opinion
of another affected by the allegations and surmises
of a social gossip. Such people always suppose the
worst, and readily pervert the most unselfish actions
into moral offences. The harm they do is incalcu-
lable."

"And, as in the present case," remarked Mrs.
Johns, "they make others responsible for their base
suggestions. Had Mrs. Little not coupled your name
with the implied charges against Mrs. Harding, my
mind would not have been poisoned against her."

"While not a breath of suspicion had ever crossed
mine until Mrs. Little came in, and wantonly inter-
cepted the stream of benevolence about to flow forth
to a needy, and, I doubt not, most worthy object."

"We have made of her an enemy. At least you
have; for you spoke to her with smarting plainness,"
said Mrs. Johns.

"Better the enmity of such than their friendship,"
replied Mrs. Miller. "Their words of detraction
cannot harm so much as the poison of evil thoughts

toward others, which they ever seek to infuse. Your dearest friend is not safe from them, if she be pure as an angel. Let her name but pass your lips, and instantly it is breathed upon, and the spotless surface grows dim."

THE YOUNG MOTHER.

[The following brief passage is from our story, "The Wife," in the series "Maiden," "Wife," and Mother."]

A NEW chord vibrated in Anna's heart, and the music was sweeter far in her spirit's ear, than any before heard. She was changed. Suddenly she felt that she was a new creature. Her breast was filled with deeper, purer, and tenderer emotions. She was a mother! A babe had been born to her! A sweet pledge of love lay nestling by her side, and drawing its life from her bosom. She was happy—how happy cannot be told. A mother only can *feel* how happy she was on first realizing the new emotions that thrill in a young mother's heart.

As health gradually returned to her exhausted frame, and friends gathered around her with warm congratulations, Anna felt that she was indeed beginning a new life. Every hour her soul seemed to enlarge, and her mind to be filled with higher and purer thoughts. Before the birth of her babe, she suffered much more than even her husband had sup

posed, both in body and mind. Her spirits were
often so depressed that it required her utmost effort
to receive him with her accustomed cheerfulness at
each period of his loved return. But, living as she
did in the ever active endeavour to bless others, she
strove daily and hourly to rise above every infirmity.
Now, all was peace within—holy peace. There
came a Sabbath rest of deep, interior joy, that was
sweet, unutterably sweet. Body and spirit entered
into this rest. No wind ruffled the still, bright
vaters of her life. She was the same, and yet not
the same.

"I cannot tell you, dear husband! how happy I
am," she said, a few weeks after her babe was born.
"Nor can I describe the different emotions that per-
vade my heart. When our babe is in my arms, and
especially when it lies at my bosom, it seems as if
angels were near me."

"And angels are near you," replied her husband.
"Angels love innocence, and especially infants, that
are forms of innocence. They are present with
them, and the mother shares the blessed company,
for she loves her babe with an unselfish love, and
this the angels can perceive, and, through it, affect
her with a measure of their own happiness.

"How delightful the thought! Above all, is the
mother blessed. She suffers much—her burden is
hard to bear—the night is dark—but the morning
that opens upon her is the brightest a human soul
knows during its earthly pilgrimage. And no wonder. She has performed the highest and holiest of
offices—she has given birth to an immortal being—
and her reward is with her."

Hartley had loved his wife truly, deeply, tenderly. Every day, he saw more and more in her to admire. There was an order, consistency, and harmony in her character as a wife, that won his admiration. In the few months they had passed since their marriage, she had filled her place to him, perfectly. Without seeming to reflect how she should regulate her conduct toward her husband, in every act of her wedded life she had displayed true wisdom, united with unvarying love. All this caused his heart to unite itself more and more closely with hers. But now, that she held to him the twofold relation of a wife and mother, his love was increased fourfold. He thought of her, and looked upon her, with increased tenderness.

"Mine, by a double tie," he said, with a full realization of his words, when he first pressed his lips upon the brow of his child, and then, with a fervour unfelt before, upon the lips of his wife. "As you have been a good wife, you will be a good mother," he added, with emotion.

THE GENTLE WARNING.

"Do not accept the offer, Florence," said her friend Carlotti.

A shade of disappointment went over the face of the fair girl, who had just communicated the pleasing fact that she had received an offer of marriage.

"You cannot be happy as the wife of Herman Leland," added Carlotti.

"How little do you know this heart," returned the fond girl.

"It is because I know it so well that I say what I do. If your love be poured out for Herman Leland, Florence, it will be as water on the desert sand."

"Why do you affirm this, Carlotti?"

"A woman can truly love only the moral virtue of her husband."

"I do not clearly understand you."

"It is only genuine goodness of heart that conjoins in marriage."

"Well?"

"Just so far as selfish and evil affections find a place in the mind of either the husband or wife, will be the ratio of unhappiness in the marriage state. If there be any truth in morals, or in the doctrine of affinities, be assured that this is so. It is neither intellectual attainments nor personal attractions that

make happiness in marriage. Far, very far from it.
All depends upon the quality of the affections. If
these be good, happiness will come as a natural
consequence; but if they be evil, misery will inevitably follow so close a union."

"Then you affirm that Mr. Leland is an evil-
minded man?"

"Neither of us know him well enough to say this
positively, Florence. Judging from what little I
have seen, I should call him a selfish man; and no
selfish man can be a good man, for selfishness is the
basis of all evil."

"I am afraid you are prejudiced against him,
Carlotti."

"If I have had any prejudices in the matter,
Florence, they have been in his favour. Well-educated, refined in his manners, and variously accomplished, he creates, on nearly all minds, a favourable
impression. Such an impression did I at first feel.
But the closer I drew near to him, the less satisfied
did I feel with my first judgment. On at least
two occasions, I have heard him speak lightly of
religion."

"Of mere cant and sectarianism, perhaps."

"No; he once spoke lightly of a mother for making it a point to require all her children to repeat
their prayers before going to bed. On another
occasion, he alluded to one of the sacraments of the
church in a way that produced an inward shudder.
From that time, I have looked at him with eyes from
which the scales have been removed; and the more
I seek to penetrate beneath the surface of his character, the more do I see what repels me. Florence,

6*

dear, let me urge you, as one who tenderly loves you and earnestly desires to see you happy, to weigh the matter well ere you assent to this proposal."

"I'm afraid, Carlotti," said Florence in reply to this, "that you have let small causes influence your feelings toward Mr. Leland. We all speak lightly, at times, even on subjects regarded as sacred—not because we despise them, but from casual thoughtlessness. It was, no doubt, so with Mr. Leland on the occasion to which you refer."

"We are rarely mistaken, Florence," replied Carlotti, "as to the real sentiment involved in the words used by those with whom we converse. Words are the expressions of thoughts, and these the form of affections. What a man really feels in reference to any subject, will generally appear in the tones of his voice, no matter whether he speak lightly or seriously. Depend upon it, this is so. It was the manner in which Leland spoke that satisfied me as to his real feelings, more than the language he used. Judging him in this way, I am well convinced that, in his heart, he despises religion; and no man who does this, can possibly make a right-minded woman happy."

The gentle warning of Carlotti was not wholly lost on Florence. She had great confidence in the judgment of her friend, and did not feel that it would be right to wholly disregard her admonitions.

"What answer can I make?" said she, drawing a long sigh. "He urges an early response to his suit."

"Duty to yourself, Florence, demands a time for

consideration. Marriage is a thing of too vital moment to be decided upon hurriedly. Say to him in reply, that his offer is unexpected, and that you cannot give an immediate answer, but will do so at the earliest possible moment."

"So cold a response may offend him."

"If it does, then he will exhibit a weakness of character unfitting him to become the husband of a sensible woman. If he be really attracted by your good qualities, he will esteem you the more for this act of prudence. He will understand that you set a high regard upon the marriage relation, and do not mean to enter into it unless you know well the person to whom you commit your happiness in this world, and, in all probability, the next."

"A coldly calculating spirit, Carlotti, that nicely weighs and balances the merits and defects of one beloved, is, in my view, hardly consonant with true happiness in marriage. All have defects of character. All are born with evil inclinations of one kind or another. Love seeks only for good in the object of affection. Affinities of this kind are almost spontaneous in their birth. We love more from impulse than from any clear appreciation of character—perceiving good qualities by a kind of instinct rather than searching for them."

"A doctrine, Florence," said Carlotti, "that has produced untold misery in the married life. As I said at first, it is only the moral virtue of her husband that a woman can love—it is only this, as a uniting principle, that can make two married partners one. The qualities of all minds express themselves in words and actions, and, by a close observance of these latter, we may determine the nature of the former. We cannot perceive them with sufficient clearness to arrive at a sound judgment: the only safe method is to determine the character of the tree by its fruits. Take sufficient time to arrive at a knowledge of Mr. Leland's character by observation, and then you can accept or reject him under the fullest assurance that you are acting wisely."

"Perhaps you are right," murmured Florence. "I will weigh carefully what you have said."

And she did so. Much to the disappointment of Mr. Leland, he received a reply from Florence asking a short time for reflection.

When Florence next met the young man, there was, as a natural consequence, some slight embarrassment on both sides. On separating, Florence experienced a certain unfavourable impression toward him, although she could not trace it to any thing he had said or done. At their next meeting, Leland's reserve had disappeared, and he exhibited a better flow of spirits. He was more off his guard than usual, and said a good many things that rather surprised Florence.

Impatient of delay, Leland again pressed his suit; but Florence was further than ever from being ready to give an answer. She was not prepared to reject him, and as little prepared to give a favourable answer. Her request to be allowed further time for consideration, wounded his pride; and, acting under its influence, he determined to have his revenge on her by suing for the hand of another maiden, and bearing her to the altar while she was hesitating over the offer he had made. With this purpose in view, he penned a kind and polite note, approving her deliberation, and desiring her to take the fullest time for reflection. "Marriage," said he, in this note, "is too serious a matter to be decided upon hastily. It is a life-union, and the parties who make it should be well satisfied that there exists a mutual fitness for each other."

Two days passed after Florence received this note before seeing her friend Carlotti. She then called upon her in order to have further conversation on the subject of the proposal she had received. The tenor of this note had produced a favourable change in her feelings, and she felt strongly disposed to make a speedy termination of the debate in her mind by accepting her attractive suitor.

"Are you not well?" was her first remark on seeing Carlotti, for her friend looked pale and troubled.

"Not very well, dear," replied Carlotti, making an effort to assume a cheerful aspect.

The mind of Florence was too intent on the one interesting subject that occupied it to linger long on any other theme. But a short time elapsed before she said, with a warmer glow on her cheeks—

"I believe I have made up my mind, Carlotti."

"About what?"

"The offer of Mr. Leland."

"Well, what is your decision?" Carlotti held her breath for an answer.

"I will accept him."

Without replying, Carlotti arose, and going to a drawer, took therefrom a letter addressed to herself, and handing it to Florence, said—

"Read that."

There was something ominous in the manner of Carlotti, which caused Florence to become agitated. Her hands trembled as she unfolded the letter. It bore the date of the day previous, and read thus:—

"MY DEAR CARLOTTI: From the first moment I saw you, I felt that you were the one destined to make me happy or miserable. Your image has been present to me, sleeping or waking, ever since. I can turn in no way that it is not before me. The oftener I have met you, the more have I been charmed by the gentleness, the sweetness, the purity, and excellence of your character. With you to walk through life by my side, I feel that my feet would tread a flowery way; but if heaven have not this blessing in store for me, I shall be, of all men, most miserable. My heart is too full to write more. And have I not said enough? Love speaks in brief but eloquent language. Dear young lady, let me hear from you speedily. I shall be wretched until I know your decision. Heaven give my suit a favourable issue! Yours, devotedly,

"HERMAN LELAND."

A deadly paleness overspread the countenance of Florence as the letter dropped from her hands; and she leaned back against her friend to prevent falling to the floor. But, in a little while, she recovered herself.

"And this to *you?*" said she, with a quivering lip, as she gazed earnestly into the face of her friend.

"Yes, Florence, that to *me.*"

"Can I trust my own senses? Is there not some illusion? Let me look at it again."

And Florence stooped for the letter, and fixed her eyes upon it once more. The language was plain, and the handwriting she knew too well.

"False-hearted!" she murmured, in a low and mournful voice, covering her face and sobbing.

"Yes, Florence," said her friend, he is false-hearted. How thankful am I that you have escaped! Evidently in revenge for your prudent deliberation, he has sought an alliance with another. Had that other one accepted his heartless proposal, he would have met your favourable answer to his suit with insult."

For a long time, Florence wept on the bosom of her friend. Then her feelings grew calmer, and her mind became clear.

"What an escape!" fell from her lips as she raised her head and turned her still pale face toward Carlotti. "Thanks, my wiser friend, for your timely, yet gentle warning! Your eyes saw deeper than mine."

"Yes, yes; you have made an escape!" said Carlotti. "With such a man, your life could only have been wretched."

"Have you answered his letter?" asked Florence.

"Not yet. But if you are inclined to do so, we will, on the same sheet of paper and under the same envelope, each decline the honour of an alliance. Such a rebuke he deserves, and we ought to give it."

And such a rebuke they gave.

A few months later, and Leland led to the altar a young lady reputed to be an heiress.

A year afterward, just on the eve of Florence's marriage to a gentleman in every way worthy to take her happiness in his keeping, she sat alone with her fast friend Carlotti. They were conversing of the bright future.

"And for all this joy, in store for me, Carlotti," said Florence, leaning toward her friend and laying her hand affectionately on her cheek, "I am indebted to you."

"To me? How to me, dear?" asked Carlotti.

"You saved me from an alliance with Leland. Oh, into what an abyss of wretchedness would I have fallen! I heard to-day that, after cruelly abusing poor Agnes in Charleston, where they removed, he finally abandoned her. Can it be true?"

"It is, I believe, too true. Agnes came back to her friends last week, bringing with her a babe. I have not seen her; but those who have tell me that her story of suffering makes the heart ache. She looks ten years older."

"Ah me!" sighed Florence. "Marriage—how much it involves! Even now, as I stand at its threshold, with so much that looks bright in the future, I tremble. Of Edward's excellent character and goodness of heart, all bear testimony. He is every thing I could wish; but will I make him happy?"

"Not all you could wish," said Carlotti, seriously. "None are perfection here; and you must not expect this. You will find, in your husband's character, faults. Anticipate this; but let the anticipation prepare you to bear with rather than be hurt when they appear, and do not seek too soon to correct them. It is said by a certain deeply-seeing writer on spiritual themes, that when the angels come to try one, they explore his mind only to find the good therein, that they may excite it to activity. Be, then, your husband's angel; explore his mind for the good it contains, and seek to develop and strengthen it. Looking intently at what is good in him, you will not be likely to see faults looming up and assuming a magnitude beyond their real dimensions. But when faults appear, as they assuredly will, compare them with your own; and, as you would have him exercise forbearance toward you, do you exercise forbearance toward him. Be wise in your love, my friend. Wisdom and love are married partners. If you separate them, neither is a safe guide. But if you keep them united, like a rower who pulls both oars, you will glide swiftly forward in a smooth sea."

Florence bent her head as she listened, and every word of her friend made its impression. Long after were they remembered and acted upon, and they saved her from hours of pain. Florence is a happy wife; but how near did she come to making shipwreck of her love-freighted heart? There are times when, in thinking of it, she trembles.

KATE'S EXPERIMENT.

KATE HARBELL, a high-spirited girl, who had a pretty strong will of her own, was about being married. Like a great many others of her age and sex who approach the matrimonial altar, Kate's notions of the marriage relation were not the clearest in the world.

Ferdinand Lee, the betrothed of Kate, a quiet, sensitive young man, had, perhaps, as strong a will as the young lady herself, though it was more under the control of reason. He was naturally impatient of dictation or force, and a strong love of approbation made him feel keenly any thing like satire, ridicule or censure. To point him to a fault was to wound if not offend him. Here lay the weakness of his character. All this, on the other side, was counterbalanced by kind feelings, good sense, and manly principles. He was above all meanness or dishonour.

Of course, Kate did not fully understand his character. Such a thing as a young girl's accurate knowledge of the character of the man she is about to marry, is of very rare occurrence. She saw enough of good qualities to make her love him with tenderness and devotion; but she also saw personal defects that were disagreeable in the object of her affections. But she did not in the least doubt that all these she could easily correct in him after she became his wife.

From a defect of education, or from a natural want of neatness and order, Ferdinand Lee was inclined to carelessnes in his attire; and also exhibited a certain want of polish in his manners and address that was, at times, particularly annoying to Kate.

"I'll break him of that when I get him," said the young lady to a married friend, alluding to some little peculiarity both had noticed.

"Don't be too certain," returned the lady, smiling.

"You'll see."

Kate tossed her head in a resolute way.

"I'll see you disappointed."

"Wait a little while. Before I'm his wife six months, you'll hardly know the man, there'll be such a change."

"The change is far more likely to take place in you."

"Why do you say that, Mrs. Morton?" inquired Kate, looking grave.

"Because I think so. Men are not so easily brought into order, and the attempt at reformation and correction by a young wife generally ends in painful disappointment. If you begin this work you will, in all probability, find yourself tasked beyond your ability. I speak from some experience, having been married for about ten years, and having seen a good many young girls come up into our ranks from the walks of single blessedness. Take my advice, and look away from Frederick's faults and disagreeable peculiarities as much as possible, and think

more of his manly traits of character—his fine sentiments, and honourable principles."

"I do look at them and love them," replied Kate,
with animation. "These won my heart at first, and
now unite me to him in bonds that cannot be broken.
But if on a precious gem there be a slight blemish
that mars its beauty, shall we not seek to remove
the defect, and thus give the jewel a higher lustre?
Will you say, no?"

"I will, if in the act there be danger of injuring
the gem."

"I don't understand you, Mrs. Morton?"

"Reflect for a moment, and see if my meaning is
not apparent."

"You think I will offend him if I point out a
fault, or seek to correct it?"

"A result most likely to follow."

"I will not think so poorly of his good sense,"
answered Kate, with some gravity of manner. The
suggestion half offended her.

"None are perfect, my young friend; don't forget
that," said Mrs. Morton, with equal seriousness.
"To think differently is a common mistake of persons circumstanced as you are."

"It's no mistake of mine, let me assure you," replied Kate. "I can see faults as quickly as any
one. Love can't blind me. It is because I see defects in Frederick that I wish to correct them."

"And you trust to his good sense to take the
work of correction kindly?"

"Certainly I do."

"Then you most probably think him more perfect than he really is. Very few people can bear

to be told of their faults, and fewer still to be told of them by those they love. Love is expected to be blind to defects; therefore, when it is seen looking at and pointing them out, the feeling produced is, in the very nature of things, a disagreeable one. Take my advice, and let Frederick's faults alone, at least for a year after you are married; and even then put your hand on them very lightly, and as if by accident."

"Do you think I could see him lounge, or, rather, slide down in his chair in that ungraceful way, and not speak to him about it? Not I. It makes me nervous now; and, if I wasn't afraid he might take it unkindly, would call his attention to it."

"Do you think he will be less likely to take it unkindly after marriage?"

"Certainly. Then I will have a right to speak to him about it."

"Then marriage will give you certain rights over your husband?"

"It will give him rights over me, and a very poor rule that is which doesn't work both ways. Marriage will make him my husband; and, surely, a wife may tell her husband that he is not perfect, without offending him."

"Kate, Kate; you don't know what you are talking about, child!"

"I think I do."

"And I know you don't."

"Oh, well, Mrs. Morton, we won't quarrel about it," said Kate, laughing. "I mean to make one of the best of wives, and have one of the best of husbands to be found. He will require a little fixing up to

7*

make him just to my mind, but don't you fear but what I'll do it in the gentlest possible manner. Women have more taste than men, you know, and a man never looks and acts just right until he gets a woman to take charge of him."

A happy bride Kate became a few months after this little conversation took place, and Lee thought himself the most fortunate of men in obtaining such a lovely, accomplished, and right-minded woman for a wife. Swiftly glided away the sweet honey-moon, without a jar of discord, though, during the time, Kate saw a good many things not exactly to her mind, and which she set down as needing correction.

One evening, it was just five weeks after the marriage, and when they were snugly settled in their own house, Frederick Lee was seated before the grate, in a handsome rocking-chair, his body in a position that it would have required a stretch of language to pronounce graceful or becoming. He had drawn off one of his boots, that was lying on the floor, and the leg from which it had been taken was hanging over an arm of his chair. He had slipped forward in the chair—his ordinary mode of sitting, or, rather, lying—so far that his head, which, if he had been upright, would have been even with the top of the back, was at least twelve inches below it. To add to the effect of his position, he was swinging the bootless leg that hung across the arm of the chair with a rapid, circling motion. He had been reclining in this inelegant attitude for about ten minutes, when Kate, who had permitted herself to become a good deal annoyed by it, said to him, rather earnestly—

"Do, Frederick, sit up straight, and try and be a little more graceful in your positions."

"What's that?" inquired the young man, as if he had not heard distinctly.

"Can't you sit up straight?"

Kate smiled; but Lee saw that it was a forced smile.

"Oh, yes," he answered, indifferently. "I can sit up straight as an arrow, but I find this attitude most agreeable."

"If you knew how you looked," said Kate.

"How do I look?" asked the young man, playfully.

"Oh! you look—you look more like a country clod-hopper than any thing else."

There was a sharpness in Kate's tones that fell unpleasantly on the ears of the young man.

"Do I, indeed!" was his rather cold remark. Yet he did not change his position.

"Indeed, you do," said the wife, who was, by this time, beginning to feel a good deal of irritation; for she saw that Frederick was not inclined to respond in the way she had hoped, to her very reasonable desire that he would assume a more graceful attitude. "The fact is," she continued, impelled to further utterance by the excited state of her feelings, although she was conscious of having already said more than was agreeable to her husband, "you ought to correct yourself of these ungraceful and undignified habits. It shows a want of"——

Kate stopped suddenly. She felt that she was about using words that would inevitably give offence.

"A want of what?" inquired Lee, in a low, firm

voice, while he continued to look his young wife steadily in the face.

Kate's eyes fell to the floor and she remained silent.

"Ungraceful and undignified. Humph!"

Lee was evidently hurt at this allegation, as the tone in which he repeated the words clearly showed.

"Do you call your present attitude graceful?" Kate asked, rallying herself under the reflection that she was right.

"It is comfortable for me; and, therefore, ought to be graceful in your eyes," was the young man's perverse answer. Not the slightest change had yet taken place in his position.

This was beyond what the high spirited lady could bear, and she retorted with more feeling than discretion:

"Love is not blind in my case, I can assure you, Frederick, and never will be. You are very ungraceful and untidy, and annoy me, sometimes, excessively. I wish you would try to correct these things."

"You do?"

There was something cool and provoking in the way Lee said this.

"I do, Frederick, and I'm in earnest."

The cheeks of Kate were in a glow, and her eyes lit up, and her lips quivering.

"How long since you made the discovery that I was only a country clod-hopper?" said Lee, who was particularly annoyed by Kate's unexpected charges against his good-breeding.

"I didn't say you were only a country clod-hop-per," replied Kate.

"I believe you used the words. My ears rarely deceive me. I must own to feeling highly compli-mented."

"Do sit up straight, Frederick! Do take your leg from over the arm of that chair! You make me so nervous that I can hardly contain myself."

"Really! I thought a man was privileged to sit in any position he pleased in his own house."

The excitement of Kate's mind had, by this time, reached a crisis. Bursting into tears, she hurried from the room, and went sobbing up to her chamber.

Here was a fine state of affairs, indeed! Was ever a man so perverse and unreasonable?

Did Frederick Lee follow, quickly, his weeping wife? No; his pride was too deeply wounded for that.

"A country clod-hopper! Undignified and un-graceful! Upon my word!" Such were some of his mental ejaculations. And then, as his feelings grew excited, he started up from his chair and began pacing the floor, muttering, as he did so—

"It is rather late in the day to make this dis-covery! Why didn't she find it out before? Humph!"

Meanwhile, Kate had thrown herself across her bed, where she lay, weeping bitterly.

What a storm had suddenly been blown about their ears!

It was fully an hour before Frederick Lee's dis-turbed feelings began to run at all clear. He was both surprised and offended. What could all this mean? What had all at once come over his young wife?

"A country clod-hopper!" he muttered to himself over and over again. "Ungraceful—ungenteel, and all that! Very complimentary, indeed!"

When Lee joined his wife in their chamber, two hours after she had left him, he found that she had retired to bed and was sleeping.

On the next morning both looked very sober, and both were cold and distant. A few words only passed between them. It was the same when they met at dinner-time, and the same when Lee came home in the evening. During the whole of this day, the thought of each was upon the other; but it was not a forgiving thought. Kate cherished angry feelings toward her husband; and Lee continued to be offended at the freedom of expression which his young wife had ventured to use toward him. Of course, both were very unhappy.

The formal intercourse of the tea-table having ended, Lee, feeling little inclined to pass the evening with his reserved and sober-looking partner, put on his hat, and merely remarking that he would not return until bed-time, left the house. This act startled Kate. With the jar of the closing door came a gush of tears. The evening was passed alone. How wretched she felt as the hours moved slowly on!

It was nearly eleven o'clock when Lee came home. By that time, the mind of Kate was in an agony of suspense. More than once the thought that he had abandoned her intruded itself, and filled her with fear and anguish. What a relief to her feelings it was when she heard the rattle of his night-key in the lock! But she could not meet him with a smile. She could not throw her arms around his neck, and press her hot cheek to his. No: for she felt that he was angry with her without just cause. and had visited with unjust severity a light offence— if, so far as she was concerned, her act were worthy to be called an offence.

And so they looked coldly upon each other when they met, and then averted their eyes.

The morning broke, but with no fairer promise of a sunny day. Clouds obscured their whole horizon. Coldly they parted after the brief and scarcely tasted meal. How wretched they were!

During the forenoon, Mrs. Morton, the friend of Mrs. Lee, called in to see her young friend.

"Why, Kate! What has happened?" she exclaimed, the moment she saw her.

Mrs. Lee tried to smile and look indifferent, as she answered—

"Happened? Why do you say that?"

"You look as if you hadn't a friend left in the world!"

"And I don't know that I have," said Mrs. Lee, losing, all at once, her self-command, and permitting the ready tears to gush forth.

"Why, Kate, dear!" exclaimed Mrs. Morton, drawing her arm around the neck of her young friend. "What is the meaning of all this? Something wrong with Frederick?"

Kate was silent.

Mrs. Morton reflected for a moment, and then said—

"Been trying to correct some of his faults, ha?"

No answer. But the sobbing became less violent.

"Ah, Kate! Kate! I warned you of this."

"Warned me of what?"

Mrs. Lee lifted her head, and tried to assume an air of dignity as she spoke.

"I warned you that Frederick would not bear it, if you attempted to lay your hand upon his faults."

Kate raised her head higher, and compressed her lips.   Still she did not answer.

"A young husband, naturally enough, thinks himself faultless—at least in the eyes of his wife."

"Very far from faultless is Frederick in my eyes," said Kate.   "My love is not blind, and so I told him."

"You did!"

"Yes, I did, and in so many words," replied Kate, with spirit.

"Ah, silly child!" returned her friend.   "Already you have the reward of your folly.   I forewarned you how it would be."

"Are my wishes, feelings, and taste to be of no account whatever?" said Kate, warmly.   "Frederick is to be and do just what he pleases, and I must say nothing, do nothing, and bear every thing.   Was this the contract between us?   No, Mrs. Morton!"

The bright eyes of Mrs. Lee flashed with indignant fire.

"Come, come, Katy, dear!   Don't let that impulsive heart of thine lead thee too far aside from the path of prudence and safety.   I am sure that Frederick Lee is no self-willed, exacting, domestic tyrant. I could not have been so deceived in him.   But tell me the particular cause of your trouble.   What has been said and done?   You have given offence, and he has become offended.   Tell me the whole story,

Kate, and then I'll know what to say and do for the restoration of your peace."

"You are aware," said Kate, after a brief pause, and with a deepening flush on her cheeks, "how awkward and untidy Frederick is at times,—how he lounges in his chair, and throws his body into all manner of ungraceful attitudes."

"Well?"·

"This, as you know, has always annoyed me sadly. Night before last, I felt so worried with him, that I could not help speaking right out."

"Ah! when you were worried?"

"Of course. If I hadn't felt worried, I wouldn't have said any thing."

"Indeed! Well, what did you say? Was your tone of voice low and full of love, and your words as gentle as the falling dew?"

"Mrs. Morton!"

There was a half-angry, indignant expression in the voice of Kate.

"Did you lay your hand lightly, like the touch of a feather, upon the fault you designed to correct, or did you grasp it rudely and angrily?"

Kate's eyes drooped beneath those of her friend.

"You were annoyed and excited," continued Mrs. Morton. "This by your own acknowledgment, and, in such a frame of mind, you charged with faults the one who had vainly thought himself, at least in your eyes, perfect. And he, as a natural consequence, was hurt and offended. But what did you say to him?"

"I hardly know what I said, now," returned Kate. "But I know I used the words ungraceful, undignified, and country clod-hopper."

"Why, Kate! I am surprised at you! And this to so excellent a man as Frederick, who, from all the fair and gentle ones around him, chose you to be his bosom friend and life companion. Kate, Kate! That was unworthy of you. That was unkind to him. I do not wonder that he was hurt and offended."

"Perhaps I was wrong, Mrs. Morton," said Kate, as tears began to flow again. "But Frederick's want of order, grace, and neatness, is dreadful. I cannot tell you how much it annoys me."

"You saw all this before you were married."

"Not all of it."

"You saw enough to enable you to judge of the rest."

"True; but then I always meant to correct these things in him. They were but blemishes on a jewel of surpassing value."

"Ah, Kate, you have proved the truth of what I told you before your marriage. It is not so easy a thing to correct the faults of a husband—faults confirmed by long habit. Whenever a wife attempts this, she puts in jeopardy, for the time being at least, her happiness, as you have done. A man is but little pleased to make the discovery that his wife thinks him no better than a country clod-hopper; and it is no wonder that he should be offended, if she, with strange indiscreetness and want of tact, tells him in plain terms what she thinks Your husband is sensitive, Kate."

"I know he is."

"And keenly alive to ridicule."

"I am not aware of that."

"Then your reading of his character is less accurate than mine. Moreover, he has a pretty good opinion of himself."

"We all have that."

"And a strong will, quiet as he is in exterior."

"Not stronger, perhaps, than I have."

"Take my advice, Kate," said Mrs. Morton, seriously, "and don't bring your will in direct opposition to his."

"And why not? Am I not his equal? He is no master of mine. I did not sell myself as his slave, that his will should be my law!"

"Silly child! How madly you talk!" said Mrs. Morton. "Not for the world would I have Frederick hear such utterance from your lips. Does he not love you tenderly? Has he not, in every way, sought your happiness thus far in your brief married life? Is he not a man of high moral virtue? Does not your alliance with him rather elevate than depress you in the social rank? And yet, forsooth, because he lounges in his chair, and permits his body, at times, to assume ungraceful attitudes, you must throw the apple of discord into your pleasant home to mar its beautiful harmonies."

"Surely, a wife may be permitted to speak to her husband, and even seek to correct his faults," said Kate.

"Better shut her eyes to his faults, if seeing them is to make them both unhappy. You are in a very strange mood, Kate."

"Am I?" returned Mrs. Lee, querulously.

"You are; and the quicker it passes away, the better for both yourself and husband."

"I don't know how soon it will pass away," sighed Kate, moodily.

"Good-morning," said Mrs. Morton, rising and making a motion to depart.

"You are not going?"

Kate glanced up with a look of surprise.

"Yes; I am afraid to stay here any longer," was the affected serious reply. "I might catch something of your spirit, and then my husband would find a change in his pleasant home. Good-morning. May I see you in a better state of mind when we meet again."

And saying this, Mrs. Morton passed from the room so quickly that Kate could not arrest the movement; so she remained seated, though a little disturbed by her friend and monitor's sudden departure.

What Mrs. Morton had said, although it seemed not to impress the mind of her young friend, yet lingered there, and now began gradually to do its work.

As for Frederick Lee, he was unhappy enough. The words of Kate had stung him severely.

"And so, in her eyes, I am no better than a country clod-hopper!"

Almost every hour was this repeated—sometimes mentally and sometimes aloud; and at each repetition, it disturbed his feelings and awakened an unforgiving spirit.

"A clod-hopper, indeed! Wonder she never made this discovery before!"

This was the thought of Lee as he left his place of business to return home, on the evening of the

day on which Mrs. Morton called upon Kate. Why
would he not look away from this? Why would he
ponder over and magnify the offence of Kate? Why
would he keep this ever before his eyes? His self-
love had been wounded. His pride had been touched.
The weapon of ridicule had been used against him,
and to ridicule he was morbidly sensitive. Kate
should have read his character more closely, and
should have understood it better. But she was
ignorant of his weaknesses, and bore heavily upon
them ere aware of their existence.

It was in this brooding, clouded, and unforgiving
state of mind that Frederick Lee took his way homeward. On entering his dwelling, which he did almost
noiselessly, he went into the parlour and seated himself in the very place where he was sitting when
Kate began, so unexpectedly to him, her unsuccessful work of reformation. Every thing around reminded him of that unfortunate evening—even the
lounging position he so naturally assumed, sliding
down, as he did, in the chair, and throwing one of
his legs over the arm.

"It is comfortable for me," said he, moodily to
himself; "and it's my own house. If she don't like
it, let her——"

He did not finish the sentence, for he felt that
his state of mind was not what it should be, and
that to speak thus of his wife was neither just nor
kind.

Unhappy young man! Is it thus you visit the
light offence—for it was light, in reality—of the
loving and gentle young creature who has given her
happiness, her very life into your keeping? Could

8*

you not bear a word from her? Are you so perfect, that her eyes must see no defect? Is she never to dare, on penalty of your stern displeasure, to correct a fault—to seek to lift you, by her purer and better taste, above the ungraceful and unmanly habits consequent upon a neglected boyhood? What if her hand was laid rather heavily upon you? What if her feelings did prompt her to use words that had better been left unsaid? It was the young wife's pride in her husband that warmed her into undue excitement, and this you should have at once comprehended.

If Frederick Lee did not think precisely as we have written, his thoughts gradually inclined in that direction. Still he felt moody, and his feelings warmed but little toward Kate.

Thus he sat for some ten or fifteen minutes. At the end of this time, he heard light footsteps coming down the stairs. He knew them to be those of his wife. He did not move nor make a sound, but rather crouched lower in his chair, the back of which was turned toward the door. But his thought was on his wife. He saw her with the eyes of his mind—saw her with her clouded countenance. His heart throbbed heavily against his side, and he partially held his breath.

Now her footsteps moved along the passage, and now he was conscious that she had entered the room where he sat. Not the slightest movement did he make—not a sign did he give of his presence. There he sat, shrinking down in his chair, moody. gloomy, and angry with Kate in his heart.

Was she aware of his presence? Had she heard

him enter the house? Such were the questioning thoughts that were in his mind.

Footsteps moved across the room. Now Kate was at the mantel-piece, a few feet from the chair he occupied, for he heard her lay a book thereon. Now she passed to the back window, and throwing it up, pushed open the shutters, giving freer entrance to the waning light.

A deep silence followed. Now the stillness is broken by a gentle sigh that floats faintly through the room. How rebukingly smote that sigh upon the ears of Lee! How it softened his heart toward Kate, the young and loving wife of his bosom! A slower movement in the current of his angry feelings succeeds to this. Then it becomes still. There is a pause.

But where is Kate? Has she left the room? He listens for some movement, but not the slightest sound meets his ear.

"Kate!" No, he did not utter the word aloud, in tender accents, though it was in his heart and on his tongue. Nor did he start up or move. No, as if spell-bound, he remained crouching down in his chair.

All at once he is conscious that some one is bending above him, and, in the next moment, warm lips touch his forehead, gently, hesitatingly, yet with a lingering pressure.

"Kate! Dear Kate!"

He has sprung to his feet, and his arms are flung around his wife.

"Forgive me, Frederick, if I seemed unkind to you," sobbed Kate, as soon as she could command her voice. "There was no unkindness in my heart —only love."

"It is I who most need to ask forgiveness," replied Lee. "I who have——"

"Hush! Not a word of that now," quickly returned Kate, placing her hand upon his mouth. "Let the past be forgotten."

"And forgiven, too," said Lee, as he pressed his lips eagerly to those of his wife.

How happy they were at this moment of reconciliation! How light seemed the causes which had risen up to mar the beautiful harmony of their lives! How weak and foolish both had been, as their acts now appeared in eyes from which had fallen the scales of passion!

Both were wiser than in the aforetime. Kate tried to look away, as much as possible, from the little faults which at first so much annoyed her; while her husband turned his thoughts more narrowly upon himself, at the same time that he made observation of other men, and was soon well convinced that sundry changes in his habits and manners might be made with great advantage. The more his eyes were opened to these little personal defects, the more fully did he forgive Kate for having in the beginning laid her hand upon them, though not in the gentlest manner.

"Six months have passed since you were married," said Mrs. Morton one day to Kate.

"Yes, six months have flown on wings of perfume," replied the happy wife.

"I saw Frederick yesterday."

"Did you?"

"Yes; and I knew him the moment my eyes rested upon him."

"Knew him! Why shouldn't you know him?"

Kate looked a little surprised.

"I thought he was to be so changed under your hands in six months, that I would hardly recognise him."

There was an arch look in Mrs. Morton's eyes, and a merry flutter in her voice.

"Mrs. Morton! Now that is too bad!"

"Your experiment failed, did it not, dear?"

The door of the room in which the ladies were sitting opened at the moment, and Frederick Lee entered.

"Not entirely," whispered Kate, as she bent to the ear of her friend. "He is vastly improved—at least, in my eyes."

"And in others' eyes, too," thought Mrs. Morton, as she arose and returned the young man's smiling salutation.

"MY FORTUNE'S MADE."

My young friend, Cora Lee, was a gay, dashing girl, fond of dress, and looking always as if, to use a common saying, just out of a bandbox. Cora was a belle, of course, and had many admirers. Among the number of these, was a young man named Edward Douglass, who was the very "pink" of neatness in all matters pertaining to dress, and exceedingly particular in his observance of the little proprieties of life.

I saw, from the first, that if Douglass pressed his suit, Cora's heart would be an easy conquest, and so it proved.

"How admirably they are fitted for each other!" I remarked to my husband, on the night of their wedding. "Their tastes are similar, and their habits so much alike, that no violence will be done to the feelings of either in the more intimate associations that marriage brings. Both are neat in person and orderly by instinct, and both have good principles."

"From all present appearances, the match will be a good one," replied my husband. There was, I thought, something like reservation in his tone.

"Do you really think so?" I said, a little ironically, for Mr. Smith's approval of the marriage was hardly warm enough to suit my fancy.

"Oh, certainly! Why not?" he replied.

I felt a little fretted at my husband's mode of speaking, but made no further remark on the subject. He is never very enthusiastic nor sanguine, and did not mean, in this instance, to doubt the fitness of the parties for happiness in the marriage state—as I half imagined. For myself, I warmly approved of my friend's choice, and called her husband a lucky man to secure, for his companion through life, a woman so admirably fitted to make one like him happy. But a visit which I paid to Cora one day about six weeks after the honeymoon had expired, lessened my enthusiasm on the subject, and awoke some unpleasant doubts. It happened that I called soon after breakfast. Cora met me in the parlour, looking like a very fright. She wore a soiled and rumpled morning wrapper; her hair was in papers; and she had on dirty stockings, and a pair of old slippers down at the heels.

"Bless me, Cora!" said I. "What is the matter? Have you been sick?"

"No. Why do you ask? Is my dishabille rather on the extreme?"

"Candidly, I think it is, Cora," was my frank answer.

"Oh, well! No matter," she carelessly replied, "my fortune's made."

"I don't clearly understand you," said I.

"I'm married, you know."

"Yes; I am aware of that fact."

"No need of being so particular in dress now."

"Why not?"

"Didn't I just say?" replied Cora. "My fortune's made. I've got a husband."

Beneath an air of jesting, was apparent the real earnestness of my friend

"You dressed with a careful regard to taste and neatness, in order to win Edward's love?" said I.

"Certainly I did."

"And should you not do the same in order to retain it?"

"Why, Mrs. Smith! Do you think my husband's affection goes no deeper than my dress? I should be very sorry indeed to think that. He loves me for myself."

"No doubt of that in the world, Cora. But remember that he cannot see what is in your mind except by what you do or say. If he admires your taste, for instance, it is not from any abstract appreciation thereof, but because the taste manifests itself in what you do. And, depend upon it, he will find it a very hard matter to approve and admire your correct taste in dress, for instance, when you appear before him, day after day, in your present unattractive attire. If you do not dress well for your husband's eyes, for whose eyes, pray, do you dress? You are as neat when abroad as you were before your marriage."

"As to that, Mrs. Smith, common decency requires me to dress well when I go upon the street or into company, to say nothing of the pride one naturally feels in looking well."

"And does not the same common decency and natural pride argue as strongly in favour of your dressing well at home, and for the eye of your husband, whose approval and whose admiration must be dearer to you than the approval and admiration of the whole world?"

"But he doesn't want to see me rigged out in silks and satins all the time. A pretty bill my dressmaker would have against him! Edward has more sense than that, I flatter myself."

"Street or ball-room attire is one thing, Cora, and becoming home apparel another. We look for both in their places."

Thus I argued with the thoughtless young wife, but my words made no impression. When abroad, she dressed with exquisite taste, and was lovely to look upon; but at home, she was careless and slovenly, and made it almost impossible for those who saw her to realize that she was the brilliant beauty they had met in company but a short time before. But even this did not last long. I noticed, after a few months, that the habits of home were confirming themselves, and becoming apparent abroad. Her "fortune was made," and why should she now waste time or employ her thoughts about matters of personal appearance?

The habits of Mr. Douglass, on the contrary, did not change. He was as orderly as before, and dressed with the same regard to neatness. He never appeared at the breakfast-table in the morning without being shaved; nor did he lounge about in the evening in his shirt-sleeves. The slovenly habits into which Cora had fallen annoyed him seriously; and still more so, when her carelessness about her appearance began to manifest itself abroad as well as at home. When he hinted any thing on the subject, she did not hesitate to reply, in a jesting

9

manner, that her fortune was made. and she need not trouble herself any longer about how she looked.

Douglass did not feel very much complimented; but as he had his share of good sense, he saw that to assume a cold and offended manner would do no good.

"If your fortune is made, so is mine," he replied on one occasion, quite coolly and indifferently. Next morning he made his appearance at the breakfast table with a beard of twenty-four hours' growth.

"You haven't shaved this morning, dear," said Cora, to whose eyes the dirty-looking face of her husband was particularly unpleasant.

"No," he replied, carelessly. "It's a serious trouble to shave every day."

"But you look so much better with a cleanly-shaved face."

"Looks are nothing—ease and comfort every thing," said Douglass.

"But common decency, Edward."

"I see nothing indecent in a long beard," replied the husband.

Still Cora argued, but in vain. Her husband went off to his business with his unshaven face.

"I don't know whether to shave or not," said Douglass next morning, running his hand over his rough face, upon which was a beard of forty-eight hours' growth. His wife had hastily thrown on a wrapper, and, with slip-shod feet and head like a mop, was lounging in a large rocking-chair, awaiting the breakfast-bell.

"For mercy's sake, Edward, don't go any longer

with that shockingly dirty face," spoke up Cora. "If you knew how dreadfully you look!"

"Looks are nothing," replied Edward, stroking his beard.

"Why, what's come over you all at once?"

"Nothing; only it's such a trouble to shave every day."

"But you didn't shave yesterday."

"I know; I am just as well off to-day as if I had. So much saved, at any rate."

But Cora urged the matter, and her husband finally yielded, and mowed down the luxuriant growth of beard.

"How much better you do look!" said the young wife. "Now don't go another day without shaving."

"But why should I take so much trouble about mere looks? I'm just as good with a long beard as with a short one. It's a great deal of trouble to shave every day. You can love me just as well; and why need I care about what others say or think?"

On the following morning, Douglass appeared not only with a long beard, but with a bosom and collar that were both soiled and rumpled.

"Why, Edward! How you do look!" said Cora. "You've neither shaved nor put on a clean shirt."

Edward stroked his face and run his fingers along the edge of his collar, remarking, indifferently, as he did so—

"It's no matter. I look well enough. This being so very particular in dress is waste of time, and I'm getting tired of it."

And in this trim Douglass went off to his business, much to the annoyance of his wife, who could not bear to see her husband looking so slovenly.

Gradually the declension from neatness went on, until Edward was quite a match for his wife; and yet, strange to say, Cora had not taken the hint, broad as it was. In her own person she was as untidy as ever.

About six months after their marriage, we invited a few friends to spend a social evening with us, Cora and her husband among the number. Cora came alone, quite early, and said that her husband was very much engaged, and could not come until after tea. My young friend had not taken much pains with her attire. Indeed, her appearance mortified me, as it contrasted so decidedly with that of the other ladies who were present; and I could not help suggesting to her that she was wrong in being so indifferent about her dress. But she laughingly replied to me—

"You know my fortune's made now, Mrs. Smith. I can afford to be negligent in these matters. It's a great waste of time to dress so much."

I tried to argue against this, but could make no impression upon her.

About an hour after tea, and while we were all engaged in pleasant conversation, the door of the parlour opened, and in walked Mr. Douglass. At first glance I thought I must be mistaken. But no, it was Edward himself. But what a figure he did cut! His uncombed hair was standing up, in stiff spikes, in a hundred different directions; his face could not have felt the touch of a razor for two or three days; and he was guiltless of clean linen for at least the same length of time. His vest was soiled; his boots unblacked; and there was an unmistakable hole in one of his elbows.

"Why, Edward!" exclaimed his wife, with a look of mortification and distress, as her husband came across the room, with a face in which no consciousness of the figure he cut could be detected.

"Why, my dear fellow! What is the matter?" said my husband, frankly; for he perceived that the ladies were beginning to titter, and that the gentlemen were looking at each other, and trying to repress their risible tendencies; and therefore deemed it best to throw off all reserve on the subject.

"The matter? Nothing's the matter, I believe. Why do you ask?" Douglass looked grave.

"Well may he ask, what's the matter?" broke in Cora, energetically. "How could you come here in such a plight?"

"In such a plight?" And Edward looked down at himself, felt his beard, and ran his fingers through his hair. "What's the matter? Is any thing wrong?"

"You look as if you'd just waked up from a nap of a week with your clothes on, and come off without washing your face or combing your hair," said my husband.

"Oh!" And Edward's countenance brightened a little. Then he said with much gravity of manner—

"I've been extremely hurried of late; and only left my store a few minutes ago. I hardly thought it worth while to go home to dress up. I knew we were all friends here. Besides, *as my fortune is made*"—and he glanced with a look not to be mis-

9*

taken toward his wife—"I don't feel called upon to give as much attention to mere dress as formerly. Before I was married, it was necessary to be particular in these matters, but now it's of no consequence."

I turned toward Cora. Her face was like crimson. In a few moments she arose and went quickly from the room. I followed her, and Edward came after us pretty soon. He found his wife in tears, and sobbing almost hysterically.

"I've got a carriage at the door," said he to me, aside, half laughing, half serious. "So help her on with her things, and we'll retire in disorder."

"But it's too bad in you, Mr. Douglass," replied I.

"Forgive me for making your house the scene of this lesson to Cora," he whispered. "It had to be given, and I thought I could venture to trespass upon your forbearance."

"I'll think about that," said I, in return.

In a few minutes Cora and her husband retired, and in spite of good breeding and every thing else, we all had a hearty laugh over the matter, on my return to the parlour, where I explained the curious little scene that had just occurred.

How Cora and her husband settled the affair between themselves, I never inquired. But one thing is certain, I never saw her in a slovenly dress afterward, at home or abroad. She was cured.

THE GOOD MATCH.

"My heart is now at rest," remarked Mrs. Presstman to her sister, Mrs. Markland. "Florence has done so well. The match is such a good one."

Mrs. Presstman spoke with animation, but her sister's countenance remained rather grave.

"Mr. Barker is worth at least eighty thousand dollars," resumed Mrs. Presstman. "And my husband says, that if he prospers in business as he has done for the last ten years, he will be the richest merchant in the city. Don't you think we have been fortunate in marrying Florence so well?"

"So far as the securing of wealth goes, Florence has certainly done very well," returned Mrs. Markland. "But, surely, sister, you have a higher idea of marriage than to suppose that wealth in a husband is the primary thing. The quality of his mind is of much more importance."

"Oh, certainly, that is not to be lost sight of. Mr. Barker is an excellent man. Every one speaks well of him. No one stands higher in the community than he does."

"That may be. But the general estimation in which a man is held does not, by any means, determine his fitness to become the husband of one like Florence. I think that when I was here last spring,

there was some talk of her preference for a young
physician.   Was such really the case?"

"There was something of that kind," replied Mrs.
Presstman, the colour becoming a very little deeper
on her cheek—"a foolish notion of the girl's.   But
that was broken off long ago.   It would not do.   We
could not afford to let her marry a young doctor with
a poor practice.   We knew her to be worthy something much higher, as the result has shown."

"Doctor Estill, I believe, was his name?"

"Yes."

"I remember him very well—and liked him much.
Was Mr. Barker preferred by Florence to Doctor
Estill?"

"Why, yes—no—not at first," half-stammered
Mrs. Presstman.   "That is, you know, she was foolish, like all young girls, and thought she loved him.
But that passed away.   She is now as happy as she
can be."

Mrs. Markland felt that it was not exactly right to
press this matter now that the mischief, if any there
were, had been done, and so remarked no further
upon the subject.   But the admission made in her
sister's reply to her last question pained her.   It
corroborated a suspicion that crossed her mind, when
she saw her niece, that all was not right within—
that the good match which had been made was only
good in appearance.   She had loved Florence for
the innocence, purity, and elevation of soul that so
sweetly characterized her.   She knew her to be sus-
ceptible of tender impressions, and capable of loving
deeply an object really worthy of her love.   This
plant had been, she feared, removed from the warm

green-house of home, where the earth had touched tenderly its delicate roots, while its leaves put forth in a genial air, and placed in a hard soil and a chilling atmosphere, still to live on, but with its beauty and fragrance gone. She might be mistaken. But appearances troubled her.

Mrs. Markland lived in a neighbouring city, and was on a visit to her sister. During the two weeks that elapsed, while paying this visit, she heard a great deal about the excellent match that Florence had made. No one of the acquaintances of the family had any thing to say that was not congratulatory. More than one mother of an unmarried daughter, she had good cause for concluding, envied her sister the happiness of having the rich Mr. Barker for a son-in-law. When she parted with her niece, on the eve of her return home, there were tears in her mild blue eyes. It was natural—for Florence loved her aunt, and to part with her was painful. Still, those tears troubled Mrs. Markland. She thought of them hours, and days, and months after, as a token that all was not right in her gentle breast.

Briefly let us now sketch a scene that passed twenty years from this period. Twenty years! That is a long time. Yes—but it is a period that tests the truth or falsity of the leading principles with which we set out in life. Twenty years! Ah! how many, even long before that time elapses, prove the fallaciousness of their hopes! discover the sandy foundation upon which they have built!

Let us introduce Mrs. Barker. Her husband has realized even more than he had hoped for, in the item of wealth. He is worth a million.

Rather a small sum in his eye, it is true, now that
he possesses it. And from this very fact, its small-
ness, he is not happy—for is not Mr. T—— worth
three millions of dollars? Mr. T——, who is no
better, if as good as he is? But what of Mrs.
Barker? Ah, yes. Let us see how time has passed
with her. Let us see if the hours have danced along
with her to measures of glad music, or in cadence
with a pensive strain. Has hers indeed been a *good
match?* We shall see.

Is that sedate-looking woman, with such a cold
expression upon her face, who sits in that elabo-
rately furnished saloon, or parlour, dreamily looking
into the glowing grate, Mrs. Barker? Yes, that is
the woman who made a *good match.* Can this indeed
be so? I see, in imagination, a gentle, loving creature, whose eyes and ears are open to all things
beautiful in creation, and whose heart is moved by
all that is good and true. Impelled by the very nature into which she has been born—woman's nature
—her spirit yearns for high, holy, interior companionship. She enters into that highest, holiest, most
interior relationship—marriage. She must be purely
happy. Is this so? Can the woman we have introduced at the end of twenty years be the same being
with this gentle girl? Alas! that we should have it
to say that it is so. There has been no affliction to
produce this change—no misfortune. The children
she has borne are all about her, and wealth has been
poured liberally into her lap. No external wish has
been ungratified. Why, then, should her face wear
habitually so strange an expression as it does?

She had been seated for more than half an hour

in an abstract mood, when some one came in. She knew the step. It was that of her husband. But she did not turn to him, nor seem conscious of his presence. He merely glanced toward his wife, and then sat down at some distance from her, and took up a newspaper. Thus they remained until a bell announced the evening meal, when both arose and passed in silence to the tea-room. There they were joined by their four children, the eldest at that lovely age when the girl has blushed into young womanhood. All arranged themselves about the table, the younger children conversing together in an under tone, but the father, and mother, and Florence, the oldest child, remaining silent, abstracted, and evidently unhappy from some cause.

The mother and daughter eat but little, and that compulsorily. After the meal was finished, the latter retired to her own apartment, the other children remained with their books in the family sitting-room, and Mr. and Mrs. Barker returned to the parlour.

"I am really out of all patience with you and Florence!" the former said, angrily, as he seated himself beside his wife, in front of the grate. "One would think some terrible calamity were about to happen."

Mrs. Barker made no reply to this. In a moment or two her husband went on, in a dogmatical tone.

"It's the very best match the city affords. Show me another in any way comparable. Is not Lorimer worth at least two millions?—and is not Harman his only son and heir? Surely you and the girl must both be beside yourselves to think of objecting for a single moment."

"A good match is not always made so by wealth," Mrs. Barker returned, in a firm voice, compressing her lips tightly, as she closed the brief sentence.

"You are beside yourself," said the husband, half sneeringly.

"Perhaps I am," somewhat meekly replied Mrs. Barker. Then becoming suddenly excited from the quick glancing of certain thoughts through her mind, she retorted angrily. Her husband did not hesitate to reply in a like spirit. Then ensued a war of words, which ended in a positive declaration that Florence should marry Harman Lorimer. At this the mother burst into tears and left the room.

After that declaration was made, Mrs. Barker knew that further opposition on her part was useless. Florence was gradually brought over by the force of angry threats, persuasions, and arguments, so as finally to consent to become the wife of a man from whom her heart turned with instinctive aversion. But every one called it such a good match, and congratulated the father and mother upon the fortunate issue.

What Mrs. Barker suffered before, during, and after the brilliant festivities that accompanied her tenderly-loved daughter's sacrifice, cannot all be known. Her own heart's history for twenty long years came up before her, and every page of that history she read over, with a weeping spirit, as the history of her sweet child for the dreary future. How many a leaf in her heart had been touched by the frost; had withered, shrunk, and dropped from affection's stem—how many a bud had failed to show its promised petals—how many a blossom had drooped and died ere the tender germ in its bosom could come forth into hardy existence. Inanimate golden leaves, and buds, and blossoms—nay, even fruits were a poor substitute for these. A woman's heart cannot be satisfied with them.

In her own mind, obduracy and coldness had supervened to the first states of disappointed affection. But her heart had rebelled through long, long years against the violence to which it had been subjected—and the calmness, or rather indifference, that at last followed was only like ice upon the surface of a stream—the water still flowing on beneath. Death to the mother would have been a willing sacrifice, could it have saved her child from the living death that she had suffered. But it would not. The father was a resolute tyrant. Money was his god, and to that god he offered up even his child in sacrifice.

Need the rambling hints contained in this brief sketch—this dim outline—be followed by any enforcing reflections? An opposite picture, full of light and warmth, might be drawn, but would it tend to bring the truth to clearer perception, where mothers —true mothers—mothers in spirit as well as in name—are those to whom we hold up the first picture? We think not.

Wealth, reputation, honours, high intelligence in a man—all or either of these—do not constitute him a good match for your child. Marriage is of the heart—the blending of affection with affection, and thought with thought. How, then, can one who loves all that is innocent, and pure, and holy, become interiorly conjoined with a man who is a gross,

selfish sensualist? a man who finds happiness only
in the external possession of wealth, or honours, or
in the indulgence of luxuries? It is impossible! Take
away these, and give her, in their stead, one with
whom her affections can blend in perfect harmony—
one with whom she can become united as one—and
earth will be to her a little heaven.

In the opposite course, alas! the evil does not
always stop with your own child. The curse is too
often continued unto the third and fourth genera-
tion—yea, even through long succeeding ages—to
eternity itself! Who can calculate the evil that may
flow from a single perversion of the marriage union—
that is, a marriage entered into from other than the
true motives? None but God himself!

THE BROTHER'S TEMPTATION.

"COME, Henry," said Blanche Armour to her brother, who had seemed unusually silent and thoughtful since tea time,—"I want you to read while I make this cap for ma."

"Excuse me, Blanche, if you please, I don't feel like reading to-night," the brother replied, shading his face both from the light and the penetrating glance of his sister, as he spoke.

Blanche did not repeat the request, for it was a habit with her never to urge her brother; nor, indeed, any one, to do a thing for which he seemed disinclined. She, therefore, took her work-basket, and sat down by the centre-table, without saying any thing farther, and commenced sewing. But she did not feel quite easy, for it was too apparent that Henry was disturbed about something. For several days he had seemed more than usually reserved and thoughtful. Now he was gloomy as well as thoughtful. Of course, there was a cause for this. And as this cause was hidden from Blanche, she could not but feel troubled. Several times during the evening she attempted to draw him out into conversation, but he would reply to her in monosyllables, and then fall back into his state of silent abstraction of mind. Once or twice he got up and walked across the floor, and then again resumed his seat, as if he had compelled himself to sit down by

a strong effort of the will. Thus the time passed
away, until the usual hour of retiring for the night
came, when Blanche put up her work, and rising
from her chair by the centre-table, went to Henry,
and stooping down over him, as he lay half reclined
upon the sofa, kissed him tenderly, and murmured
an affectionate " good night."

" Good night, dear," he returned, without rising
or adding another word.

Blanche lingered a moment, and then, with a repressed sigh, left the room, and retired to her chamber. She could not understand her brother's strange
mood. For him to be troubled and silent was altogether new. And the cause? Why should he conceal it from her, toward whom, till now, he had never
withheld any thing that gave him either pleasure or
pain?

The moment Blanche retired, the whole manner
of Henry Armour changed. He arose from the sofa
and commenced walking the floor with rapid steps,
while the deep lines upon his forehead and his
strongly compressed lips showed him to be labouring
under some powerful mental excitement. He continued to walk thus hurriedly backward and forward for the space of half an hour; when, as if
some long debated point had been at last decided,
he grasped the parlour door with a firm hand, threw
it open, took from the rack his hat, cloak, and cane,
and in a few moments was in the street.

The jar of the street door, as it closed, was
distinctly heard by Blanche, and this caused the
troubled feeling which had oppressed her all the
evening, to change into one of anxiety. Where could

Henry be going at this late hour? He rarely stayed out beyond ten o'clock; and she had never before known him to leave the house after the usual bedtime of the family. His going out had, of course, something to do with his unhappy mood. What could it mean? She could not suspect him of any wrong. She knew him to be too pure-minded and honourable. But there was mystery connected with his conduct—and this troubled her. She had just laid aside a book, that she had taken up for the purpose of reading a few pages before retiring for the night, and commenced disrobing herself, when the sound of the door closing after her brother startled her, and caused her to pause and think. She could not now retire, for to sleep would be impossible. She, therefore, drew a shawl about her, and again resumed her book, determined to sit up until Henry's return. But little that she read made a very distinct impression on her mind. Her thoughts were with her brother, whom she tenderly loved, and had learned to confide in as one of pure sentiments and firm principles.

While Henry Armour still lingered at home in moody indecision of mind, a small party of young men were assembled in an upper room of a celebrated refectory, drinking, smoking, and indulging in conversation, a large portion of which would have shocked a modest ear. They were all members of wealthy and respectable families. Some had passed their majority, and others still lingered between nineteen and twenty-one,—that dangerous age for a young man—especially if he be so unfortunate as to have little to do, and a liberal supply of pocket money.

O*

"Confound the fellow! What keeps him so long?" said one of the company, looking at his watch "It's nearly ten o'clock, and he has not made his appearance."

"Whom do you mean? Armour?" asked another.

"Certainly I do. He promised to join us again to-night."

"So he did! But I'll bet a pewter sixpence he won't come."

"Why?"

"His sister won't let him. Don't you know that he is tied to her apron string almost every night, the silly fellow! Why don't he be a man, and enjoy life as it goes?"

"Sure enough! What is life worth, if its pleasures are all to be sacrificed for a sister?" returned the other, sneeringly.

"Here! Pass that champagne," interrupted one of the company. "Let Harry Armour break his engagement for a sister if he likes. That needn't mar our enjoyment. There are enough of us here for a regular good time."

"Here's a toast," cried another, as he lifted a sparkling glass to his lips—"Pleasant dreams to the old folks!"

"Good! Good! Good!" passed round the table, about which the young revellers were gathered, and each drained a glass to the well understood sentiment.

In the mean time, young Armour had left his home, having decided at last, and after a long struggle with himself, to join this gay company, as he had agreed to do. It was, in fact, a little club, formed a short time previous, the members of which met once a week to eat, drink, smoke, and corrupt each other by ridiculing those salutary moral restraints which, once laid aside, leave the thoughtless youth in imminent danger of ruin.

Henry Armour had been blessed with a sister a year or two older than himself, who loved him tenderly. The more rapid development of her mind, as well as body, had given her the appearance of maturity that enabled her to exercise a strong influence over him. Of the dangers that beset the path of a young man, she knew little or nothing. The constant effort which she made to render home agreeable to her brother by consulting his tastes, and entering into every thing that seemed to give him pleasure, did not, therefore, spring from a wish to guard him from the world's allurements; it was the spontaneous result of a pure fraternal affection. But it had the right effect. To him, there was no place like home; nor any smile so alluring, or voice so sweet, as his sister's. And abroad, no company possessed a perfect charm, unless Blanche were one of its members.

This continued until Henry gained his twenty-second year, when, as a law student, he found himself thrown more and more into the company of young men of his own age, and the same standing in society. An occasional ride out with one and another of these, at which times an hour at least was always spent in a public house, opened to him new scenes in life, and for a young man of lively, buoyant mind, not altogether unattractive. That there was danger in these paths he did not attempt to disguise from himself. More than one, or two, or three, whom he met on almost every visit he made to a fashionable resort for young men, about five miles from the city, showed too strong indications of having passed beyond the bounds of self-control, as well in their use of wines and stronger drinks as in their conduct, which was too free from those external decent restraints that we look for even in men who make no pretensions to virtue. But he did not fear for himself. The exhibitions which these made of themselves instinctively disgusted him. Still, he did not perceive that he was less and less shocked at some things he beheld, and more than at first inclined to laugh at follies which verged too nearly upon moral delinquencies.

Gradually his circle of acquaintance with young men of the gay class extended, and a freer participation with them in many of their pleasures came as a natural consequence.

"Come," said one of them to him, as the two met in the street, by accident, one evening,—"I want you to go with me."

"But why should I go with you? Or, rather, where are you going?" asked Armour.

"To meet some of our friends down at C——'s," replied the young man.

"What are you going to do there?" farther inquired Armour.

"Nothing more than to drink a glass of wine, and have some pleasant chit-chat. So come along."

"Will I be welcome?"

"Certainly you will. I'll guarantee that. Some half dozen of us have formed a little club, and each member has the privilege of inviting any one he pleases. To-night I invite you, and on the next evening I expect to see you present, not as a guest, but as a member. So come along, and see how you like us."

Armour had no definite object in view. He had walked out, because he felt rather listless at home, Blanche having retired with a sick headache. It required, therefore, no persuasion to induce him to yield to the friend's invitation. Arrived at C——'s, a fashionable house of refreshment, the two young men passed up stairs and entered one of the private apartments of the house, which they found handsomely furnished and brilliantly lighted. In this, gathered around a circular, or rather oblong table, were five or six young men, nearly all of them well known to Armour. On the table were bottles of wine and glasses—the latter filled.

"Just in time!" cried the president of the club. "Henry Armour, I bid you welcome! Here's a place waiting for you," placing his hand upon a chair by his side as he spoke. "And now," as Armour seated himself, "let me fill your glass. We were waiting for a sentiment to find its way out of some brain as you came in, and our brimming glasses had stood untasted for more than a minute. Can't you help us to a toast?"

"Here's to good fellowship!" said Armour, promptly lifting his glass, and touching it to that of the president.

"To be drunk standing," added the president.

All rose on the instant, and drank with mock solemnity to the sentiment of their guest.

Then followed brilliant flashes of wit, or what was thought to be wit. To these succeeded the song, the jest, the story,—and to these again the sparkling wine-cup. Gayly thus passed the hours, until midnight stole quietly upon the thoughtless revellers. Surprised, on reference to his watch, to find that it was one o'clock, Armour arose and begged to be excused.

"I move that our guest be excused on one condition," said the friend who had brought him to the company. "And that is, on his promise to meet with us again, on this evening next week."

"What do you think of the condition?" asked the president, who, like nearly all of the rest, was rather the worse for the wine he had taken, looking at Armour as he spoke.

"I agree to it with pleasure," was the prompt reply.

"Another drink before you go, then," said the president, "and I will give the toast. Fill up your glasses."

The bottle again passed round the table.

"Here's to a good fellow!" was the sentiment announced. It was received standing. Armour then retired with bewildered senses. The gay scene that had floated before his eyes, and in which himself had been an actor, and the freedom with which he had taken wine, left him confused, almost in regard to his own identity. He did not seem to himself the same person he had been a few hours before. A new world had opened before him, and he had, almost involuntarily, entered into, and become a citizen of that world. Long after he had reached his home, and retired to his bed, did his imagination revel amid the scenes he had just left. In sleep, too, fancy was busy. But here came a change. Serpents would too often glide across the table around which the gay company, himself a member, were assembled; or some other sudden and more appalling change scatter into fragments the bright phantasma of his dreams.

The sober morning found him in a soberer mood. Calm, cold, unimpassioned reflection came. What had he been doing? What path had he entered; and whither did it lead? These were questions that would intrude themselves, and clamour for an answer. He shut his eyes and endeavoured again to sleep. Waking thoughts were worse than the airy terrors which had visited him in sleep. At length he arose, with dull pains in his head, and an oppressive sluggishness of the whole body. But more painful than his own reflections, or the physical consequences of the last night's irregularity, was the thought of meeting Blanche, and bearing the glance of her innocent eyes. He felt that he had been among the impure, —and worse, that he had enjoyed their impure sentiments, and indulged with them in excess of wine. The taint was upon him, and the pure mind of his sister must instinctively perceive it. These thoughts made him wretched. He really dreaded to meet her. But this could not be avoided.

"You do not look well, brother," said Blanche, almost as soon as she saw him.

"I am not well," he replied, avoiding her steady look. "My head aches, and I feel dull and heavy."

"What has caused it, brother?" the affectionate girl asked, with a look and voice of real concern.

Now this was, of all others, the question that Henry was least prepared to answer. He could not utter a direct falsehood. From that his firm principles shrunk. Nor could he equivocate, for he considered equivocation little better than a direct falsehood. "Why should I wish to conceal any part of my conduct from her?" he asked himself, in his dilemma. But the answer was instant and conclusive. His participation in the revelry of the last night was a thing not to be whispered in her ear. Not being prepared, then, to tell the truth, and shrinking from falsehood and equivocation, Armour preferred silence as the least evil of the three. The question of Blanche was not, therefore, answered. At the breakfast-table, his father and mother remarked upon his appearance. To this, he merely replied that he was not well. As soon as the meal was over, he went out, glad to escape the eye of Blanche, which, it seemed to him, rested searchingly upon him all the while.

A walk of half an hour in the fresh morning air dispelled the dull pain in his head, and restored his whole system to a more healthy tone. This drove away, to some extent, the oppressive feeling of self-condemnation he had indulged. The scenes of the previous evening, though silly enough for sensible young men to engage in, seemed less objectionable than they had appeared to him on his first review. To laugh involuntarily at several remembered jests and stories, the points of which were not exactly the most chaste or reverential, marked the change that

a short period had produced in his state of mind.
During that day, he did not fall in with any of his
wild companions of the last evening, too many of
whom had already fairly entered the road to ruin.
The evening was spent at home, in the society of
Blanche. He read while she sewed, or he turned
for her the leaves of her music book, or accompanied
her upon the flute while she played him a favourite
air upon the piano. Conversation upon books,
music, society, and other topics of interest, filled up
the time not occupied in these mental recreations,
and added zest, variety, and unflagging interest to
the gently-passing hours. On the next evening
they attended a concert, and on the next a party.
On that succeeding, Henry went out to see a friend
of a different character from any of those with whom
he had passed the hours a few nights previous—a
friend about his own age, of fixed habits and principles, who, like himself, was preparing for the bar.
With him he spent a more rational evening than
with the others, and, what was better, no sting was
left behind.

Still, young Armour could never think of the
"club" without having his mind thrown into a
tumult. It awoke into activity opposing principles.
Good and evil came in contact, and battled for su-
premacy. There was in his mind a clear conviction
that to indulge in dissipation of that character,
would be injurious both to moral and physical health.
And yet, having tasted of the delusive sweets, he
was tempted to further indulgence Meeting with
ome two or three of the "members' during the
week, and listening to their extravagant praise of

11

the "club," and the pleasure of uniting in unrestrained social intercourse, made warm by generous wine, tended to make more active the contest going on within—for the good principles that had been stored up in his mind were not to be easily silenced. Their hold upon his character was deep. They had entered into its warp and woof, and were not to be eradicated or silenced in a moment. As the time for the next meeting of the club approached, this battle grew more violent. The condition into which it had brought him by the arrival of the night on which he had promised again to join his gay friends, the reader has already seen. He was still unable to decide his course of action. Inclination prompted him to go; good principles opposed. "But then I have passed my word that I would go, and my word must be inviolable." Here reason came in to the aid of his inclinations, and made in their favour a strong preponderance.

We have seen that, yet undecided, he lingered at home, but in a state of mind strangely different from any in which his sister had ever seen him. Still debating the question, he lay, half reclined upon the sofa, when Blanche touched her innocent lips to his, and murmured a tender good-night. That kiss passed through his frame like an electric current. It came just as his imagination had pictured an impure image, and scattered it instantly. But no decision of the question had yet been made, and the withdrawal of Blanche only took off an external restraint from his feelings. He quietly arose and commenced pacing the floor. This he continued for some time. At last the decision was made.

"I have passed my word, and that ends it," said he, and instantly left the house. Without permitting himself to review the matter again, although a voice within asked loudly to be heard, he walked hastily in the direction of the club-room. In ten minutes he gained the door, opened it without pausing, and stood in the midst of the wild company within. His entrance was greeted with shouts of welcome, and the toast, "Here's to a good fellow!" with which he had parted from them, was repeated on his return, all standing as it was drunk.

To this followed a sentiment that cannot be repeated here. It was too gross. All drunk to it but Armour. He could not, for it involved a foul slander upon the other sex, and he had a sister whose pure kiss was yet warm upon his lips. The individual who proposed the toast marked this omission, and pointed it out by saying—

"What's the matter, Harry? Is not the wine good?"

The colour mounted to the young man's face as he replied, with a forced smile—

"Yes, much better than the sentiment."

"What ails the sentiment?" asked the propounder of it, in a tone of affected surprise.

"I have a sister," was the brief, firm reply of Armour.

"So Charley, here, was just saying," retorted the other, with a merry laugh; "and, what is more, that he'd bet a sixpence you were tied to her apron-string, and would not be here to-night! Ha! ha!"

The effect of this upon the mind of Armour was decisive. He loved, nay, almost revered his sister.

She had been like an angel of innocence about his
path from early years. He knew her to be as pure
as the mountain snow-flake. And yet that sister's
influence over him was sneered at by one who had
just uttered a foul-mouthed slander upon her whole
sex. The scales fell instantly from his eyes. He
saw the dangerous ground upon which he stood;
while the character of his associates appeared in a
new light. They were on a road that he did not
wish to travel. There were serpents concealed
amid the flowers that sprung along their path, and
he shuddered as he thought of their poisonous fangs.
Quick as a flash of light, these things passed through
his mind, and caused him to act with instant resolution. Rising from the chair he had already taken,
he retired, without a word, from the room. A
sneering laugh followed him, but he either heard it
not or gave it no heed.

The book which Blanche resumed after she had
heard her brother go out, soon ceased to interest
her. She was too much troubled about him to be
able to fix her mind on any thing else. His singularly disturbed state, and the fact of his having
left the house at that late hour, caused her to feel
great uneasiness. This was beginning to excite her
imagination, and to cause her to fancy many reasons
for his strange conduct, none of which were calculated in any degree to allay the anxiety she felt.
Anxiety was fast verging upon serious alarm, when
she heard the sound of footsteps approaching the
house. She listened breathlessly. Surely it was
the sound of Henry's footsteps! Yes! Yes! It
was indeed her brother. The tears gushed from her

eyes as she heard him enter below and pass up to his chamber. He was safe from harm, and for this her heart lifted itself up in fervent thankfulness! How near he had been to falling, that pure-minded maiden never knew, nor how it had been her image and the remembrance of her parting kiss that had saved him in the moment of his greatest danger. Happy he who is blest with such a sister! And happier still, if her innocence be suffered to over-shadow him in the hours of temptation!

THE HOME OF TASTE.

THERE are three words, in the utterance of which more power over the feelings is gained than in the utterance of any other words in the language. These are "Mother," "Home," and "Heaven." Each appeals to a different emotion—each bears influence over the heart from the cradle to the grave.—And just in the degree that this influence is active, are man's best interests secured for time and eternity.

Only of "home" do we here intend to speak; and, in particular, as to the influence of the home of taste. We hear much, in these days, of enlarging the sphere of woman's social duties; as if, in the sphere of home, nothing remained to be done, and she must either fold her hands in idleness, or step

forth to engage with man in life's sterner conflicts.
But it is not true that our homes are as they might
be, if their presiding genius fully comprehended all
that was needed to make home what the word im-
plies. Among those in poorer circumstances, this
is especially so. They are too apt to regard matters
of taste as mere superfluities; to speak lightly of
order, neatness, and ornament; to think time and
money spent on such things as useless. But this is
a serious mistake, involving, often, the most lament-
able consequences.

If we expect our children to grow up with a love
for things pure and orderly, we must surround them
with the representations thereof in the homes where
first impressions are formed. The mind rests upon
and is moulded by things external to a far greater
extent than many suppose. These are not only a
mirror, reflecting all that passes before the surface, but
a highly sensitive mirror, that, like the Daguerreotype
plate, retains the image it receives. If the image
be orderly and beautiful, it will ever have power to
excite orderly and beautiful thoughts in the mind;
but if it be impure and disorderly, its lasting influence will be debasing. If you meet with a coarse,
vulgar-minded man or woman, and are able to trace
back the thread of life until the period of early
years, you will be sure to find the existence of coarse
and vulgar influences; and, in most cases, the opposite will alike be found to hold good.

There is no excuse for disorder in a household, no
matter how small or how low the range of income,
but idleness or indifference. The time required to
maintain neatness, order, and cleanliness, is small,

it the will is active and the hands prompt. Every home, even the poorest, may become a home of taste, and present order and forms of beauty, if there is only a willing purpose in the mind.

It is often charged upon men—particularly operatives with low wages—that they do not love their homes, preferring to spend their evening hours in bar-rooms, or wandering about with other men as little attracted by the household sphere as themselves, until the time for rest. If you were to go into the homes of such, in most cases, you would hardly wonder at the aversion manifested. The dirty, disordered rooms, which their toiling wives deem it a waste of time and labour to make tidy and comfortable for their reception, it would be a perversion to call homes. Home attracts; but these repel. And so, with a feeling of discomfort, the men wander away, fall into temptation, and usually spend, in self-indulgence, money that otherwise would have gone to increase home comforts, if there had been any to increase. And so it is, in its degree, in the homes of every class. The more pleasant, orderly, and tasteful home is made, in all its departments and associations, the stronger is its attractive power, and the more potent its influence over those who are required to go forth into the world and meet its thousand allurements. If every thing is right there, it will surely draw them back, with a steady retraction, through all their absent moments, and they will feel, on repassing the threshold, that, in the wide, wide world, there is no spot to them so full of blessings.

What true woman does not aspire to be the genius of such a home?

THE TWO SYSTEMS.

"It's no use to talk; I can't do it. The idea of punishing a child in cold blood makes me shiver all over. I certainly think that, in the mind of any one who can do it, there must be a latent vein of cruelty."

This remark was made by Mrs. Stanley to her friend and visiter Mrs. Noland.

"I have known parents," she continued, "who would go about executing some punishment with a coolness and deliberation that to me was frightful. No promise, no appeal, no tear of alarm or agony, from the penitent little culprit, would have the least effect. The law must be fulfilled even to the jot and tittle."

"The disobedient child, doubtless, knew the law," remarked Mrs. Noland.

"Perhaps so. But even if it did, great allowance ought to be made for the ardor with which children seek the gratification of their desires, and the readiness with which they forget."

"No parent should lay down a law not right in itself; nor one obedience to which was not good for the child."

"But it is very hard to do this We have not the

wisdom of Solomon. Every day, nay, almost every hour, we err in judgment; and especially in a matter so little understood as the management of children."

"Better, then, have very few laws, and them of the clearest kind. But, having them, implicit obedience should be exacted. At least, that is my rule."

"And you punish for every infraction?"

"Certainly. But, I am always sure that the child is fully aware of his fault, and let my punishment be graduated according to the wilfulness of the act."

"And you do this coolly?"

"Oh, yes. I never punish a child while I am excited with a feeling of indignation for the offence."

"If I waited for that to pass off, I could never punish one of my children."

"Do you find, under this system, that your children are growing up orderly and obedient?"

"No, indeed! Of course I do not. Who ever heard of orderly and obedient children? In fact, who would wish their children to be mere automatons? I am sure I would not. They are, by nature, restless, and impatient of control. It will not do to break down their young spirits. As for punishments, I don't believe much in them, any how. I have an idea that the less they are brought into requisition the better. They harden children. Kindness, long suffering, and forbearance will accomplish a great deal more, and in the end be better for the child."

At this moment a little fellow came sliding into the parlour, with a look that said plainly enough, "I know you don't want me here."

"Run out, Charley, dear," said Mrs. Stanley, in a mild voice.

But Charley did not seem to notice his mother's words, for he continued advancing toward her, until he was by her side, when he paused and looked the visiter steadily in the face.

"Charley, you must run out, my dear," said Mrs. Stanley, in a firmer and more decided voice.

But Charley only leaned heavily against his mother, not heeding in the smallest degree her words. Knowing how impossible it would be to get the child out of the room, without a resort to violence, Mrs. Stanley said no more to him, but continued the conversation with her friend. She had only spoken a few words, however, before Charley interrupted her by saying—

"Mother!—Mother!—Give me a piece of cake."

"No, my son. You have had cake enough this afternoon," replied Mrs. Stanley.

"Oh yes, do, mother, give me a piece of cake."

"It will make you sick, Charley."

"No, it won't. Please give me some."

"I had rather not."

"Yes, mother. Oh do! I want a piece of cake.'

"Go 'way, Charles, and don't tease me."

There was a slight expression of impatience in the mother's voice. The child ceased his importunities for a few moments, but just as Mrs. Stanley had commenced a sentence, intended to embody some wise saying in regard to the management of children, the little boy broke in upon her with—

"I say, mother, give me a piece of cake, won't you?" in quite a loud voice.

Mrs. Stanley felt irritated by this importunity, but she governed herself. Satisfied that there would be no peace unless the cake were forthcoming, she said, looking affectionately at the child :

"Poor little fellow ! I suppose he does feel hungry. I don't think another piece of cake will hurt him Excuse me a moment, Mrs. Noland."

The cake was obtained by Charley in the very way he had, hundreds of times before, accomplished his purpose, that is, by teasing it out of his mother. For the next ten minutes the friends conversed, unmolested. At the end of that time Charley again made his appearance.

"Go up into the nursery, and stay with Ellen," said Mrs. Stanley.

The child took no notice, whatever, of this direction, but walked steadily up to where his mother was sitting, saying, as he paused by her side—

"I want another piece of cake."

"Not any more, my son."

"Yes, mother. Give me some more."

"No." This was spoken in a very positive way.

Charley began to beg in a whining tone, which, not producing the desired effect, soon rose into a well-defined cry.

"I declare ! I never saw such a hungry set as my children are. They will eat constantly from morning until night." Mrs. Stanley did not say this in the most amiable tone of voice.

"Mother ! I want a piece of cake," cried Charley.

"I'll give you one little piece more ; but, remember, that it will be the last ; so don't ask me again."

Charley stopped crying at once. Mrs. Stanley went out with him. As soon as she was far enough from the parlour not to be heard, she took Charley

by the shoulders, and giving him a violent shake,
said—

"You little rebel, you! If you come into the parlour again, I'll skin you!"

The cake was given. Charley cared about as much
for the threat as he did for the shaking. He had
gained his end.

"I pray daily for patience to bear with my children," said Mrs. Stanley, on returning to the parlour.
"They try us severely."

"That they do," replied Mrs. Noland. "But it
is in our power, by firmness, consistency, and kindness, to render our tasks comparatively light."

"Perhaps so. I try to be firm, and consistent,
and kind with my children; to exercise toward them
constant forbearance; but, after all, it is very hard
to know exactly how to govern them."

"Mother, can't I go over into the square?" asked
Emma, looking into the parlour just at this time. She
was a little girl about eight years old.

"I would rather not have you go, my dear," returned Mrs. Stanley.

"Oh yes, mother, do let me go," urged Emma.

"Ellen can't go with you now; and I do not wish
you to go alone."

"I can go well enough, mother."

"Well, run along then, you intolerable little tease,
you!"

Emma scampered away, and Mrs. Stanley remarked—

"That is the way. They gain their ends by importunity."

"But should you allow that, my friend?"

"There was no particular reason why Emma should not go to the square. I didn't think, at first, when I said I would rather not have her go, or I would have said 'yes' at once. It is so difficult to decide upon children's requests on the spur of the moment."

"But after you had said that you did not want her to go to the square, would it not have been better to have made her abide by your wishes?"

"I don't think it would have been right for me to have deprived the child of the pleasure of playing in the square, from the mere pride of consistency. I was wrong in objecting at first—to have adhered to my objection would have been still a greater wrong;—don't you think so?"

"I do not," returned Mrs. Noland. "I know of no greater evil in a family, than for the children to discover that their parents vacillate in any matter regarding them. A denial once made to any request should be positive, even if, in a moment after, it be seen to have been made without sufficient reason."

"I cannot agree with you. Justice, I hold, to be paramount in all things. We should never wrong a child."

The third appearance of Charley again broke in upon the conversation.

"Give me another piece of cake, mother."

"What! Didn't I tell you that there was no more for you? No! you cannot have another morsel."

"I want some more cake," whined the child.

"Not a crumb more, sir."

The whine rose into a cry

"Go up stairs, sir."

Charley did not move.

"Go this instant."

"Give me some cake."

"No."

The cry swelled into a loud bawl.

Mrs. Stanley became excessively annoyed. "I never saw such persevering children in my life," said she, impatiently. "They don't regard what I say any more than if I had not spoken. Charles! Go out of the parlour this moment!"

The tone in which this was uttered the child understood. He left the parlour slowly, but continued to cry at the top of his voice. The parlour bell was rung, and Ellen the nurse appeared.

"Do, Ellen, give that boy another piece of cake! There is no other way to keep him quiet."

In about three minutes after this direction had been given, all was still again. Mrs. Stanley now changed the topic of conversation. Her manner was not quite so cheerful as before. The conduct of Charley had worried and mortified her.

The last piece of cake had not been really wanted. Charley asked for it because a spirit of opposition had been aroused, but he had no appetite to eat it. It was crumbled about the floor and wasted. His mother had peace for the next hour. After that she went into the kitchen to give directions, and make some preparations for tea. Charley was by her side.

"Ellen, take this child out," said she.

Ellen took hold of Charley's arm.

"No!—no!— Go 'way, Ellen!" he screamed.

"There !—there !—never mind: Let him stay,' said the mother.

A jar of preserved fruit was brought forth.

"Give me some?" asked Charley.

"No, not now. You will get some at the table."

"I want some now. Give me some now."

A spoonful of the preserves was put into a saucer, and given to the child.

"Give me some more," said he, holding up his saucer in about half a minute.

"No. Wait until tea is ready."

"Give me some sweetmeats. I want more, mother!"

"I tell you, no."

A loud bawl followed.

"I declare this child will worry me to death!" exclaimed the mother, her mind all in confusion, lading out a large spoonful of the fruit, and putting it into his saucer.

When this was eaten, still more was demanded, and peremptorily refused. Crying was resorted to, but without effect, though it was loud and deafening. Finding this unsuccessful, the spoiled urchin determined to help himself. As soon as his mother's back was turned, he clambered up to the table and seized the jar containing the preserves. In pulling it over far enough to get his spoon into it, the balance of the jar was destroyed, and over it went, rolling off upon the floor, and breaking with a loud crash. At the moment this occurred, Mrs. Stanley entered the room. Her patience, that had been severely tried, was now completely overthrown. She was angry enough to punish her child, and feel a delight in doing so. Seizing him by one arm, she lifted him from the floor, as if he had been but a feather, and hurried with him up to her chamber. There she whipped him unmercifully, and then put him to bed. He conti nued to cry after she had done so, when she commanded him to stop in a voice that he dared not disobey. An hour afterward, when much cooled down, she passed through the chamber. She looked down upon her little boy with a feeling of repentance for her anger and the severity of her punishment. This feeling was in no way mitigated on hearing the child sob in his sleep. The mother felt very unhappy.

So much for Mrs. Stanley—so much for her tenderness of feeling—so much for her warm-blooded system. Its effects need not be exposed further. Its folly need not be set in any plainer light.

Some weeks afterward she was spending an afternoon with Mrs. Noland. Her favourite topic was the management of children, and she introduced it as usual, inveighing as was her wont against the cruelty of punishing children—especially in cold blood, as she called it. For her part, she never punished except in extreme cases, and not then, unless provoked to do so. Unless she felt angry, and punished on the spur of the moment, she could not do it at all. During the conversation, which was led pretty much by Mrs. Stanley, a child, about the age of Charley, came into the parlour. He walked up to his mother and whispered some request in her ear.

"Oh no, Master Harry!" was the smiling, but decided reply.

The child lingered with a look of disappointment. At length he came up, and kissing his mother, asked

again, in a sweet, earnest way, for what he had been
at first denied.

"After I said no!" And Mrs. Noland looked
gravely into his face.

Tears came into Henry's eyes. But he said no
more. In a moment or two he silently left the
room.

"Mrs. Noland! How could you resist that dear
little fellow? I declare it was right down cruel in
you."

The eyes of Mrs. Stanley glistened as she spoke.

"It would have been far more cruel to him if I
had yielded, after once having said 'no'—far more
cruel had I given him what I knew would have in-
jured him."

"But, I don't see how you could refuse so dear a
child, when he asked you in such a sweet, affectionate
manner. I should have given him any thing in the
world he had asked for."

"That's not my way. I say 'no' only when I have
good reason, and then I never change."

"Never?"

"Never."

Henry appeared at the parlour door again.

"Come in, dear," said Mrs. Noland.

The child came quickly forward, put up his mouth
to kiss her, and then nestled closely by his mother's
side. The conversation continued, without the slightest
interruption from him.

"Dear little fellow," said Mrs. Stanley, once or
twice, looking into the child's face, and smoothing
his hair with her hand.

When the tea bell rung, the family assembled in

the dining-room. A visiter made it necessary that one of the children should wait. Henry was by the table as usual.

"Harry, dear," said his mother, "you will have to wait and come with Ellen."

The child felt very much disappointed. He looked up into his mother's face for a moment, and then, without a word, went out of the room.

"Poor little fellow! It is really a pity to make him wait; and he is so good," said Mrs. Stanley. "I am sure we can make room for him. Do call him back, and let him sit by me."

And she moved close to one of the older children as she spoke. "Here is plenty of room."

Mrs. Noland thought for a moment, and then told the waiter to call Henry back. The child came in as quietly as he had gone out, and came up to his mother's side.

"My dear," said Mrs. Noland, "this good lady here has made room for you by her side. You can go and sit by her."

The child's face brightened. He went quickly and took the offered seat. By the time tea was over, Henry had fallen asleep in his chair. Mrs. Noland, when all arose from the table, took Henry in her arms, and went with him, accompanied by Mrs. Stanley, to her chamber, where she undressed him, and kissing fondly his bright young cheek, laid him in his little bed.

Mrs. Stanley stood for some moments over the sleeping child, and looked down upon his calm face. As she did so, she remembered her own little Charley, and under what different circumstances and feelings ne had been put to bed on the evening of Mrs. Noland's visit to her.

Whether the contrast did her any good, we have no means of knowing. We trust the lesson was not without its good effect upon her.

THE EVENING PRAYER.

"Our Father."

"OUR Father." The mother's voice was low, and tender, and solemn.

"Our Father." On two sweet voices the words were borne upward. It was the innocence of reverent childhood that gave them utterance.

"Who art in the heavens."

"Who art in the heavens," repeated the children, one with her eyes bent meekly down, and the other looking upward, as if she would penetrate the heavens into which her heart aspired.

"Hallowed be Thy name."

Lower fell the voices of the little ones. In a gentle murmur they said: "Hallowed be Thy name."

"Thy kingdom come."

And the burden of the prayer was still taken up by the children—"Thy kingdom come"

"Thy will be done on earth, as it is done in heaven."

Like a low, sweet echo from the land of angels— "Thy will be done on earth, as it is done in heaven," filled the chamber.

And the mother continued—"Give us this day our daily bread."

"Our daily bread" lingered a moment on the air, as the mother's voice was hushed into silence.

"And forgive us our debts, as we also forgive our debtors."

The eyes of the children had drooped for a moment. But they were uplifted again as they prayed —"And forgive us our debts, as we also forgive our debtors."

"And lead us not into temptation; but deliver us from evil. For Thine is the kingdom, and the power, and the glory, for ever. Amen."

All these holy words were said, piously and fervently, by the little ones, as they knelt with clasped hands beside their mother. Then, as their thoughts, uplifted on the wings of prayer to their heavenly Father, came back again and rested on their earthly parents, a warmer love came gushing from their hearts.

Pure kisses—tender embraces—the fond "good night." What a sweet agitation pervaded all their feelings! Then two dear heads were placed side by side on the snowy pillow, the mother's last kiss given, and the shadowy curtains drawn.

What a pulseless stillness reigns throughout the chamber! Inwardly the parents' listening ears are bent. They have given these innocent ones into the keeping of God's angels, and they can almost hear the rustle of their garments as they gather around their sleeping babes. A sigh, deep and tremulous, breaks on the air. Quickly the mother turns to the father of her children, with a look of earnest inquiry on her countenance. And he answers thus her silent question.

"Far back, through many years, have my thoughts been wandering. At my mother's knee thus said I nightly, in childhood, my evening prayer. It was that best and holiest of all prayers, "Our Father," that she taught me. Childhood and my mother passed away. I went forth as a man into the world, strong, confident, and self-seeking. Once I came into great temptation. Had I fallen in that temptation, I would have fallen, I sadly fear, never to have risen again. The struggle in my mind went on for hours. I was about yielding. All the barriers I could oppose to the in-rushing flood seemed just ready to give way, when, as I sat in my room one evening, there came from an adjoining chamber, now first occupied for many weeks, the murmur of low voices. I listened. At first, no articulate sound was heard, and yet something in the tones stirred my heart with new and strange emotions. At length, there came to my ears, in the earnest, loving voice of a woman, the words—'Deliver us from evil.' For an instant, it seemed to me as if the voice were that of my mother. Back, with a sudden bound through all the intervening years, went my thoughts; and, a child in heart again, I was kneeling at my mother's knee. Humbly and reverently I said over the words of the holy prayer she

had taught me, heart and eyes uplifted to heaven.
The hour and the power of darkness had passed. I
was no longer standing in slippery places, with a
flood of waters ready to sweep me to destruction ;
but my feet were on a rock. My mother's pious
care had saved her son.   In the holy words she
taught me in childhood, was a living power to resist
evil through all my after life.   Ah! that unknown
mother, as she taught her child to repeat his evening prayer, how little dreamed she that the holy
words were to reach a stranger's ears, and save him
through memories of his own childhood and his own
mother !   And yet it was so.   What a power there
is in God's Word, as it flows into and rests in the
minds of innocent children !"

Tears were in the eyes of the wife and mother as
she lifted her face, and gazed with a subdued tenderness upon the countenance of her husband.   Her
heart was too full for utterance.   A little while she
thus gazed, and then, with a trembling joy, laid her
head upon his bosom. Angels were in the chamber
where their dear ones slept, and they felt their holy
presence.

A PEEVISH DAY, AND ITS CONSE-QUENCES.

"It is too bad, Rachael, to put me to all this trouble; and you know I can hardly hold up my head!"

Thus spoke Mrs. Smith, in a peevish voice, to a quiet-looking domestic, who had been called up from the kitchen to supply some unimportant omission in the breakfast-table arrangement.

Rachael looked hurt and rebuked, but made no reply.

"How could you speak in that way to Rachael?" said Mr. Smith, as soon as the domestic had withdrawn.

"If you felt just as I do, Mr. Smith, you would speak cross too!" Mrs. Smith replied a little warmly. "I feel just like a rag; and my head aches as if it would burst."

"I know you feel badly, and I am very sorry for you. But still, I suppose it is as easy to speak kindly as harshly. Rachael is very obliging and attentive, and should be borne with in occasional omissions, which you of course know are not wilful."

"It is easy enough to preach," retorted Mrs. Smith, whose temper, from bodily lassitude and pain, was in quite an irritable state. The reader will understand at least one of the reasons of this, when he is told that the scene here presented occurred during the last oppressive week in August.

Mr. Smith said no more. He saw that to do so would only be to provoke instead of quieting his wife's ill-humour. The morning meal went by in silence, but little food passing the lips of either. How could it, when the thermometer was ninety-four at eight o'clock in the morning, and the leaves upon the trees were as motionless as if suspended in a vacuum? Bodies and minds were relaxed—and the one turned from food, as the other did from thought, with an instinctive aversion.

After Mr. Smith had left his home for his place of business, Mrs. Smith went up into her chamber, and threw herself upon the bed, her head still continuing to ache with great violence. It so happened that a week before, the chambermaid had gone away sick, and all the duties of the household had in consequence devolved upon Rachael, herself not very well. Cheerfully, however, had she endeavoured to discharge these accumulated duties, and but for the unhappy, peevish state of mind in which Mrs. Smith indulged, would have discharged them without a murmuring thought. But, as she was a faithful, conscientious woman, and, withal, sensitive in her feelings, to be found fault with worried her exceedingly. Of this Mrs. Smith was well aware, and had, until the latter part of the trying month of August, acted toward Rachael with consideration and forbearance. But the last week of August was too much for her. The sickness of the chambermaid threw such heavy duties upon Rachael, whose daily headaches and nervous relaxation of body were borne without a complaint, that their perfect performance was almost impossible.   Slight omissions, which were next to unavoidable under the circumstances, became so annoying to Mrs. Smith, herself, as it has been seen, labouring under great bodily and mental prostration, that she could not bear them.

"She knows better, and she could do better, if she chose," was her rather uncharitable comment often inwardly made on the occurrence of some new trouble.

After Mr. Smith had taken his departure on the morning just referred to, Mrs. Smith went up into her chamber, as has been seen, and threw herself languidly upon a bed, pressing her hands to her throbbing temples, as she did so, and murmuring,

"I can't live at this rate!"

At the same time, Rachael set down in the kitchen the large waiter upon which she had arranged the dishes from the breakfast-table, and then sinking into a chair, pressed one hand upon her forehead, and sat for more than a minute in troubled silence. It had been three days since she had received from Mrs. Smith a pleasant word; and the last remark, made to her a short time before, had been the unkindest of all.   At another time, even all this would not have moved her—she could have perceived that Mrs. S. was not in a right state—that lassitude of body had produced a temporary infirmity of mind. But, being herself affected by the oppressive season almost as much as her mistress, she could not make these allowances.   While still seated, the chamber-bell was rung with a quick, startling jerk.

"What next?" peevishly ejaculated Rachael, and then slowly proceeded to obey the summons.

"How could you leave my chamber in such a condition as this?" was the salutation that met her ear,
as she entered the presence of Mrs. Smith, who, half
raised upon the bed, and leaning upon her hand,
looked the very personification of languor, peevish-
ness, and ill-humour. "You had plenty of time
while we were eating breakfast to have put things a
little to rights!"

To this Rachael made no reply, but turned away
and went back into the kitchen. She had scarcely
reached that spot, before the bell rang again, louder
and quicker than before; but she did not answer it.
In about three minutes it was jerked with an energy
that snapped the wire, but Rachael was immovable.
Five minutes elapsed, and then Mrs. Smith, fully
aroused from the lethargy that had stolen over her,
came down with a quick, firm step.

"What's the reason you didn't answer my bell?
say!" she asked, in an excited voice.

Rachael did not reply.

"Do you hear me?"

Rachael had never been so treated before; she
had lived with Mrs. Smith for three years, and had
rarely been found fault with. She had been too
strict in regard to the performance of her duty to
leave much room for even a more exacting mistress
to find fault; but now, to be overtasked and sick,
and to be chidden, rebuked, and even angrily assailed, was more than she could well bear. She did not
suffer herself to speak for some moments, and then
her voice trembled, and the tears came out upon her
cheeks.

"I wish you to get another in my place. I find

I don't suit you. My time will be up day after to-morrow."

"Very well," was Mrs. Smith's firm reply, as she turned away, and left the kitchen.

Here was trouble in good earnest. Often and often had Mrs. Smith said, during the past two or three years—"What should I do without Rachael?" And now she had given notice that she was going to leave her, and under circumstances which made pride forbid a request to stay. Determined to act out her part of the business with firmness and decision, she dressed herself and went out, hot and oppressive as it was, and took her way to an intelligence office, where she paid the required fee and directed a cook and chambermaid to be sent to her. On the next morning, about ten o'clock, an Irish girl came and offered herself as a cook, and was, after sundry questions and answers, engaged. So soon as this negotiation was settled, Rachael retired from the kitchen, leaving the new-comer in full possession. In half an hour after she received her wages, and left, in no very happy frame of mind, a home that had been for three years, until within a few days, a pleasant one. As for Mrs. Smith, she was ready to go to bed sick; but this was impracticable. Nancy, the new cook, had expressly stipulated that she was to have no duties unconnected with the kitchen. The consequence was, that notwithstanding the thermometer ranged above ninety, and the atmosphere remained as sultry as air from a heated oven, Mrs. Smith was compelled to arrange her chamber and parlours. By the time this was done, she was in a condition to go to bed, and lie until dinner-time.

The arrival of this important period brought new troubles and vexations. Dinner was late by forty minutes, and then came on the table in a most abominable condition. A fine sirloin was burnt to a crisp. The tomatoes were smoked, and the potatoes watery. As if this was not enough to mar the pleasure of the dinner hour for a hungry husband, Mrs. Smith added thereto a distressed countenance and discouraging complaints. Nancy was grumbled at and scolded every time she had occasion to appear in the room, and her single attempt to excuse herself on account of not understanding the cook-stove, was met by, "Do hush, will you! I'm out of all patience!"

As to the latter part of the sentence, that was a needless waste of words. The condition of mind she described was fully apparent.

About three o'clock in the afternoon, just as Mrs. Smith had found a temporary relief from a troubled mind, and a most intolerable headache, in sleep, a tap on the chamber-door awoke her, and there stood Nancy, all equipped for going out.

"I find I won't suit you, ma'am," said Nancy, "and so you must look out for another girl."

Having said this, she turned away and took her departure, leaving Mrs. Smith in a state of mind, as it is said, "more easily imagined than described."

"Oh dear! what shall I do?" at length broke from her lips, as she burst into tears, and burying her face in the pillow, sobbed aloud. Already she had repented of her fretfulness and fault-finding temper, as displayed toward Rachael, and could she have made a truce with pride, or silenced its whispers, would have sent for her well-tried domestic, and endeavoured to make all fair with her again. But, under the circumstances, this was now impossible. While yet undetermined how to act, the street-bell rung, and she was compelled to attend the door, as she was now alone in the house. She found, on opening it, a rough-looking country girl, who asked if she were the lady who wanted a chambermaid. Any kind of help was better than none at all, and so Mrs. Smith asked the young woman to walk in. In treating with her in regard to her qualifications for the situation she applied for, she discovered that she knew "almost nothing at all about any thing." The stipulation that she was to be a doer-of-all-work-in-general, until a cook could be obtained, was readily agreed to, and then she was shown to her room in the attic, where she prepared herself for entering upon her duties.

"Will you please, ma'am, show me what you want me to do?" asked the new help, presenting herself before Mrs. Smith.

"Go into the kitchen, Ellen, and see that the fire is made. I'll be down there presently."

To be compelled to see after a new and ignorant servant, and direct her in every thing, just at so trying a season of the year, and while her mind was "all out of sorts," was a severe task for poor Mrs. Smith. She found that Ellen, as she had too good reason for believing, was totally unacquainted with kitchen-work. She did not even know how to kindle a coal fire; nor could she manage the stove after Mrs. Smith had made the fire for her. All this did not in any way tend to make her less unhappy or more patient than before. On retiring for the night

13*

she had a high fever, which continued unabated until morning, when her husband found her really ill; so much so as to make the attendance of a doctor necessary.

A change in the air had taken place during the night, and the temperature had fallen many degrees. This aided the efforts of the physician, and enabled him so to adapt his remedies as to speedily break the fever. But the ignorance and awkwardness of Ellen, apparent in her attempts to arrange her bed and chamber, so worried her mind, that she was near relapsing into her former feverish and excited state. The attendance of an elder maiden sister was just in time. All care was taken from her thoughts, and she had a chance of recovering a more healthy tone of mind and body. During the next week, she knew little or nothing of how matters were progressing out of her own chamber. A new cook had been hired, of whom she was pleased to hear good accounts, although she had not seen her; and Ellen, under the mild and judicious instruction of her sister, had learned to make up a bed neatly, to sweep, and dust in true style, and to perform all the little etceteras of chamber-work, greatly to her satisfaction. She was, likewise, good-tempered, willing, and to all appearance strictly trustworthy.

One morning, about a week after she had become too ill to keep up, she found herself so far recovered as to be able to go down stairs to breakfast. Every thing upon the table she found arranged in the neatest style. The food was well cooked, especially some tender rice cakes, of which she was very fond.

"Really, these are delicious!" said she, as the

finely flavoured cakes almost melted in her mouth. "And this coffee is just the thing! How fortunate we have been to obtain so good a cook! I was afraid we should never be able to replace Rachael. But even she is equalled, if not surpassed."

"Still she does not surpass Rachael," said Mr. Smith, a little gravely. "Rachael was a treasure."

"Indeed she was. And I have been sorry enough I ever let her go," returned Mrs. Smith.

At that moment the new cook entered with a plate of warm cakes.

"Rachael!" ejaculated Mrs. Smith, letting her knife and fork fall. "How do you do? I am glad to see you! Welcome home again!"

As she spoke quickly and earnestly, she held out her hand, and grasped that of her old domestic warmly. Rachael could not speak, but as she left the room she put her apron to her eyes. Hers were not the only one's dim with rising moisture.

For at least a year to come both Mrs. Smith and her excellent cook will have no cause to complain of each other. How they will get along during the last week of next August we cannot say, but hope the lesson they have both received will teach them to bear and fo bear.

SISTERS.

[We make the following extract from one of our books—
"Advice to Young Men on their Duties and Conduct in
Life."]

IF you have younger sisters, who are just entering
society, all your interest should be awakened for
them. You cannot but have seen some little below
the surface, and already made the discovery that too
few of the young men who move about in the various social circles to which you have admission, are
fit associates for a pure-minded woman. Their
exterior, it is true, is very fair; they sing well, they
dance well, their persons are elegant, and their
manners attractive; but you have met them when
they felt none of the restraints of female society,
and seen them unmask their real characters. You
can remember the ribald jest, the obscene allusion,
the sneer at virtue, the unblushing acknowledgment
of licentiousness. You have heard them speak of
this sweet girl, and that pure-minded woman, in
terms that would have roused your deepest indignation, had your own sister been the subject of
allusion.

You may know all these things, but your innocent
sisters at home cannot know them, nor see reason

152

for shunning the society of those whose real characters, if revealed, would cause them to turn away
in disgust and horror. From the dangers of an
acquaintanceship with such young men it is your
duty to guard your sisters; and you must do this
more by warding off the evil than by warnings
against it. In order to this, you should make it a
point of duty always to go with your sisters into
company, and to be their companion, if possible, on
all public occasions. By so doing, you can prevent
the introduction of men whose principles are bad;
or, if such introductions are forced upon them in
spite of you, can throw in a timely word of caution.
This latter it may be too late to do after an acquaintanceship is formed with a man whose character is
detestable in your eyes, provided he have a fair
exterior. Your sister will hardly be made to believe
that one who is so attractive in all respects, and who
can converse of virtue and honour so eloquently,
can possibly have an impure or vicious mind. She
will think you prejudiced. The great thing is to
guard, by every means in your power, these innocent ones from the polluting presence of a bad man.
You cannot tell how soon he may win the affections
of the most innocent, confiding, and loving of them
all, and draw her off from virtue. And even if his
designs be honourable—if he win her but to wed
her—her lot will be by no means an enviable one;
he cannot make her happy; for happy no pure-
minded woman ever has been, or ever can be made,
by a corrupt, evil-minded, and selfish man.

You are a brother; your position is one of great
responsibility; let this be ever before your mind.

On your faithfulness to your duty, may depend a lifetime of happiness or misery for those who are, or ought to be, very dear to you. But not only should you seek to guard them from the danger just alluded to—your affection for them should lead you to enter into their pleasures as far as in your power to do so; to give interest and variety to the home circle; to afford them, at all times, the assistance of your judgment in matters of trivial as well as grave importance. By this you will gain their confidence and acquire an influence over them that may, at some later period, enable you to serve them in a moment of impending danger.

We very often—indeed, far too often—see young men with sisters who appear to be entirely indifferent in regard to them. They rarely visit together; their associates, male and female, are strangers to each other; they appear to have no common interests. This state of things is the fault, nine times in ten, of the young men. It is the result of their neglect and indifference. There are very few sisters who do not love with a most tender and unselfish regard their brothers, especially their elder brothers, and who would not feel happier in being their companions than in the companionship of almost any one. Notwithstanding all this neglect and indifference, how willingly is every little office performed that adds to the brother's comfort! How much care is there for him who gives back so little in return! The sister's love is as unselfish as it is unostentatious. It is shown in acts, not in professions. How can any young man be indifferent to such love? How can he fail in its full and free reciprocation?

A regard for himself, as well as for his sisters, should lead a young man to be much with them. Their influence in softening, polishing, and refining his character, will be very great. They have perceptions of the propriety and fitness of things far quicker than he has ; and this he will soon see if he observe their remarks upon the persons with whom they come in contact, and the circumstances that transpire around them. While he is reasoning on the subject, and balancing many things in his mind before coming to a satisfactory conclusion, they, by a kind of intuition, have settled the whole matter, and settled it, he will find, truly. In the graver things of life, a man's judgment is more to be relied upon than a woman's, because here a regular course of reasoning from premises laid down is required, and this a man is much more able to do than a woman ; but in matters of taste and propriety, and in the quick appreciation of character, a woman's perceptions are worth far more than a man's judgment. And in the more weighty and serious matters of life, a man will always find that he will receive aid, in coming to a nice decision, from a wife or sister who loves him, if he will only carefully lay the whole subject before her, with the reasons that appeal to his judgment, and be guided in some measure by her perceptions of what is right. This is because man is in the province of the understanding, which acts by thought, and woman in the province of the affections, which act by perceptions; not that a man does not have perceptions and a woman reason, but the leading characteristic difference between the sexes is as stated, and each comes to conclusions mainly by either the one or the other of these two modes. This position, which we believe to be the true one in regard to the difference between the sexes, demonstrates the great use of female society, especially the society of those who feel some interest in and affection for us. In such society, there is a reciprocation of benefits that is nearly, if not quite, equal. And nowhere can this reciprocation be of greater utility than among brothers and sisters, just entering upon life, with all their knowledge of human character and human life to gain.

BROTHERS.

[The following suggestions, on the relation and duties of a sister to her brother, are taken from a volume by the Author of this book, entitled, "Advice to Young Ladies on their Duties and Conduct in Life."]

OLDER brothers are not usually as attentive to their younger sisters as the latter would feel to be agreeable. The little girls that were so long known as children, with the foibles, faults, and caprices of children, although now grown up into tall young ladies, who have left or are about leaving school, are still felt to be children, or but a little advanced beyond childhood, by the young men who have had some three or four years experience in the world. With these older brothers, there will not usually be, arising from this cause, much confidential and unreserved intercourse; at least, not until the sisters have added two or three years more to their ages, and assumed more of the quiet dignity of womanhood.

Upon these older brothers, therefore, the conduct of sisters cannot, usually, have much effect. They are removed to a point chiefly beyond the circle of their influence. But upon brothers near about their own age, and younger than themselves, the influence of sisters may be brought to bear with the most salutary results.

The temptations to which young men are exposed, when first they come in contact with the world, are many, and full of the strongest allurements. Their virtuous principles are assailed in a thousand ways; sometimes boldly, and sometimes by the most insidious arts of the vicious and evil-minded. All, therefore, that can make virtue lovely in their eyes, and vice hideous, they need to strengthen the good principles stored up, from childhood, in their minds. For their sakes, home should be made as attractive as possible, in order to induce them frequently to spend their evenings in the place where, of all others, they will be safest. To do this, a young lady must consult the tastes of her brothers, and endeavour to take sufficient interest in the pursuits that interest them, as to make herself companionable. If they are fond of music, one of the strongest incentives she can have for attaining the highest possible skill in performing upon the piano, will be the hope of making home, thereby, the most attractive place where they can spend their evenings. If they are fond of

14

reading, let her read, as far as she can, the books that interest them, in order that she may take part in their conversations; and let her, in every other possible way, furnish herself with the means of making home agreeable.

There is no surer way for a sister to gain an influence with her brother, than to cultivate all exterior graces and accomplishments, and improve her mind by reading, thinking, and observation. By these means she not only becomes his intelligent companion, but inspires him with a feeling of generous pride toward her, that, more than any thing else, impresses her image upon his mind, brings her at all times nearer to him, and gives her a double power over him for good.

The indifference felt by brothers toward their sisters, when it does exist, often arises from the fact that their sisters are inferior, in almost every thing, to the women they are in the habit of meeting abroad. Where this is the case, such indifference is not so much to be wondered at.

Sisters should always endeavour to gain, as much as possible, the confidence of their brothers, and to give them their confidence in return. Mutual good offices will result from this, and attachments that could only produce unhappiness may be prevented. A man sees more of men than woman does, and the same is true in regard to the other sex. This being so, a brother has it in his power at once to guard his sister against the advances of an unprincipled man, or a man whose habits he knows to be bad; and a sister has it in her power to reveal to her brother traits of character in a woman, for whom he is about forming an attachment, that would repel rather than attract him.

Toward her younger brother a sister should be particularly considerate. In allusion to this subject, Mrs. Farrar has written so well that we cannot repress our wish to quote her. "If your brothers are younger than you, encourage them to be perfectly confidential with you; win their friendship by your sympathy in all their concerns, and let them see that their interests and their pleasures are liberally provided for in the family arrangements. Never disclose their little secrets, however unimportant they may seem to you; never pain them by an ill-timed joke; never repress their feelings by ridicule; but be their tenderest friend, and then you may become their ablest adviser. If separated from them by the course of school and college education, make a point of keeping up your intimacy by full, free, and affectionate correspondence; and when they return to the paternal roof, at that awkward age between youth and manhood, when reserve creeps over the mind like an impenetrable vail, suffer it not to interpose between you and your brothers. Cultivate their friendship and intimacy with all the address and tenderness you possess; for it is of unspeakable importance to them that their sisters should be their confidential friends. Consider the loss of a ball or party, for the sake of making the evening pass pleasantly to your brothers at home, as a small sacrifice —one you should unhesitatingly make. If they go into company with you, see that they are introduced to the most desirable acquaintances, and show their that you are interested in their acquitting themselves well."

Having quoted thus much from the "Young Lady's Friend," we feel inclined to give a few passages more from the author's admirable remarks on the relation of brother and sister.

"So many temptations beset young men, of which young women know nothing, that it is of the utmost importance that your brothers' evenings should be happily passed at home; that their friends should be your friends; that their engagements should be the same as yours; and that various innocent amusements should be provided for them in the family circle. Music is an accomplishment usually valuable as a home enjoyment, as rallying round the piano the various members of a family, and harmonizing their hearts, as well as their voices, particularly in devotional strains. I know no more agreeable and interesting spectacle than that of brothers and sisters playing and singing together those elevated compositions in music and poetry which gratify the taste and purify the heart, while their parents sit delighted by. I have seen and heard an elder sister thus leading the family choir, who was the soul of harmony to the whole household, and whose life was a perfect example of those virtues which I am here endeavouring to inculcate. Let no one say, in reading this chapter, that too much is here required of sisters; that no one can be expected to lead such a self-sacrificing life; for the sainted one to whom I refer was all that I would ask my sister to be; and a happier person never lived. 'To do good and make others happy,' was the rule of her life; and in this she found the art of making herself so.

"Brothers will generally be found strongly opposed to the slightest indecorum in sisters. . . . . Their intercourse with all sorts of men enables them to judge of the construction put upon certain actions, and modes of dress and speech, much better than women can; and you will do well to take their advice on all such points.

"I have been told by men, who had passed unharmed through the temptations of youth, that they owed their escape from many dangers to the intimate companionship of affectionate and pure-minded sisters. They have been saved from a hazardous meeting with idle company by some home engagement, of which their sisters were the charm; they have refrained from mixing with the impure, because they would not bring home thoughts and feelings which they could not share with those trusting and loving friends; they have put aside the wine-cup, and abstained from stronger potations, because they would not profane with their fumes the holy kiss, with which they were accustomed to bid their sisters goodnight."

HOME.

SOCIETY is marked by greater and smaller divisions, as into nations, communities, and families. A man is a member of the commonwealth, a smaller community, as a hamlet or city, and his family at the same time; and the more perfectly all his duties to his family are discharged, the more fully does he discharge his duties to the community and the nation; for a good member of a family cannot be a bad member of the commonwealth, for he that is faithful in what is least, will also be faithful in what is greater. Indeed, the more perfectly a man fulfils all his domestic duties, the more perfectly, in that very act, has he discharged his duty to the whole; for the whole is made up of parts, and its health depends entirely upon the health of the various parts. There are, of course, general as well as specific duties; but the more conscientious a man is in the discharge of specific duties, the more ready will he be to perform those that are general; and we believe that the converse of this will be found equally true, and that those who have least regard for home—who have, indeed, no home, no domestic circle—are the worst citizens. This they may not be apparently; they may not break the laws, nor do any thing to call down upon them censure from the community, and yet, in the secret and almost unconscious dissemination of demoralizing principles, may be doing a work far more destructive of the public good than if they had committed a robbery.

We always feel pain when we hear a young man speak lightly of home, and talk carelessly, or, it may be, with sportive ridicule, of the "old man" and the "old woman," as if they were of but little consequence. We mark it as a bad indication, and feel that the feet of that young man are treading upon dangerous ground. His home education may not have been of the best kind, nor may home influences have reached his higher and better feelings; but he is at least old enough now to understand the causes, and to seek rather to bring into his home all that it needs to render it more attractive, than to estrange himself from it and expose its defects.

Instances of this kind are not of very frequent occurrence. Home has its charms for nearly all, and the very name comes with a blessing to the spirit. This, however, is more the case with those who have been separated from it, than it is with those who yet remain in the old homestead with parents, brothers, and sisters, as their friends and companions.

The earnest love of home, felt by nearly all who have been compelled to leave that pleasant place, is a feeling that should be tenderly cherished: and this love should be kept alive by associations that have in them as perfect a resemblance of home as it is possible to obtain. It is for this reason that it is bad for a young man to board in a large hotel, where there is nothing in which there is even an image of the home-circle. Each has his separate chamber; but that is not home. All meet together at the common table; but there is no home feeling there, with its many sweet reciprocations. The meal completed, all separate, each to his individual pursuit or pleasure. There is a parlour, it is true; but there are no family gatherings there. One and another sit there, as inclination prompts; but each sits alone, busy with his own thoughts. All this is a poor substitute for home. And yet it offers its attractions to some. A young man in a hotel has more freedom than in a family or private boarding-house. He comes in and goes out unobserved; there is no one to say to him, "why?" or "wherefore?" But this is a dangerous freedom, and one which no young man should desire.

But mere negative evils, so to speak, are not the worst that beset a young man who unwisely chooses a public hotel as a place for boarding. He is much more exposed to temptations there than in a private boarding-house, or at home. Men of licentious habits, in most cases, select hotels as boarding-places; and such rarely scruple to offer to the ardent minds of young men, with whom they happen to fall in company, those allurements that are most likely to lead them away from virtue. And, besides this, there being no evening home-circle in a hotel, a young man who is not engaged earnestly in some pursuit that occupies his hours of leisure from business has nothing to keep him there, but is forced to seek for something to interest his mind elsewhere, and is, in consequence, more open to temptation.

Home is man's true place. Every man should have a home. Here his first duties lie, and here he finds the strength by which he is able successfully to combat in life's temptations. Happy is that young man who is still blessed with a home—who has his mother's counsel and the pure love of sisters to strengthen and cheer him amid life's opening combats.

A GLEAM OF SUNSHINE ON THE PATH OF A MONEY-LENDER.

Mr. Edgar was a money-lender, and scrupled not in exacting the highest "street rates" of interest that could be obtained. If good paper were offered, and he could buy it from the needy seeker of cash at two or even three per cent. a month, he did not hesitate about the transaction on any scruples of justice between man and man. Below one per cent. a month, he rarely made loans. He had nothing to do with the question, as to whether the holder of bills could afford the sacrifice. The circle of his thoughts went not beyond gain to himself.

Few days closed with Mr. Edgar that he was not able to count up gains as high as from thirty to one hundred dollars: not acquired in trade—not coming back to him as the reward of productive industry —but the simple accumulation of large clippings from the anticipated reward of others' industry. Always with a good balance in bank, he had but to sign his name to a check, and the slight effort was repaid by a gain of from ten to fifty dollars, according to the size and time of the note he had agreed to discount. A shrewd man, and well acquainted with the business standing of all around him, Mr. Edgar rarely made mistakes in money transactions. There was always plenty of good paper offering, and he never touched any thing regarded as doubtful.

Was Mr. Edgar a happy man? Ah! that is a home question. But we answer frankly, no. During his office hours, while his love of gain was active —while good customers were coming and going, and good operations being effected—his mind was in a pleasurable glow. But, at other times, he suffered greatly from a pressure on his feelings, the cause of which he did not clearly understand. Wealth he had always regarded as the greatest good in life. And now he not only had wealth, but the income therefrom was a great deal more than he had any desire to spend. And yet he was not happy—no, not even in the thought of his large possessions. Only in the mental activity through which more was obtained, did he really find satisfaction; but this state was only of short duration.

Positive unhappiness, Mr. Edgar often experienced. Occasional losses, careful and shrewd as he always was, were inevitable. These fretted him greatly. To lose a thousand dollars, instead of gaining, as was pleasantly believed, some sixty or seventy, was a shower of cold water upon his ardent love of accumulation: and he shivered painfully under the infliction The importunities of friends who needed money, and to whom it was unsafe to lend it, were also a source of no small annoyance. And, moreover, there was little of the heart's warm sunshine at home. As Mr. Edgar had thought more of laying up wealth for his children than giving them the true riches of intellect and heart, ill weeds had sprung up in their minds. He had not loved them with an unselfish love, and he received not a higher affection than he had bestowed. Their prominent thought, in regard to him, seemed ever to be the obtaining of some concession to their real or imaginary wants; and, if denied these, they reacted upon him in anger, sullenness, or complaint.

Oh, no! Mr. Edgar was not happy. Few gleams of sunshine lay across his path. Life to him, in his own bitter words, uttered after some keen disappointment, had "proved a failure." And yet he continued eager for gain; would cut as deep, exact as much from those who had need of his money in their business, as ever. The measure of per centage was the measure of his satisfaction.

One day a gentleman said to him—

"Mr. Edgar, I advised a young mechanic who has been in business for a short time, and who has to take notes for his work, to call on you for the purpose of getting them cashed. He has no credit in bank, and is, therefore, compelled to go upon the street for money. Most of his work is taken by one of the safest houses in the city; his paper is, therefore, as good as any in market. Deal as moderately with him as you can. He knows little about these matters, or where to go for the accommodation he needs."

"Is he an industrious and prudent young man?" inquired Mr. Edgar, caution and cupidity at once excited.

"He is."

"What's his name?"

"Blakewell."

"Oh, I know him. Very well; send him along, and if his paper is good, I'll discount it."

"You'll find it first-rate," said the gentleman.

"How much shall I charge him?" This was Mr. Edgar's first thought, so soon as he was alone. Even as he asked himself the question, the young mechanic entered.

"You take good paper, sometimes?" said the latter, in a hesitating manner.

The countenance of Mr. Edgar became, instantly, very grave.

"Sometimes I do," he answered, with assumed indifference.

"I have a note of Leyden & Co.'s that I wish discounted," said Blakewell.

"For how much?"

"Three hundred dollars—six months;" and he handed Mr. Edgar the note.

"I don't like over four months' notes," remarked the money-lender, coldly. Then he asked, "What rate of interest do you expect to pay?"

"Whatever is usual. Of course, I wish to get it done as low as possible. My profits are not large, and every dollar I pay in discounts is so much taken from the growth of my business and the comfort of my family."

'You have a family?"

"Yes, sir.   A wife and four children."

Mr. Edgar mused for a moment or two.   An unselfish thought was struggling to get into his mind.

"What have you usually paid on this paper?" he asked.

"The last I had discounted cost me one and a half per cent. a month."

"Notes of this kind are rarely marketable below that rate," said Mr. Edgar. He had thought of exacting two per cent.   "If you will leave the note, and call round in half an hour, I will see what can be done."

"Very well," returned the mechanic.   "Be as moderate with me as you can."

For the half hour that went by during the young man's absence, Mr. Edgar walked the floor of his counting-room, trying to come to some decision in regard to the note. Love of gain demanded two per cent. a month, while a feeble voice, scarcely heard so far away did it seem, pleaded for a generous regard to the young man's necessities. The conflict taking place in his mind was a new one for the money-lender. In no instance before had he experienced any hesitation on the score of a large discount. Love of gain continued clamorous for two per cent. on the note; yet, ever and anon, the low voice stole, in pleading accents, to his ears.

"I'll do it for one and a half," said Mr. Edgar, yielding slightly to the claim of humanity, urged by the voice, that seemed to be coming nearer.

Love of gain, after slight opposition, was satisfied.

15

But the low, penetrating voice asked for something better still.

"Weakness! Folly!" exclaimed Mr. Edgar. "I'd better make him a present of the money at once."

It availed nothing. The voice could not be hushed.

"One per cent! He couldn't get it done as low as that in the city."

"He is a poor young man, and has a wife and four little children," said the voice. "Even the abstraction of legal interest from his hard earnings is defect enough; to lose twice that sum, will make a heavy draught on his profits, which, under the present competition in trade, are not large. He is honest and industrious, and by his useful labour is aiding the social well-being. Is it right for you to get his reward?—to take his profits, and add them to your already rich accumulations?"

Mr. Edgar did not like these home questions, and tried to stop his ears, so that the voice could not find an entrance. But he tried in vain.

"Bank rates on this note," continued the inward voice, "would not much exceed nine dollars. Even this is a large sum for a poor man to lose. Double the rate of interest, and the loss becomes an injury to his business, or the cause of seriously abridging his home comforts. And how much will nine dollars contribute to your happiness? Not so much as a jot or a tittle. You are unable, now, to spend your income."

The young mechanic entered at this favourable moment. The money lender pointed to a chair;

then turned to his desk, and filled up, hurriedly, a
check. Blakewell glanced at the amount thereof as
it was handed to him, and an instant flush of surprise
came into his face.

"Haven't you made a mistake, Mr. Edgar?"
said he.

"In what respect?"

"The note was for three hundred dollars, six
months, and you have given me a check for two
hundred and ninety dollars, forty-three cents."

"I've charged you bank interest," said Mr. Edgar,
with a feeling of pleasure at his heart so new, that
it sent a glow along every nerve and fibre of his
being.

"Bank interest! I did not expect this, sir," replied the young man, visibly moved. "For less
than one and a half per cent. a month, I have not
been able to obtain mone. One per cent. I wou'
have paid you cheerfully. Eighteen dollars saved.
How much good that sum will do me! I could not
have saved it—or, I might say, have received it—
more opportunely. This is a kindness for which I
shall ever remember you gratefully."

Grasping the money-lender's hand, he shook it
warmly; then turned and hurried away.

Only one previous transaction had that day been
made by Mr. Edgar. In that transaction, his gain
was fifty dollars, and much pleasure had it given
him. But the delight experienced was not to be
compared with what he now felt. It was to him a
new experience in life—a realization of that beautiful
truth, "It is more blessed to give than to receive."

Once or twice during the day, as Mr. Edgar dwe

on the little circumstance, his natural love of gain caused regret for the loss of money involved in the transaction to enter his mind. How cold, moody, and uncomfortable he instantly became! Self-love was seeking to rob the money-lender of the just reward of a good deed. But the voice which had prompted the generous act was heard, clear and sweet, and again his heart beat to a gladder measure.

Evening was closing in on the day following. It was late in December, and winter had commenced in real earnest. Snow had fallen for some hours. Now, however, the sky was clear, but the air keen and frosty. · The day, to Mr. Edgar, was one in which more than the usual number of "good transactions" had been made. On one perfectly safe note he had been able to charge as high as three per cent. per month. Full of pleasurable excitement had his mind been while thus gathering in gain, but now, the excitement being over, he was oppressed. From whence the pressure came, he did not know. A cloud usually fell upon his spirits with the closing day; and there was not sunshine enough at home to chase it from his sky.

As Mr. Edgar walked along, with his eyes upon the pavement, his name was called. Looking up, he saw, standing at the open door of a small house, the mechanic he had befriended on the day before.

"Step in here just one moment," said the young man. The request was made in a way that left Mr. Edgar no alternative but compliance. So he entered the humble dwelling. He found himself in a small, unlighted room, adjoining one in which a lamp was burning, and in which was a young woman, plainly but neatly dressed, and four children, the youngest lying in a cradle. The woman held in her hand a warm Bay State shawl, which, after examining a few moments, with a pleased expression of countenance, she threw over her shoulders, and glanced at herself in a looking-glass. The oldest of the children, a boy, was trying on a new overcoat; and his sister, two years younger, had a white muff and a warm woollen shawl, in which her attention was completely absorbed. A smaller child had a new cap, and he was the most pleased of any.

"Oh, isn't father good to buy us all these? and we wanted them so much," said the oldest of the children. "Yesterday morning, when I told him how cold I was going to school, he said he was sorry, but that I must try and do without a coat this winter, for he hadn't money enough to get us all we wanted. How did he get more money, mother?"

"To a kind gentleman, who helped your father, we are indebted for these needed comforts," replied the mother.

"He must be a good man," said the boy. "What's his name?"

"His name is Mr. Edgar."

"I will ask God to bless him to-night when I say my prayers," innocently spoke out the youngest of the three children.

"What does all this mean?" asked the money-lender, as he hastily retired from the room he had entered.

"If you had charged me one per cent. on my note, this scene would never have occurred," answered the mechanic. "With the sum you generously saved me, I was able to buy these comforts. My heart blesses you for the deed; and if the good wishes of my happy family can throw sunshine across your path, it will be full of brightness."

Too much affected to reply, Mr. Edgar returned the warm pressure of the hand which had grasped his, and glided away.

A gleam of sunshine had indeed fallen along the pathway of the money-lender. Home had a brighter look as he passed his own threshold. He felt kinder and more cheerful; and kindness and cheerfulness flowed back to him from all the inmates of his dwelling. He half wondered at the changed aspect worn by every thing. His dreams that night were not of losses, fires, and the wreck of dearly-cherished hopes, but of the humble home made glad by his generous kindness. Again the happy mother, the pleased children, and the grateful father, were before him, and his own heart leaped with a new delight.

"It was a small act—a very light sacrifice on my part," said Mr. Edgar to himself, as he walked, in a musing mood, toward his office on the next morning. "And yet of how much real happiness has it been the occasion! So much that a portion thereof has flowed back upon my own heart."

"A good act is twice blessed." It seemed as if the words were spoken aloud, so distinctly and so suddenly were they presented to the mind of Mr. Edgar.

Ah, if he will only heed that suggestion, made by some pure spirit, brought near to him by the stirring of good affections in his mind! In it lies the secret of true happiness. Let him but act therefrom, and the sunshine will never be absent from his pathway.

ENGAGED AT SIXTEEN.

"MRS. LEE is quite fortunate with her daughters," remarked a visitor to Mrs. Wyman, whose oldest child, a well grown girl of fifteen, was sitting by.

"Yes; Kate and Harriet went off in good time. She has only Fanny left."

"Who is to be married this winter."

"Fanny?"

"She is engaged to Henry Florence."

"Indeed! And she is only just turned of sixteen. How fortunate, truly! Some people have their daughters on their hands until they are two or three-and-twenty, when the chances for good matches are very low. *I* was only sixteen when *I* was married."

"You?"

"Certainly; and then I had rejected two or three young men. There is nothing like early marriages, depend upon it, Mrs. Clayton. They always turn out the best. The most desirable young men take their pick of·the youngest girls, and leave the older ones for second-rate claimants."

"Do you hear that, Anna?" Mrs. Clayton said, laughing, as she turned to Mrs. Wyman's daughter. "I hope you will not remain a moment later than your mother did upon the maiden list."

Anna blushed slightly, but did not reply. What had been said, however, made its impression on her mind. She felt that to be engaged early was a matter greatly to be desired.

"My mother was married at sixteen, and here am I fifteen, and without a lover." So thought Anna, as she paused over the page of a new novel, some hours after she had listened to the conversation that passed between her mother and Mrs. Clayton, and mused of love and matrimony.

From that time, Anna Wyman was another girl. The sweet simplicity of manner, the unconscious innocence peculiar to her age, gradually vanished. Her eye, that was so clear and soft with the light of girlhood's pleasant fancies, grew earnest and restless, and, at times, intensely bright. The whole expression of her countenance was new. It was no longer a placid sky, with scarce a cloud floating in its quiet depths, but changeful as April, with its tears and smiles blending in strange beauty. Her heart, that had long beat tranquilly, would now bound at a thought, and send the bright crimson to her cheek—would flutter at the sight of .the very individual whom she, a short time before, could meet without a single wave ruffling the surface of her feelings. The woman had suddenly displaced the girl; a sisterly regard, that pure affection which an innocent maiden's heart has for all around her had expired on the altar where was kindling up the deep passion called *love*. And yet Anna Wyman had not reached her sixteenth year.

All at once, she became restless, capricious, unhappy. She had been at school up to this period, but now insisted that she was too old for that; her mother seconded this view of the matter, and her father, a man of pretty good sense, had to yield.

"We must give Anna a party now," said Mrs. Wyman, after their daughter had left school.

"Why so?" asked the father.

"Oh—because it is time that she was beginning to come out."

"Come out, how?"

"You are stupid, man. Come out in the list of young ladies. Go into company."

"But she is a mere child, yet—not sixteen."

"Not sixteen! And how old was *I*, pray, when you married me?"

The husband did not reply.

"How old was I, Mr. Wyman?"

"About sixteen, I believe."

"Well; and was I a mere child?"

"You were rather young to marry, at least," Mr. Wyman ventured to say. This remark was made rather too feelingly.

"Too young to marry!" ejaculated the wife, in a tone of surprise and indignation—"too young to marry; and my husband to say so, too! Mr. Wyman, do you mean to intimate—do you mean to say?—Mr. Wyman, what do you mean by that remark?"

"Oh, nothing at all," soothingly replied the hus
band; "only that I"——

"What?"

"That I don't, as a general thing, approve of very
early marriages. The character of a young lady is
not formed before twenty-one or two; nor has she
gained that experience and knowledge of the world
that will enable her to choose with wisdom."

"You don't pretend to say that my character was
not formed at sixteen?" This was accompanied by
a threatening look.

Whatever his thoughts were, Mr. Wyman took
good care not to express them. He merely said—

"I believe, Margaret, that I haven't volunteered
any allusion to you."

"Yes, but you don't approve of early marriages."

"True."

"Well, didn't I marry at sixteen? And isn't your
opinion a reflection upon your wife?"

"Circumstances alter cases," smilingly returned
Mr. Wyman. "Few women at sixteen were like
you. Very certainly your daughter is not."

"There I differ with you, Mr. Wyman. I believe
our Anna would make as good a wife now as I did
at sixteen. She is as much of a woman in appearance; her mind is more matured, and her education
advanced far beyond what mine was. She deserves
a good husband, and must have one before the lapse
of another year."

"How can you talk so, Margaret? For my part,
I do not wish to see her married for at least five
years."

"Preposterous! I wouldn't give a cent for a

marriage that takes place after seventeen or eighteen.
They are always indifferent affairs, and rarely ever
turn out well. The earlier the better, depend upon
it First love and first lover, is my motto."

"Well, Margaret, I suppose you will have these
matters your own way; but I don't agree with you
for all."

"Anna must have a party."

"You can do as you like."

"But you must assent to it."

"How can I do that, if I don't approve?"

"But you must approve."

And Mrs. Wyman persevered until she made him
approve—at least do so apparently. And so a party
was given to Anna, at which she was introduced to
several dashing young men, whose attentions almost
turned her young head. In two weeks she had a
confidante, a young lady named Clara Spenser, not
much older than herself. The progress already made
by Anna in love matters will appear in the following conversation held in secret with Clara.

"Did you say Mr. Carpenter had been to see you
since the party?" asked Clara.

"Yes, indeed," was the animated reply.

"He's a love of a man!—the very one of all others
that I would set my cap for, if there was any hope.
But you will, no doubt, carry him off."

Anna coloured to the temples, half with confusion
and half with delight.

"He used to pay attention to Jane Sherman, I'm
told."

"Yes; but you've cut her out entirely. Didn't

you notice how unhappy she seemed at the par
whenever he was with you?"

"No; was she?"

"Oh, yes; everybody noticed it. But you can
carry off all of her beaux; she's a mere drab of a
girl. And, besides, she's getting on the old maids'
list; I'm told she's more than twenty."

"She is?"

"It's true."

"Oh, dear;" there's no fear of her then. If I
were to go over sixteen before I married, I should be
frightened to death."

"Suppose Carpenter offers himself?"

"I hope he won't just yet."

"Why?"

"I want two or three strings to my bow. It would
be dangerous to reject one unless I had another
in my eye."

"Reject? Nonsense! Why should you reject
an offer?"

"My mother had three offers before she was sixteen, and rejected two of them."

"Was she married so early?"

"Oh, yes; she was a wife at sixteen, and I'm not
going to be a day later, if possible. I'd like to decline *three* offers and get married into the bargain
before a year passes. Wouldn't that be admirable?
It would be something to boast of all my life."

Pretty well advanced!—the reader no doubt ex-
claims; and so our young lady certainly was. When
a very young girl gets into love matters, she "does
them up," as the saying is, quite fast; she doesn't
mince matters at all. A maiden of twenty is cooler,

more thoughtful, and more cautious. She thinks a good deal, and is very careful how she lets any one —even her confidante, if she should happen to have one, (which is doubtful)—know much beyond her mere external thoughts. Four or five years make a good deal of difference in these things. But this need hardly have been said.

"You are going to Mrs. Ashton's on Wednesday evening, of course?" said Clara Spenser to Anna, on visiting her one morning, some weeks after the introduction to Carpenter had taken place.

"Oh, certainly; their soirées, I'm told, are elegant affairs."

"Indeed they are; I've been to two of them. Fine music, pleasant company, and so much freedom of intercourse—oh, they are delightful!"

"Did you ever see Mr. Carpenter there?"

"Oh, yes; he always attends."

"I shall enjoy myself highly."

"That you will—the young men are so attentive."

Wednesday night soon came round, and Anna was permitted to go, unattended by either of her parents, to the so-called soirée at Mrs. Ashton's. As she had hoped and believed, Carpenter was there. His attentions to her were constant and flattering; he poured many compliments into her ears, talking to her all the time in a low, musical tone. Anna's heart fluttered in her bosom with pleasure; she felt that she had made a conquest. But the fact of bringing so charming a young man to her feet, and that so speedily, quickened her pride, and made it seem the easiest thing in the world to be able to reject three

16

lovers and yet be engaged, or even married, at six teen.

Besides Carpenter, there was another present who saw attractions about Anna Wyman. He wore a moustache, and made quite a dashing appearance. In the language of many young ladies, who admired him, he was an elegant-looking young man—just the one to be proud of as a beau. His name was Elliott.

As soon as he could get access to the ear of the young and inexperienced girl, he charmed it with a deeper charm than Carpenter had been able to in part. She felt almost like one within a magic circle. His eye fascinated her, and his voice murmured in her ear like low, sweet music.

A short time before parting from her, he said— "Miss Wyman, may I have the pleasure of calling upon you at your father's house?"

"Oh, yes, sir; I shall be most happy to see you." She spoke with feeling.

"Then I shall visit you frequently. In your society I promise myself much happiness."

Anna's eyes fell to the floor, and the colour deep ened on her cheeks. When she looked up, Elliott was gazing steadily in her face, with an expression of admiration and love.

Her heart was lost. Carpenter, that love of a man, was not thought of—or, only as one of her re jected lovers.

When Anna laid her head upon her pillow that night, it was not to sleep. Her mind was too full of pleasant images, central to all of which was the elegant, accomplished, handsome Mr. Elliott. He had, she conceived, as good as offered himself, and she much as she wished to reject three lovers before she accepted one, felt strongly inclined to accept him, and so end the matter.

Now, who was Mr. Thomas Elliott? A few words will portray him. Mr. Elliott was twenty-six; he kept a store in the city; had been in business for some years, but was not very successful. His habits of life were not good; his principles had no sound, moral basis. He was, in fact, just the man to make a silly child like Anna Wyman wretched for life. But why did he seek for one like her? That is easily explained. Mr. Wyman was reputed to be pretty well off in the world, and Mr. Elliott's affairs were in rather a precarious condition; but he managed to keep so good a face upon the matter, that none suspected his real condition.

After visiting Anna for a short time, he offered his hand. If it had not been that her sixteenth birthday was so near, Anna would have declined the offer, for Thomas Elliott did not grow dearer to her every day. There were young men whom she liked much better; and if they had only come forward and presented their claims to favour, she would have declined the offer. But time was rapidly passing away. Anna was ambitious of being engaged before she was sixteen, and married, if possible. Her mother had rejected two offers, and she was anxious to do as much. Here was a chance for one rejection—but was she sure of another offer in time? No! There was the difficulty. For some days she debated the question, and then laid it before her mother. Mrs. Wyman consulted her husband, who did not much like Elliott; but the mother felt the necessity of an early marriage, and overruled all objections. Her advice to Anna was to accept the offer, and it was accepted accordingly.

A fond, wayward child of sixteen may chance to marry and do well, spite of all the drawbacks she will meet; but this is only in case she happen to marry a man of good sense, warm affections, and great kindness, who can bear with her as a father bears with a capricious child; can forgive much and love much. But give the happiness of such a creature into the keeping of a cold, narrow-minded, selfish, petulant man, and her cup will soon run over. Bitter, indeed, will be her lot in life.

Just such a man was Thomas Elliott. He had sought only his own pleasures, and had owned no law but his own will. For more than ten years he had been living without other external restraints than those social laws that all must observe who desire to keep a fair reputation. He came in when he pleased and went out when he pleased. He required service from all, and gave it to none—that is, so far as he needed service, he exacted it from those under him, but was not in the habit of making personal sacrifices for the sake of others. Thus, his natural selfishness was confirmed. When he married, it was with an end to the good he should derive from the union—not from a generous desire to make another happy in himself. Anna was young, vivacious, and more than ordinarily intelligent and pretty. There was much about her that was attractive, and Elliott really imagined that he loved her; but it was himself that he loved in her fascinating qualities. These were all to minister to his pleasure. He never once thought of devoting himself to her happiness.

On the night of the wedding, which took place soon after Anna's sixteenth birthday, the bride was in that bewildered state of mind which destroys all the rational perceptions of the mind. Her whole soul was in a pleasing tumult, and yet she did not feel happy; and why? Spite of the solemn promise she had made to love and honour her husband above all men, she felt that there were others whom she could have loved and honoured more than him, were they in his place. But this, reason told her, was folly. They had not presented themselves, and he had. They could be nothing to her—he must be every thing. To secure a husband early was the great point, and that had been gained. This thought, whenever it crossed her mind, would cause her to look around upon her maiden companions with proud self-complacency. They were still upon the shores of expectancy. She had launched her boat upon the sunny sea of matrimony, and was already moving steadily away under a pleasant breeze.

Alas! young bride, thy hymeneal altar is an altar of sacrifice. Love is not the deity who is presiding there. Little do they dream who have led thee, poor lamb! garlanded with flowers, to that altar, how innocent, how true, how good a heart they were offering up upon its strange fires. But they will know in time, and thou wilt know when it is too late.

Two years from the period of their marriage, Elliott and his wife were seated in a small room moderately well furnished. He was leaning back in

16*

a chair, with arms folded, and his chin resting on his bosom. His face was contracted into a gloomy scowl. Anna, who looked pale and troubled, was sewing and touching with her foot a cradle, in which was a babe. The little one seemed restless. Every now and then it would start and moan, or cry out. After a time it awoke and commenced screaming. The mother lifted it from the cradle and tried to hush it upon her bosom, but the babe still cried on. It was evidently in pain.

"Confound you! why don't you keep that child quiet?" exclaimed the husband, impatiently casting at the same time an angry look upon his wife.

Anna made no reply, but turned half away from him, evidently to conceal the tears that suddenly started from her eyes, and strove more earnestly to quiet the child. In this she soon succeeded.

"I believe you let her cry on purpose, whenever I am in the house, just to annoy me," her husband resumed in an ill-natured tone.

"No, Thomas, you know that I do not," Anna said.

"Say I lie, why don't you?"

"Oh, Thomas, how can you speak so to me?" And his young wife turned toward him an earnest, tearful look.

"Pah! don't try to melt me with your crying. I never believed in it. Women can cry at any moment."

There was a convulsive motion of Mrs. Elliott's head as she turned quickly away, and a choking sound in her throat. She remained silent, ten minutes passed, when her husband said in a firm voice,

"Anna, I'm going to break up."

Mrs. Elliott glanced around with a startled air.

"It's true, just what I say—your father may think that I'm going to make a slave of myself to support you, but he's mistaken. He's refused to help me in my business one single copper, though he's able enough. And now I've taken my resolution. You can go back to him as quick as you like."

Before the brutal husband had half finished the sentence, his wife was on her feet, with a cheek deadly pale, and eyes almost starting from her head. Thomas Elliott was her husband and the father of her babe, and as such she had loved him with a far deeper love than he had deserved. This had caused her to bear with coldness and neglect, and even positive unkindness without a complaint. Sacredly had she kept from her mother even a hint of the truth. Thus had she gone on almost from the first; for only a few months elapsed before she discovered that her image was dim on her husband's heart.

"You needn't stand there staring at me like one moon-struck"—he said, with bitter sarcasm and a curl of the lip. "What I say is the truth. I'm going to give up, and you've got to go home to them that are more able to support you than I am; and who have a better right, too, I'm thinking."

There was something so heartless and chilling in the words and manner of her husband, that Mrs. Elliott made no attempt to reply. Covering her face with her hands, she sunk back into the chair from which she had risen, more deeply miserable than she had ever been in her life. From this state she was aroused by the imperative question,

"Anna, what do you intend doing?"

"That is for you to say"—was her murmured reply.

"Then, I say, go home to your father, and at once."

Without a word the wife rose from her chair, with her infant in her arms, and pausing only long enough to put on her shawl and bonnet, left the house.

Mr. and Mrs. Wyman were sitting alone late on the afternoon of the same day, thinking about and conversing of their child. Neither of them felt too well satisfied with the result of her marriage. It required not even the close observation of a parent's eye, to discover that she was far from happy.

"I wish she were only single"—Mr. Wyman at length said. "She married much too young—only eighteen now, and with a cold-hearted and, I fear, unprincipled and neglectful husband. It is sad to think of it."

"But I was married as young as she was, Mr. Wyman?"

"Yes; but I flatter myself you made a better choice. Your condition at eighteen was very different from what hers is now. As I said before, I only wish she were single, and then I wouldn't care to see her married for two or three years to come."

"I can't help wishing she had refused Mr. Elliott. If she had done so, she might have been married to a much better man long before this. Mr. Carpenter is worth a dozen of him. Oh dear! this marriage is all a lottery, after all. Few prizes and many blanks. Poor Anna! she is not happy."

At this moment the door opened, and the child of whom they were speaking, with her infant in her arms, came hurriedly in. Her face was deadly pale, her lips tightly compressed, and her eyes widely distended and fixed.

"Anna!" exclaimed the mother, starting up quickly and springing toward her.

"My child, what ails you?" was eagerly asked by the father, as he, too, rose up hastily.

But there was no reply. The heart of the child was too full. She could not utter the truth. She had been sent back to her parents by her husband, but her tongue could not declare that! Pride, shame, wounded affections, combined to hold back her words. Her only reply was to lay her babe in her mother's arms, and then fling herself upon the bosom of her father.

All was mystery then, but time soon unveiled the cause of their daughter's strange and sudden appearance, and her deep anguish. The truth gradually came out that she had been deserted by her husband; or, what seemed to Mrs. Wyman more disgraceful still, had been sent home by him. Bitterly did she execrate him, but it availed nothing. Her ardent wish had been gratified. Anna was engaged at sixteen, and married soon after; but at eighteen, alas! she had come home a deserted wife and mother! And so she remained. Her husband never afterward came near her. And now, at thirty, with a daughter well grown, she remains in her father's house, a quiet, thoughtful, dreamy woman, who sees little in life that is attractive, and who rarely stirs beyond the threshold of the house that shelters her. There are those who will recognise this picture

So much for being engaged at sixteen!

THE DAUGHTER.

It often happens that a daughter possesses greatly superior advantages to those enjoyed, in early years, by either her father or mother. She is not compelled to labour as hard as they were obliged to labour when young; and she is blessed with the means of education far beyond what they had. Her associations, too, are of a different order, all tending to elevate her views of life, to refine her tastes, and to give her admission into a higher grade of society than they were fitted to move in.

Unless very watchful of herself and very thoughtful of her parents, a daughter so situated will be led at times to draw comparisons between her own cultivated intellect and taste and the want of such cultivation in her parents, and to think indifferently of them, as really inferior, because not so well educated and accomplished as she is. A distrust of their judgment and a disrespect of their opinions will follow, as a natural consequence, if these thoughts and feelings be indulged. This result often takes place with thoughtless, weak-minded girls; and is followed by what is worse, a disregard to their feelings, wishes, and express commands.

A sensible daughter, who loves her parents, will hardly forget to whom she is indebted for all the superior advantages she enjoys. She will also readily perceive that the experience which her parents have acquired, and their natural strength of mind, give them a real and great superiority over her, and make their judgment, in all matters of life, far more to be depended upon than hers could possibly be. It may be that her mother has never learned to play upon the piano, has never been to a dancing-school, has never had any thing beyond the merest rudiments of an education; but she has good sense, prudence, industry, economy; understands and practises all the virtues of domestic life; has a clear, discriminating judgment; has been her husband's faithful friend and adviser for some twenty or thirty years; and has safely guarded and guided her children up to mature years. These evidences of a mother's title to her respect and fullest confidence cannot long be absent from a daughter's mind, and will prevent her acting in direct opposition to her judgment.

Thoughtless indeed must be that child who can permit an emotion of disrespect toward her parents to dwell in her bosom for more than a single moment!

Respect and love toward parents are absolutely necessary to the proper formation of the character upon that true basis which will bring into just order and subordination all the powers of the mind. Without this order and subordination there can be no true happiness. A child loves and respects his parents, because from them he derived his being, and from them receives every blessing and comfort. To them, and to them alone, does his mind turn as the authors of all the good gifts he possessed. As a mere child, it is right for him thus to regard his parents as the authors of his being and the originators of all his

blessings.   But as reason gains strength, and he sees
more deeply into the nature and causes of things,
which only takes place as the child approaches the
years of maturity, it is then seen that the parents
were only the agents through which life, and all the
blessings accompanying it, came from God, the great
Father of all.   If the parents have been loved with
a truly filial love, then the mind has been suitably
opened and prepared for love toward God, and an
obedience to his divine laws, without which there can
be no true happiness.   When this new and higher
truth takes possession of the child's mind, it in no
way diminishes his respect for his earthly parents,
but increases it.   He no longer obeys them because
they command obedience, but he regards the truth
of their precepts, and in that truth hears the voice
of God speaking to him.   More than ever is he now
careful to listen to their wise counsels, because he
perceives in them the authority of reason, which is
the authority of God.
     Most young ladies, on attaining the age of respon-
sibility, will perceive a difference in the manner of
their parents.   Instead of opposing them, as heretofore, with authority, they will oppose them with reason, where opposition is deemed necessary.   The
mother, instead of saying, when she disapproves any
thing, "No, my child, you cannot do it;" or, "No,
you must not go, dear;" will say, "I would rather
not have you do so;" or, "I do not approve of your
going."   If you ask her reasons, she will state them,
and endeavour to make you comprehend their force.
It is far too often the case, that the daughter's desire to do what her mother disapproves is so active,

that neither her mother's objections nor reasons are strong enough to counteract her wishes, and she follows her own inclinations instead of being guided by her mother's better judgment. In these instances, she almost always does wrong, and suffers therefore either bodily or mental pain.

Obedience in childhood is that by which we are led and guided into right actions. When we become men and women, reason takes the place of obedience; but, like a young bird just fluttering from its nest, reason at first has not much strength of wing; and we should therefore suffer the reason of those who love us, like the mother-bird, to stoop under and bear us up in our earlier efforts, lest we fall bruised and wounded to the ground. To whose reason should a young girl look to strengthen her own, so soon as to her mother's, guided as it is by love? But it too often happens that, under the first impulses of conscious freedom, no voice is regarded but the voice of inclination and passion. The mother may oppose, and warn, and urge the most serious considerations, but the daughter turns a deaf ear to all. She thinks that she knows best.

"You are not going to-night, Mary?" said a mother, coming into her daughter's room, and finding her dressing for a ball. She had been rather seriously indisposed for some days, with a cold that had fallen upon her throat and chest, which was weak, but was now something better.

"I think I will, mother, for I am much better than I was yesterday, and have improved since morning. I have promised myself so much pleasure at this ball, that I cannot think of being disappointed."

17

The mother shook her head.

"Mary," she replied, "you are not well enough to go out. The air is damp, and you will inevitably take more cold. Think how badly your throat has been inflamed."

"I don't think it has been so *very* bad, mother."

"The doctor told me it was badly inflamed, and said you would have to be very careful of yourself, or it might prove serious."

"That was some days ago. It is a great deal better now."

"But the least exposure may cause it to return."

"I will be very careful not to expose myself. I will wrap up warm and go in a carriage. I am sure there is not the least danger, mother."

"While I am sure that there is very great danger. ou cannot pass from the door to the carriage without the damp air striking upon your face, and pressing into your lungs."

"But I must not always exclude myself from the air, mother. Air and exercise, you know, the doctor says, are indispensable to health."

"Dry, not damp air. This makes the difference. But you must act for yourself, Mary. You are now a woman, and must freely act in the light of that reason which God has given you. Because I love you, and desire your welfare, I thus seek to convince you that it is wrong to expose your health to-night. Your great desire to go blinds you to the real danger, which I can fully see."

"You are over-anxious, mother," urged Mary. "I know how I feel much better than you possibly can, and I know I am well enough to go."

"I have nothing more to say, my child," returned the mother. "I wish you to act freely, but wisely. Wisely I am sure you will not act if you go to-night. A temporary illness may not alone be the consequence; your health may receive a shock from which it will never recover."

"Mother wishes to frighten me," said Mary to herself, after her mother had left the room. "But I am not to be so easily frightened. I am sorry she makes such a serious matter about my going, for I never like to do any thing that is not agreeable to her feelings. But I must go to this ball. William is to call for me at eight, and he would be as much disappointed as myself if I were not to go. As to making more cold, what of that? I would willingly pay the penalty of a pretty severe cold rather than miss the ball."

Against all her mother's earnestly urged objections, Mary went with her lover to the ball. She came home, at one o'clock, with a sharp pain through her breast, red spots on her cheeks, oppression of the chest, and considerable fever. On the next morning she was unable to rise from her bed. When the doctor, who was sent for, came in, he looked grave, and asked if there had been any exposure by which a fresh cold could be taken.

"She was at the ball last night," replied the mother.

"Not with your approval, madam?" he said quickly, looking with a stern expression into the mother's face.

"No, doctor. I urged her not to go; but Mary thought she knew best. She did not believe there was any danger."

A strong expression rose to the doctor's lips, but he repressed it, lest he should needlessly alarm the patient. On retiring from her chamber, he declared the case to be a very critical one; and so it proved to be. Mary did not leave her room for some months; and when she did, it was with a constitution so impaired that she could not endure the slightest fatigue, nor bear the least exposure. Neither change of climate nor medicine availed any thing toward restoring her to health. In this feeble state she married, about twelve months afterward, the young man who had accompanied her to the ball. One year from the period at which that happy event took place, she died, leaving to stranger hands a babe that needed all her tenderest care, and a husband almost brokenhearted at his loss.

This is not merely a picture from the imagination, and highly coloured. It is from nature, and every line is drawn with the pencil of truth. Hundreds of young women yearly sink into the grave, whose friends can trace to some similar act of imprudence, committed in direct opposition to the earnest persuasions of parents or friends, the cause of their premature decay and death. And too often other, and sometimes even worse, consequences than death, follow a disregard of the mother's voice of warning.

PASSING AWAY.

[From our story of "The Two Brides," we take a scene, in which some one sorrowing as those without hope may find words of consolation.]

IN the very springtime of young womanhood, the destroyer had come; and though he laid his hand upon her gently at first, yet the touch was none the less fatal. But, while her frail body wasted, her spirit remained peaceful. As the sun of her natural life sunk low in the sky, the bright auroral precursor of another day smiled along the eastern verge of her spiritual horizon. There was in her heart neither doubt, nor fear, nor shrinking.

"Dear Marion!" said Anna, dropping a tear upon her white transparent hand, as she pressed it to her lips, a few weeks after the alarming hemorrhage just mentioned; "how can you look at this event so calmly?"

They had been speaking of death, and Marion had alluded to its approach to Anna, with a strange cheerfulness, as if she felt it to be nothing more than a journey to another and far pleasanter land than that wherein she now dwelt.

"Why should I look upon this change with other than tranquil feelings?" she asked.

"Why? How can you ask such a question, sister?' returned Anna. "To me, there has been

17*   19'

always something in the thought of death that made the blood run cold about my heart."

"This," replied Marion, with one of her sweet smiles, "is because your ideas of death have been, from the first, confused and erroneous. You thought of the cold and pulseless body; the pale winding-sheet; the narrow coffin, and the deep, dark grave. But, I do not let my thoughts rest on these. To me, death involves the idea of eternal life. I cannot think of the one without the other. Should the chrysalis tremble at the coming change?—the dull worm in its cerements shrink from the moment when, ordained by nature, it must rise into a new life, and expand its wings in the sunny air? How much less cause have I to tremble and shrink back as the hour approaches when this mortal is to put on immortality?"

"Yours is a beautiful faith," said Anna. "And its effects, as seen now that the hour from which all shrink approaches, are strongly corroborative of its truth."

"It is beautiful because it is true," replied Marion. "There is no real beauty that is not the form of something good and true."

"If I were as good as you, I might not shrink from death," remarked Anna, with a transient sigh.

"I hope you are better than I am, dear; and think you are," said Marion.

"Oh, no!" quickly returned Anna.

"Do you purpose evil in your heart?" asked Marion, seriously.

Anna seemed half surprised at the question.

"Evil! Evil! I hope not," she replied, as a shadow came over her face.

"It is an evil purpose only that should make us fear death, Anna; for therein lies the only cause of fear. Death, to those who love themselves and the world above every thing else, is a sad event; but to those who love God and their neighbour supremely, it is a happy change."

"That is all true," said Anna. "My reason assents to it. But, in the act of dissolution—in that mortal strife, when the soul separates itself from the body—there is something from which my heart shrinks and trembles down fainting in my bosom. Ah! In the crossing of that bourne from which no traveller has returned to tell us of what is beyond, there is something that more than half appals me."

"There is much that takes away the fear you have mentioned," replied Marion. "It is the uncertain that causes us to tremble and shrink back. But, when we know what is before us, we prepare ourselves to meet it. Attendant upon every one who dies, says a certain writer, are two angels, who keep his mind entirely above the thought of death, and in the idea of eternal life. They remain with him through the whole process—protecting him from evil spirits—and receive him into the world of spirits after his soul has fully withdrawn itself from the interior of the body. The last idea active in the mind of the person before death, is the first idea in his mind after death, when his consciousness of life is restored; and it is some time after this conscious life returns before he is aware that he is dead. Around him he sees objects similar to those seen in the natural

world.   There are houses and trees, streams of water and gardens.   Men and women dressed in variously fashioned garments.   They walk and converse
together, as we do upon earth.   When, at length,
he is told that he has died, and is now in a world
that is spiritual instead of natural—that the body in
which he is, is a body formed of spiritual instead of
natural substances, he is in a measure affected with
surprise, and for the most part a pleasing surprise.
He wonders at the grossness of his previous ideas,
which limited form and substances to material things;
and now, unless he had been instructed during his
life in the world, begins to comprehend the truth
that man is a man from the spirit, not from the body."

Anna, who had been listening intently, drew a
long breath, as Marion paused.

"Dead, and yet not know the fact!" said she,
with an expression of wonder.   "It seems incredible.
And all this you fully believe?"

"Yes, Anna; as entirely as I believe in the existence of the sun in the firmament."

"If these doctrines can take away the fear of
death, which so haunts the mind of even those who
are striving to live pure lives, they are indeed a
legacy of good to the world.   Oh, Marion, how much
I have suffered, ever since the days of my childhood,
from this dreadful fear!"

"They do take away the fear of death," returned
Marion; "because they remove the uncertainty which
has heretofore gathered like a gloomy pall over the
last hours of mortality.   When the soul of lover or
friend passed from this world, it seemed to plunge
into a dark profound, and there came not back an

echo to tell of his fate. 'The bourne from which no traveller returns!' Oh! the painful eloquence of that single line. But, now, we who receive the doctrine of which I speak, can look beyond this bourne; and though the traveller returns not, yet we know something of how he fared on his entrance into the new country."

"Then we need not fear for you," said Anna, tenderly, "when you are called to pass this bourne?"

"No, sister," replied Marion, "I know in whom I have believed, and I feel sure that it will be well with me, so far as I have shunned what is evil and sought to do good. Do not think of me as sinking into some gloomy profound; or awakening from my sleep of death, startled, amazed, or shocked by the sudden transition. Loving angels will be my companions as I descend into the valley and the shadow of death; and I will fear no evil. Upon the other side I will be received among those who have gone before, and I will scarcely feel that there has been a change. A little while I will remain there, and then pass upward to my place in heaven."

The mother of Marion entered her room at this moment, and the conversation was suspended. But it was renewed again soon after, and the gentle-hearted, spiritual-minded girl continued to talk of the other world as one preparing for a journey talks about the new country into which he is about going, and of whose geography, and the manners and customs of whose people, he has made himself conversant from books.

Not long did she remain on this side of the dark valley, through which she was to pass. A few months wound up the story of her earthly life, and she went peacefully and confidently on her way to her eternal dwelling-place. It was a sweet, sad time, when the parting hour came, and the mother, brother, and dearly loved adopted sister, gathered around Marion's bed to see her die. That angels were present, each one felt; for the sphere of tranquillity that pervaded the hearts of all was the sphere of heaven.

"God is love," said Marion, a short time before she passed away. She was holding the hand of her mother, and looking tenderly in her face. "How exquisite is my perception of this truth? It comes upon me with a power that subdues my spirit, yet fills it with ineffable peace. With what a wondrous love has he regarded us! I never had had so intense a perception of this as now."

Marion closed her eyes, and for some time lay silent, while a heavenly smile irradiated her features. Then looking up, she said, and as she spoke she took the hand of Anna and placed it within that of her mother—

"When I am gone, let the earthly love you bore me, mother, be added to that already felt for our dear Anna. Think of me as an angel, and of her as your child."

In spite of her effort to restrain them, tears gushed from the eyes of Mrs. Lee, and fell like rain over her cheeks. For a short time she bent to her dying one, and clasped her wildly to her bosom. But the calmness of a deeply-laid trust in Providence was soon restored to her spirit, and she said, speaking of Anna—

"Without her, how could we part with you? I do not think I could bear it."

"I shall go before you only a little while," returned Marion, "only a very little while. A few years—how quickly they will hurry by! A few more days of labour, and your earthly tasks will be done. Then we shall meet again. And even in the days of our separation we shall not be far removed from each other. Thought will bring us spiritually near, and affection conjoin us, even though no sense of the body give token of proximity. And who knows but to me will be assigned the guardianship of the dear babe given to us by Anna? Oh! if love will secure that holy duty, then it will be mine!"

A light, as if reflected from the sun of heaven, beamed from the countenance of Marion, who closed her eyes, and, in a little while, fell off into a gentle sleep. Silently did those who loved her with more than human tenderness—for there was in their affec· tion a love of goodness for its own sake—bend over and watch the face of the sweet sleeper, even until there came stealing upon them the fear that she would not waken again in this world. And the fear was not groundless; for thus she passed away. To her death came as a gentle messenger, to bid her go up higher. And she obeyed the summons without a mortal fear.

No passionate grief at their loss raged wildly in the bosoms of those who suffered this great bereavement. For years, the mother and son had daily striven against selfish feelings as evil; and now, comprehending with the utmost clearness that Marion's removal was, for her, a blessed change, their hearts were thankful, even while tears wet their cheeks. They mourned for her departure, because they were human; they suffered pain, for ties of love the most tender had been snapped asunder; they wept, because in weeping nature found relief. Yet, in all, peace brooded over their spirits.

When the fading, wasting form of earth which Marion's pure spirit had worn, as a garment, but now laid aside forever, was borne out, and consigned to its kindred clay, those who remained behind experienced no new emotions of grief. To them Marion still lived. This was the old mortal body, that vailed, rather than made visible, her real beauty. Now she was clothed in a spiritual body, that was transcendently beautiful, because it was the very form of good affections. To lay the useless garment aside was not, therefore, a painful task. This done, each member of the bereaved family returned to his and her life-tasks, and, in the faithful discharge of daily duties, found a sustaining power. But Marion was not lost to them. Ever present was she in their thought and affection, and often, in dreams, she was with them,—yet, never as the suffering mortal; but as the happy, glorified immortal. Beautiful was the faith upon which they leaned. To them the spiritual was not a something vague and undeterminate; but a real entity. They looked beyond the grave, into the spiritual world, as into a better country, where life was continued in higher perfection, and where were spiritual ultimates, as perfectly adapted to spiritual sense as are the ultimates of creation to the senses of the natural body.

THE LOVE SECRET.

"EDWARD is to be in London next week," said Mrs. Ravensworth; "and I trust, Edith, that you will meet him with the frankness he is entitled to receive."

Edith Hamilton, who stood behind the chair of her aunt, did not make any answer.

Mrs. Ravensworth continued—"Edward's father was your father's own brother. A man of nobler spirit never moved on English soil; and I hear that Edward is the worthy son of a worthy sire."

"If he were as pure and perfect as an angel, aunt," replied Edith, "it would be all the same to me. I have never seen him, and cannot, therefore, meet him as one who has a right to claim my hand."

"Your father gave you away when you were a child, Edith; and Edward comes now to claim you by virtue of this betrothal."

"While I love the memory of my father, and honour him as a child should honour a parent," said Edith, with much seriousness, "I do not admit his right to give me away in marriage while I was yet a child. And, moreover, I do not think the man who would seek to consummate such a marriage contract worthy of any maiden's love. Only the heart that yields a free consent is worth having, and the man who would take any other is utterly unworthy of

any woman's regard. By this rule I judge Edwar
to be unworthy, no matter what his father may have
been."

"Then you mean," said Mrs. Ravensworth, "de-
liberately to violate the solemn contract made by
your father with the father of Edward?"

"I cannot receive Edward as any thing but a
stranger," replied Edith. "It will not mend the
error of my father for me to commit a still greater
one."

"How commit a still greater one?" inquired Mrs.
Ravensworth.

"Destroy the very foundation of a true marriage
—freedom of choice and consent. There would be
no freedom of choice on his part, and no privilege
of consent on mine. Happiness could not follow
such a union, and to enter into it would be doing a
great wrong. No, aunt, I cannot receive Edward in
any other way than as a stranger—for such he is."

"There is a clause in your father's will that you
may have forgotten, Edith," said her aunt.

"That which makes me penniless if I do not
marry Edward-Hamden?"

"Yes."

"No—I have not forgotten it, aunt."

"And you mean to brave that consequence?"

"In a choice of evils we always take the least."
Edith's voice trembled.

Mrs. Ravensworth did not reply for some moments. While she sat silent, the half-closed door
near which Edith stood, and toward which her aunt's
back was turned, softly opened, and a handsome
youth, between whom and Edith glances of intelli-

gence instantly passed, presented the startled maiden with a beautiful white rose, and then noiselessly retired.

It was nearly a minute before Mrs. Ravensworth resumed the light employment in which she was engaged, and as she did so, she said—

"Many a foolish young girl gets her head turned with those gay gallants at our fashionable watering-places, and imagines that she has won a heart when the object of her vain regard never felt the throb of a truly unselfish and noble impulse."

The crimson deepened on Edith's cheeks and brow, and as she lifted her eyes, she saw herself in a large mirror opposite, with her aunt's calm eyes steadily fixed upon her. To turn her face partly away, so that it could no longer be reflected from the mirror, was the work of an instant. In a few moments she said—

"Let young and foolish girls get their heads turned if they will. But I trust I am in no danger."

"I am not so sure of that. Those who think themselves most secure are generally in the greatest danger. Who is the youth with whom you danced last evening? I don't remember to have seen him here before."

"His name is Evelyn." There was a slight tremor in Edith's voice.

"How came you to know him?"

"I met him here last season."

"You did?"

"Yes, ma'am. And I danced with him last night. Was there any harm in that?" The maiden's voice had regained its firmness.

"I didn't say there was," returned Mrs. Ravensworth, who again relapsed into silence. Not long after, she said—"I think we will return to London on Thursday."

"So soon!" Edith spoke in a disappointed voice.

"Do you find it so very pleasant here?" said the aunt, a little ironically.

"I have not complained of its being dull, aunt," replied Edith. "But if you wish to return on Thursday, I will be ready to accompany you."

Soon after this, Edith Hamilton left her aunt's room, and went to one of the drawing-rooms of the hotel at which they were staying, where she sat down near a recess window that overlooked a beautiful promenade. She had been here only a few minutes, when she was joined by a handsome youth. to whom Edith said—

"How could you venture to the door of my aunt's parlour? I'm half afraid she detected your presence, for she said, immediately afterward, that we would return to London on the day after to-morrow."

"So soon? Well, I'll be there next week, and it will be strange if, with your consent, we don't meet often."

"Edward Hamden is expected in a few days," replied Edith, her voice slightly faltering.

Her companion looked at her searchingly for a few moments, and then said—

"You have never met him?"

"Never."

"But when you do meet him, the repugnance you now feel may instantly vanish."

A shadow passed over Edith's face, and she

answered in a voice that showed the remark—the tone of which conveyed more than the words themselves—to have been felt as a question of her constancy.

"Can one whose heart is all unknown to me, one who must think of me with a feeling of dislike because of bonds and pledges, prove a nearer or a dearer friend than——"

Edith did not finish the sentence. But that was not needed. The glance of rebuking tenderness cast upon her companion expressed all that her lips had failed to utter.

"But you do not know me, Edith," said the young man.

"My heart says differently," was Edith's lowly spoken reply.

Evelyn pressed the maiden's hand, and looked into her face with an earnest, loving expression.

Mrs. Ravensworth, to whose care Edith had been consigned on the death of her father, had never been pleased with the unwise contract made by the parents of her niece and Edward Hamden. The latter had been for ten years in Paris and Italy, travelling and pursuing his studies. These being completed, in obedience to the will of a deceased parent, he was about returning to London to meet his future wife. No correspondence had taken place between the parties to this unnatural contract; and from the time of Edward's letter, when he announced to Mrs. Ravensworth his proposed visit, it was plain that his feelings were as little interested in his future partner as were hers in him.

During the two or three days that Mrs. Ravensworth and her niece remained at the watering-place, Edith and young Evelyn met frequently; but, as far as possible, at times when they supposed the particular attention of the aunt would not be drawn toward them in such a manner as to penetrate their love secret. When, at length, they parted, it was with an understanding that they were to meet in London.

On returning to the city, the thoughts of Edith reverted more directly to the fact of Edward Hamden's approaching visit; and, in spite of all her efforts to remain undisturbed in her feelings, the near approach of this event agitated her. Mrs. Ravensworth frequently alluded to the subject, and earnestly pressed upon Edith the consideration of her duty to her parent, as well as the consequences that must follow her disregard of the contract which had been made. But the more she talked on this subject, the more firm was Edith in expressing her determination not to do violence to her feelings in a matter so vital to her happiness.

The day at length came upon which Edward Hamden was to arrive. Edith appeared, in the morning, with a disturbed air. It was plain to the closely observing eyes of her aunt, that she had not passed a night of refreshing sleep.

"I trust, my dear niece," she said, after they had retired from the breakfast table, where but little food had been taken, "that you will not exhibit toward Edward, on meeting him, any of the preconceived and unjust antipathy you entertain. Let your feelings, at least, remain uncommitted for or against him.

"Aunt Helen, it is useless to talk to me in this

way," Edith replied, with more than her usual warmth. "The simple fact of an obligation to love puts a gulf between us. My heart turns from him as from an enemy. I will meet him with politeness; but it must be cold and formal. To ask of me more, is to ask what I cannot give. I only wish that he possessed the manliness I would have had if similarly situated. Were this so, I would now be free by his act, not my own."

Seeing that all she urged but made the feelings of Edith oppose themselves more strongly to the young man, Mrs. Ravensworth ceased to speak upon the subject, and the former was left to brood with a deeply disturbed heart over the approaching inter-view with one who had come to claim a hand that she resolutely determined not to yield.

About twelve o'clock, Mrs. Ravensworth came to Edith's room and announced the arrival of Edward Hamden. The maiden's face became pale, and her lips quivered.

"If I could but be spared an interview," she murmured. "But that is more than I can ask."

"How weak you are, Edith," replied her aunt, in a tone of reproof.

"I will join you in the drawing-room in half an hour," said Edith, speaking more calmly.

Mrs. Ravensworth retired, and left Edith again to her own thoughts. She sat for nearly the whole of the time she had mentioned. Then rising hurriedly, she made a few changes in her attire; after which she descended to the drawing-room with a step that was far from being firm.

So noiselessly did she enter the apartment where

Hamden awaited her, that neither her aunt nor the young man perceived her presence for some moments, and she had time to examine his appearance, and to read the lineaments of his half-averted face. While she stood thus observing him, her countenance suddenly flushed, and she bent forward with a look of surprise and eagerness. At this moment the young man became aware that she had entered, and rising up quickly, advanced to meet her.

"Evelyn!" exclaimed Edith, striking her hands together, the moment he turned toward her.

"Edith! my own Edith!" returned the young man, as he grasped her hand, and ventured a warm kiss on her beautiful lips. "Not Evelyn, but Hamden. Our parents betrothed us while we were yet too young to give or withhold consent. Both, as we grew older, felt this pledge as a heart-sickening constraint. But we met as strangers, and I saw that you were all my soul could desire. I sought your regard and won it. No obligation but love now binds us."

The young man then turned to Mrs. Ravensworth, and said—

"You see, madam, that we are not strangers."

Instead of looking surprised, Mrs. Ravensworth smiled calmly, and answered—

"No—it would be singular if you were. Love-tokens don't generally pass, nor familiar meetings take place between strangers."

"Love-tokens, Aunt Helen?" fell from the lips of Edith, as she turned partly away from Hamden, and looked inquiringly at her relative.

"Yes, dear," returned Mrs. Ravensworth. "White

roses, for instance. You saw your own blushing face in the mirror, did you not ?"

"The mirror! Then you saw Edward present the rose ?"

"And did you know me ?" inquired the young man.

"One who knew your father as well as I did could not fail to know the son. I penetrated your love secret as soon as it was known to yourselves."

"Aunt Helen !" exclaimed Edith, hiding her face on the neck of her kind relative, "how have I been deceived !"

"Happily, I trust, love," returned Mrs. Ravensworth, tenderly.

"Most happily! My heart swells with gladness almost to bursting," came murmuring from the lips of the joyful maiden.

THE END.

STEREOTYPED BY L. JOHNSON & CO.
PHILADELPHIA.